WOMAN OF THE INNER SEA

BY THOMAS KENEALLY

Fiction

The Place at Whitton
The Fear
Bring Larks and Heroes
Three Cheers for the Paraclete
The Survivor
A Dutiful Daughter
The Chant of Jimmie Blacksmith
Blood Red, Sister Rose
Gossip from the Forest
Season in Purgatory
A Victim of the Aurora
Passenger
Confederates
The Cut-Rate Kingdom
Schindler's List
A Family Madness
The Playmaker
To Asmara
Flying Hero Class
Woman of the Inner Sea

Nonfiction

Outback
Now and in Time to Come
The Place Where Souls Are Born:
    A Journey to the Southwest

For children

Ned Kelly and the City of Bees

THOMAS KENEALLY

Woman

of the

Inner Sea

NAN A. TALESE
DOUBLEDAY
New York London Toronto Sydney Auckland

PUBLISHED BY NAN A. TALESE
an imprint of Doubleday,
a division of Bantam Doubleday Dell Publishing Group, Inc.
666 Fifth Avenue, New York, New York 10103

DOUBLEDAY and the portrayal of an anchor
with a dolphin are trademarks of
Doubleday, a division of Bantam Doubleday Dell
Publishing Group, Inc.

Library of Congress Cataloging-in-Publication Data

Keneally, Thomas.
Woman of the inner sea/Thomas Keneally.
   p. cm.
I. Title.
PR9619.3.K46W65 1993
823—dc20 92-28554
CIP

ISBN 0-385-46795-8

To Jane, my valiant and worldly daughter

WOMAN OF THE INNER SEA

One

A WOMAN IN HER EARLY THIRTIES, our traveler, the handsome but slightly frowning Kate Gaffney-Kozinski, running across the rain-glossed pavement in Potts Point, saw from a poster in front of the closed newsagent's that her defrocked uncle had given another interview to one of those smooth-paged magazines.

She stopped in front of this poster. As an artifact she found it hard and sad to believe in. Her hand sought—beneath the neck of her dress—the scar tissue behind her left shoulder. She had no time —the delicatessen was about to close and she had no coffee for Murray—but she stopped, shuddered, let her breath go in large gasps of steam and began to weep.

She knew it was the wrong block to start crying so openly. Two blocks further up the road, where the elegance gave way to backpackers' hostels, to brown houses with opaque windows where men went to have their groins massaged by bored Maori girls from over the Tasman Sea . . . *there* people wept and laughed and made the sort of big, loud, mad-city speeches you heard only in big, loud, mad cities.

But art deco flats and nineteenth-century mansions reserved this end of the street for more orderly emotions than these that were rocking her.

Weeping Kate could not understand why her uncle should piss away his gifts like that, into the ear of some uncomprehending girl journalist, some popsy who came of Latvian or Greek or—worst of all—North Shore Protestant parents. Some little tart who knew sweet nothing about Uncle Frank's godhead, or his astounding view of government and the universe.

Kate could imagine him even with the weight of accusation

around him twinkling away at some two-dimensional little hack. Some little hoyden who believed in nothing yet still wanted to ask him the big, vulgar question. Father O'Brien, why don't you stand for the same prissy Christ all those cops and Legislative Assembly backbenchers make a gesture toward at Sunday Mass? Why aren't you like His Eminence Fogarty?

This Celtic city—named Sydney by accidents of history and displaced to the Southwest Pacific—*really* worshiped scoundrel gods and tart goddesses and gave only token nods to the Other, the Dressed-up One. This city's true deities were Cuchulain the cattle-duffer and divine horse-thief, or the Fianna his bagmen and party machine followers, and the great bullshitter and cocksman Finn MacCool, who once built a causeway from Antrim to Scotland to enable him to go and seduce a Scots goddess, and who ultimately sailed into this Pacific city in the company of arse-out-of-the-trousers Scots and Irish convicts or immigrants.

Anyone who knew the not-so-Reverend Uncle Frank knew he came from one of these other more dualist gods, from a god with warts. A Celtic-mist god who counted cunning more important than virtue. As Uncle not-so-Reverend Frank himself would say, *a fooking scoundrel.*

Uncle Frank had a very inexact knowledge of folklore, of course. But by this stage of Kate's history he had said regularly that Kate was a queen of *the Sorrows.* Sometimes he would use the name of what he saw as a prototype of Kate's condition. He would advance the name Deirdre. Deirdre of the capital S Sorrows. The royal daughter of Ulster. When she was born, it was predicted she would bring nothing but grief to Ulster. Uncle Frank didn't know the details of the story, so he used the term sloppily. A glib phrase. Deirdre of the Sorrows because—as Uncle Frank said during a prison visit—*some poor bitch has to be.*

Her Uncle Frank was the only person in the world who knew what he was talking about in matters to do with grief. At funerals and in the mortuary parlor of his friend O'Toole the mortician, he had given people essential clues to their loss and they had never forgotten it. And he had given his niece Kate Gaffney-Kozinski the clue that *someone* had, breath by breath, to find the universe too massive to support; someone, transfixed by it, had thereby to hold it in place. It was she who was appointed to contribute so often the mute rain with her own unbidden tears. That was the rule.

Except that *he, himself,* the old fraud, the family shaman, in jail for violations of the New South Wales Gaming Act, for fraud and bribery and tax evasion, still somehow a glamour puss to the press, was the one to do it to her this time. *He* had caused her unbidden tears.

The Queen of Sorrows as envisaged by Uncle Frank:

Never less than fatedly and palely beautiful, yet fatally touched by love.

Nice bone structure, high cheekbones.

Even when the sun shone, always a woman of rain.

The Queen of Sorrows's shoulders still itched with the burn of suns other people have forgotten.

Through the front glass of the news agency, she could see Uncle Frank grin out of the poster inset. The silly old bugger had always insisted on wearing his Roman collar everywhere. He might even wear it under his overalls in the Central Industrial Prison. With criminal charges proven, his photographed jaw sat supported by that buttress of white celluloid. Hardly any *licit* priests wore the damn thing anymore. *He* did it for the sake of the old days. When for instance men of the cloth were let into the Sydney Cricket Ground for free by sentimental gatemen called Hogan and Clancy. In the postindustrial, cybernetic, space and nuclear age, the not-so-Reverend Frank still loved all that antediluvian clerical stuff.

—And how are you today, Father?

—I'll be all right so long as the fellers get their defense organized.

—Oh, I think they might miss Lyons at five-eighth, Father. I've got my money on the others.

—Well, it's not in our hands. We'll see, we'll see.

He really believed he still lived in a world where that white celluloid meant something.

Cardinal Fogarty might and *did* say, even in the *Sydney Morning Herald,* that Uncle Frank no longer had faculties. But there were men who'd worked for the Cricket Ground Trust for years who knew Uncle Frank and believed him still a priest—in Uncle Frank's pompous terms—*of the order of Aaron and Melchizedech.*

The last-mentioned two Hebrews were as shady yet powerful in his imagination as Deirdre.

Uncle Frank was therefore no scholar; went to a lesser diocesan seminary in Cavan and never got the prize for canon law. But he doesn't let any of that stop him from uttering such suggestive phrases as *Deirdre of the Sorrows* and *According to the order of Aaron and Melchizedech.*

Her tears stopped at last. She had torn her eyes from the magazine poster and was walking again. Soon she had bought the coffee for Murray and some ice cream to honor him for his careful way of life and his gentleness of method. She knew she wanted a third of a liter of scotch and some brutish sex, a universal rut to answer the universe of tears momentarily imposed on her by the poster of the silly old bugger, the not-so-Reverend Uncle Frank.

Happily, it did not take too much to turn Murray into that species of lover. Seemly in his public demeanor, he *could* become someone furious who carried off the memory of rain. Kate remembered how it had been managed before this, first by a lagoon in Fiji, after the tragedy this story will concern itself with. She had for a start dictated his moves, but in the end he'd gone screaming like a hurricane through all the doors and windows.

Good old Murray who did not and never would inhabit one of Uncle Frank's myths. She meant to marry him for that reason. There was mileage in him, and nothing strange and nothing cursed. Even the wreck of his marriage had been an average wreck. Though he'd taken it as if it was a fearsome grief. To Kate, his innocence was of an erotic scale.

Two

THIS KATE is daughter of James Gaffney, owner of a cinema chain and builder of the city's first hypercinema, a complex of hotels and shops arranged around a series of cinemas: venue above all for film festivals all held under the one roof. And of Katherine O'Brien, a woman of deep yet primitive compassion, a virago, and sister to Uncle Frank.

Thus to head off any whingeing about mother and daughter having the same name:

James Gaffney m. Kate O'Brien—sister of Frank O'Brien
|
Kate Gaffney-Kozinski

People found Mrs. Gaffney (née O'Brien) abrasive, and in uttering that opinion of her always balanced it by saying that Jimmy Gaffney was so diplomatic. Kate O'Brien—mother to the Kate of our story—is a fury. Her brother is a wild Druid, and her daughter Deirdre of the Sorrows.

Some people, the daughter Kate Gaffney herself, the woman who has just stopped crying in time to buy coffee and ice cream, have been known to wonder what sort of children Kate senior and her brother Frank O'Brien were together. Even those who love them know they might have been monstrous, furious children.

So there it is: Mrs. O'Brien-Gaffney, Kate Gaffney-Kozinski's mother, is a known difficult woman, and the difficulties her brother has had are written large in feature articles composed by one girl-hack after another.

Mrs. Kate Gaffney and the barely Reverend Frank O'Brien had grown up together in a dismal town in Limerick where anything might be going on behind the stucco shopfronts and the blinded windows. Whereas Jimmy Gaffney—*our* Kate's father—grew up in working-class Leichhardt in the honest Australian sun.

The barely Reverend Frank had to travel some counties away from home before he found a seminary willing to half-educate him, and then he volunteered to serve in a remote bush diocese, and next in the archdiocese of Sydney (to be close, he argued, to the Randwick and Rose Hill races). His sister Kate O'Brien followed him to Sydney from Ireland and met Jimmy Gaffney at a Children of Mary picnic.

Our Kate, born just short of nine months after her parents' marriage in 1958, is on the night of her tears thirty-two years of age. She is close to average height, and her fairness of complexion and light brown hair come from Jim Gaffney's side. She inherits her figure from her ardent mother, and older women have occasionally—at her wedding, for example, where these conversations are customary—spent time discussing whether her fine-drawn features qualify her to be called pretty or beautiful. She has been married once, to Paul Kozinski, the son of Polish refugees. Her marriage I can tell you at once has been annulled both by the archdiocesan court and by civil divorce.

Old Mr. Kozinski, Paul Kozinzki's father, used to boast with what Kate once saw as reasonable pride that he began in Australia with a wheelbarrow, and built that wheelbarrow—load of cement by load of cement—into one of the nation's five largest construction companies.

Andrew Kozinski m. Maria Kozinski
|
Paul Kozinski

Even during Paul's courtship of her, Kate Gaffney had suspected the regularity with which old Mr. Kozinski said that—*one of the five largest*. It wasn't that it wasn't the truth. It was that Mr. Kozinski was honest enough to say *one of the five largest*, but not honest enough to say *the fifth largest*. It was probably too extreme though to see this simple vanity as an unheeded early warning.

Paul Kozinski had been educated by the Jesuits. He worked part time as a rigger while acquiring a degree in economics. He was lanky, had brown hair with a cowlick, and a philosophic grin. There was something in his family's peasant background which fitted in perfectly with his Australian upbringing. Something to do with egalitarian impulse and lands of opportunity. *That* was Australia. Only peasants need apply.

He founded and managed the real estate development side of Kozinski Constructions. He carried his power with an easy charm. He was athletic. He could make loving jokes about his parents. That is, he seemed to observe the Kozinskis' wheelbarrow dynasty from outside itself.

This night when Kate sees her uncle's dog-collared head-and-shoulders, the enterprises of the Kozinskis are ailing. The Kozinskis' whereabouts are such as we cannot divulge so early in the story. But in the boom times of the 1980s, Paul took the development arm of Kozinski Constructions into California malls, borrowing up junk-bond money for expansion. In that mad decade he was praised for it in the business sections of magazines. He has not been the only prince of industry caught in a squeeze. If what had turned foul between Kate and himself had been nothing more than an average marital breakdown, she might have been happy—in a rancorous way—about his sufferings, or companionably distressed for him, as some ex-wives were for former adventurous spouses.

As it happens she finds either attitude an irrelevance. The photographs she has seen of him more recently in journals like the *Financial Review* are chosen for the shadowiness of his face, the suggestion of stubble, the shiftiness of the eyes. The snide captions of the past year, the ones that indicated he was in a mess, the reports that the National Securities Commission had interviewed him, that the Commission of Inquiry into the Building Industry had gathered anecdotal evidence of him from those who once received his favors—all that is so incidental to reality it has sometimes made her furious, made her crumple the pages in her fists. Not out of anger at *him*, but because the issues are such pallid ones.

The real question has always been his guilt in matters the National Securities Commission doesn't even inquire into. Matters beyond the purview too of the Commission of Inquiry into the Building Industry.

Paul Kozinski and Kate Gaffney were married by Uncle Frank, whose own crimes had not at that stage been established and who charmed all Kate's and Paul's friends so thoroughly that people asked, in those days before his faults had been catalogued in the *Sydney Morning Herald*, Why isn't he a monsignor?

Mrs. Kozinski regretted that boozy Reverend Frank had been the officiating priest. Her husband was such a good friend of young Monsignor Pietecki, who was reduced at the Gaffney-Kozinski wedding to the stature of mere concelebrant of the Wedding Mass.

Loreto Girls and Saint Ignatius boys! Marriages made in heaven and consummated in mutual ignorance. *Omnes ethnici sunt periculosi*, as Uncle Frank had said in the garden on the day of the wedding. All foreigners are dangerous. Said as a fancy clerical joke, but of course she remembers it as a warning now. What it meant roughly was that just because a boy goes to the Jesuits doesn't mean you have anything in common with him. History is everything. People will not in the end forgive you for not having shared theirs.

Three

HERE ARE THE BACKGROUNDS:
1. Kate Gaffney graduated in a staid time for students and with a Distinction in the unexceptional area of Pacific History. This was a favorite subject of radicals, since it had to do with all the inroads of cruel European culture and all the plunderings of Poly-, Mela- and Micronesia. Just the same, she did not have the makings of a student radical. For a start, she had not suffered any alienations from her parents. An enchantment with Uncle Frank and regard for her parents kept her fairly observant of what Uncle Frank called—almost with a wink—*the Faith*.

2. Adolescent, she saw that the not-so-Reverend Uncle Frank's Faith was connected not only to mysteries of religion but to certain cultural mysteries such as SP bookmaking, liquor, irreverence for government. Whereas the Kozinskis' "Faith" was different from Uncle Frank's. One of the Kozinski mysteries was that Jewish property developers—many of whom had come in the same ship as the Kozinskis—played all games by secret and preferential rules, hammered out in the Sinai Desert in Moses' day and employed to kill the Son of God and make things hard for ambitious Catholics. Veneration of the Virgin, which had somehow diminished in the Gaffney household since Kate's childhood, flourished in the Kozinski household. The Black Virgin of Czestochowa, the easternmost great Madonna, the last before the Muscovites began, *and*—Paul once remarked with an engaging Polish slyness—the Madonna who had the honor of being closest to Auschwitz, was something of a familiar of Mrs. Kozinski's.

Czestochowa's smoke-stained Virgin will later have reason to visit Kate frequently enough in sleep. But we are ahead of ourselves.

3. Before marrying Paul Kozinski, Kate worked for a film pub-

licity company. She had met its principal, a man called Bernie Astor, at a cocktail party her father had given to representatives of the film distribution business. At it she had seen a fellow feeling easily exercised between Jim Gaffney and Bernard Astor. Bernard's presence seemed to free Jim Gaffney to be a little loud and risqué. Her mother, Kate Gaffney née O'Brien, had worried about Bernie, about his intentions, since he had had a reputation and been recently divorced when she had first met him in the fifties, a decade when no one but libertines got divorced. Kate O'Brien's motherly suspicion annoyed Kate Gaffney the younger—mothers who mistrusted their daughters' talents always seemed to attribute their girl children's small successes to intentions of lechery harbored by bosses. In fact Bernie became a good friend. He was cozily married, observed Shabbat, read widely, had the wryness to prove it, was loved in his profession, and delighted in films.

4. At the time Kate got her job with Bernie, the glamorous American word *gopher* had not come into common use except in businesses like Bernie's, ones to do with the film industry. These were the terms on which Bernie employed her, as his office gopher. The word wasn't just a pun to Kate Gaffney. It carried undertones of unsung cleverness and hidden energy. The older women in Bernie's office, some of whom were rumored to have had affairs on tour with directors and actors, began by resenting her, misjudging her as a rich girl filling in time before marriage. It was delicious to disprove—through *gophering*—all their prejudice.

Kate took to profaning with the same dry, antipodean energy the others showed. She worked long hours for which Bernie did not pay her overtime. But then he and she had an unspoken agreement—he would teach her everything in return for her ill-paid but willing labor. Sometimes he would ask her to stay behind and join himself and a number of the city's more artistically inclined lawyers and businessmen, in watching some new film from France or Czechoslovakia or Brazil, and devising means to save it from the oblivion the distributors had planned for it.

5. Bernie's more senior people, sometimes Bernie himself, began to give her itineraries to prepare for the startling names and faces she'd met only in her father's darkened picture houses. She found herself deciding what time Meryl Streep or Kevin Kline, Dennis Hopper or Robert Duvall should appear on a lunchtime television show in Sydney and still be in to Melbourne in time for a rest, the

premiere, the subsequent cocktail party. She decided which directors would talk at the Film and Television School, which didn't have the time. She brought new-wave directors up from Melbourne, literate, tentative, spiky young men and women who would, within a few years, find their names in Academy Awards nominations. She got to know and respect the physical and mental duty under which *soi-disant* stars lived.

6. She received sexual offers from four famous men and two famous women, generally late at night after mellow, heartfelt conversations. She knew it was pride or self-esteem as much as virtue which kept her out of their arms. (There was of course the question, and she recognized it, of whether virtue and pride were the one beast.) Perhaps if she could have believed that on their return the famous, particularly the men, would call her from Los Angeles and New York and say, I cannot forget you . . . !

7. She received overtures too from a young but berserkly successful Australian director of Italian descent, yielded thoroughly to them, and—through the erotic momentum of events—was educated by her helplessness. The director's name was Pellegrino: Pilgrim.

Pellegrino called a halt, went back to America and wrote twice. They were moist, regretful letters. He was already engaged to a girl from New York. Enjoying all the radiance of a kindly affair, she had known he would soon be engrossed by someone else.

Kate already had in mind anyhow the Slavic darkling, Paul Kozinski, with whom she was soon making love at every chance. She had a life plan, a fine thing to have in a nation which allows you to have one. Her life's plan was: once she knew Bernie Astor's business, she would marry Paul. She would give some five to seven years to motherhood, an exalted form of gophering. And then she would return to the industry.

Paul Kozinski had not been raised to like the idea of his wife going back to anything which was chimerical in fact yet had the arrogance to call itself *the industry*. A woman should if possible be kept at home amongst the domestic icons, seated contentedly with other madonnas over coffee at some long cedar table. But his opposition never got beyond a snide joviality.

For her desire for children validated him as his parents' son. He knew he was safe with his parents in marrying a woman who had sworn off the idea of going straight from the labor ward back to some supposed profession.

She spoke a little vainly of her *mothering phase,* the half-decade or so of raising infants. She used the word *sabbatical.* And—thinking of it in those terms—she looked for a place of retreat. She did not want to wait for motherhood in Paul's apartment looking out on the harbor. She sensed there was sterility to that. She desired a beach. The sea would mother her children as well.

Imagine such resources. The beloved to the lover: I think the beach is the place. The lover to the beloved: I like beaches myself. A beach was an *Australian place,* he said, to raise children.

Kozinski Constructions owned a seventy-two-foot cruising yacht called *Vistula,* named after the river which flowed through the Kozinski parents' home city. The *Vistula* could have sailed to Tahiti, the Kozinskis boasted, and then on to San Diego. None of them would ever have the time to make such a voyage. The *Vistula* —aboard which Paul once took Kate for a weekend at anchor— was moored at Pittwater, a delicious arm of water north of Sydney: green-blue water, the banks bushclad, along whose terraces of sandstone wallabies and kangaroos still rested and bounded, across the faces of whose eucalypts the most brilliant white and yellow, black and red cockatoos flitted; and rainbow lorikeets.

> The lorikeet, indecent bright,
> Compels the homage of my sight . . .

Just a little way from Pittwater where the *Vistula* was moored, just a little way across Sydney's Northern Peninsula, was Palm Beach. This Palm Beach was named not in imitation of Miami but because cabbage-tree palms still grew there, the palms out of which convicts and settlers had once made their hats. It was one of those places that was characterized by rich people's holiday homes and the not-quite-so-superb residences of the permanent population. The wealthy visited only on fashionable weekends and public festivals.

Kate and Paul agreed quite peaceably to break the pattern. They intended to live at Palm Beach all the time during their children's first years. Paul argued he didn't mind the long drive to town. It was compensated for by the short drive to the *Vistula* on weekends. And their children would be sun-kissed, Australian *Herren-volk*.

Convinced of the imminent idyll, they bought a three-story sandstone house facing north toward Barrenjoey lighthouse and the illimitable promise of the Pacific. The living room filled with winter sunshine and was the size of half a football field. The sun-deck was large enough for a child to ride a bike. Even indoors, the small Kozinskis would be as good as outdoors, looking out at an ocean which absorbed and humanized the sun itself. Out the back, in a natural amphitheater created by ledges of sandstone, a land-scaped subtropic garden embowered an area of turf apt for child-play and exploration.

There is a trap in every milieu. Everyone knew that the trap here, on this paradisal strand, was the funnel-web spider, the earth's most venomous. The beautiful peninsula was its native place. Kate, before proceeding to contract on the place, had an insect expert survey the garden and the foundations. There were, he reassured her at the end, no visible signs of large funnel-web infestation. She should take all the normal precautions—knocking shoes together before putting them on, inspecting sand pits, buckets and spades before children were allowed to handle them. But the Gaffney-Kozinskis, the expert implied, would have very little to fear. No black-carapaced arachnid would come ravening out of the bush to envenomate their happiness.

The marriage drew near in an air of exact accounting practice. A family trust was drawn up as a means of diminishing taxation. There were legal arrangements to be made and documents signed. These were drawn up by conscientious lawyers who seemed genially to desire nothing less than the young couple's happiness. Years earlier Kate had signed similar but not so sweeping documents to do with her father's corporation and her sleeping share in it. During this premarital signing, though, Kate becoming extremely paper-rich for the sake of tax-sharing, an accountant who knew Paul said. You just better not get bloody well divorced too soon, Paul. That's all.

The idea of it caused laughter.

Her father had once said, making a speech at some family occasion, I distribute the mysteries of light, and Uncle Frank distributes the mysteries of faith. Who is the luckier of the two? I think Uncle Frank is. Because the mysteries of faith survive when the light goes out.

Polite family applause.

For this was Australia, where no one trusted eloquence. Where the man of the aphorism had to be watched. The elevated wit of Europe was the chain which had bound a thousand felons and provoked a million emigrations. In Ireland, said the not-so-Reverend Uncle Frank, you got a thousand years of oppression, and all that came out of it was a nancy boy called Oscar Wilde uttering a few epigrams.

Australians—the Gaffney and O'Brien relatives—knew in their blood that epigram wasn't worth the price, since it was their heredity who'd paid the piper.

So it was her courtly father, Jim Gaffney, who was considered the fanciful one, the one given to excess of nicety and even oratory, and Uncle Frank was the *man's man*, who knew horses and which referee kept a good five meters; who knew how to be utterly comfortable in company, who was in fact eloquent, but seamlessly. The not-so-Reverend Frank *did* speak in high color, but according to the idioms they were accustomed to.

Yet at some times in her childhood it seemed to Kate that all Uncle Frank's most serious statements had been directed at her. There was a night—it was the start of the Australian Jockey Club's spring season, in which a horse her father Jim had a share in had run second in the Doncaster Handicap—when she had gotten up from her fourteen-year-old bed and seen her father help Uncle Frank into a limousine, one from the company her father had an account with. And as Uncle Frank got in—so rarefied with booze that even his sister was moved to ask the next morning, Why do they say drunk as a lord when we have Frank to go by?—Uncle Frank had looked up at her window and yelled:

—Do you think the Pope is a higher being than the Prime Minister of the Commonwealth of Australia? It's the processes, see. The processes are designed for gobshites. And they both oblige the processes by *being* gobshites!

She believed Uncle Frank was sure she was listening. Acquiring a very ordinary political and ecclesiastical education: not shattering news, but received a little earlier than most of her sister students at Loreto Convent were receiving it.

But before this ordinary heresy could escape too pervasively into the Eastern Suburbs air, her father had lovingly pushed Uncle Frank into the back of the limousine.

There had always been that nearly embarrassing feeling of personal communication. This scandalous priest, rumored to have investments in hotels and racehorses, would—often at the height of a binge, even at the point where incoherence threatened—raise his large prophetic jaw and utter a message which seemed to his niece to be meant for her.

Slowly she had gathered a portmanteau of usable Uncle Frankisms. Things barely worth saying in themselves but having force as said. All plain truths, or truisms. But there was something about the force of truisms when they're uttered by certain mouths, and Uncle Frank's mouth had that force for her. Uncle Frank was her *teller* in the furnace. The way lovers dealt in banal yet always refreshing praise, Uncle Frank dealt in banal but always refreshing truth. As essential as a lover is a *teller!* And the greater was the art of the teller, since with the right resonant dictum, you could understand even a loveless universe.

When she was quite young, even before she had identified Uncle Frank as her shaman, she noticed that other people, the parents of her schoolfriends, would sometimes denounce the not-so-Reverend Frank with a special fury. Their faces would close down. They talked about his imported cars, his alpaca suits, and his gambling and drinking as if he were the only priest guilty of such things. The Archdiocese of Sydney, whether Anglican or Roman Catholic, had never been intensely penitential. As in the brash city itself, the visionary or the mystic had never been encouraged. Generally a lower-middle-class virtuousness was counted more highly than searing faith.

Grafted on to these ambitions of low church respectability, which in Sydney were always breaking down anyhow into graft and saturnalia, was the tradition of the Irish working-class priesthood as perceived by someone of Jim Gaffney's and of Uncle Frank's generation. The priest was heterosexual (after all, how else was he to be conventionally tempted and proven?), a gambler, a drinker, a sporting man. He was even *entitled* to be. It was sufficient that he edify by being a eunuch for Christ's sake. If you permitted him access to the bottle and the sporting field, then he was less likely to look wistfully toward the marriage bed. He was not the great Bull of Coole. He was a steer for higher causes. So he was entitled to eat well and drive well, to put money on the backs of footballers and racehorses—yes, even though an ordinance of the Archdiocese of Sydney forbade priests to attend racecourses, since the possibility of obsession existed there. But after all, gambling was venial, and copulation was mortal.

The reason people muttered about the not-so-Reverend Frank O'Brien was, Kate would realize much later, that they thought he was getting the lot: the racing, the football, the whiskey, the alpaca coat, the Jaguar or the BMW, and the arms of a woman as well. The woman being his business partner, the widowed Mrs. Fiona Kearney.

This was an O'Brien-Gaffney scandal even before the action of this book begins. But the rumors about Mrs. Kearney and Uncle Frank were well suppressed in the household. Kate did not pick them up herself until she was in the first year of her degree at university. Perhaps Kate's ignorance was a chosen one; it is astounding what people can fail to notice if it suits them. Hearing Uncle Frank put forward in some undergraduate debate as a fargone example of institutional hypocrisy, she understood certain fights her tempestuous mother, Mrs. Kate Gaffney, had had at friends' places.

Kate was pleased she hadn't inherited the jawline of the O'Briens, but she would have liked to have inherited more of the O'Brien social fortitude, the principles of tribal loyalty and of sisterly decency which let, and *made* Kate Gaffney the elder stamp out of some prim Christmas party as soon as she heard any excessive or stupid word against the Reverend Frank; made her walk down through the garden amongst the clicking of Christmas beetles and the barking of cicadas, and drive away.

Honest Jim Gaffney had married an elemental force. Kate Gaffney the junior surmised that he might have been amply rewarded —her mother, she understood these days, was likely to have been a furious and rugged lover.

So Jim bore bravely too the weight of that other elemental force, his brother-in-law the not-so-Reverend Frank.

Just before her wedding to Paul Kozinski, Jim sat with his daughter, drinking a bottle of wine on the balcony of her flat. He looked out at the stupefying dazzle of the Harbour and said with discreet daring, Of course, Frank should never have been a priest. He would have been a better trade unionist. And a marvelous politician. A football coach. His forwards would die for him! Or a trainer. God, his jockeys would pull any race for him. But maybe he shouldn't have been a priest.

He'd looked at her directly.

—It was poverty and limited opportunity that put him in a Roman collar.

This was a rare and heretical outburst, and it was something Kate believed he would not in his right mind say to his wife.

In the end-state in which we first encountered her though, looking at Uncle Frank's poster in the rain, Kate Gaffney believes that if Uncle Frank hadn't been what Uncle Frank *was*, she might now be dead. It is not that at the end of everything she was delighted to be alive. But she recognizes her survival as a phenomenon, of equal value to other phenomena, as the continuance of sunlight, say, or the persistence of magnetism in some objects. She knows that if the Reverend Frank had been a Labor Party number-cruncher, or president of the Australian Council of Trade Unions, or president of the Republic of Eire, or coach of Parramatta Rugby League, then she would not still be here. Some other poor bitch would have had to be levered into place as Uncle Frank's Queen of Sorrows.

Four

WE ALL KNOW from our own histories or else from observation how a marriage between two families of different ethnic derivation generates clan rancor:

how Uncle Frank would say one Christmas at the Gaffney home in Double Bay, That old Polish harridan Kozinski doesn't like me one bit. Straight out of the muck of some Polish cowyard, and she behaves like one of the fooking Hapsburgs;

how the two clans danced around each other at public festivals with a brittle joviality;

how Paul, enriched for now by love, entered into a plot with Kate to rise above, to take a mocking stance on all this, laughing equally at the peasant priest O'Brien as at his own peasant mother, Maria Kozinski;

how Mrs. Kozinski continued—with no theological basis—to mistrust the validity of sacraments as administered by the not-so-Reverend Frank, and so the validity of her son's casual and self-assured happiness;

how Jim Gaffney crossed the vast Gaffney living room, traveling from one tribe to the other, pouring wine and offering soothing compliments;

how Kate O'Brien-Gaffney's watchful and tigerish love of her brother ensured that everyone knew Frank was the Gaffney officiator; and how this fact needed to be balanced out against Mrs. Kozinski's concern to have an impeccable Polish priest involved at all Kozinski rites;

how, as you know, the wedding vows between Paul and Kate Gaffney were administered by Uncle Frank, while a Polish monsignor stood by to co-administer, to put licit value into the pledging of troth.

□ □ □ □

A year later, at the baptism of Kate Gaffney-Kozinski's first-born, a daughter named Siobhan, the ceremony was again performed by Uncle Frank, but a Polish priest, Monsignor Pietecki, assisted Frank in wresting Siobhan's soul from Satan.

A similar arrangement was made for her son Bernard, named in honor of the great Carthusian mystic (at least, that is what Jim Gaffney would softly tell Mrs. Kozinski) and of Bernie Astor, the publicist.

It was only later that these politic ceremonial balancings would take on a height of meaning in Mrs. Maria Kozinski's mind. It was only later that the Kozinskis would begin to believe that Uncle Frank had poisoned the marriage and even the breath of the infants right at the source, on the altar steps and at the font of baptism. It also came to be believed that the tainted priest had insinuated into Kate Gaffney-Kozinski's heart the frenzy of motherhood which left her husband lonely and drove him out amongst the whores.

To Mrs. Kozinski then, Uncle Frank was first the disreputable clown, and then the malign wizard who brought curses on her son, the prince of mall development in six Australian states, two Federal Territories and large swaths of California. Everything Mrs. Kozinski had heard and been through in the Polish mud told her that where there is a prince, there is also a smiling maledictor. So Mrs. Kozinski attended to the broader question of how some visiting Polish monsignor might inject legitimacy into the barbarous baptisms the not-so-Reverend Frank had performed on her grandchildren.

In the amplitude of love between Kate and Paul, all primitive mothers were seen to be mere primitive mothers. She who believed that her bloodline had been hijacked and transmuted into Siobhans and Bernards was amusing for the moment. Paul grinned handsomely, suppressing the laugh with an upthrust lower lip so that it came out through his nose like a series of snorts. It was one of those surprisingly entrancing mannerisms of his.

—Babushka wants you to call the poor little bugger Casimir after her uncle in the Resistance. Can you imagine what would happen in any schoolyard to a kid with a name like Casimir?

It was later, in the savagery after loss, that Paul would climb back into his mother's world scheme.

—And *Bernard?* I don't go along with Hitler. I never went along with Hitler. I bled under Hitler. It doesn't mean you need to dance with Jews, or name your children after them.

Another of Mrs. Kozinski's continual griefs—that people might think her family was related to that novelist, the one who was a friend of the child-molester Polanski. Polanski had tainted the name Roman for centuries to come. The novelist had not done such a thorough job on tainting Jerzy. To Mrs. Kozinski, said Paul, *Jerzy* had a relatively short taint life of perhaps one hundred years.

Five

WHEN KATE LOOKS BACK to her children's brief rearing, she always sees the beach. The beach is her garden and her age of innocence. To sunbathe then with merely a high-factor sunscreen was still considered safe and rational. In the year Siobhan was born, the sun was in its last four or five summers of being considered nutritious and kindly.

Kate sees Sydney sand, that ideal childhood sand—not powdery and bleached, not black and volcanic, not shingly and hostile to bare feet. Soft enough for a child to launch himself onto, shoulder or stomach first, without pain; compact enough for the constructions of fantasy. It is made of fragments of ocher-yellow sandstone, and may have been stone and alluvium, stone and sand again and again, many times over. A granular sand therefore with a residual memory of its other forms.

In the surf-fed pool at the south end of the beach, in the dense and buoyant sea water, Siobhan could swim twenty-five meters by the age of two and a half. Bernard would prove slower than his sister. His tottering walk, his tendency to subside while in thought, indicated that he might not become a sportsman. His interest in specific rock pools along the sandstone platforms below the house was greater than his interest in the immense sea. He was an eternity-in-a-grain-of-sand man.

In the spirit of Kate's memory of it all, Siobhan accepted the surf, even at its roughest, as if it were some Gaffney-Kozinski backyard beast. But the smallest waves at the sheltered southern end knocked Bernard on his backside. People—even the not-so-Reverend Frank—commented on the contrast. Most of them came to see that these observations were not popular with Kate Gaffney-Kozinski. Since Bernard was in no way affronted or humbled at being knocked on his arse by moving water, it merely indicated to her that he was growing in a different but equally meritorious manner. Had he been offended or oppressed by water—that would have been a different question.

Jim Gaffney, inventor of the hypercinema, was one of the few who could talk about young Bernard's poor balance and lack of an eye for moving objects without having Kate fall away into a threatening, primal silence.

—It's just this, said honest Jim. School's hard on a boy who hasn't got a sort of bodily aptitude. It's not as bad as it was in the days when the teachers saw sport as a holy Australian duty. But schoolboys are pretty primitive about these things, Kate.

Jim now sat back to gauge the effect of his words. To see if he was still in business with his daughter.

—There are clinics. Thank God there are. There weren't any clinics in my day. The Christian brothers just beat the shit out of you instead.

So Kate would strap young Bernard into her wedding-present BMW and drive him an hour into the University of Sydney, where in a brightly painted clinic attended by poorly coordinated and beloved children, he learned to catch those future balls which would never be thrown to him. To his enormous credit with his wife, Paul Kozinski sometimes took his son there. Another time, rushing from one building site to another, he called in to see his son swimming in the clinic pool. He was gratified the way a parent should be: by his son's minute advances.

—You've really taught him well, Kate. Good to see him away from his sister. Beside her, he swims like a sinking container ship, doesn't he?

He took equal joy in Bernard's lumpy progress through the water as in Siobhan's Olympian smoothness. He implied that all styles that worked were of equal value. That was an unexpected latitude of mind to find in a tycoon. In a man who—as she suspected—could in other contexts speak in harsh and primitive idioms: the language, for example, of the Builders Labourers' Federation, a rough language, the roughest language there was.

Her vanity was to believe this democratic frame of mind of Paul's would last a lifetime. She did not know it would be chaff in the furnace.

By the end of his brief time at the clinic, Bernard was catching small hard balls. He did it with a little bark of laughter which showed he didn't quite understand what the point was but was pretty well enjoying himself. There had been a minor lesion in one of his synapses at birth, a little tear in the normal human aptitudes, caused perhaps by a two-second delay in taking his first breath. But now he was the coordination clinic's summa cum laude. He was certified to pass on into a world of catching, tumbling and side-stepping.

He was still reflective on the beach, however. He could spend an hour peering into the mute mouth of some shell.

It was appropriate for a mother to look in two directions: the mercurial child first, then the hypnotically reflective one. Then back to the mercurial, who in one of Bernard's mesmerized instants would have leapt or swum further than you might believe likely.

All on a beach so often shaded from the prevailing south wind by its tiers of south-end sandstone, that it served for winter celebrations almost as well as it had for summer.

In a decade of boom, Paul and his father were heroes of the Polish community in Sydney. They were generous to and were honored by the Polish Association, the Polish Club, the Polish Centre, the Polish War Memorial Chapel. They endowed the Polish Performing Arts Theatre and the Polish Sports, Recreation and Social Centre. Their faces were fixtures in the *Polish News*. Their name ran like wine on Polish Ethnic Radio.

For a time Kate sat in the front row of the Polish Theatre, or watched teams called Polska and Krakowa play tight games of basketball. She attended the dinners at which the Kozinskis were acclaimed and at which they gave of their plenty. She listened to the immigrants of the 1950s greet each other in that spiky, assertive tongue, evoking memories of vanished women from Lodz or Wroclaw or Bydgoszcz, of black marketeers in Olsztyn or Bialystok or Lublin, of close shaves with Germans or Soviet policemen in Ostrowiec or Leszno, Opole or Katowice. It was peculiar to come from a blithe society and to find yourself envying them their Polishness, their historic misery.

Here is Mr. Kozinski senior's favorite after-dinner joke about the Polish lust for vengeance and wry acceptance of suffering:

A Pole in one of those primeval Slavic woods finds a tarnished lamp hidden amongst the roots of a tree. He extracts it, brushes it off. The genie of the lamp appears and announces that the Pole should make three wishes—the usual arrangement, one per year for the next three years. The first wish the Pole makes is that the Chinese army should come to Poland, should bayonet, plunder, ravage its people, put it to the torch, and then go home. The genie —as always in these jokes—considers this a strange request. But he obliges, and within two months the Red Army is at the gates of Warsaw. After a season of pillage, they retreat.

A year passes. The Pole approaches the lamp again, and the genie appears, and the man makes the same request with the same results. When, once again the following year, the man makes this identical wish for the third time, the genie consents to it but is possessed by curiosity and asks why. Because, says the Pole, every time they march into Poland and then go home, they have to cross Russia twice.

Mr. Kozinski senior considered this story a key to the Polish soul. Kate looked at all the Slavs around the dinner tables on which sat raw Polish wine and good vodka, and she wondered if life could ever be as bitter as that, where all that could be achieved was a scale of relative torments.

Mr. Kozinski often repeated the joke to Jim and Kate Gaffney before saying, There you are, darlings. We're just like the Irish. No wonder we fit right into Sydney.

Mrs. Kate Gaffney, our Kate's mother, who *did* know something of grief and oppression, would not say anything; she had no intention of admitting Mrs. Kozinski to *her* sisterhood of suffering. She would remark too that in the construction business, Mr. Kozinski senior was himself the equivalent of a plundering army.

Kate was aware her husband had a partisan toughness of the kind typified by the joke. His was not an industry for the timid or for those with obscure incentives to failure. The dealings with the unions alone absorbed more daring and caused more nervous trauma in a week than orthodontists or lawyers expended in a year, and on top of that there were shire councils and environmentalists and politicians as well to be talked to, soothed and—sometimes this was implied in mutters—frightened off.

Early in her marriage though, Kate did not find this Kozinski style forbidding. She liked to listen to old Andrew Kozinski make his observations on the Slavic soul and come up with his little tales to validate them. She was perplexed though by the old question: how a man who could handle whatever governments and unions threw at him could tolerate having his family agendas set by Mrs. Kozinski. It must be true, she thought, what the social scientists said, that to men power in the more visible arenas was the desired power. If they had that, they were quite content to be dominated at home.

She looked at roguish, pleasant Andrew Kozinski, at calm, mediating, whimsical Jim Gaffney. She considered the wives. Everyone believed the wives turbulent, caricatures—in their different ways—of the tribal mother. Kate wondered how she might stop herself going that way. Were Mrs. Kozinski and Mrs. O'Brien-Gaffney suffering from an unacknowledged pain, from having spouses considered powerful in what you could call *the larger sphere?* The raising of Siobhan and Bernard seemed to her the most spacious of human endeavors. Had Mrs. Kozinski once felt the same way about young Paul? Had Kate O'Brien about young Kate Gaffney? And yet both still ended up spiky, discontent pulling at the corners of their handsome mouths.

The Gaffney-Kozinskis did much of their entertaining in Pittwater, on the Kozinski corporate yacht, the *Vistula.* I have already mentioned sublime Pittwater. So exquisite that one English business associate murmured to Paul, And to think we sent you here for punishment!

Kate came to dislike the *Vistula,* however, because Paul was never himself aboard it anymore. Under pressure of the growth of Kozinski Constructions' development arm, *his* arm, he invited aboard not friends but people he wanted to use, and pretended with an overeager smile to want to please them at all costs. One of those people was Kozinski Constructions' chief of security, a tall, cropped-haired, meaty man, a former footballer of some renown, named Burnside.

When Burnside swung Bernard in the air, as if Bernard too was going to grow to be a great, beefy enforcer, Kate felt a contraction of her womb.

An infection of Siobhan's upper respiratory tract gave Kate her first excuse for failing to attend a building industry dinner, the sort of event at which the Kozinski boys, father and son, were able to flex their social charm and show their princely power.

She found that she liked staying home. She liked taking all the medical precautions—flattering Siobhan into swallowing a child's dose of aspirin, a child's dose of elixir. Then the long tale-reading session which sedated the children. She loved to emerge then into a living room in which she could feel the voiceless motors of her children's sleep. She sat down, taking a glass of wine and the *Sydney Morning Herald,* or she poured herself vodka and watched some current affairs program.

She felt no guilt at liking such evenings better than anything else. She presumed she was for the moment in a primal mode, and like a nomadic mother, like someone in touch with the passages of the sun and the tides of the moon, she savored everything being the same every day and every night. Sameness was blessed. A social calendar was a low form of sport and a torment of the spirit. She was willing to fulfill obligations only for Paul's sake.

So she found herself—to her own astonishment—content with that commonwealth of three. Kate, Siobhan, Bernard.

Afterwards it would always amaze Kate how the eternal banalities had been proven by her case. The banality that a man who is allowed to socialize without his wife will speak to and be spoken to by other women in a way he wouldn't be if the wife were there.

In staying home from the dinners, she forfeited, she was penalized, and ultimately she paid gigantic tolls. Because she didn't know she was a player in the trite game. She thought she transcended all that.

Paul's first affair, so far as she knew the record of his affairs, was not with his own secretary but with old Andrew's. This was a minor adventure. The real thing began—by irony—at a dinner at which film distributors honored Jim Gaffney. Paul met the great obsessive love, the one who demented him, for whom he felt not simply desire but a delirium, for whom he would willingly and in the end devour fire, be damned, walk through hell.

Kate happened to be there; an off-the-shoulder dress in the days before her shoulders were scar tissue. If Paul's affair had not become the heroic obsession it did, Kate might have thought that the Gaffney-esque quality of the evening might have been what led Paul to take a little conscious or intuitive vengeance against the Gaffney family by seducing a stranger.

The woman's name was Perdita. She was angular like Paul and had fine skin and blond hair. Kate knew and could recite all her features; Perdita and her Croatian-born husband were regulars on Palm Beach during the summer, so that Kate even knew how Perdita looked in a bikini. So did Paul. But it seemed he did not really notice her in that superheated and single-minded way until he was seated beside her at the Gaffney dinner. Anyone would have said that neither her conversation nor her beauty came to explain the hectic and disordered devotion which possessed Paul Kozinski from that point on.

Paul's affair with Perdita Krinkovich began soon after the Gaffney dinner. It caused Kate the usual anguish. But what she most hated about it was that it altered the terms under which planet Palm Beach maintained itself. It brought to an end the ecstatic age—the one in which by choice she dispensed the laughter and the sunlight while the divine children, with easy and infallible grace, availed themselves of it all.

For their sake and by choice she had been in social exile. Now she was a social exile by Paul's choice. He found reasons to stay in the flat at Double Bay during the week. When he came to the beach on weekends, he slept a great deal on Saturdays. He and Kate would go out to dinner together on Saturday nights, but the conversation would be tentative and sporadic and would turn gratefully to questions and anecdotes about the children.

He would take a boatload of targeted people out on the *Vistula* on Sundays. Though she sometimes took the children so that they could swim with their father, she often found a pretext not to go. She hated the sight of Burnside and the others.

The plain, square-faced man Murray first came to Kate's door with a petition he wanted her to sign. She'd had him pointed out to her once on the beach. He was a lawyer who worked for a merchant bank. Now he was engaged in an uncharacteristic act of overt politics—gathering signatures.

Someone wanted to build a two-story restaurant on Palm Beach. Its roof would break the pure sweep of Pacific he could see from his sun deck. It would also go bust and stand vacant or become a disco. The roads out here weren't built for that sort of traffic. They were not built for young men to drive on fueled with grog (he used the old-fashioned, convict-naval term) while showing off to some tanned girl passenger.

The strain of all this activism just about made him sound pompous. But little ironies in his manner kept saving him.

Murray Stannard: an old-fashioned honorable man of the Anglo-Australian tradition, the way Jim Gaffney was an old-fashioned man in the Celtic vein. Two very different kinds of creatures nonetheless. He was never as funny as Jim. He had values, and she quite rightly thought the day he first visited to get her signature that he was bemused, that there was an intensity to his desire for petitions which perhaps his stated cause itself didn't justify. That he was trying to preserve more than he said he was trying to preserve.

There were rumors his marriage was going wrong. The conventional wisdom was that it had happened because he was a man who typified the values of the early 1950s. His young wife, a seventies child, more of a freebooter in sex and culture, in reading and opinion, originally attracted by his quaintness, now couldn't stand it.

—Of course (he said) people think it's only because of my view I'm tramping round like this. It's more than that. People come here from all over the world just because the view isn't broken by structures. The building itself, Mrs. Kozinski, is—I admit—inoffensive by comparison with other buildings elsewhere. But that's not the point. This is nothing else but Sydney's last chance. If this view goes, then the whole coastline's brutalized for the whole community. We have a concrete coast from Wollongong to Palm Beach!

She signed, yet she was sure he would take the list of signatories home and bore his wife with it.

There were plenty of people to tell her what was happening between Perdita Krinkovich and Paul Kozinski. Some did so with malice and some with concern. Krinkovich was—by report—delighted. He had a girlfriend of his own. He wanted to get out cheaply too, and he was most likely to do that if his wife married another of the group known as "Big Developers."

Her mother, Kate O'Brien-Gaffney, demanded that she do something tough about Paul. Her mother-in-law advised her to be kinder and to go to more parties with him.

In the summer before the cataclysm, people could sometimes sit on Palm Beach and see with one sweep of the eye the parties to the three drowning marriages—the Krinkoviches, the Kozinskis and the Stannards (Murray and his wife). Not that people talked excessively about or were amazed by such things in Sydney.

If Reg Krinkovich however was said to take love easy, Paul Kozinski only pretended to.

Someone at the coordination clinic had mentioned that dance classes might be good for little Bernard. Dance appealed to Bernard temperamentally, Kate could tell, and might even unleash in him the athleticism looked for in antipodean males.

The classes begun, Siobhan managed in no time robust pliés and arabesques. Bernard achieved a more intense form of balance.

Attending a Christmas concert at the dance school Mrs. Maria Kozinski, always alert for signs of a malign destiny for her grandson, said, But there is only one other little boy in the class.

The curse inherent in the improper baptism and the Jewish first name continued to display its omens to Paul's mother.

—I want you to speak to her, Kate told Paul. When we see them on Christmas Day.

—Why don't you? She listens to you.

—No. You tell her to leave him alone. None of this, *Wouldn't you like to play a game that other boys play?*

—Come on. You haven't actually heard her say that to him, have you?

—She's come close to it.

—And you say *she* misjudges *you?*

—She'll be influenced by you, Paul. For God's sake, just warn her off. Bernard may never keep wickets for Australia, but he's got a greater strength than that. He takes things as they come. He's practically the only boy in the dance class, but he doesn't see it in those terms. They're all just other dancers to him. His sister's just another dancer. He sees her do some lairy *grand jeté*, but he doesn't think: I don't want to do that because it's a girl doing it. And he doesn't think: I don't want to do it because I can't. He just rejoices, that's all. And I don't want her messing him up, Paul.

She could tell Paul thought all this was only a matter of making an adjustment in the balance of rivalries between his wife and his mother.

He was in any case already bored with Kate and the tussle for Bernard's unimpaired soul.

There was a thin freckled girl called Denise who had been coming for the past two years into the Gaffney-Kozinski household to help with the children. She was gentle. She had trekked in the Himalayas again and again. The Himalayan journey had become one of the rites of passage of the Australian young in the 1980s. They helped pollute the slopes of the mountains, even of Everest itself, but they also learned from the Nepalese to be vegetarian and studiously gentle. Denise was a vegetarian and intended to go on periodically trekking until she was thirty-five. She lived with her parents, who were bemused by her, her penitence, her lack of concern over real estate and career and all the rest. She had a special feeling for Bernard, and her Zen sense of the priority of all acts, human and animal, drove Siobhan to paroxysms of somersaults and jetés. She never drank, and for an ascetic, she drove well. It became an established pattern that she drove the children to their Tuesday dance classes.

Arriving home early during the summer one Tuesday afternoon, Paul found Kate sitting sun-dazed in an armchair, sipping a substantial glass of vodka and reading the *Bulletin*.

Kate felt bound to explain herself.

—The days Denise takes them to dance classes, I indulge myself. She couldn't help sounding defensive.

—Drinking to the overthrow of old mother Kozinski, said Paul, and poured himself a drink, and sat and looked out to sea.

There were a few such Tuesdays, when he got home early to sit with her and join in her hour-and-a-half party. Usually, he would be traveling or would not get home until late, drugged with fatigue, complaining about the long drive from the city.

He woke one night as she was returning from the bathroom with a bottle of sedatives in her hands.

—You're taking too many of those, he complained, his side of the story for their cold bed. And she was. She was taking plenty. Probably twenty milligrams too much per night, and she was drinking extra vodka too. Marriage was a state of such rigidity. All the other people's marriages seemed flexible and escapable. It was well known that people went for the bottle or the dalliance before they went for the lawyer. Another banal rule whose force had fallen on the Gaffney-Kozinski household.

—I hope you're clearheaded when you're driving the kids, he said.

Paul on his own could be happy for her to go on being mother to his children when the marriage ended. But Mrs. Kozinski might inflame her son, calling on his pride with the idea of extricating her grandchildren from the frightful ambience of the not-so-Reverend, from the flawed sacraments. Evidence such as the use of liquor and drugs were a gift to his case.

Preparing for unconsciousness at last, Kate envisaged some court scene, and a brief astringent sweat broke on the surface of her skin.

—Mr. Kozinski, did you ever remonstrate with your wife over the use of sedatives?

—I remember one night, when I saw her returning from the bathroom with a pill bottle in her hands. I complained then. I was worried about her competence to drive the children . . .

Kate took the interior oath to live in Guatemala with them if she had to. Or on the beaches of Costa Rica. She had a nightmare in which they went driving blithely away in a black car at whose wheel sat smiling Burnside, Kozinski Constructions' heavy and enforcer.

She thought of asking Paul if the sight of her taking sedatives made it easier for him to sleep with Perdita. And then she thought that she was too tired to sustain the loudness this would generate.

That counting of small costs was a sign. They were near an end.

And then the features of a pleasant man, a man who would never be vengeful over children, broke with that random sort of clarity. The man who had come for the petition. Murray. A man who didn't simulate.

Uncle Frank used sometimes to come to see her and the children on Mondays. Most of his confreres played golf that day, but he was already not so much a pariah but a sign of contradiction amongst his fellow priests, even though his cardinal archbishop had not yet—to use his own whimsical phrase—pulled his plug.

He was always restless on Mondays. Jim Gaffney said, Monday's Frank's black sabbath. He's got to wait for the midweek race meetings before he can have another bet!

But the not-so-Reverend Frank had by now become more abstemious with liquor than he once was. Cronies in the police force and the magistracy who would have protected him had he driven boozed in the past were now retired or else facing charges. At Kate's place, he sipped white wine on the sun deck and discussed politics. Cuchulain between cattle raids.

—If your poor grandmother could see us here in the sun, drinking this golden wine, she'd understand what all the suffering was for. Just the same, Kate darling, things aren't good with your man, that bloody Pole . . .

—Not good, Uncle Frank, she admitted, against all the urgings of her passion for privacy.

—Oh, Jesus, he said. Marriage is a bugger, you see. It can aggrandize ordinary people. It can make extraordinary ones miserable. Do you love him still, this Paul Kozinski?

She had no answer. He had been easy to love in the celebratory sweetness of the first six or so years. Could he be said to be loved in the cunning warfare of the present?

—Dear Kate, breathed Uncle Frank. I suppose your parents will want you to undergo the entire canonical circus of annulment. All that stuff's easier these days. To have a contract, according to little canonical weasels like Monsignor Slattery, you need material appropriate to a contract, suitable persons, mutual consent, and full knowledge. Now anyone can prove that one of those was missing. And I suppose you'll want to go through all that. After all, it's tradition. And tradition's worth something. If the faithful realized how easy it was—and if they could afford it—half of them would be divorced right now.

—We'll just see. The marriage can be retrieved, Uncle Frank.

But he had obviously heard differently. Everyone was hearing differently. Paul Kozinski bore all the marks of a man far gone.

—Do you ever wonder about Mrs. Kearney and myself? Uncle Frank asked, to show the extent to which he was willing to raise his questions above the level of domestic gossip.

Mrs. Kearney, widow of Alderman Pat Kearney. Mrs. Fiona Kearney—the name you were better not to utter in the presence of the Reverend Frank's volatile sister, Kate O'Brien.

—I put this woman's name in safe deposit with you, Kate, so you'll know I'm not kidding around. I could always talk to you.

By the time you were two years we were coconspirators. And you used to tell me anything when you were a kid—fourteen years old and so on. Remember I took you to a bloody awful Kiss concert, and we saw those rock hoodlums with paint on their faces, and the sound was coming up through the cement stand into my spine, Kate. But you looked at me and you were seraphic, and I thought, *To hell with it all, if it makes her happy.* That's why I bring up Mrs. Kearney, Kate, to show we're soul mates. I would surely do anything for you. And that's why I bring up that name. Whatever complexion your sainted mother puts on it, darling Kate.

He waited for her to bring her eyes back to him, and she rushed to do it. She smiled to signify that Uncle Frank had safely mentioned and exorcised the name of his woman.

—Now I don't want to make a meal out of mea culpas. The Irish are so buggered up with Manichaeanism and self-hate that all that comes without effort. But I would have to say I'm a profoundly flawed man. At the archdiocesan chancellery, they're queuing up to say that's what I am. Profoundly flawed. I mean, you're looking at a fellow who, though breathed upon by the Holy Spirit, can barely get through today without a flutter on a horse. In my case, I admit, it's not exactly a flutter. It's more like a fooking myocardial infarction.

—Now other men in my situation have given up and renounced the collar, and got a bit of paper from the Vatican that says they're all square and fit for gambling and matrimony. But I'm too bloody proud and rebellious, Kate, and I won't let a load of Dago gobshites in some congregation in Rome force me out of my chosen path.

He drank on that, and then continued.

—I am, Kate, a priest according to the order of Aaron and Melchizedech. When I was a little feller in Ireland of the sorrows, they used to tell this story about the eternity of the thing. How a priest chased women and became a drunk and had been stripped of his powers by his bishop. But still one night, when he came to a bakery window full of bread, he had the power to consecrate the lot, every ounce within reach of his voice. *For this is my body . . .* Pausing by a bakery window in some miserable little lace-curtained town in the Bogs, he transformed an entire windowful of bread into *mysterium fidei.*

—Now see, that's how I see the value of what I've taken on. In those terms. What you'd call *inescapability*. And no little gang of Italian monsignors is going to cast me out on the street like that poor feller in the story. I'm just letting you know, Kate, because you must wonder where I stand and what keeps me going in this stubborn way. You *must* look at a feller like me and often wonder. Even when you were a kiddie you must have looked at me and found it all mystifying. So I wanted to set the story straight for you, Kate darling. I keep to what I'm doing out of bloodymindedness. I'm blasphemous enough to think that even I might know more about love than they do in the joyless chambers of the Vatican.

Though Kate found it hard for some reason to control her tears at the end of these confessions, Uncle Frank was beaming and exalted.

—And let me tell you something else . . . Well, maybe after I pour myself another glass of this golden wine from the Hunter Valley . . .

And, holding up his glass, he burst into a parenthesis of song:

> —Oh I wish I was in sweet Dunlow
> And seated on the grass.
> And by my hand a bottle of wine.
> And on my knee a glass . . .

He sipped a mouthful and gasped and said that life was grand beyond our deserts! And then he composed himself and was ready to go on.

—What I'm telling you, Kate, is that I know you're unhappy. I grieve for your sake. There are two people on earth I'd go to hell for. One of them is not—I'm sad to say—my good sister, your mother. It embarrasses me that I'm on her go-to-hell list, and she's not on mine. She'd do anything for me. Blind to my faults, etc., etc. But the two people *I'd* go to hell for are you and Fiona Kearney. There it is. The story of Frank O'Brien, priest of the order of Melchizedech and living bloody shame. So it comes down to this. What can I do for you, Kate?

But of course, he knew and she knew that as soothing as it was to be told that the not-so-Reverend Frank would die for you, there was nothing he could do. Avuncular love, even unto hell, availed nothing when set up against Paul Kozinski's absorption in Perdita Krinkovich.

His speech was not futile, though. She found to her surprise that she too had a list she had not been aware of owning, and that without even thinking of it she had fantastically considered Uncle Frank a possible parent for her children if, for example, as loving partners on a holiday, she and Paul fell from the sky in a helicopter or were lost sailing the *Vistula* to Tahiti. Bernard would grow up to be a bookmaker. Siobhan would own pubs, as Uncle Frank and Mrs. Kearney did, and none of that seemed such a bad thing.

The rumor was that Frank and Fiona owned eight pubs between them. Even more, that he had a share of a funeral parlor owned by his friend O'Toole, where on the positive side he spent a lot of evenings consoling the bereaved in the comfortable front parlors.

Uncle Frank said, Just watch him. He's an intense sort of lad.

—What do you mean?

—Those Slavs are sort of emotionally concentrated.

—But his father's always saying they're just like you.

—Well, they're not. We're intense, sure. But in a different way. We drink to bleed the pressure off. They drink so they'll never forget. You ought to watch them, and call on me in any circumstances.

Six

APRIL IS A SWEET MONTH on the beaches north of Sydney. It is considered autumn, but would pass for summer in another place. There is a public holiday then—Anzac Day—the celebration of the sacrifice of young Australians and New Zealanders on the shores of the Hellespont in 1915. The day was generally so benign in disposition that the Gaffney-Kozinskis could spend it on the sand as if high summer still prevailed.

In that year, the holiday came on a Monday. Bernard walked the water line looking for mussels to inspect. Siobhan did her faultless *fouettés en tournant* on firm sand below the tide line. Paul Kozinski was strangely compliant that morning. He claimed he had to fly to Melbourne later, so the day would be foreshortened. But he smiled. He was not abstracted.

Just the same, he brought with him not so much the musk of other women. It was the musk of another preoccupation, the way he played politely at being the husband and the father.

—Two years ago we would have had a barbecue, and thirty or forty people would have come out here.

—It's nicer *en famille*.

They had moved into this phase of guarded pleasantries. It was a brittle state, thinner than a filament.

Sometimes at this time of year the Pacific grew still and earned its name. That day it was the sort of sea in which you could imagine yourself swimming all the way from Palm Beach south along the ramparts of sandstone cliff to the next beach south, which was named Whale. That afternoon she even thought in a random way of getting Denise to stay with the children on the shore, and of heading out on a surf-ski to paddle miles down the coast. A modest adventure was open to a mother on such a day, with the slightest utterance of a southerly breeze still two hundred miles away. If she only had Paul to pick her up at, say, Newport.

But she understood that she had no one but Denise to call on. She would be humiliated to ask her father or Uncle Frank, and even though—if he hadn't been going to Melbourne—Paul might in fact willingly do it, she did not want, aglow with the energy of her rowing, to encounter the mute Perdita-dazzlement in his eyes as he asked for the sake of form, How was it?

Thus, after Paul left to pack and go to Melbourne, she went exploring ledges of rock left bare only once or twice a year by rare, low, tranquil seas like this one. Siobhan and Bernard were such consummate beach folk now. They knew to the nearest square meter of stone what rocks generally lay below the sea. They got a thrill from walking on surfaces usually deep beneath a growing surf. If you wanted shells not normally encountered, and strange sea animals left behind in isolated pockets of lenslike water, then both were available to you when the Pacific was low and imitated its tranquil name.

On a great sandstone boulder above where Siobhan and Bernard and she were fossicking she saw a man holding binoculars. His head and shoulders were completely covered with a large beach towel. Under the beach towel he wore the sort of floppy white hat favored by aesthetes or pedophiles in British films about the Mediterranean in the Edwardian era. He was wearing long white trousers too; either careful of the sun even as late as now, when it was on its way back north, or else wanting to show he didn't intend to take part in water sports. He was in fact taken up entirely with what he could see through the binoculars. Kate idly followed the line his lenses were aimed along and saw a little way out what looked like porpoises or oily flaps of seaweed. The shapes, however, then defined themselves as two divers in wet suits, lying with their backs and their calves breaking the surface, their airtanks discernible but their heads under, fixed on the sub-aqueous planet. They moved barely but both at once, browsing.

They must have wanted simultaneously to see more closely what was there, because in unison they kicked up two sets of flippers in the air, and went—communally fascinated—for the bottom. Now they were utterly out of sight.

The man dropped his binoculars for a second, though his eyes kept to the point the two had disappeared from. It was Murray, the seeker of signatures for petitions. And now—it seemed from all of the protective clothing he wore—the sun hater.

She drew level with him and called out hello.

—Kate Kozinski. I'm sorry you didn't stop the restaurant.

—Hello, he said. I'm sorry too.

Then he returned his glance to the point where the flippers had risen above the surface of the sea and vanished in harmony.

She was shocked and annoyed. He had been urbane enough when he'd wanted her to sign his petition. And it was known that he was supposed to have charm and was so obviously a different kind of man from the rough-edged media and law barons who populated Palm Beach on weekends. They would have given you that sort of answer: Hello. I'm sorry too. Go to hell.

Murray's young wife spoke freely to people. That was how it was known that she considered her husband almost grotesquely well bred. He was from some supposedly elegant British family— again according to his wife's free conversation. His mother, a hand-reared but unmarried English girl, had flown to Australia especially to have him and had raised him for a potential return to the motherland. He had gone to the imitation English grammar schools the Australians ran to knock the rough edges off themselves, and was such a good cricketer that he was first selected for the New South Wales Sheffield Shield team at the age of twenty. His mother's hope was that he'd return to England in an Australian test cricket team, and that the relatives who had wanted his mother to raise him in uncouth Australia would meet him at Lord's in the tea break and write to her and say, You've done a wonderful job after all. He's just like one of us.

Is it worthwhile making him talk? she wondered. It would have been natural to her to do that—but what was the value of it now? However, the impulse to try was almost habitual. To test this man who had rabbited on to get her signature to a petition which in the world's scales meant damnall. To jostle up against the surface of his hand-rearing, and see what it was worth.

—I wouldn't mind being out there with them, she called up to him.

He did not take his eyes away from the line which connected him to the last certain sight he'd had of the divers. She could see that his face, from which he now dropped the towel, had gone a vivid red. Straight away Kate repented of the game. Because it was his wife out there gamboling in the water with someone else. Possibly going for that extreme act of subsurface communion, sucking oxygen from the same face mask and the same tank and blowing it into each other's mouth.

So he too was in the same old stupid torment. And he didn't have the divine relief of Siobhan the flash swimmer or Bernard and his new gifts as a catcher. He was stuck solitary on his sandstone slab.

If she climbed up to him what would she say?

—Listen, put the glasses down. Turning the focus knob won't make anything better. My husband is out of sight, on his way to talk to Hungarian property people and city officials and trade unionists, and I can't see him. But I know Perdita's there too. *Perdita:* the Lost One. Certainly lost to Mr. Krinkovich. Gone a million. And your wife is a cricket ball's throw away, a shorter distance than from deep fine leg to the stumps, but you can't see her either. She and her diver, who could be called anything. What's his name? What smiling name is carried by your grief?

But in his state of brusqueness, in his heavily clothed denial of the sun, Murray wouldn't like to be visited. He was foolish enough to think he was going to learn something when his wife and the unnamed resurfaced.

Her own weariness, her own inexpectancy of finding out anything whenever Paul resurfaced, made her feel unstrung. To be restored, she chose to forget Murray and to go chasing after Bernard.

Knowing she was spending lonely evenings, Jim Gaffney thought she might want to attend one of his political dinners with him.

—But why?

—It's a distraction. It's a sport. They'll put us at the same table as a cabinet minister. You can ask a few polite questions and feel close to the power. It's a night out. I'll send a car out for you.

It was not her normal idea of a night out. She went, though, to show her parents she was still in business, still possessed of a nice line in table talk.

Some of the dinner guests would know she was Paul Kozinski's apparently spurned wife.

As Denise arrived to be with the children, Kate dressed herself painstakingly. She knew it was her duty to take a sort of rugged joy out of looking good for its own sake, or for Jim's, so that he could be fatherly proud. Looking in her mirror at the finished effect, she thought abstractedly of Frank Pellegrino the film-maker, a token man from somewhere in the ether who would—given the chance—approve of and desire her.

The Minister for Immigration sat at their table—the Prime Minister and the Treasurer were at adjoining ones. The conversation at Jim's table was all about the difference between economic and political refugees.

—What's to stop a Chinese student from deliberately getting into political trouble with his government? asked a broker at the table. Demonstrating in front of the Chinese Embassy in Canberra, for example, and getting his face on TV?

A thoughtful man from Perth's outer suburbs, the minister, not quite the sort of argumentative mauler and spoiler the Labor Party produced in Sydney, sister city of Tammany and Boston, frowned. To demonstrate outside the embassy was a risk, one not lightly undertaken. After all, most of the Chinese who did so had vulnerable relatives back on the Chinese mainland.

Not even for the sake of peace over the dessert would the broker agree. He wanted his children to inherit an Australia which was different in as few aspects as could be managed from the one which prevailed tonight, in this metropolis between the Pacific and the Blue Mountains. There was a kind of love in his anxiety. Why don't I feel this anxiety for Bernard and Siobhan? Kate thought. She didn't see their blood as under siege from Koreans or boat people or quick-moving Hong Kong or mainland Chinese.

The time of the evening came when the Prime Minister gave a speech about banking deregulation and growth indices, and then guests began to table-hop in earnest. She noticed that everyone, the Prime Minister and Treasurer as well, called Jim Gaffney by his first name and shook his hand with a direct warmth. The politicians and trade unionists who crowded up to say hello to him had been boys of the Christian Brothers when he was a boy at the Christian Brothers. They talked to each other in a language, an argot if you liked, they brought with them out of the common past. Jim Gaffney had a primal attachment to the political party of his parents and of his childhood. Kate wasn't sure at all that he even voted Labor anymore. She was certainly sure that he didn't vote Labor all the time. Nonetheless, the *idea* of Labor was part of his religion and his system.

This new Labor Party represented in Macquarie Street tonight had however become the preserve of young technocrats and middle-class ideologues. Some of the old holiness still attached just the same. And in this company, amongst men and women from the House of Representatives of the Commonwealth of Australia, men and women from the Legislative Council and Legislative Assembly of New South Wales, Jim was an insider, a reliable man to call on for government commissions and for counsel.

Apart from the tribes of Jim's boyhood and the new party visionaries, there came also to these Macquarie Street dinners tycoons from advertising, the television industry, banking, mining, development and construction—from the whole rugged and eccentric apparatus, that is, of antipodean thrust, enterprise and acquisitiveness. She had been lucky so far, and seen very little of them.

Dessert had been eaten and Kate was refusing port when a man with a square face and groomed and dyed hair came to the table, got down on his haunches beside her chair, and began to talk in a hushed voice.

She recognized it was Reg Krinkovich. She had seen him before only a few times, in the near-nakedness of meetings on the beach.

—I wanted to say hello, Kate.

Unlike Paul Kozinski, Reg still had traces of an immigrant accent, in his case Yugoslav. He retained also a kind of Adriatic courtliness. But he was informal enough to table-flit and to crouch by somebody else's chair in this casual way.

—Could I see you before you go home?

At other dinners in Sydney it would have been impossible for Krinkovich to talk like this to the wife of the man who was *on*, involved with, and by his own confession achieving ecstasy with your wife.

But in this company, the chief gossip was political gossip.

—What about the lobby out there? she suggested.

—Let's meet out in the lobby in three minutes.

There, surrounded by portraits of former premiers of New South Wales, they could talk in the remaining minutes before the Prime Minister rushed out to his car and initiated a general departure.

□   □   □   □

Reg and Kate met as arranged then and sat down on upholstered seats around an indoor fountain.

—I don't enjoy meeting this way.

Reg thereby through accident made it sound as if this was an assignation. As he should have known, the assignations were elsewhere.

He knit together the fingers of both hands. They looked fairly well kept hands for a man who began his business more or less the same way as old Mr. Kozinski—with one truck, one cement mixing machine, one barrow.

—Listen, Kate, I'm talking about rumors I keep hearing. Let me start like this. When I married Perdita, I wanted to write her into my business. Okay, there were tax reasons for doing it. But it was meant to be a gesture of love too.

He half smiled at that and shook his head at his own recent innocence.

—Anyhow, my lawyer is a wise old bloke, Jewish, you know. A Polish Jew. With his head screwed on. He's like a father to me. I know Yugoslavs don't have any reputation for liking Jews, but I love this old bugger. Anyhow, he said to me, Reg, don't do it. He meant, There's other ways of minimizing tax, and other ways of showing devotion. He said, I know you're going to live with her forever in happiness. But her background's different, she's Australian born and bred. She's sort of Anglo-Saxon or something like that. Hard as it is to imagine now, you might have problems. So just be wary. Think about it.

A few trade union officials, meaty-faced, meaty-handed, muttering like extras in a Renaissance tapestry, went by on their way to the toilets.

—So I thought about it, and I wrote her into the industrial waste disposal division—I wanted to give her something no one could take away. There's an income for her in that, no one could ever take from her. That's the way I thought at the time. I was pretty pleased with myself. Even now I don't begrudge her that.

—Pardon me, Reg, but there's actually a rumor you might be happy to get rid of her.

He unknitted his hands.

—Three months ago, before she and Paul started, I would have said yes. But it isn't true now. I'm not enjoying myself these days.

There were sudden tears in his eyes, falling down the cheeks which looked so well tended, waxed and hairless.

—These days I really can't stand the idea of him rooting her.

It evinced tears in Kate's eyes too.

—Well, I can't either.

But saying it brought its own anxiety. Because if he stopped the affair, she believed she could restore the marriage very easily. But she didn't perceive Paul as of the essence, the way Reg Krinkovich claimed he saw Perdita.

Seeing Krinkovich cry, the absolutism of his love or his pride, she knew that only the children were supreme with her. While Kate could shed tears for Paul, all living cells were magnetized toward Bernard and Siobhan. They were her unarguable north. And they hadn't noticed anything yet—the long absences had come on at a gradual pace. There had not yet been any of the questions normally spoken by the children of a marriage like hers; there had been no *Is he going to go away forever?* Since Paul hadn't distressed the children at the core, had distressed only her, the thing could be managed and mediated, could be healed and redeemed.

So the tears, the wistfulness, the lack of usual Croatian anger in Krinkovich spoke for the idea that his soul cried out for her. For the strayed Perdita.

Now Krinkovich had, almost by will, vaporized the tears. His face was utterly clear again.

Reg said, I've heard from reliable sources that you've got tremendous power, Kate. You know, by comparison with my wife. Because Paul signed you right into the heart of his business, just like I wanted to do with Perdita. Very passionate people, the two of us, that prick of a husband of yours and me. But it means you can really cause the bastard a lot of financial pain, Kate. You can bring him back to reality with the biggest bloody thud he's felt since old Mrs. Kozinski gave birth to him on some Polish shitheap. The bastard.

Krinkovich's idea terrified her. She looked around. She was anxious that her father might appear, or one of the ministers or back benchers or trade unionists he'd gone to school with, someone who'd try to trade a few sentences with her. Soon surely the Prime Minister and his retinue would come stamping out. He always wanted to return to Kirribilli House as early as he could.

She had to talk quickly, before prime ministerial fatigue set in.

—I suppose you'd want me to tell him the corporate facts? All Perdita will bring to a marriage with him is the waste disposal business? While with the right lawyer I can really tie his assets up. Or end up splitting them out from beneath him. Selling them to someone he hates!

Reg was looking expectant.

—That's exactly right, Kate. You've always had a clue or two. Tell him you'll do him over, eh. Remind him of the real world, love. Be fair dinkum with him.

He'd become more colloquial now that he saw hope.

She wondered how he could believe that would work. He wanted her to use an abstract legal stratagem as if there wouldn't be a resultant long, killing hate.

—I'd use your method, Reg, if it would work. But I know it won't.

Krinkovich tossed his head. He was disgusted. He cast his eyes up.

—Look, love, let me tell you something. Paul is scared of only two people in this world. His father and his mother. If the father and mother *knew* that you intended to rip into Paul, turn him upside down, empty his fucking pockets, ride off with half the assets—*they* would really start treading on the bastard. They're two old crocodiles. They'd bully him into seeing you like an innocent, a woman he's treated like shit . . .

This was now such a tempting scenario that she had to think quickly about why it was the wrong one.

—If I took half his business away, wouldn't I take half his liabilities as well? The malls in California. They're geared to hell.

—Christ!

Krinkovich had stood up.

—Have you got some boyfriend or something? You just don't want to save your fucking marriage!

—I want to do it on terms I can tolerate.

—That's just indulgent bullshit.

He put on a fake female voice.

—*I want to be able to respect myself.* You're talking about people—the fucking Kozinskis—who don't give a flying fuck for their self-respect. All they want is to get to the top of the shitheap. Most of these people lived under Hitler *and* Stalin. The SS made them fuck their sisters in public. They know shame never killed anyone. What people die of is of not fucking winning! For Christ's sake, wake up, Australia!

She stood up. She'd been stupid to talk to him. She couldn't learn anything from Krinkovich, who even the Kozinskis said was a gangster.

—And let's cut out the building-site profanity. I'm not a site supervisor.

Even so, she was thinking, Why can't I do it? It *would* work in a way.

Plausibly handsome Reg Krinkovich looked away and gathered himself.

—Sorry.

But then his anger reasserted itself.

—Look, there are a lot of people who say you encouraged this. You never go out to official dinners with Paul. You're out tonight. But who with? Your bloody *father*. You need to be there to keep an eye on Paul. Jesus, I watch Perdita like a hawk.

She could have said, had she wanted to draw blood, *And it didn't do you much good, did it?*

—Jesus, I can't understand you Australian-born bitches. You just don't play for keeps like girls from the old country. For Christ's sake, you've got to get him back on side, and hammer him down. That's just good sense. That's what wives are bloody-well for. Cramp his style. And use a bloody baby-sitter more.

—Don't tell me what to do when it comes to my children!

—Oh Jesus, yes. I forgot about that. Living like a fucking hippie at Palm Beach. You're the Madonna, and they're the Immaculate Conception, I suppose.

She had listened foolishly and too long. She walked back toward the dining room. She turned though for a second, speaking as softly as she could, Run your own marriage any way you like. Don't hive the blame off onto others, Reg.

Unhappily, the Prime Minister and his entourage emerged just as she reached the doorway of the dining room. He turned his craggy face and avian eyes toward her. He grinned the crooked grin which was worth a fortune electorally.

—It's the handsome Kate O'Brien, he said. Still voting for us, Kate?

She smiled but felt awkward.

—Of course, Prime Minister.

She cursed herself for the demure sound of that. He was the sort of man who would have appreciated her saying something ironic —he liked irreverent, tough women. She could have said, How else are you still winning, Prime Minister? But Reg Krinkovich had taken her impetus away from her.

So the Prime Minister spent no more time there. She feared he went thinking, *Silly, stiff bitch.* The Labor Party gets them out of the working class, and in two generations they become *her!*

She contemplated his receding back. *He* had been a womanizer, the nation's most famous. Self-confessed. The runs on the board. The indiscretions so much on the record that they had ceased to become indiscreet. Not as monogamous a creature as Paul. But at least he would never develop the sort of monomania Paul had. He would never give up a perfectly workable and extant wife and children for a furious delusion about another woman.

She realized that like most perfect mothers whose major jealousies were for their children, she would have preferred the ironic womanizer, for he at least came home in the end. He was not— even in your very *presence*—an absentee.

Jim Gaffney had provided a limousine for her, and the driver asked her which way he was to take her home. The Forest? he suggested. The Forest was a stretch of bush, semitropical, which connected the suburbs to the Northern Beaches. There were few distractions as you traveled through it. It was a good road for taking thought. So she agreed.

Partway into the Forest, the driver braked and pulled over into a lay-by. She-oaks, linked to each other by thick, succulent vines, with white trumpetlike blossoms nearly luminous in the night, pressed close up to the windows.

The driver looked at her by means of the rearview mirror.

—Is there any way I can help you, madam?

—Help me?

—It's just that sometimes I can be of assistance . . .

—I don't understand what you mean.

—Look, madam, if there's been a misunderstanding . . .

—I want to get home, she told him. To my children.

—Of course. I just thought . . .

—There's no mechanical problem, is there?

—No.

To show there wasn't, he started up the engine.

When they emerged from the Forest into lit streets, she asked, What did you do before this?

—I was a mixed farmer, sheep and wheat. I do hope madam will overlook the misunderstanding.

—You're talking like a European serf . . .

—Yes, he said. Well.

—Back in the Forest, were you *really* offering . . . ?

—Well, some women ask for me, you see. They always say, Let's go by way of the Forest.

—That's incredible.

She sounded so prim, but the genuine sociological wonder of it amazed her.

She saw him grin tentatively in the mirror.

—It was a mix-up this time . . .

She said nothing. She wondered why such an adventure shouldn't be welcome. She wished she could see it in those terms.

Seven

WE'RE GETTING TO THE CORE, the frightful trigger. Let's not worry about the threadbare trickery of it all—it's the frightfulness of that day which is hard for us to contemplate.

That is why we postpone its literal accounting until later and here deal only with its lesser chronology and its domestic detail, sinister only in hindsight.

So weather:

the morning had been squally;

great thunderheads hung over the Pacific, that arm of it which is also called the Tasman Sea and which is so dangerous in days of cyclone;

the surf was pounding and emphatic, scraping the embankments of ocher sand away.

Siobhan was now a student at the state school at Avalon Beach. She had begun that February, in the same fog of humidity in which Australian children always commence their academic year. Jim and Kate Gaffney senior had stated the expected surprise that their daughter had not chosen the parish school. But Kate had formulated her program: expose her daughter to the full plurality for the first six years—for Siobhan was a girl made for pluralism—and then send her to Loreto or Sacré Coeur for the academic excellence.

Today, however, she did not send Siobhan to school. Nor did she send Bernard to the small nursery school he attended without any apparent fear or enthusiasm three mornings a week. Both the children had been fevered overnight and called out in their sleep. Mad fevers swept across the history of any childhood. There were women Kate knew who had been convinced that these viral squalls were a sign of unhappiness.

But it would not be sensible to send them out in their yellow oilskins and gumboots on an uncertain morning like this; a change-of-season morning in the luxuriant Northern Beaches, when plants released the strange allergic exhalations of April.

That morning Paul Kozinski was, by his own report, in Brisbane on more mall business. He had plans to go to Southern California, to Sherman Oaks—one mall development—and down to La Jolla —another—within the month. She supposed Perdita might find a way of going also.

For Kate could too easily think of Paul and Perdita side by side in some cabin above the Pacific. She soothed herself by pouring out felt-tip pens and lumps of play dough for the children. She talked to them with a feverish jolliness—she was beginning to indulge in frenetic conversations, which she feared the children could sense were too much of a good thing.

—You are so excited, Siobhan had told her earlier.

—You are so excited, said Bernard. For him glamour was whatever Siobhan had just done.

As the storms closed in, Bernard grew sleepy. He staggered to a couch and threw himself on it. Wary of the fever, Kate covered him with a blanket. But Siobhan worked on, drawing away with pencils and felt-tips and talking furiously. She gave the figures she drew fictional names.

—This is my friend, Carstanz. She is a very good dancer. The entire village flocks to see her dance . . .

At noon the sun came out. The wind dropped a little, the surf moderated. Bernard was asleep, Siobhan was deep in her own fiction, and Kate in that of a British feminist novelist.

She heard heavy boots coming down the sandstone staircase from the street and across the bridge of red cedar to the door. She did not expect a plumber or any delivery, so she went to look through the spy-hole at who it was. Siobhan was still too engrossed in the dancer whom everyone flocked to see to know that her mother had even risen from the table.

Kate saw through the little lens in her doorway that it was Murray, the lawyer-cum-banker, approaching. In the fish-eye portrait the viewing hole gave her, his skin looked bruised, in tune with the morning's weather. He was not so much unsteady as strangely deliberate. He rang the doorbell, and she counted to a certain number before opening it.

There should be no objection to the banality of his phone being out of order. May I assure you that in that section of Sydney, telephone cables are often brought down in storms like the one Kate and the children woke to this morning.

—Hello, Murray, she said fairly briskly. She remembered how he'd been abrupt on Anzac Day. Even in our extremest miseries, she thought, it's still exciting to keep the score.

—Mrs. Kozinski, I have a favor to ask.

—Of course.

She didn't ask him inside yet, nor was he comfortable with the idea of coming inside before he'd made himself as clear as he could.

—You must have thought I was pretty crass. You know, the day you spoke to me, round on the rocks. I was preoccupied.

He was certainly shaved, but not up to his normal standard. He had missed a patch on the side of his neck. In this imperfection he looked almost Italianate.

—Please. I'd forgotten that.

—Now my telephone won't work. A branch brought the cable down last night.

She saw tears come into his eyes. This was an exceptional event for him, asking a neighbor for the use of something, weeping in front of her. But of course he had chosen her already, without knowing it, as a fallback. Exactly the way she'd chosen him. The nose for who can become a lover is never as strong as the nose for who can become a haven.

She said he ought to come in, and swung the door wide. He entered the hallway. Siobhan still recounted her tale to herself in the living room.

—So the teacher came and said to her, *We need you, Carstanz. For a special performance* . . .

Murray leaned against the wall.

—I haven't been to work yet this week.

—It's only Tuesday.

But she knew that to a man like him it was an extraordinary nihilism to have missed Monday and have no scars to show by way of excuse. And now to be missing Tuesday . . . !

She told him to come into the kitchen. She led him in and she began to make some coffee. She put the beans in the grinder and depressed the lid of the thing, and felt the blades chop the beans from Kenya into fragments. What a satisfying thing, a little Lethean rite.

—Nearly all these houses are empty during the week. But I knew you'd be here. Your phone?

—Of course. There's one around the corner there in my study. I'd say pour yourself a vodka. But you may not want one.

—No.

But he did not go at once.

—Can you tell me why the phone should go off now? Why now? I woke up yesterday and I couldn't even call the office. I had to go down through the storm to the beach. That phone booth there.

He looked demented. The moisture in his eyes increased.

—I remember her saying that she was taking him back up to town. That was Sunday night. I don't know what time. I was absolutely shot. Inebriated. I think if you'd pushed me, the scotch would have run out of the corners of my eyes. That's not my normal condition.

—I think everyone knows that.

Kate is in her way a strong character. She's not like someone out of Ionesco. It is all very well for novelists not to believe in character, but what if the characters themselves have been raised to believe in it?

Kate believes she is a structural being and not a thing of air. Yet even so—that day before much had befallen her—the river is flowing in one side of her brain, and its voice is taking up what was already said inside her on the day of the petition.

Thus: *If ever I console myself, this is the sort of man. But he'll have to pull himself together. He'll have to get back to being the fellow he was, the polite, serious, manly fellow he was.*

—That's the last I saw of her. I didn't call until after midnight— that was before the phone line went down. I kept on calling *his* number. You know he's a former protégé of mine. But I only get the barbarous answering machine and his voice. A wonder of communication? A wonder of punishment if you ask me.

—Come on, said Kate, pouring his coffee. You're allowed to say you hate the fucking things, Murray. You don't have to be gentle-manly any more.

—I *do* hate the fucking things. What good does that do me? Where is your telephone again?

She had to lead him to it. She left him by it then, but he was back in the kitchen very soon, looking even more attenuated in the face, more hollowed out.

—You got the answering machine again?

—I'm going up there. As soon as I'm fit to drive.

—Very well. I know you think you have to rush. But I don't think rush makes any difference.

Such a sage, when it comes to other people's spoiled love.

—I'm ashamed to say I know nothing's going to work. But I have to test it out.

He looked at the ceiling and his eyes overflowed.

—My mother was many years younger than my father. She never treated him like this.

—Different times. And a different sort of girl.

Murray was talking about his stepfather, of course, a Sydney stockbroker who had fallen for the young *widow* from England and her Australian-born son.

He decided to go and prepare himself for his futile journey.

—Thank you, Mrs. Kozinski. I hope they fix my phone soon, and I won't have to worry you.

She regretted having to show him out. She knew that once he was gone, she would be alone with the rage of the surf and with Siobhan still deep in the meat of her tale of ballerinas, where an evil rival had entered.

—But you can't dance Giselle, Siobhan was saying in a malice-charged voice. Giselle is for me.

Kate opened the door on the garden and the wall of sandstone rising to the road. There was a wanness to sandstone after rain. She didn't want to rush him away.

—I know it's hard to talk to people frankly like this. I'm very pleased you feel you can.

—Oh well. I remembered you'd seen me at my worst. When I was sheltering under that towel. That terrible day. How long ago was that?

—Only the week before last.

—Oh God.

He began to contemplate the cedar planking of the footbridge.

—You're very sympathetic, Kate.

—Will you let me know what becomes of it all? she asked in a voice of such forced casualness she was sure he could hear the device behind it.

But without any irony he said he would. He was ready to go yet did not. He looked at her and there was a rictus of a smile. This was a very painful thing to see on such an honest face. You could imagine that face, fifteen to twenty years younger, rising out of the creams of a New South Wales Sheffield Shield team picture. People seeing it and saying a lovely boy, a tryer, pity he mightn't make the test team because he's just the sort of sporting ambassador we need. The face of a man who believed there were rules and that he had clearly played by them, and was now doubting his own wisdom.

—Pardon me saying this, Kate, but I know you have problems of your own. I think it's all a virus. I think it's almost as if it's a virus that wasn't even there in my mother's day.

—It was there. People feel more entitled now, that's all. You know, to have obsessions. To have malice. It's a sense of latitude. It's not a virus.

—But I can't imagine what lies on the other side of this sort of thing. A wife running away. There aren't any precedents. Not in my experience.

—There aren't any precedents for any of us, Murray. We discover the precedents as we go.

In a mode for departure, Murray still kept deciding to delay. He began to gesture toward the rubber bushes, the tea tree, the liana, the palms which cascaded down the slope from the road to the Kozinskis' front garden, embowering the bridge with their fronds. He was attempting to work up a theorem out of them.

—I'd better get back and sober up. In any case the technicians will come and fix the phone.

He did manage to convey, almost despite himself, that once he sobered up and the phone was fixed he would not have any future need to expose his grief to any outsider.

Bernard awoke, and Kate made him a sandwich. In strengthening light, perhaps she could open the doors to the sun deck soon and let the sea air discreetly in.

But then thunderheads bulked up around the headland again.

The telephone rang and it was Jim Gaffney, master of the hyper-cinema.

—I was thinking. Your mother is going to the ballet with her group.

For Mrs. Gaffney had become in middle life a balletophile, if not -maniac. She had discovered the work of a Sydney choreographer called Graeme Murphy, and had taken to the dance with very nearly the same degree of loyalty she displayed to her brother, the fallen priest.

—I believe Paul is away in Brisbane, said Jim, always better at intelligence than anyone ever expected. I think this is a good chance for us to have dinner.

—I'd have to see how Denise is placed.

—You ought to get a live-in nanny.

—I'm a professional mother, as everyone kindly points out. I don't need a nanny yet.

—What if we went to Bilson's and looked down on Sydney Cove? asked Jim. Where it all began, eh? Phillip and the convicts. Father and daughter?

—Have you been talking to Uncle Frank?

—Well, I don't have to talk to Uncle Frank to work out what's happening.

—I don't need comforting.

Jim said, not quite plausibly, I'm the one who needs comfort. I haven't seen my daughter sufficiently.

She made a number of excuses. For this was supposed to be the afternoon for the dancing lesson. There were balletomanes in this household too. She wanted to be home for them when Denise brought them back from their class. However, since they had colds, she doubted she would send them to the dancing class.

She asked Jim to wait a moment. On the rule of thumb that if the child was sick, she would say, *No, I want you to stay with me,* she went and asked Siobhan whether she would like Denise to come and stay with her that evening.

Siobhan did not even take her eyes from the page on which she was drawing a dancer, yet another one.

—No worries, she told Kate.

The idiom of the Avalon playground was there. *No worries.*

Bernard had just woken and had overheard the question. He sat up, greeting the idea by clapping both hands in front of his face. A memorable gesture, to do with life's abundance.

We can indulge and find outright poignant Kate's minor flush of jealousy. It had been apparent for some years that Denise the baby-minder was not merely a substitute Kate. She was autonomous in the children's order of things.

It worried Kate that envy arose even so minutely. The chance was inherent of slipping into the habit of resentment, of growing up to become Mrs. Kozinski senior, whose life consisted of the bitter assertion of the primacy of her own vision of Paul; of pushing the idea that nobody understood Paul as she did, that in connecting with Kate he had placed himself in the hands of a base interpreter.

Kate went back to the telephone and told Jim that—dependent on Denise being free—she could meet him. She felt like something quiet and less special-occasion than Bilson's, though.

He nominated a restaurant in Double Bay, one of his favorites though not one of hers. He liked hearty meals. He was not an enthusiast of nouvelle cuisine.

—Shall I send a car? he asked.

But then she remembered what had happened in the Forest last time, and couldn't accommodate any more misunderstandings of that nature.

—No, I'll drive myself.

As was usual, he wanted to dine early. It was his working-class origins, he said. Six-thirty.

Worn out from the strenuous business of creating a universe of balletic success for her central character, Siobhan now fell asleep. Kate read to the refreshed Bernard on the couch.

There were more weather changes that day than she could keep count of. It rained and stopped. The sun struck the beach. Then it rained again. The light came back from its drenching a second time very subtle. She would remember the nuances of that afternoon's pendulum swing from storm to tranquillity and back. She was at the same time utterly concentrated on reading aloud, on the quiet ecstatic playing out of stories of wombats and badgers, of Madeleine the smallest girl in the Paris school, of the Magic Pudding and the Giant Peach, all into Bernard's unflinching appetite for tales.

Denise was there on time at half past four. A newly awoken Siobhan somersaulted to mark the arrival. The light was thinning. The sun had nearly gone now behind the sharp hillside above Palm Beach.

She dressed and kissed the children goodbye and went outside. From the corner by the open-sided and doorless garage, the sort of garage people favored at the beach even though it let the salt at the metalwork, she looked back at the house. Because it had struck her again that her children did not ask her the question children were supposed to ask in marital tragedies.

Her car wouldn't start. It had always been so reliable. German engineering, as Mr. Kozinski senior always said, slapping it on the bonnet with perverse and grudging Polish admiration. It had never failed to start at the first turn of the key up to now. Perhaps she had left lights on by accident. She inspected the dashboard but there was no explanation.

There wasn't time to call for mechanical help. She would call Totally Tom's Garage in Avalon the next day. She went back to the house and rang for a taxi. It took some twenty-five minutes for a cab to reach her remote arm of the Northern Beaches. In that time her children played with Denise and were less likely than ever to ask questions about Paul.

Double Bay was touted as a cosmopolitan part of town. It had a high number of Middle and East European refugees who had flourished in Sydney's Eastern Suburbs. It had European-style cafés and exorbitant boutiques. The indications were that it was about to acquire a new wave of immigrants and refugees, South Africans, Hong Kong Chinese, Japanese. What were considered the niftiest kind of immigrants: the ones who brought their wealth with them.

The French restaurant which Jim Gaffney had nominated was a hybrid, actually run by Hungarians. The sauces were baroque rather than delicate. There were hunting horns on the wall, and the decor strove to imitate a German beer cellar.

—Look, Kate told Jim Gaffney as she arrived, I couldn't get my car started. And I'm going home by cab. I don't want any argument about that.

She felt that she'd be safe with a working cab driver. They didn't normally stop in the middle of the journey and offer the passenger extra services.

Jim argued. You could get anyone driving a cab. The Koreans, he said, were totally berserk. He wouldn't want her to drive all the way to Palm Beach with one of them.

Kate decided to be brisk with Jim Gaffney.

—This is exactly the conversation I didn't come to Double Bay to have.

He relented. But she had not yet finished.

—And there's another sort of conversation I didn't come to have.

He looked at his hands.

—I know exactly which one you *didn't* come to have, Kate. That's why your mother's not here.

He grinned. His volatile wife would quickly raise the matter of Paul Kozinski, urge Kate to compel him home or seek a divorce. But she was safe with this parent.

—We could talk about your girlfriends, she told him, wanting to display her humor intact, and certain he had no mistress.

It wasn't simply that he was her father. He *was* monogamous, almost by temperament, and he lived too packed a day. Before six o'clock he was in Centennial Park riding his racing bicycle. By six-thirty he was at Tattersall's Club swimming laps. By a quarter to eight he was at his desk. He went to sleep early. He was a happy man.

Over plates of onion soup, they spoke of the children and of Uncle Frank. At that stage Uncle Frank was still a parish priest in the Archdiocese of Sydney. But he was already under threat from Cardinal Archbishop Fogarty. Jim Gaffney could see extenuating causes which favored Uncle Frank, at least in Jim Gaffney's eyes.

—Admittedly Sydney is very straitlaced. Very narrow. I didn't know it when I was a kid. It's one of the revelations that came when I traveled. In any case the Cardinal thinks Frank has overdone it. Frank has stood guarantor on various loans his friend has taken. He's technically in violation of the letter of canon law. He's just bought another two pubs in the Western Suburbs. They're in the woman's name of course.

He always called Mrs. Kearney *the woman,* or *his friend.*

—There's apparently an item of canon law which forbids priests to own inns. Did you know about that, Kate? Anyhow, in the midst of it all, the most astounding phenomenon is that of Uncle Frank's people. I still can't get over that. Former parishioners. People he's said a few words to in O'Toole's mortuary. And they never forget. That's Frank's great gift—attracting people's loyalty.

He lowered his voice.

—But he's not embarrassed to ask for a payoff on any spiritual comfort he gives people. He's an amazing operator, the old Frank.

—He's never asked me for anything.

—Well, he loves you beyond measure, Kate. You know what he is, Kate? He's a bandit chieftain.

And again he smiled. When he said *bandit chieftain* he was probably thinking of O'Dwyer, the Wicklow chieftain, a man held up as something of a martyr and hero to the sort of good Catholic boy Jim Gaffney had once been. O'Dwyer hero of the '98. Earning the respect even of the British. Transported to Australia and lying now in an ornate grave in Waverley cemetery. Someone who like Uncle Frank partook in the holiness of the illicit and subversive.

—Then there are the haters too. There's a letter-writing campaign against Frank. I met his old friend Monsignor Bryant out at Royal Sydney the other day. Bryant told me it's a planned attack. They're getting forty or fifty letters every Monday or Tuesday at the chancellery. People actually go to Mass to get a thrill out of seeing what they consider a scandalous priest up there, and then they come home and write their cowardly little missives.

—But if they *spoke* to Uncle Frank, asked Kate, would he change his ways?

Jim did not answer that. Uncle Frank, the barely Christian wizard, evaded that sort of inquiry.

There was little doubt Jim Gaffney would have made a better priest than Uncle Frank. Jim Gaffney would have been a bishop. He wouldn't have been a sign of contradiction like the not-so-Reverend Frank.

—You mightn't know it, said the potentially episcopal Jim Gaffney, trying to adjust the scales of discussion, but your uncle puts the entire income from his pub at the Flemington markets into the home for aged priests. I'm sure that never gets mentioned in the complaining letters to the Cardinal.

    ▫   ▫   ▫   ▫

They talked about the passage of time. For she was near the end of what she called her sabbatical. Bernard would be at school within eighteen months. She had begun to tell people she could now see reasons for waiting till Bernard was seven before she went back to work for Bernie Astor.

—It has to be an office job anyhow. I won't be able to travel round with film stars anymore.

Jim said, You're such a good mother.

She shrugged.

—It isn't much of a father-daughter night, is it? All we've talked about is Uncle Frank's failed priesthood, and my failed marriage.

—No, no. In my opinion, neither is failed. Or at least the failure's not your fault, and perhaps not even Frank's.

If *he* had been Uncle Frank's bishop, there would have been mutual diplomacy and a modus vivendi. Uncle Frank was nearing sixty. Time and a new age would soon take better care of him than diocesan edicts could.

Just as gossip then, though it was to her more than gossip, she told him about Murray, about Murray's young wife, about the diving, how Murray's young wife and her boyfriend had hidden from Murray beneath the surface of the sea, and how Murray had become deranged, not the merchant-banker, Sheffield-Shield-cricketer Murray everyone expected he would always be. She felt—strangely—that even in reflecting on all this in her father's company she was somehow misusing Murray, taking his pain as entertainment to distract her father from mentioning her own.

A Slovenian waiter, with the Italian manner all Yugoslav waiters in Sydney seemed to adopt, came and told Jim Gaffney there was a telephone call for him.

—I told my mistress not to call me here, he joked as he went off to answer it.

She sat there inspecting her hand. She still wore her wedding ring and, from habit, an ancestral piece of Polish jewelry which had survived World War II and which Mrs. Kozinski had given her in the first flush of the engagement with Paul.

It struck her as she looked at these gifts from the Kozinskis, *mère et fils,* that Paul could with plausible justice have said to her, *You find time to dine with your father, quicker than you do to dine with me.*

It hadn't occurred to her till now that perhaps she should have

considered working in that business, that industry which, whatever you said about the people in it, was a *genuine* industry. There
were gifts she had which could equally be applied there. So she
had the stratagem available to her of becoming her husband's left
or right hand? Indispensable and unsackable not only because she
once signed trustee documents in some lawyer's office. Indispensable in the strict terms of daily business.

It was an idea—at least—to give room to. She gave some room
to it. Then it came to her with a little surprise that her father had
been at the telephone for a long time. She looked up to the bar,
where calls were normally taken, but her father was not there. The
maître d' saw her confusion and came across to her. He also was a
Slovenian masquerading to be either an Italian or a Hungarian,
only so that he did not have to waste time explaining to ignorant
clients where Slovenia was, and he did not want to describe himself as Yugoslav.

—Mrs. Kozinski, your father has taken the telephone call in my
office.

She watched the office door for a time, but Jim Gaffney did not
re-emerge. The manager reappeared and offered her a liqueur, but
she declined.

At last Jim came from the office and crossed the floor to her. He
looked stricken and more wizened than he had earlier. There were
vacancies beneath his cheekbones where solidity should be. He
began to speak to the Slovenian maître d', who kept nodding as if
saying, Of course, any arrangement you want to make.

What entitled Jim to such serious obedience?

That settled, Jim approached her.

—Kate, we have to go.

She asked him what was the matter. He said it was best not to
talk there. Standing, urged upright by his hands, she said, It's
mother, isn't it?

He seemed more confused still, as if his exact anxiety had been
forgotten and replaced by numbness.

—Mother? No, it's nothing like that.

But then he waved this aside with his hand.

—It's something. But we can't talk here.

At that point she saw the line of his mouth threaten to crumble.
She walked with him amongst the tables, making for the door.

—It *is* mother, she said.

—No! I told you. We have to go, Kate.

They had to leave this bright place full of easeful people. They had been disqualified from it.

—Then it's Paul. It's Paul! Tell me! He's had an accident! With that tart Perdita!

—Kate, come with me. We'll talk in the car.

—The children. My God, it's Siobhan and Bernard!

—Stop talking like that! he told her, and in his desperation he had genuine command. Everyone is all right.

But he was evasive about the *everyone*. She could tell it infallibly. The children might be all right, but not *everyone* was.

—Mother.

—For sweet Jesus' sake, Kate, stop saying it. Come with me.

She would always remember afterwards that at that time she had *had* the image of Paul and Mrs. Krinkovich dying together in something that involved an impact—a limousine which collided with a fuel tanker, for example; or a plane crash, as rare as air disasters were meant to be in Australia's kindly skies.

—I won't go to the car until you *do* tell me, said Kate on the pavement. I'll get a cab and go and check on everyone.

Jim's face threatened to collapse in upon itself even further. He pleaded.

—Please, Kate. I'll tell you everything once we get to the car.

It was parked outside a boutique run by a Hungarian couturier whom Kate had met at parties. Jim Gaffney seemed to have trouble opening the vehicle. His keys stabbed at metal.

—Do you want me to come round there and help you?

—No, no. But if you don't mind, when the door's opened, I won't come round and hand you in.

At last Jim managed the task, and his door opened and the central locking was released. Kate got in her side. Her father seemed to be using the steering wheel to keep himself upright in his seat.

—Let me drive, she insisted.

—No, no, no, he muttered in an attenuated voice. He already knew, as incapacitated as he was, that soon she would be left limbless, a woman stripped of everything, and every vital function turned to ice.

—Well, turn the key and tell me, she demanded.

He started the car and pulled out, circling the block to come to

New South Head Road, the artery which fed all Sydney's fancy Eastern Suburbs.

—Well? she asked, after he had negotiated the right turn safely.

But she did not press it, because she could see that he should not be pressed, and she made a decision to submit her anguish to his apparently greater pain.

—A moment, he kept saying. The moment lasted quite a time. Through Kings Cross and down William Street, where the sixteen-year-old tarts wore crotch-high leather skirts and high heels this night of wind and squalls.

It lasted too through a right turn from William Street, past the Domain, the back of the Mitchell Library, the tunnel under Macquarie Street. Breaking from that tunnel was always a moment of exaltation to Sydney-siders, for the Harbour presented itself, Sydney Cove. Where the ceramic sails of Sydney's Opera House were visible.

There were dangers here too, because lanes came together. The extraordinary Harbour Bridge was a mechanism of annoyance for drivers, and they showed it by behaving recklessly on all its approaches. Where the lanes merged then, a large truck loaded with vegetables came raging into Jim Gaffney's track, coming close to obliterating the front end of his Jaguar. It was in fact so close that Jim braked and began to weep and say, Oh God, oh God.

The vegetable truck was disappearing into the further tunnel which would take it right onto the bridge. Its driver would not know, Kate was sure, that he had unmanned Jim Gaffney, creator of the hypercinema.

Jim merely sat panting over the steering wheel, and other drivers made annoyed swerves to bypass him. Shaking his head to clear his vision, he hit the hazard light button.

—You can't stay here, Kate reminded him.

And then Jim dragged his attention to Kate. And he told her.

Eight

NEARLY THREE MONTHS have passed. The injuries have healed and the fever has burned out, and the Black Virgin of Czestochowa no longer occupies her hospital room and upbraids her. Her shoulders have healed to a pink lumpiness. A surgeon has been to her and canvassed the option of skin grafts.

Murray has agreed to collect her at noon and take her to her parents' flat above the harbor. Jim Gaffney let her nominate Murray, knowing that if his wife Kate O'Brien and he came to collect her it would all grow to be fussy.

She had with her in her hospital room a full bottle of vodka, its label torn. The only relic of her house. On the night, a young man wearing some sort of civil mercy uniform—State Emergency, Fire Brigade—had made his way a little distance down the corridor and, probing round the corner, had grabbed the thing, brought it out, and in the end pushed it into her hands. Stupefied, she had carried it away from the scene. At her parents' place it had stood on a table by her bed. The Gaffney parents could not bear to mix the bottle in amongst the other liquors in their cocktail cabinet, even if Kate had permitted them to. It also seemed wrong to think of pouring it out or throwing it away. It had the sort of holiness which attaches to unlikely survival.

There can be little doubt she looked upon it as an essential item, took it to Fiji with her, and had it now in hospital. It was a fragment out of which the whole might be able to be built again. Given that she had a journey in mind, and a transformation, and that the transit she was now about to undertake might become too heated for mere glass, she'd grabbed the chance offered by a visit from Uncle Frank. She was, she said, anxious that her parents might out of kindness want to do away with the one artifact she had carried away from the disaster. She wanted him to take it and keep it safe and separate.

Of course Uncle Frank, from his long experience of the demented in the presbytery parlor or in O'Toole's mortuary, knew exactly what she wanted. Understood very closely all the saving illogic of grief.

—You wouldn't drink any of it or mix it in, would you?

—Mother of God, what manner of gobshite do you think I am?

So she had arranged sanctuary for the last thing taken from her house, and was now a free traveler.

A number of nurses would call in to say goodbye to her. It was not that she had been an endearing patient. But they were professionally endowed to look the demon in the eye, to be familiar with the ghosts of loss. She did not appall them as she appalled the populace at large.

On top of that, she noticed with a mute astonishment that they seemed to feel warmly for her, though she was not conscious of having put any thought into her connection with them. So was it real regard, or was it rough-handed pity? She did not so much want to work her way to a zone where she could answer such a question. She wanted to work her way to a zone, though, where it wouldn't even come up.

It is hard to define the remoteness of the sadness she feels for Murray. He has arranged his work so that he can have the afternoon free to ease her back into her girlhood household, where Jim and Kate edgily wait for her. She does not have resources to feel any remorse for them, for they are in the game of disappointment after all. They are parents. Parents always deserved better and could be expected not to come anywhere close to getting it. She knew from television that Jim and Kate Gaffney were bearing another grief too:

Uncle Frank had been suspended at last by Fogarty, and some Uncle Frank–supporter in the diocesan chancellery seemed to have leaked the fact to the press so that His Eminence would be abashed. Saint or rogue? was the burden of an item a current affairs program had done on Uncle Frank. People swore by him, and others at him. In the light of Father O'Brien's recent family tragedy, some people said, His Eminence Fogarty might have shown more tact.

But—judging by his visits to her hospital bed—Uncle Frank seemed to take with good humor the cancellation of his right to preach and marry people and say Mass in public. He was talking of a lawsuit. He had a high if raw sense that even priests could appeal to civil courts for equity.

Though the not-so-Reverend was her Deity, *she* was only his niece. In the corner of the room she has left her larger suitcase with all her best clothes in it, including the blouse and skirt she wore from the airport the day they shipped her here in an ambulance. She has taped to the bag a letter with Murray's name on it, and a second letter for Jim and Kate and Uncle Frank to share.

Murray's read:

Dearest Murray,
Please, my dearest Murray. You won't find me when you come for me because I haven't had time yet to let things settle. As you know, I've drunk a great deal and kept myself dazed with your friendship. On top of that I hugged the sun like some moth. So I've been utterly distracted.

If I'd known someone like you—a straitlaced Anglo-Saxon— was so tender and so erotically proficient, dearest Murray, I might have turned to you in girlhood.

That sentence was deliberately flippant, but an instinct told her you had to put in some flippancy. It convinced people you were sane, that you could be safely permitted to go off alone. It also said, This is all our holiday in Fiji counted for: a bit of anthropology. It had been that in one sense. She had been surprised by the narcotic, raging hours with Murray. He took it as a given that this meant serious business between them. She lacked the history to take on any more serious business. His confusion wouldn't kill him. He could find other women. He had a track record now.

More of the letter:

I'm sorry, but I don't know when I will be coming back. So I plead with you, Murray, if you want to do me a large favor, don't make any inquiries about me. I think you are aware of the simple equation, Murray—either I do this or I shoot myself. By not following me up you will let me breathe. If you can, discourage my family from searching too. Ask my uncle the heretic and the ex-communicant to say the Mass of the Angels for me and the children.

So let me put it clearly. I owe you a great amount, Murray, and as exactly as I can say this to anyone, I say it to you. I love you. But the sentence doesn't mean in my mouth what it would mean in the mouths of real people. You know that, how accurately I'm speaking, Murray.

Yours sincerely, Kate

For her departure she wore a bulky light blue sweater and green pants. They both happened to be of first-class quality, but she proposed to make a dent in that. She wanted to be able to turn up in a town like Trangie or Coonamble and ask for a job in a motel and not have the manager be confused by her clothes. So she was dressed in the lingua franca of couture. She owned a plastic bag with one Tampax in it. She had not menstruated for three months, but—since she was fitted with a device—she knew it was not pregnancy. In any case, would nature and chemistry dare that? She carries in her airline bag a few basic cosmetics, some underwear, and some potent sleeping tablets she was allowed to swallow as long as she was not simultaneously drunk. On the road she could take the banal way out, if she chose, and swallow the lot.

She carries her airline bag unzipped to convey casualness and now that she is in the corridor, she mimics casualness too. She tells the nurse at the nursing station that she is going to the communal toilets to put on makeup.

This is the private hospital. The toilets are as painstakingly kept as those in a five-star hotel. Sitting on one of the seats, she realizes that this is probably the most elegant Women's she'll encounter for some time to come. The reflection causes a shift in her soul. It is not joy, but the shadow of joy, a reflex thing, a twitch of joy's seared musculature.

We can see her, so casual in the lift too. She makes small talk with two hospital acquaintances of hers, a woman who has had a hysterectomy, another with thyroid trouble. In the lobby she looks around once, and then walks out into Darlinghurst Road and is struck with the awful familiarity of this city. It is difficult for her to believe it merely two centuries old. This town was aged before the Nineteenth Dynasty of Egypt.

She catches a cab to Martin Place. Her intention is to live rough, but she draws $10,000 out of her own account. The bank treats the transaction with boredom, since it retains the mammoth's share of all Kozinski money in all Kozinski accounts.

She goes on to Central Railway, one of those cathedrals of steam. You could live in the Eastern Suburbs or on the Northern Beaches of Sydney and never see this place for years, this great arched roof you walk beneath to find trains. She hasn't been here since a train journey she made as a child with her mother. The main hall is dressed and painted up now. It is more than a hundred years old, and so has a history. The country trains sit waiting at a dozen platforms for travelers who cannot afford planes or are bound for destinations too obscure to have an airport.

The faces she sees in here, under the great arches, are the faces of an earlier and less complicated Australia. Country faces for country trains. No cosmopolites. Few Asians. Just the plain, worn, meat-and-potatoes of the bush. Anglo-Celts, as people liked now to say in the feature articles, jamming two ancestral enemies together with the ease of a hyphen. Patchy faces, sun-blasted. Often spotted with small sun cancers. Eyes which had squinted across great distances into earth-stripping winds and murderous suns and were even here, beneath the dome of Central, half closed. Features which had been yielded up to the elements.

The electronic screen told her that two trains would be leaving within the next quarter of an hour, and then none for nearly forty-five minutes. She would like to have wandered and had greater leisure than a quarter of an hour, but she was worried that Murray or someone else might come looking for her.

The first train was an express northward, along the coast to Grafton. A coastal option. The second interested her more. Its itinerary, detailed on the board, brimmed with stops, and for a woman who wished to avoid the reproach inherent in the sea it was perfect, since it went inland, northwest to an interior where, Australians always liked to believe, either answers or nullities could be found. The litany of this train was so soothing too. Bathurst, said the board, Orange, Wellington. The British names reaching a certain way inland, but then the native ones taking command. Dubbo, Narromine, Trangie, Nevertire, Mullengudgery, Myambagh, Nyngan, where you changed for Hermidale, Canbelego and Cobar, or else kept on to Girilambone, Coolabah,

Byrock, Boorindal. Before arriving at Bourke named for a colonial governor, and sitting on a river named for another—Darling.

As you may know, Bourke was a town people mentioned when they were talking of something which sat on the edge of the vacancy inherent in the words like *never never,* in terms like *back of beyond* and *gone bush.* All these phrases soothed her. Yet every name on that string of track, Bathurst to Bourke, a chance. A perhaps ideal town.

She did not buy a first class ticket. There was nothing to be had from first class on the Bourke line which would compensate for the present balance of the universe. She wanted to be amongst those country faces anyhow. She wanted to *feed* numbly on them. From the present, poisoned world, she wanted to track back with the help of those faces to the safer Australia, to Jim Gaffney's version, the Australia where people called lunch *dinner* and dinner *tea;* where they referred to their suitcases as *ports;* called all dairy farmers *titstrippers* and *cowcockies;* cooked on wood-burning stoves which had belonged to their grandmothers, and might with the greatest of ease give you a comparative rundown of the drought or flood of 1964 as against the drought or flood of 1986.

She bought a ticket which would take her all the way to Bourke. But she might not go all the way. She reserved the right to get off at the place which gave off the exact echo.

Nothing she saw from the train window drew her until she was across the mountains and rolling into the coal town of Lithgow, hunched hard up against the backside of the mountains. The fringes of its streets gleamed with fragments of anthracite dropped by passing trucks. Promising enough in that it was so spread out and Australian—every miner and his wife living on their own quarter-acre block, in a house which refused to share any wall with another. Lithgow, however, was not correct; still—in a massive country—too close in to Sydney and the Kozinski towers.

But then the sheep and cattle pastures set in, and the earth turned brown, and the paddocks began to look drier. Great, tough, iconic eucalypts grew out of the middle of pastorages and the false green of fodder crops. Wherever the train crossed rivers, she would see herds making their way uphill to the milking sheds, to meet their afternoon farmers. There was a kind of sedation in the sight. The passive habit behind it all, the unfussed lope of the beasts. She wanted to find similar sedating habits of her own, to succumb to their narcosis, to reduce herself to a few primal timetables and expectations. Out here, she thought, out here I might even be in some senses saved.

But most of the scenes were static. This was grazing country, and herds—if you saw them at all—grazed so slowly, sunk in the great, triumphant boredom of the ruminant.

Broad serpentine rivers marked some towns, and the plains were broad, always with a far-off mountain chain of teal or green. She considered herself blessed to be in country where towns delivered themselves up to view according to the same principle again and again. Towns began with a stutter of outbuildings, and then churches and banks and municipal halls, all of them utterly interchangeable with their counterparts in other towns. The civic buildings nineteenth-century brick or sandstone. Or else cream brick from the 1950s or '60s, another era of high wool and meat prices, a boom time for the bush. And all the Victorian pubs which bore the same names, town by town, the Railway, Tattersall's, the Federal, the Victoria, the Royal, the Commercial.

It struck her that she ought to stay in a pub. Until now she had imagined herself renting a room in some large weatherboard house amongst pepper trees. But now she decided she would stay in a hotel called the Railway, in a narrow room with a single bed and no pictures, and a women's bathroom at the end of the hall. Given that anonymity was her ambition, then the universal Railway Hotel was the go.

All morning and half the afternoon she let the recurrent wide-spaced towns educate her. A little after four o'clock, while the train was moving gingerly across an aqueduct beneath which no water flowed, she was presented with a town. Held intimately in a bow of river, it had a distant view of a worn-down, sea-green set of mountains. It looked most eminently a town of habit. It looked as if it would grow achingly still once the sun set.

And since this is May, and the clocks have gone forward, the sun *will* soon set.

Nine

SHE GATHERED HER GRIP and moved to the end of the carriage before the train had even applied its brakes. The station buildings still carried the ancient yellow paint which had been on country ticket offices when she had last made a train journey as a child. She got down onto the gravel platform and made for that primeval yellow, carrying her grip. The ticket collector at the gate told her to wait until he was finished with other passengers and then fill in a form for a refund of the unexpended part of her ticket. He was mystified that she didn't want to, that she should own a ticket good all the way to Bourke, and yet have got off here, two hundred and fifty miles short.

She was gratified that he was puzzled. She wanted a town where everything was so habitual. Where there were hardly any flighty choices made. When a man would remember, as the highlight of his working day, as something to tell his wife, that a particular unknown woman had for some reason, with a perfectly good ticket to Bourke, got off at Myambagh and had failed to apply for a refund. If this was Myambagh's version of meeting and admitting *all kinds,* then it was a safe place to spend time.

Outside the station, in the railway freight yard, grass grows in clumps. There are a few strings of bulk grain wagons.

Beyond them, a broad street fringed with peppercorns. Imperial surveyors, trained in India, laid these towns out in hopeful eras, and made the thoroughfare faubourg-broad just in case.

A convent large and once, in the great days of the bush, when small farmers could subsist and when labor was widely needed, full of eager nuns from the same genetic pool as her mother, Kate O'Brien-Gaffney. The tasteful Anglican church, a sober Uniting. And the nineteenth-century courthouse in whose stone cornice are cut the lion and the unicorn and the letters VR. A few Aboriginals, and white boys in lumpy sweaters, wait on chairs on the verandah to face the last minor charges of the day.

And then she comes level to a rail crossing, with the little yellow painted cottage beside it where once a gatekeeper's family sustained their unwritten history, and here she sees it, back across the lines, on the north side. Two stories, wide verandahs. On its fascia boards, MURCHISON'S RAILWAY HOTEL. Separated by the railway line from major institutions of the township. *That* was in its favor.

The train had left and had vanished further west, and as she crossed the rails by the gatekeeper's abandoned cottage, she heard the steel sing in a silence which lasted a hundred miles eastward, back through silent towns, or ones where all that was heard were the complaints of crows and of old trucks suffering through gearshifts.

Murchison's Railway Hotel. Deep-brown brick walls, the bricks a dainty size which had not been manufactured now for perhaps ninety years. Semicircular writing on frosted windows. *Railway Hotel.* Licensees' names painted over the main bar entrance: *John Patrick Murchison* and *Constantia V. Murchison*.

She did not go into the bar, but entered through a door beyond which a stairwell rose to upstairs rooms. She thought there might have been a registration desk there. But no, this was one of those pubs where you registered in a book they kept at the bar, where if you could not survive the scrutiny of the drinkers you should not stay. A pub, that is, where beer was the main order of business, and accommodation had its place because the licensing laws were so written.

In the bar sat a few old men and some swarthy travelers who wore large stockman's hats even indoors. At a servery window, a hefty woman was delivering steak sandwiches. The manager looked up from pouring beers and yelled, Okay, boys!

He moved to fetch the sandwiches and put them in front of the travelers. As he did it of course he noticed Kate.

At this first sighting of Jack Murchison, owner-manager of the Myambagh Railway Hotel, Kate thought he looked unreliable. He was tall but carried weight at his middle. He had an appeasing quickness to the way he delivered the sandwiches and worked the beer taps. He had been very ready to laugh when one of the travelers made some joke over the meat in the sandwich.

All this is to say that he looked the way the licensee of a pub like this should look according to the program in Kate's head. He was properly wary as he approached Kate. Though she had dressed down, her manner wasn't right by him. He did not know that she wanted his tolerance. She hoped that he would understand she was in earnest transition. The tragedy had to be fully absorbed into the cells yet.

—Help you, dear? he asked edgily.

—I was looking for accommodation.

She could not stop her head from shaking slightly sideways—that had been happening, a flick of the head which might look deliberate but which was beyond her will.

—We've got some rooms.

He cried out over a shoulder.

—Connie, watch the bar will you?

A woman's voice, young, asked why. It sounded querulous in a habitual way.

—Someone wants to look at a room.

One of the travelers at the bar said, Jesus, Jack, you'd better get that lady up the stairs before Connie sees you.

There was a waspish titter from the old man at the end of the bar. A knowing rustle of resigned and barely requited male desire. Jack turned to the traveler in the big hat.

—Get fucked, Ian.

The publican grabbed a key from the wall beneath the rum and whiskey bottles. He signaled to Kate that she should move parallel to him along the bar and meet around the corner in the saloon. So it happened. The saloon was a little bar. It would be cozier on a winter's night.

He then led her out into the hallway where she'd first entered and up the stairway. Paneled in cedar, its texture had been subdued by layers of varnish. The upper walls were metal molding, the sort of thing those Victorians and Edwardians who had desired to fill the world with mass-produced houses and hotels had manufactured and sent to the remotest places. Fleur-de-lis pattern, all painted cream.

The large man called Jack was half turned back to her, looking down as he climbed the stairs.

—You know we've got a lot of tradesmen here, working on the flood damage.

—No, I didn't know that.

—Thought you might.

—No.

—That bugger down there's right. Connie'll give me hell. So no contract exists between you and me, love. I'm just showing you the room, as required by the licensing law, and that's it. I'm not saying I'm renting it yet. I need to know a few things . . .

Kate felt a sort of mist of fatigue rise up her limbs.

—What things?

—Look, you don't look like a traveling woman. Just the same, you can't work out of a place like this. If that's what you want. I'd lose my license.

—Work? No one's mentioned *work* to you.

—You know what I mean, love. I've had girls stay here before and try to work the bar. The former owner ran the place like that. He took the risk. I can't, love. Because (a) I'm mortgaged up to my armpits. (b) Connie wouldn't let it happen. (c) There's such a thing as the bloody licensing laws of New South Wales.

—You think I'm a prostitute? I simply want a room. Though if you wanted a reliable employee . . .

—Christ, an employee?

He had paused on the top step, by the gigantic, dark upstairs corridor of Murchison's Railway Hotel.

—You know how to do that, love? Barmaiding?

—I believe I could learn pretty fast.

—You believe . . .

He shook his vast, meaty head in a twice-shy way.

—Not that it's simple, I know. But I would really love to do some work like that. Repetitive. I could wash up if you wished.

—What work did you do before?

—I worked in an office.

—What's your name?

—Kate Gaffney.

—Have you been in jail or something? Or a psychiatric hospital? Something like that?

—No. Do I look like it?

—Well, a man can always use barstaff from Thursday onwards. But Jesus, you're a good-looking girl. Connie wouldn't trust me round you. Look, I never go near other women. *Thou shalt not covet thy neighbor's wife.* But Connie doesn't believe in me, I know it. It's her way.

—I might try one of the other places.

—Hold hard. I'd hate to see someone as pretty as you go off to the Federal or the Commercial. There are some pretty rough pubs in this town. I know you're thinking how I don't look like a disciplinarian. But I bloody am. I keep a good discipline. On myself, too. Pub discipline starts with the publican. Jesus, there's some awful bastards in a town like this. Blokes from up the river who attack their little sisters. You'd be safe here, but I wouldn't swear by the other places, not at all.

They were in the comfortless dark upstairs corridor now.

—Look, I've got to be square with you. I can see you being okay for business here. But Jesus, we don't even know each other. Kate, is it? Look at the room for a start, Kate.

He opened a door. It was the very essence of room, the room she'd dreamed of on the train. Three-quarter bed, a lowboy. A blind. A bedlamp. A chair and a washbasin. One picture—a scene of the Gwydir River, cut from a calendar and framed.

—Ladies' along the verandah. It's not the Regent Hotel, but we keep it clean. The artwork isn't exactly Picasso.

He tapped the glass of the picture.

—Eighteen dollars for breakfast and dinner. Hearty bush tucker, I can promise you. We can make an arrangement on a weekly rate *if* . . .

—If Connie likes me.

—Exactly, love. And not only that. You bring one man across this threshold, and you're on your lovely little backside out in the street. I don't care if it's the middle of the night. I'm still finding my way with the licensing police up here. You do understand me, don't you?

Kate was tiring of Jack Murchison's instructive tone. She undid the top button of her cardigan and dragged both the wool and the shirt beneath it away to expose her left shoulder.

—Do you see that?

Jack squinted at what Kate knew confidently to be a disfigured, deathly, lumpy parody of flesh.

—Jesus!

—Hard to make a living as a tart with shoulders like that.

—Jesus. Sorry, love.

His head was half turned away, and he was anxious for her to cover her shoulders again.

—Room's yours.

—And what about the job?

—You stick round till Poet's Day, we'll try you out.

—Poet's Day?

—Yes. Friday, love. Piss Off Early Tomorrow's Saturday. Poet's Day.

—And you're Mr. Murchison?

—Jack. Wife's Connie. She's an ethnic. Greek. Old man owns a café in Goondiwindi. Set us up in this place. Really did me a favor. Jesus!

He was not ironic about it. He was filially grateful.

From the bottom of the stairs, the Greek wife could be heard crying.

—Jack? Jack? You have to rig up another CO-two canister.

He smiled and whispered indulgently.

—She knows I'm with another woman. You watch yourself with the blokes, love. To some of them, handicaps mean nothing.

Kate had cause all at once to think of her burns as handicaps. It put them in a new light. There were kindnesses strangers did for you even with their misnomers.

—Handicaps? I can run. I can dance and even swim.

—Okay. Between now and Poet's, you can have a good look at our metropolis, love. Should take you all of three minutes. They just closed the public baths last week for the winter. Should have left 'em till the northerlies started. Used 'em as an ice rink eh?

She found herself following him like a chatelaine to the top of the stairs. He took two steps down and then turned again.

—Connie'll look after you, love. She'll scare the buggers off.

The idea of Connie the virago seemed to tickle him. He laughed all the way to the bottom of the stairs.

Ten

S HE WANTED TO VERIFY that it was a three-minute town so
she crossed the railway line again to examine things as laid out
so cleverly and essentially.

Some things she was looking at for a second time, but now she
had a room in town, the angle of inquiry was different. She found
what she wanted. She found for example that the little Congrega-
tional church carried a fading pastel poster on its noticeboard:
Myambagh is not Your Ambagh. It's God's Ambagh! She wanted
to see, and found, the town baths with a drained pool, a high wire
fence and a locked gate with the sign THE FLORENCE TRELOAR MEMO-
RIAL POOL.

She wanted to see the other two-story pubs, the Royal and Tattersall's, whose polarity on the south side of the line kept Murchison's Railway Hotel in its place on the north. She wanted to see
the standard war memorial, the putteed World War I digger, fore-
arms folded on the butt of his bayonet-down rifle. She wanted to
read the never before encountered and yet familiar names of those
who had gone from Myambagh into a distant furnace: Ainsworth,
Brady, Clarke, Dankworth, Egan, Flannery, Gordon, Gogarty,
Harris, Ireton, Jenkins, Kelly, Lloyd, Mangan . . . Not expecting
a second conflagration, the civic fathers of Myambagh had not left
room for the new generation of dead in '39–'45. Their names were
crowded onto one remaining side: Lavery, McIntosh, MacMillan,
O'Leary, Phillips.

The numbing, familiar names whose sacrifice served now, each
one, as a little specific of two or three syllables to take the edge off
Kate Gaffney's dementia.

Near the War Memorial, a little metal sculpture of a merino
sheep in honor of Horace Wrangle, native of Devon, Myambagh's
founding pastoralist.

On a corner the Bowling Club, such lovingly cared-for greens, such friendly knots of the middle-aged and the elderly in white flannels and skirts and cardigans. At the end of the greens, which had the even plushness of an untouched snooker table, a licensed clubhouse. Kate could see the barman from the street—he wore a little black bow tie on a muscular throat. Above him, the photograph of the Monarch, and the gold-leafed Roll of Honour which said who had won the mixed doubles in 1984.

One more corner along, the Returned Services League: *Age shall not weary them.* At its front desk, she could see, an elderly man was dozing. She could hear the metallic stammer of a poker machine within. The pokies, the bandits. The dispensers of small fortunes and manageable griefs, the devourers of addicted wives' housekeeping. *Age shall not weary them* . . . Only in Kate's nation, only in Australia and in every town, this nexus between one-armed-bandits and the holy memory of boys dead on the Kokoda Trail in 1942, in Flanders in 1917.

The high school: named after the lesser nineteenth-century explorer, discoverer of Myambagh's fatal headwaters, which seem to flood the town on a cyclical basis, and the sighter of rare species of kingfishers. The Captain John Eglington High School. A knee-high thumb of granite stood by the fence. *The Staff of the Captain John Eglington High School raised this monument in appreciation of the efforts of the students in restoring the buildings after the flood of 1986.*

Beneath that the prosaic motto: *Industry and Merit.*

Anything more remarkable would have been a stab in the bowels, a hiatus of the breath.

Around the corner, the St. John Ambulance station had its door open, and a young, moon-eyed ambulance man sat in the vehicle, chattering into a radio without conviction. It looked to Kate as if the device was new to him, as if electronics of this sophistication weren't his métier.

But she was not looking for clever countrymen.

All the doors of the shed marked Wrangle Shire Volunteer Bush Fire Brigade were properly shut. The memories of the incandescent bushfires of the past were held in place with a heavy lock.

She found herself turning in idly to the newsagents. She asked the woman who ran the cash register whether they stocked paperbacks.

—No, dear. We found there wasn't the demand.

So ever more ideal, Myambagh, Wrangle Shire's Venice, sang in her brain. Here there was a chance of being breathed in by the great antipodean stupefaction. She bought a copy of the *Wrangle Shire Times,* a photograph of three Rotary past presidents and their wives on its front page, and she walked out with its triviality wrapped under her arm, a sedative within reach. Who knew but that, before she got back to Murchison's Railway Hotel, she might need to sustain herself by reading the scores of the Myambagh Central versus Wombilil A Grade cricket final?

There was an aged man, perhaps senile, on a bench outside Dunnegan's Country Stores, who seemed to recognize her at once as a stranger.

—Have you seen our levees, dear?

—Levees?

—Flood levees, love. We're famous for floods. The levees're the most interesting thing in town. You ought to see the levees.

—I will. I'll make sure of it.

—That's the girl!

The bar when she returned was full of men in white overalls, or else with freshly scrubbed faces and combed hair, who may have recently emerged from overalls. They were the tradesmen brought in to repair the marks of the flood.

She closed herself in her room and sat on the bed.

There was a knocking on the door. Drum roll: *Shave-and-a-haircut-two-bob* knocking that wanted to show it didn't have intent. Jack Murchison was there.

—Connie wants to know would you like a cup of tea?

He made two separate significant clenchings of his brows.

She recognized this as a command of unseen Connie's. She followed the biddable Jack Murchison down the stairway and out along a verandah where the working rooms of the pub—the kitchen, the laundry, the meat-cutting room—were all located, their walls hedged in by the metal kegs waiting for collection. Kate entered the oven-warm kitchen in which Connie Murchison sat, feeding stewed pears to one of her two children who were just home from school. Jack Murchison's wife was dark-eyed and with a dark and yet at the same time pale complexion. She was severely handsome. She had bruised, aggrieved eyes, a genetic grievance her parents had passed on to her. A bitterness due to the ancient behavior of the Turks or the Macedonians.

One child, a boy, large-boned like Jack, roamed the kitchen looking for something to put on bread. A mountainous woman was cooking steaks at an enormous fuel stove. Veal and langouste and angel-hair pasta had no place in the Railway Hotel dispensation. Here you gorged on steak and eggs and white bread. You perished early of a heart clogged by hefty protein.

The steak's redolence was an omen for Kate and a navigational reminder. It told her she was on course to a tolerable end. Connie put her youngest child down and let it run out the door.

—You want a cup of tea?

—Yes.

She couldn't prevent that silly involuntary flick of the head.

—Anything the matter? asked Connie with a new kind of suspicion. The tic soothed Connie's moral concern but raised the possibility her new guest was epileptic.

Kate was aware that as she drank the tea, Connie watched her and held the discontented mouth in repose.

—We'll have lots of men in for tea. Every night we've got lots of men. Jack says he really doesn't think you know how many.

—I didn't really know. I was looking for a quiet town. But I'll see how this goes.

—Well, it's a quiet town. Except the place is full of men. This is the way Myambagh goes: we have a flood every three years, and every time it happens, the politicians come in by helicopter and promise immediate help. So they fly in tradesmen, and pay them these special rates to paint and plaster before the damn place has even dried out. And then, a year or two later, when the town *has* dried out, they send them all back again, because by then the plaster has fallen off the walls, and the paint's blistered. That's why Shirley's cooking all those steaks you see. For the men. You know.

Throughout her introduction Connie looked at Kate with cagey eyes. Again and quite frankly, the eyes of a woman who may not have seen the worst but certainly expected to.

—So you're not really keen on the town being full of men?

Kate shook her head. In fact she *was* wondering whether she would leave, go west on the unused portion of her Bourke ticket. But it would mean giving up this exactly tailored town.

—I'm not a men sort of person.

Her eyes following her smaller boy child around the kitchen, Connie gave a snort of laughter. It sounded sisterly.

—God, that's going to disappoint them.

Shirley the steak cooker laughed too.

Connie said, They really need women, those buggers. For about ten minutes a week.

Kate was emboldened now.

—I suppose I was brought in here to pass a test?

—Yeah, said Connie. Grievance came back to her face again, the sullenness which derived from before her birth. But as if to show that she had grounds for complaint in the present imperfection of things as well, she yelled, Hey, Jack! You called the distributor in Dubbo yet?

From the public bar Jack yelled, Soon darls! I've just got to broach a new keg first.

Eleven

APPROACHING POET'S DAY, Kate saw with some pleasure that her hair was getting raggier. In the spirit of this change, she maintained a savage air of separateness at dinner, and the men let her sit unmolested at her own table. The food was robust as you would expect, of vast quantity and bad for the heart. I will thicken, Kate promised herself, and my blood will thicken too to a kind of country glue. I will eat steak for breakfast. I will become a caution to the Australian Heart Foundation. I will swell their statistics for rural ill-health.

The table covers were plastic imitation lace punched out in Taiwan, and she was not worried about splashing steak juice across them as she ate her way toward becoming different.

She was aware of two types amongst the men who were painting and plastering the town.

There were some who clearly had an orderly life elsewhere. It marked the way they behaved here at the Railway Hotel, Myambagh. They'd come to a flood town to earn the good money available to those who mend disasters, and you could feel them holding themselves in against an unwise use of a dollar. They spent hardly anything in the bar. Their hair was brushed, they conversed quietly, their eyes did not jerk around the room and their elbows were tucked into their sides.

There was another breed: the escapees. Somewhere lay a city or a marriage they hated, and they were paying for taking false choices in the past. Their money would go to child maintenance or to some payment attended with high interest rates and potential loss.

The men of fixed purpose, the Monks, sat together in their own enclaves in the dining room, as did the Escapees. The Escapees were recklessly loud. Always they asked Kate if she would like a drink with them. Even if she had wanted to, she wondered could she drink what she really wanted. You were required, it seemed to her, to bludgeon yourself with the heavy beer from the taps. If she ordered a gin and tonic, it might betray and define her. She might drink, she told them, some Friday.

—That's no bloody good, love. Most of us go back home Poet's night.

She thought of the fat marbled steak she had eaten and the beer she would come to drink in time, and was gratified.

At the funeral Mrs. Kozinski's pursed mouth fell away into hysteria, yelling across the grave.

—What sort of mother? What sort of mother? If you had been a wife! Dining with your father? Of course, you dined with your father! If you had been a wife and a mother, I would have my grandchildren!

If she could clog in her blood the memory of Mrs. Kozinski's frightful plaint! She would smother it up in the wrong kind of carbohydrate. Fearing nothing except that Mrs. Kozinski's voice might not be blotted out in torrents of country food.

The Escapees went to the bar confused, the Monks went upstairs to watch a quiz or current affairs or the instigating murder of some cop show, and thence to their thrifty beds. She could feel from the bar the emanations of the Escapees' surmises: was she *on* or a teaser or a dyke? Whereas watching margarine commercials, the Monks wondered was she really a nice girl or a troublemaker? Kate hoped that these two poles of speculation held her in stupefying balance, like Buridan's ass, stuck halfway between two equidistant bundles of hay.

In a month or so, Kate was sure, neither the Monks nor the Escapees would bother entertaining such questions at all. The electricity would slacken. And if it did not, she would catch another train, looking for one apt town amongst all the others, as they dwindled away in population the nearer you got to the core of the country.

Cardinal Archbishop Fogarty was at the graveside, and Kate heard people say of Mrs. Kozinski, Imagine, behaving like that in front of the cardinal!

As if it made any difference. Cardinal Fogarty's eminential purple added a fragment of heroism to Mrs. Kozinski's scream.

Uncle Frank was too demented and Monsignor Pietecki handled the actual obsequies. And the crone yelled without restraint,

—You did not respect my motherhood, you did not give allegiance to my son. And so God came down on you like an axe.

We will see, she cried within herself, having spooned custard in to smother her heart. I will do a better job on myself than God could.

In the television room upstairs, when she looked in and beheld a curled-lipped commentator grilling a shadow minister in a manner which had the entire attention of the Monks, she noticed a bookshelf, an aging encyclopedia in it. It was perhaps a leftover from the days when Myambagh's wool and wheat earned a lot from places far removed. Or maybe Jack Murchison had bought it on an impulse at a sheep station auction.

She grabbed one volume. Back in her room, the door bolted, she sat on the bed and read studiously, since even a ghost needs news and diversion.

Volume 13—Jirásek to Lighthouses. In the casual hope of finding something new about Slavs, she turned to the opening page and read Jirásek. She found he was a Czech. 1851–1930.

—Jirásek was born at the Hronov, Bohemia, on August 23rd, 1851 and served as a high school teacher throughout his working life. His historical novels were the most famous of his era and invoked Czechoslovakian nationalism. He showed a strong interest in the Hussite period . . .

Joss, she discovered, was a pidgin English word derived from Chinese seaports and applied to idols and deities. *Jota* was a traditional Spanish dance from Aragon and exploited 3/4 rhythm. *Slobodan Jovanović* was a Serbian national lawyer, politician and historian who died in Windsor, Canada in 1962. *James Joyce—* well, she knew of James Joyce. She had failed to understand *Finnegans Wake* at university. She skipped *Judaism,* with mental apologies and a few inner tears in Bernard Astor's direction; she skipped the *Book of Judges, Julian of Norwich, Jungle warfare.* She read a little of *Jurassic,* and the section of *Jurisprudence*'s two basic concerns.

And then she came to the Ks, and at their head *Kangaroo,* the national totem. On the same page as *Kandinski.* People shot these animals. There were probably men in the bar downstairs who could tell her how you prepared yourself to execute them. Yet their placid herbivore stare, well captured in the photograph beside the entry, should have given them immunity. *Macropodidae*—Greek for *big-footed.* Of the order *Marsupialia.* The nearest living relatives: wombats and phalangers, who are also Australian. The gray kangaroo, *Macropus canguru,* had—by the time this particular encyclopedia was compiled—been clocked at twenty-eight miles an hour over the surface.

The sooty kangaroo stood about six feet, but an extinct form stood twelve. Five toes—one however missing except in *Hypsiprymnodon.* The second and third toes slender. They did not contribute to the species' gift for locomotion but were used instead to comb the fur. The tail served as a balance and a rudder during movement at speed.

The kangaroo in the photograph was leaning back a little, hind paws slightly in the air, so that *his* tail looked like a support of great solidity.

The dark brown eyes are rather large, said Volume 13. The ears are capable of being turned toward sound. Female red kangaroos have two uteri and three vaginas. Almost as soon as one infant is born from one uterus, another can be conceived in the second. Once conceived, it remains in suspended animation in the womb for five months, while its older sibling occupies its mother's pouch and feeds from one of its four teats.

Something like the shadow of rapture overcame Kate as she read of the infant's journey after birth, ploughing across the fur between the womb and the pouch of the four teats. Using its four limbs in a motion similar to the Australian crawl. It chooses the beginning of winter to make this journey, this transmaternal exodus. Red and gluey and one inch long, it makes its first and its slowest dash from one shelter to another. On its journey, Kate presumes, it learns the nature of the world and the value of established routes. Coming to haven, it takes one of the teats in its mouth. The teat expands and holds it in place. The infant stays there, in dark security, attached to the earth's bounty which enters its mother and washes down to this warm cavity. After months, it will leave the teat for a time and begin to make excursions from the pouch, until at six months it renounces the sac for good.

The gray kangaroo, born of its red mother and also known as the sooty, the boomer or the forester, lives in the grassy plains of open eucalyptus, serving the function for Australia which antelope and deer perform for other continents. Turning the earth with its gentle mouth.

Kangaroos travel in clans or troops, protected by a patriarchal kangaroo who will ultimately have to meet the challenge of young, ambitious males. While he can he defeats them by boxing with his forepaws, by punching and slashing with his large, savagely clawed hindfeet. Under siege, he enjoys the does.

The gray kangaroos—though so vigorous—are easily frightened however, Volume 13 told Kate, and in fleeing are capable of injuring themselves. They will tend to flee in a group rather than resist, but sometimes they stand and punch and strike out. There are some documented instances where they have crushed or disemboweled dogs, and there exist some nineteenth- and early twentieth-century reports of their disemboweling humans who attacked them. For a considerable time, their boxing talents were exploited by sideshow operators, who would pit them against human opponents. When boxing they throw their weight onto their tail and use only the heels of their hind legs for support.

—Don't worry, she announced to the kangaroo entry in Volume 13. Don't worry.

In one sense she had no time or sympathy for the creature in the photograph, labeled *Macropus canguru,* who with its left forefoot to its mouth stared at her from the page. It had blundered into the wrong universe, where the promise of the safe pouch was not honored on the open plain.

She had passed perhaps an hour and a half with the encyclopedia, and now someone knocked at her door. As she expected, it was Jack Murchison with his comfortable half-grin. They could have known each other for months.

—Quiet night. Thought you might like to have a look at the taps.

Are there many men down there?

—The usual suspects. Locals. Harmless old bastards.

Yet toward the bottom of the stairs he turned again.

—Everyone of them bloody famous for something in this town, though.

The saloon bar, small and designed for business and exchanges of confidence, was empty at this hour. From beyond the glass doors you could feel the determined quietude of the town. She could see more or less through the wall how the grain trucks slept in the sidings in a skein of light mist. Exactly, she told herself. Exactly. In other places, politicians might be making firm speeches about grain exports, but here in the Myambagh yard grain took its long sleep in the bellies of the wheat containers.

Jack opened the counter in the saloon and let her through to the business side of things. They could now walk through a door and emerge behind the long counter of the main bar.

She was aware that she had entered a place of holiness and taboo like other places of this nature: the weighing room at race-courses, the middle box of a confessional. Behind the bar! It felt to her as if it offered a brand of immunity. She wished they'd wait here, in the empty saloon awhile, while she absorbed the air of sanctuary. Jack thought that her delay was just a sort of confusion about the nature of his kind of proletarian pub, the geography of a place like this. His smile was forgiving. But it said too, I always suspected you belonged in bloody Marriotts and Hiltons.

Through with not enough delay, into the public bar. Sparsely populated, the way Jack had promised. She noticed by the further wall the pool table asleep under its green cloth. Its triangle hung up over that three-notch snooker device called the spider. The light out above the table itself. The last men gathered up to the bar for the final drink of an irretrievable day. Even then she had the feeling which became stronger the longer she stayed at the Railway, that they thought they were pleasing themselves but in fact were at a kind of work, fulfilling a function, occupying spaces which had to be occupied to ensure that things lasted and that constellations stayed in place.

She saw a man still in his white overalls—a local tradesman. Sheltering, she could tell, behind the simple exchanges of Jack Murchison's pub. He thought this was home—it was obvious. He didn't want the complicated market which waited for him in his marriage home, behind the walls of his plain house in a sleeping street. It stood out. You didn't need to be Sherlock Holmes . . .

In the corner by the back door, on a tall stool, a very large man.

His upper body pyramidal as he sat. Yet it could be in part a muscular fatness—you couldn't be sure it was flabbiness through and through.

His corner. God knows how you tell that. But *his* corner. Utterly without aggression, he gave off the smell of ownership. Jack said they were all famous for something. This man knew he was famous. He bore it sweetly apparently, since the face he turned toward Kate looked large and generous and without suspicion. Famous for more than his great bulk, this man.

Separated by a yard or so from the pyramid was a thin man still wearing his hat. He flashed a ferrety smile at Jack as Jack led the new woman through. He was a whippet. Kate could tell infallibly, with the judgment which came to you only on this side of the bar, that his function was that of a man who had opinions and who'd been everywhere. Not everywhere in the sense of Melbourne or San Francisco or Edinburgh or Tokyo. Everywhere in the sense of Wilcannia, Dungog, Warricknabeal, Manduramah. And of course, Myambagh, where he was now stuck.

Kate found these categories delicious. She had not been able to spot them before her catastrophe. Now there was some nutrition for her in them.

The man who'd been everywhere had a boy at his left side, a very tall boy with a Celtic smudge of a face. Those faces you saw now mainly and only in bush towns. A distillation of Connemara or the Highlands. Such a face had been sent into the bush in the nineteenth century, not always voluntarily, and had remained there in its original form, a survival, an ancient visage. You wouldn't see a better face on fishermen in the outer Hebrides.

There were also two immeasurably old and yet not quite aged men, one on the corner of the bar, one where its shorter arm met the wall. This second one sat under a plaque which said, *Placed here by Murchison's Railway Hotel Social Club in memory of Bert (Stumpy) Hogan, 1923–1989. Stumpy's Corner.*

These two old men wore hats, just as the appointed thin man, the smartalec about places, did. The one at the bar corner—the Cornerman—had what Kate thought of as a *quick* face, the way a friendly dog who wants to be involved in human games has a quick face, sifting conversations for the word which will let him in, invite him to stand on his hind legs.

By contrast, it was clearly the appointed task of the man under

Stumpy Hogan's memorial plaque—the Plaqueman—to know that though he had perhaps six and a half decades' vivid experience to exploit if called on, he would fail to be asked. He would die with all that eager material still in his veins.

For the pyramid of a man by the back door and the whippet in the stained hat were the two who controlled the traffic of discourse here. Catalyzed by Jack Murchison, they would do it in a leisurely but utterly authoritative way.

The Plaqueman understood this exquisitely, and in a more refined version of the universe would have passed it on to the Cornerman whose ears twitched so much like a willing hound's. But that was the rule too. You didn't pass it on. You had too much bloody pride.

So part of the special tension of the bar was that the two old men could have been so easily won. A crumb would have done it. The making of a minute space in a conversation. That could not happen though. For the New South Wales Liquor Licensing Board had given Jack his license for liquor, not a license to let eagerness be satisfied or diffused. The kindly-looking pyramid of a man would have lightly done it for the two older ones if it hadn't been for the operation of such rules of the universe.

Kate was astounded and reassured to know that since the first fermenting and distilling gods there'd always been such arrangements as these. A man was given his license and control of the liquors on which the deities had breathed, and all these acolytes arose from nowhere, at a summons they couldn't even hear, and came in to fulfill fragments of the liturgy, altering their dreams as they went by passing the brown fluid through their brains.

Jack, she thought, was a very lucky man. Without trying and because it was appointed, he had acquired regulars. They all interested her, including the two old men you weren't meant to talk to.

As Jack introduced her to the till, she could feel the whippet's eyes on her. He was the one who would make the prescribed jokes, the ones which weren't even funny.

—Got a new apprentice there, Jack? Bloody sight prettier than the last one.

—This button is for a middy, Jack showed her, standing before the cash register. This is for a schooner. You press this one for a nip of spirits—vodka, rum, whiskey. In a perfect bloody world, of course, you'd charge what each nip was worth, because everyone knows whiskey, vodka, gin and rum are all different prices. But the Railway Hotel is an imperfect bloody world, and you can't get staff anymore who'll keep different prices in their heads. The age of literacy is bloody dead and gone out here. Now peanuts and every other sort of rubbish we've got for sale, that's all the same price too. See the peanuts button? That's what you hit.

He cleared the cash register so she could do a few trial runs. All conversation had stopped, she was aware. Everyone was intent on Jack's instruction and trying to read its effect on her, above all waiting for some hilarious error.

—Now the taps, said Jack. Old and New and Foster's. Bulk of the trade. Guts of the business. Watch my wrist.

He took out a schooner glass from a tray of unused glasses and flourished it before her as if he might be about to make it disappear.

—All in the wrist. The big aim in life is the two-pour schooner. No beer lost through the drip tray, nice head, beautiful.

And so he demonstrated, exactly by description. One long pour, flicking the beer tap handle with a genuine elegance. Panache. It filled her with a kind of pleasure, one appropriate to the plain planet where she now lived. This wrist stuff was exquisite.

A second, shorter, sharper pour, and there was the completed column of beer, carrying the right head. You had to be careful, she knew, about heads of beer. What was normal and permitted in other nations was grounds for assault or the ruination of a pub's repute in Australia. The right head was a birthright. It applauded the drinker's existence and manhood.

She studied what Jack did, keeping in her mind the wrist motion. Flick, flick.

—Beautiful, said Jack, putting the perfect flute of beer on the bar. The fat man clapped. He was permitted. The eager old man laughed at the clapping. That was permitted and ignored.

Introductions now, in prodigal order. The large pyramidal man by the back wall was Jelly. Jelly's brown eyes, she noticed, were by nature genial, despite the seemingly cruel nickname.

But then Jack said, Nothing to do with the size of the bastard.

And Jelly laughed, hugging the joke to himself.

—He's a bloody dynamiter. Jelly for gelignite. This is Kate, Jelly.

—Okay, love. Welcome.

Jack had turned to the whippet by now.

—This is Guthega. Don't pour him a drink unless you've already got the bloody money in the till . . .

—That's all right with you, you avaricious bastard, the whippet cried. There used to be a bloody miserable publican like you in Canowindra. Ran him out of bloody town. Will you introduce my poor bloody son or what?

The whippet had gestured toward the boy with the Celtic blur of a face.

—I was getting to your son. Best bloody thing you ever had anything to do with. Though if you ask me, it was the shearer's cook. Kate, this is Guthega's son Noel.

The tall boy, so much lankier than his father, put his hand out for Kate to shake. Guthega didn't like that.

—Don't shake hands with a woman, bugger it Noel! Jesus, she's not some bloody feminist on the High Court of Australia or something!

So everyone laughed at the boy, who was genuinely uneasy. Though Kate kept a smile to herself, it was more because she had found a town where people still called their children Noel. Again, this seemed as wonderful as she could expect. A return to simple elements.

Jelly had to tell her something as soon as he could manage to swallow his merely dutiful laughter. She could see by the way his hands chopped at the surface of the bar.

—Noel is the Australian champion shearer. You wouldn't believe it. But honestly. Australian champion. With a father like that. Bloody dyslexic, hopeless father. So, you could of shook the hand of an Aussie champ.

Noel shifted from foot to foot. It was appropriate for Noel's type that they be discomfited while people chatted about their glory.

—Wide comb, miss, said Noel. Not narrow comb, like in the old days.

—Wide comb, Guthega repeated. Not like the old days. Bloody scabby wide comb shears the bloody graziers forced on us. And now here's my son the champion of the wide bloody comb. His mother and I can't hold our heads up.

Guthega had drunk too much. His son, the wide comb champion, hadn't. Kate could hear Mrs. Guthega's absent voice.

– You stick with your father and get him home okay!

Jack next told her the names of the two old men, the Cornerman and the Plaqueman. The one in the corner took it eagerly. The other with a small, contemptuous rearing of the head. He and Kate understood they had no need of each other's names. A woman who had lost hold of both her children wasn't going to hold on to two names like that.

But the Cornerman didn't know it. Without reason, he expected immediate friendship and banter. He would say, Kate! And expect to hear his name spoken in return. Like the kangaroo in Volume 13, just because he had had a convivial mother, he still believed, in his antique folly, that the world would come his way.

The man in the overalls had already left by now.

Since there was nothing more to be learned, Kate said good night in a general sort of way. She was aware that Jelly's eyes followed her in exactly the right manner: lustrous with goodwill. But not expecting anything.

Stupid Guthega though, the champ's father, thought he had a chance.

Twelve

FOR A TIME, she could tell, she made a little difference to business. Teachers from the Captain John Eglington High School and accountants from the banks: National, Westpac, State, came in to see her for novelty's sake. The Escapees asked her to a Wednesday night party at a pub further up the Eglington Highway. They could not understand that she did not need another pub, except to get away from them. Apart from them, the Railway was the idea she had been in search of.

A few attempted seductions but were easily rebuffed: a motor mechanic asked her would she like to drive out to Wrangle Reserve with him after closing, just to see the billabongs under the moon. It was lovely out there, he told her. A bookkeeper at the stock and station agent's wondered would she like to go and see the French play Australia at Wagga.

—A long drive and it'll be bloody cold, he told her as if this added allurement.

At last, muttering about her frigidity, the unusual welter of business died away.

In the mornings she ate bacon, not bothering to separate the fat from the ocher kernels of meat. She had steak at lunch and tea time. With it she consumed slices of white bread laden with packs of cold butter. Woman of starch: woman of milk!

Jack took her room and board out of her modest weekly wage. It cost ninety dollars a week to stay at Murchison's Railway Hotel and transmogrify yourself.

Yet the transformation did not always go smoothly. One morning, coming out into the brisk air which lay over inner Australia on such late autumn mornings, she heard through the kitchen window Jack and Connie debating her.

—I'm talking about *ordinary* friendliness.

—Bugger me, Connie, you were the one worried she was a tart!

—You don't have to be a tart to be a bit more friendly. She's scaring people off.

—That was all fake anyhow, love, all that extra business.

She could hear Jack making little squeaks of reason, of appeals for concession, with the corner of his mouth.

—Those blokes wouldn't have lasted as customers, he said. Artificial.

—Didn't look too damn artificial on the bank statements, said Connie, the frugal Greek. For who knew when the Turks would come and burn the village? Make business while you can.

—Listen darls, don't say anything for Christ's sake.

—She's weird.

—Yeah, but she's not dangerous is she?

Later in the kitchen, she peeled the potatoes which hefty Shirley would fry for dinner, and she let her eyes skid across the pages of newspapers. Sometimes her attention would hook on some little snag, a familiar name or an intimately known one.

Kozinskis Given Stay
On Building Commission

Mr. German Q.C., representing development tycoons Peter and Paul Kozinski, the father-and-son team of Kozinski Constructions and Kozinski International Development Corporation, were given temporary exemption from appearing before the Inquiry into the Building Industry led by Mr. Commissioner P. Roger Q.C. Mr. Roger accepted Mr. German's submission that in view of recent family tragedy, the Kozinskis had not been able to collect their thoughts for their appearance before the Commission. Mr. Roger said that although there were questions he wished to put to the Kozinskis, and though these could not be indefinitely delayed, their recent tragedy was such as would justify the sympathy of the entire community. The Commissioner was referring to events at . . .

But she did not let her eye rest long enough to encounter a cheap retelling of her own tale.

As she worked in the kitchen, scaling the bland vegetables over the generally bland newsprint, Connie set her a test.

—Jack and I are set to go to the Hereford Breeders' ball. We were wondering whether you could baby-sit the kids?

Kate closed her eyes. She didn't want these unnecessary tricks played on her.

—I'm not good at looking after children.

—D'you mean you'll look after them on protest? Or you don't want to look after them at all.

—No. I'm not good . . .

She was prepared to share the Railway Hotel with Connie's children, but she did not talk to them and avoided remembering their names. They were there, like the Cornerman and the Plaqueman in the bar.

Knowing that what she'd said to Connie had endangered her, she went to find Jack in the darkened public bar, not yet open for business.

—Listen, Jack. I'll do this whole shift.

He didn't know what she meant. He frowned earnestly.

—I mean, ten in the morning until closing. The whole day.

—You'll be buggered, love.

—I want to do some hard work. I'll sleep better.

—I don't know if I can afford you.

—Same pay. Same pay.

She wanted to fill the deserts of daytime with that simple wristwork. The two-pour schooner. Flick. Flick. Perfection.

—Listen . . . none of my business. But do you reckon you're okay? Do you reckon you ought to see a doctor?

—I saw plenty when I was in hospital.

—Hospital?

—For my burns. Do you think I might be a danger to people?

—No, not that. No fear.

And Jack made the appeasing noises which he'd used earlier with Connie. The little squeaks of rational dialogue.

But Kate could see at once that it was not quite enough to be willing to pull perfect beers for twelve hours at a stretch. Or thirteen. As always, people weren't satisfied that you did what they did. They wanted to see the wires and the struts.

It was getting complex. So she decided to be forceful.

—Look, do you want me to bloody well work here or not, Jack?

He was not good at the anger of women. He was frightened by it.

—Okay, okay. I think you're great at this, Kate.

He tapped one of the beer taps, the Toohey's New.

—Do you have a husband somewhere or something?

—I left him.

She wondered was there somewhere she could go where men, and the question of men, were not as omnipresent and would not so clearly arise. She could not think however of such a location.

—Okay, Kate. Try it if you want. What about from one o'clock in the afternoon till eleven at night? You've got to have a life to yourself, Kate.

He seemed to understand that this easy *You've got to have a life* enraged her, but he couldn't see why.

—You *will* be nice to the customers, Kate, won't you?

She knew how to answer that. The precisely effective words.

—Go to buggery!

She still could not stop her head from jerking. She was as disappointed as that: he'd said it was adequate to pour the perfect beer and not have spillage through the drip tray but it seemed that he needed to know other things as well. Jack approached these other things by talk of his wife.

—Listen, I've noticed a few similarities with you and the wife. Let me tell you . . . Connie gets depressed. But her sister was a great depressive. You see, she cut her own throat in a café the family owns at Goondiwindi. Closing time, about nine-thirty at night. She shuts the doors, goes to the sink behind the bloody counter and just cuts through her carotid, here.

He touched the corner of his neck. She could tell from the tender way he did it that his own carotid would always be safe from any violence at his hands. She found him lovely therefore in his completeness, in his beer flab and his weakness, in his height and his dark complexion and his small farting noises of appeasement.

—I don't want any emotional troubles around here. I've got my hands full looking after Connie. See?

He saw it as his task to keep Connie from handling a knife with intent.

Kate decided to laugh. He could be got at by laughter.

—So first I have to convince you I'm not a whore, and now I have to convince you I won't kill Jelly in the public bar.

He laughed at that. He was pitiably relieved at her joke.

—Sounds silly when you put it like that, he conceded.

—Of course it's fucking silly.

—Better not use that word in the bar, Kate. These blokes are pretty simple-minded. They presume any woman who uses that word is all in favor of it.

That night, without being asked, she poured a Bundaberg rum and put it in front of the pyramid, Jelly. It was his standard drink. Thoughtfully, he drank a quarter of a bottle a night. Sticky distillation of the sun, and of Queensland sugarcane. Overproof.

—What's this about you and dynamite?

She knew that Jack was listening in, though pretending to speak to someone down the bar. Jelly had, set amidst the jowls of his lower face, a well-formed set of honest features, and he could not stop them flushing with a sort of gratification, could not prevent the glitter in his green eyes.

He said, You do something once in a country town and you cop the name for life. People talk as if it's the only thing you ever done. I haven't touched bloody gelignite for years. Pardon the language, love. We're a rough pack of bastards in here.

Jack intervened, chin held high. He had to endow Jelly with a seriousness Jelly was not permitted to endow himself with.

—Be honest with the lady, eh. You got a bloody shedful of the stuff in the backyard. Maybe you'd better have a look at it, Jelly. See if it's bloody sweating.

—I've got nothing in the backyard, Kate, Jelly told her, looking up from under his eyebrows. I don't even mow the bloody backyard. Not since my wife went home to her mother. No dynamite in the backyard. No bloody dynamite in the bedroom either.

But he was just saying it to make Guthega and Jack laugh. He wasn't using it as a lever, though other men laughed as much as if it were.

—But you were a dynamiter once?

—Listen, love, I'm a pensioner. I live on bugger-all. Used to be a fancied footballer and country selector. Used to work on the railways once too.

Guthega laughed at this claim of having worked.

—Bloody nifty-fingered in the goods yard.

—Go to buggery, said Jelly to Guthega, and turned again to Kate.

—I did some dynamiting in the '62 flood. That's true.

Seemingly rehearsed, Jack had already fetched pencil and paper and now delivered it to Jelly. Jelly took both as if he expected them, as if the two of them had taken other wanderers through this tale.

Jelly drew a diamond-shaped parallelogram.

One side, he said, was the western highway named Eglington. Two others were the levee banks. The fourth side, the one closest to his right hand, was the branch railway, the Myambagh–Cobar line. The road was a natural levee, as was the railway. The two lines of citizen-made levees were on the lower ground and faced the direction the water usually came from when the whole western river system flooded. The levees completed the walls of fortress Myambagh, said Jelly. They were too low, though the Shire President McHugh said they were high enough. Everyone knew they'd have to be reinforced in floodtime with sandbags.

Within the diamond the Bourke–Sydney railway (by which Kate had arrived in town) traveled on low ground through the center of Myambagh, but it was not for the moment germane to what Jelly was telling Kate. Out of the picture, near where the Cobar spur—which was germane—broke away, it crossed the Wrangle and went off seeking other towns.

—I was a footballer in those days, prop for Western Districts. Bloody sight skinnier than I am now. Full of confidence, stupid as a rabbit. But I knew enough physics to see there weren't aqueducts under the railway to take floodwater off once it breached the levees. A man didn't need to be Einstein!

He passed the map on to Kate for her full study.

—A wall of water came in from the east, across the flats from the Bogan. As it's been doing at least since the Stone Age. And we were all working on the levees, piling up sandbags like the bloody Egyptians, but the thing broke under the force of the flood. And everyone was dithering about the railway line—the cops said one thing, and the Shire President something else.

—Old McHugh, said Guthega. Absolutely useless.

Noel gurgled. It was filial assent.

—So two other blokes and I broke into the dynamite store at the railway—gelignite, detonators—took it all out to the Cobar line. And we blew a great hole in the embankment.

He lowered his voice and sipped his rum, and then said in a

rum-aspirated voice, Before we did it, the water was already to the bloody rooftrees. Now it emptied away west. People say the jelly bloody saved the town.

—Bloody did, said Guthega.

Bloody did. The Australasian *Amen*.

Guthega turned to Noel.

—You reckon you got enough go in you to do something that size?

—I don't know, said Noel.

—I bloody do. Your moral fiber's got sapped by the bloody wide comb . . .

Noel looked away. Guthega often niggled him in the long purgatory of his dutiful nights. A champion without credit. Always invoked, always backhandedly praised to strangers, but always devalued.

—No wonder he likes the bloody scabby wide comb, said his father, nasty with booze. Fucking terrified of spiders. Wouldn't clean a fucking dead mouse out of the kitchen for his mother. Did it out of shame in the end. But you should've seen him trembling . . .

He imitated craven trembling, and only the Plaqueman laughed.

Noel had gone pale. He walked out of the bar to stop himself hitting his father.

—Jesus, Guthega, said Jack. You ought to be kinder to that boy. He's a credit to you and all you do is tear him bloody down.

—Go and apologize and tell him to come back in, Jelly instructed Guthega.

—He's entitled to come in on his own steam. If he's too thin-skinned . . .

But under the joint pressure of Jack and Jelly he was forced to rise and go to the door. Noel was waiting out there in the night, looking at the road and the peppercorns and the glint of railway lines.

—Okay son, said Guthega. Don't take it hard. Come in and have a drink with your old man.

Noel came in but with a set face. It was probably the truth that he had a phobia of small and creeping things. Otherwise he could not have looked so betrayed.

—Listen, said Guthega, turning to anecdote to make everyone

forget his meanness. Did I tell you about this big feller from Coonabarabran . . . ?

—Hang on, Jelly told Guthega. We're still on the dynamite. Who's strangling this bloody cat?

In near-silence the Plaqueman tittered once, and Jelly went on.

—Then, last time, '86, I should of done it, but I didn't. See, I was away with the footballers in Wagga. My mates from '62 . . . one had passed away and the other'd moved to North Queensland. There weren't any bloody young bulls left in town to blow the line.

Guthega said, Those emergency services blokes wouldn't know you were up 'em till you coughed.

He winked at his son.

—Well, next time, said Jelly evenly. Next time, I'm going to take no bloody notice of them at all, and I'll just do it again. Bloody useless line anyhow. Blow the shit out of it. Pardon the French, Kate.

Concluding, he conceded with a nod that she should keep his little map. His mouth looked delicate now. Myambagh's flood history and his past missed chances made him wistful. Childlike. Someone's lost darling boy. He and Jack had, she thought for an instant, been cruelly teamed *because* they were willing and expectant children.

Jelly sank the residue of his rum and, deadly white around the mouth from resolve, looked Kate in the eye.

—Are you going to let me buy you a drink, love?

All watched. She put her hand to her throat and hitched her chin. Ironic consent. She pulled up one of the schooner glasses from the tray. Even the whippet—Guthega—knew for the time being not to be snide. She knew anxious Jack weighed what was happening. He knew it all had a kind of unruly impetus.

She flicked one of the taps.

—A schooner of New, she announced to Jelly.

After the first pour had settled, she finished the big glass off smoothly; an exceptional job. Kate would have liked a vodka, but that wouldn't have thickened her adequately. She raised the schooner to her lips.

—Cheers, Jelly. Thanks.

Jelly picked up his Bundaberg rum, and before taking a sip, he said so that only she could hear, Jesus!

He meant that he didn't know what it meant, her accepting a drink. It had a kind of binding quality just the same.

When she had emptied a third of the glass, she put it down for a rest and put her hand out so that he could pay her.

Thirteen

AND SO TO PROVE her usualness to the Murchisons and the Monks and the Escapees, Kate took Jelly as her protector and her associate. No one need ask her a further question now. The burden of her suspicious soleness was borne away. Neither could Jack and Connie be too surprised at her submission, since it had not been sudden or flippant or casual, and was directed at a person of eminent worth. Secure, she listened to the conversations at the bar, to the tales of average profanity, to the numbingly plain opinions.

And Kate was salved by the utter indistinction of every word.

She listened to this gracious static all day. Barely had she time to eat her enormous breakfast, to excrete, to stun herself with some article from *Woman's Day,* and she was in the bar, claimed—for the remaining twelve hours of her daily energy—by the two-flick action of perfect pouring. Jelly arrived at six, drank a rum and ate a steak sandwich, and stayed on in his presidential corner.

The acres of newsprint in which she wrapped the morning eggshells, steak fat and potato peelings, remained as plain as the bar talk. Yet one morning when Shirley the cook's breath smoked as she entered from the brisk air outside, Kate's eye hooked on another headline, radiant with meaning even here in Myambagh.

Reverend Frank Expelled from Parish House

His Eminence Cardinal Fogarty, Archbishop of Sydney, yesterday threatened legal action against deregistered priest, the Reverend Francis O'Brien, well-known racing and sporting identity.

Cardinal Fogarty's office said that it regretted having to take such action, but Father O'Brien's refusal to vacate the presbytery had forced the Archdiocese's hand. A spokesman for the Cardinal said Father O'Brien has extensive investments in real estate, and that therefore he would not be rendered homeless by any action the Church took.

Father O'Brien was a close friend of the late Alderman Kearney, a former city of Sydney Alderman named by the Independent Commission Against Crime as a notable operator of SP bookmaking outlets. The Reverend O'Brien is believed to have entered into business partnerships with the late Mr. Kearney's widow, Mrs. Fiona Kearney.

The Reverend Frank was unavailable for comment, but his housekeeper of fifteen years, Mrs. Prendergast, says that she will go with him to manage the house in Abbotsford where the Reverend Frank intends to move now to forestall legal action by the Church. Long-time friend of the Reverend Frank, prominent Sydney mortician, Mr. Patrick O'Toole, said, Though I am a loyal son of the Church, I have to say that in this case Cardinal Fogarty has again shown that generosity of spirit is not his strong suit.

Not so much poor Uncle Frank, she thought. Poor Kate O'Brien-Gaffney. Frank would be buffered by his champions: Mrs. Prendergast, Mrs. Kearney, Mr. O'Toole, and a network of hundreds. Kate O'Brien would be his loneliest defender.

At once Kate knew that Uncle Frank did not need his niece to come out of mid-transformation to defend him in any case, even if she had resources to offer him. He must understand her purpose, and must know others would stand up for him by the busload. Remarkable that O'Toole, dependent for business on the Catholic community, as venal a man as any other, would chastise Cardinal Fogarty in Uncle Frank's divine name.

And with such help Uncle Frank did not need someone marked with scar tissue, dead except for the peeling of potatoes, the eating of steak, the performance of the two-flick pour.

So by some mysterious pressure, the news report of Uncle Frank drove her not to writing comforting letters, but to traveling—in a sense—further away. Without more than the most wooden thought of Murray, she intended to seal things with Jelly. There were no favors involved. Murray would be the favored one. Jelly would be benefited very little.

For grief had seized up her womb. She did not have her monthly bleed as women her age were meant to. She did not go through the phases of desire. She considered herself to be in cronehood. Her appetite, so high in Fiji two months before, was vanished. Poor Jelly would explore dead surfaces.

That evening ten Aborigines, seven men and three women, arrived in the barren dusk on their way through to a Sunday rodeo at Nevertire. Their children waited outside in the back of utes or station wagons, or else played hopscotch under the wide overhang of the Railway's enormous top verandah.

Then four men wearing cricket flannels turned up. Their Saturday afternoon triumph, startling end-of-season bowling figures or else quick half-centuries, had put some bark into their laughter. They were not regulars but began remaking brotherly connections with those who were, even with Jelly, who tolerantly accepted them. For they had been to school together: the cricketers and Jelly and Guthega. But this was not the cricketers' normal milieu. Usually they drank with greater comfort at the Bowling Club or Returned Soldiers.

It was hectic. The people going to the rodeo bought out the Railway's supply of peanuts to pacify their waiting children. The cricketers were on a binge and were generous with shouts.

Though the pattern by which Jelly brought Kate her pint had by now the solidity of something more aged than most civilizations, he knew somehow that within its scope she had changed by degrees.

He said this evening, Would you like to come back afterwards for a cup of tea?

His face had become white under the stress of asking. But she knew the mention of tea was more than a pretext. He often spoke affectionately of it. All the drinking he did here might have been imposed on him by his fame as dynamiter and tacit president of the bar. Drinking tea, he was a private man.

—I'll have a lot of glasses to wash, said Kate. It will be late. But yes.

And it *was* late as the cultists of the Railway drank their way into the treacly rind of their evening. The cricketers got drunk, looked at their watches, told everyone proudly what trouble they'd be in with their wives, but swore that from now on this would be their pub.

Jelly didn't believe them and said casually, Telephone's in the hall, boys. Why don't you ask them to join us?

At last, they began to gather themselves, saying again that they'd be back soon. Loudly, they wondered why they had neglected this golden place for so many years. Their tongues were thick and they had that strange wooden look behind their eyes. But they were surer of the schoolyard bonds they would now renew and cement with Jelly.

Softly belching and uttering parental threats, the Aborigines had long gone, crowding their children into their vehicles.

—By Christ, Sharon, you get in the back of that bloody truck!

Guthega was taken home by his son Noel. The Cornerman and the Plaqueman had both left an hour past. Reassured and appalled at the one time, Jack watched Kate come to the front of the bar and say to Jelly, You're ready? Jelly rose, sighing in a way which was meant to tell her not to expect Elysium.

Outside, in a northerly with red dust on its breath, he said, This isn't going to be the most exciting night of your life, love.

He touched her wrist to ensure she knew that. He did not have his truck. He believed the Myambagh police paid particular notice to drivers whose vehicles lay parked outside pubs such as the Railway for hours at a stretch. It was a safe bet that their blood alcohol was at least modestly high, as Jelly's surely was after his quarter-bottle of Bundy.

They walked down the railway line, the wind punching at their shoulders. Enormous brown-eyed Jelly, stupendous in the chest and even greater in the girth, yet with two little satchels of buttocks. Kate whose ambition to become pursy and obese and coarse had not yet quite been realized and who seems to Jelly to be the only beauty abroad at this hour. The town utterly silent, finished with its Saturday night. The oblivious town she loved beyond utterance: all the rich hours wantonly unharvested.

Across the railway lines, silvered by the moon and stretching abstractly away without any contingency of actual traffic, of diesel engine or freight trucks. A Jacob's ladder laid flat on the earth between Murchison's Railway Hotel and Jelly's cottage. Nineteenth-century pastoralists and Members of Parliament lobbied and argued and paid each other off to get the line to come here, across the Wrangle from the south, to get the spur line stretching to Cobar, the one which Jelly was famous for dynamiting. To-night, though, the rails looked a mere decorative border between Myambagh's two hemispheres.

Over the track, by the Returned Soldiers, the Cantonese husband and wife who ran the restaurant for the Returned Soldiers were leaving with plastic bags in their hands. Frugal people who had found a niche in Myambagh, nested down between the memory of wars in the RSL. Past Dunnegan's Country Stores where Kate had recently bought the gumboots she needed for hosing the pub pavement down. Left by the Captain John Eglington High School, left again at the St. John Ambulance. Bardia Street, Myambagh.

Jelly's weatherboard cottage hunched down on its foundations. It had a curved corrugated iron roof of a contour which had been thought fashionable around the time of World War I, and there was a sense of many successive families about it. Now, though, it belonged to wifeless Jelly. As he had promised, the gardening hadn't been exactly done. But at some stage, someone had planted things there, so that it looked luxuriant.

In his kitchen, by his electric stove, Jelly put on the kettle. He put a tube of tablets on the table beside the place where his teacup would go.

—Hypertension, he explained.

The kitchen was clean. Its floorboards were varnished. There was no smell of dust.

When the tea was made, he filled a cup according to her instructions and put it on her side of the table.

—Sit down.

He himself sat on his side of things and began to sip.

—Jesus. Who would have thought, Kate?

—I'm not going to marry you.

—Wouldn't worry if you were.

—But I'm not.

In the country bedroom to which Jelly leads Kate, there is a splay-footed dresser with a circular mirror. Built to carry a woman's cosmetics and mementoes, what it does carry now are three *Best and Fairest Trophy Won By* . . . The name space in each case is blank.

On the wall above the bed hangs a picture of the explorers Burke and Wills. Having crossed Australia from south to north and returned to find their Cooper's Creek depot abandoned, they sit by moonlight beneath a tree on which is marked DIG. They have unearthed a modicum of supplies the abandoning parties left cached there for them. This is a core Australian picture. Thirst and dread above the double bed.

The bed itself is high as if Jelly has reinforced it against his weight, or uses two mattresses. There is an easy chair whose seat is filled with folded newspapers, the top one with a picture of the Prime Minister who greeted the earlier Kate in Macquarie Street.

Jelly indicates a bedside lamp. Nearly without breath, he says, Do you want this left on?

—Yes.

Between the dresser and the chair she found beneath the burden of his weight his little white gland and persuaded it forth. The cries of his gratitude took away her sense of a silent midnight. He had not expected anything like this to happen to him. That was why she was doing it.

Since it was not a marriage, she left him when he was still asleep, in the profound anesthesia of 3 A.M., when even the Eglington Highway was silent and might not be able to be revived by dawn traffic. Then she went back to her cherished room at Murchison's Railway Hotel.

In the real morning she woke and went downstairs and found Connie Murchison hosing the pavement under the verandah. She or Kate did that every morning, while Jack slept off the brotherly damage his clients had done to him. Connie kept her dark eye on the thread of water, as if she feared that, unsupervised, it would stop running.

—You know he's not a well man, Jelly.

—I noticed he has to take pills.

—Okay. As long as you know.

If anyone knew it was silly to chat about the odds, it should have been Connie. Her own sister had been safe from hypertension, but had made up for that with her own hand. Kate could have told her: I had children, one of whom could do arabesques to the point of her own and the audience's exhaustion, the other a clinic-certified catcher of balls. And despite the eternity of jetés and sure fingers which seemed to be guaranteed it had meant nothing. So what did it mean? *He's not a well man.*

She knew enough though to understand she must pretend it meant something. That it might have a weight for her.

—None of my business, Connie told her. But I'm surprised he's capable of it, carrying all that weight.

Kate said nothing. Was she meant to explain how she had found his tiny, boy-thin sexual purpose, and cajoled it into surprising him?

Lying in Jelly's arms Kate listened to how thoroughly the world had elected Jelly to the status of Dynamiter.

—It's all true enough. I've got the stuff out there in the shed. Gelignite and detonators. In an Esky.

The Esky. As Australian as the dismal Burke and Wills who despaired every night over Jelly's bed. Insulated beer and picnic carrier. An item eloquent of a good life and cool beer and charred steak devoured in the mottled shade of gum trees. You unlocked its lid and—so it seemed—out came the voices of children, the busy small talk of women, the jovial bark of men. Except Jelly's Esky, which held a different sort of picnic.

—Took the stuff from the railway. Every bugger knows. Even the cops know. Pretty sure I'll look after it. If it went off, watch them disclaim all knowledge! World's full of bloody hand-wringers and hand-washers.

Whereas you could say of Kate and Jelly that they were a mating of utter destinies. No luxuries of evasion for them.

—Good condition, said Jelly, the lot of it. No sweating. I keep a dehumidifier plugged in out there, just so everything's in prime condition. Everyone wants me to do it see. Except people like the Shire President. He's got some pasturage west of the Cobar line. Higher bloody ground anyhow. And he doesn't want to be incommoded. He wants his sheep bone dry and to hell if Myambagh's awash.

How Jelly studied the water patterns on the ceiling during these quiet talks.

Kate wondered if this slander on McHugh was well founded.

—How does he get elected then?

Jelly shook his head. The electoral energy of men like that was a mystery to him.

—So . . . most ordinary people want me to blow the shit out of the Cobar line. They don't expect anyone else except Muggins here to be bloody stupid enough to do it. At least, that's their bloody story.

Under his burden, he began to gasp a little. It might have been laughter.

As she went out one morning at the Railway Hotel, along the verandah to find the women's shower which she alone used, to wash off the sweat of six or seven tranquil and undemanding hours by Jelly's side, she saw the town in all its indistinction, the red roofs of corrugated iron, in the nation which raised corrugated iron to an art form. The occasional flash brick and red tile—a bank manager's, a doctor's, a stock and station agent's. People who didn't drink—except as an aberration like the one which struck the cricketers—at the Railway Hotel. People who would never take hold of one of Kate's perfect two-pour schooners. And all of Myambagh: the vernacular corrugated iron, the more particular red tile, capping seven hundred dull breakfasts, two thousand expressions of heroically unenlightened opinion; and she felt a pulse in her from all that oblivious and peaceful ignorance, a pulse something like love, and certainly like a brand of patriotism.

Under the spray of Myambagh water, from a shower rose installed perhaps forty years ago, under that hard spray of mud-tasting water from the river or of alkaline water from deep beneath, fossil water as old as the stone, she soaked her thickening thighs and saw a dimpling on the flesh, a minor model of her shoulder scars, and she was so pleased that in mute celebration she took to scrubbing her hair with the hard soap and the obdurate water.

Returning, content after her fashion, she had to pass the men's showers, where the Monks and Escapees could be heard hooting, cursing, farting and objecting to farting, and invoking Christ when the first gush of water from the shower roses hit them. It was growing cold outdoors now in the mornings. Men often sprinted along this exposed verandah, half-naked or naked beneath over-alls. They sneezed all the time, for in the steamy and populous men's bathroom there was no chance of drying a body out properly. She was delighted that she had leisure and space to pat herself dry. It was a vengeance against the cheapness of their minds.

Striding by the steamy men's bathroom one cold blue dawn, she met the painter-plasterer who had once knocked on her door and asked her to a party in another pub. He had the same bruised look about the eyes as Connie.

—Selling yourself cheap, aren't you, love?

She could tell he assessed her again then, and saw how she had grossened, and wondered why he'd bothered coming weeks before to her door, asking for her company. In her mind she was confident that given another three months, she would no longer resemble what he counted as a woman. She was on the way to being exempt from his attention. She was in training for being beneath notice.

So she embraced Jelly's grossness because she desired it for herself. Nor could the man she met on the verandah, a reactive man, a man living by the pay packet, understand how Jelly was engorged with his dynamiting past and future. Jelly was like Uncle Frank, a lovable and inferior man claimed for diviner purposes.

—Get fucked! she told the man on the balcony.

—Nice bloody talk.

He spoke as if he took ardent comfort now from the fact he'd never held her.

Fourteen

THAT OR SOME OTHER NIGHT, an old friend of Jelly's came into the bar. He was wiry, exactly like the whippet Guthega. But he had none of Guthega's snide air. She admired the way he and Jelly greeted each other, not loudly, not wanting to impress the bar with their external mateship. He was a young enough man, perhaps close to forty, but olive-skinned and strangely leathered as if he had been that way since babyhood, or had even chosen to bear the accumulated leathering of his father and grandfather as well. Deep-set in the dark skin were glittering green eyes. He had a thatch of black hair which grew forward on his head like a hedge given a bias by the wind. He wore a gray sweater clogged with red dust, and carried an aged, big Akubra hat.

Jelly's eyes softened as Kate approached him down the bar.

—Kate, Gus Schulberger. Protégé of mine. Played for New South Wales Country and I bloody hand-selected him myself.

Kate nodded at once and smiled and shook hands, a procedure Gus Schulberger seemed unfamiliar with.

—Gus comes from out near Bourke, Jelly said, as if that explained his unhandiness with the conventions.

Australians, so addicted to brave failure, spoke of the figure called the Battler, the man cheated by banks and seasons, hope withered by drought, drowned deep by flood, et cetera. Gus Schulberger could have played the Battler in any hard-luck documentary on television. For the Battler was required to have nothing left but a reflex grin and an upright posture, and Gus Schulberger had both. So that it was impossible to look at him now and imagine the young athlete, the twinkle toes, the sure fingers, the brushed hair, whom Jelly had selected for Country Firsts, who had run forth onto the Sydney Cricket Ground.

Both Gus and Jelly had been raised in any case in the bush tradition which expected early athleticism and energy to be shown up as a vain dream.

Jelly whispered to Kate.

—My friend Gus's got outside in the back of his truck the bloody living Commonwealth of Australia coat of arms.

Kate frowned easily, knowing she was meant to. Jelly laughed at his Bundaberg rum before swallowing it, while Gus scratched his ear. Not *acting* rueful, as Guthega could. Rueful in fact and by nature. Jelly urged him.

—Give her a look, Gus.

Kate walked along the bar, past the Corner and then the Plaque men, the first of them angling for a glancing smile, and into the saloon. There Jack was talking to the accountant from one of the banks. Jack excused himself and stepped aside, and she asked him secretly could he mind the bar for a second?

With Jack's permission she emerged on the clientele's side of the bar, a matter of feet but a different continent. She saw that Jelly and Gus Schulberger were working it secretively too. Jelly pretended he needed to go out to the men's to empty his calabash of a bladder. He had to be careful, for everyone watched him so jealously—the old men, Guthega, perhaps even Noel. Wary in case he cut them out of something, of some information they required for wholeness.

Gus stood bareheaded by a small furniture removal truck parked outside the saloon. He let out one plume of breath, bunched the corner of his mouth in regret, unlocked the bolt which kept the back door in place, and slid it upwards and open.

Kate flinched; that silly flick of the head overcame her. The block of dark inside the truck gave off a sudden animal rustling, a crinkling and resting of feathers, a click of paws, which made her step back. Her head returned to its normal, controlled position and she considered what had been presented. For a second she could believe that, pressed by hard times, Gus had brought with him something absurd and repellent to show to people in towns more populous even than this one, where he had stopped simply for a drink and for the sight of an old but sadly enlarged friend.

He pulled a torch from his pocket and shone it into the truck.

—Man feels a bit of a bloody traitor!

By the beam of light, Kate saw two animals standing on a bed of straw. Their eyes picked up the beam of Gus's torch and had for a second a weird, orange luminosity. Feather and fur. So tall that it was no wonder Gus had had to borrow this truck, made for transporting sideboards and hatstands. The bird was the taller. An emu. The kangaroo was not as lofty but was vast and muscular, and delicate in the face.

The emu, reassured by Gus's musk or sight, folded its legs in a way which was the reverse of human legs and sat down all at once in its ball of body feathers. With that neck and small beaked head, it was still much higher seated than either of Connie Murchison's children standing.

—These are the poor bloody beasts, Gus told Kate.

Addressing them, he adopted a voice of pleading.

—Okay, you blokes. No worries.

He turned down the beam of the torch.

—Wife raised both of them on our place. See that bird? Menzies. She raised it from the egg. Dogs got his father. The fathers do the nest-sitting with emus. Old feller put up a great fight, but the dogs get them in the legs and bring them down. I couldn't call them off. They were right out of control, you know.

Kate was fascinated by the bird's intense bulge-eyed stare. Incapable of flight, its eyes covered all angles of attack. The head seemed in fact half eyes, half beak; all caution and appetite. Feathered and wingless, it had long ago been played some trick.

—See the big gray roo? Chifley. Wife raised him too, from the pouch. Mother was hit by a truck. Wife fed it on a titty bottle. Used to be a station hand of my father's in good times who tried to box poor bloody Chifley, you know square up to him, go two rounds. And my father said—and I agree with him—humans don't have a tail, and roos don't box. Do you Chif, eh? I hate boxing bloody kangaroos. Demeaning.

Gus's green eyes took the kangaroo's fixed gaze for a second but then turned away, sliding the torch beam away too.

—I saw an advert in the *Western Plains Gazette*—some bloke in Wagga is putting together this amusement park. He wants a roo and an emu, because at every stroke of the hour between nine and five, he's going to put on what they call a *tableau vivant* of the Australian coat of arms. He's got the Australian coat of arms standing there in the middle of his park. And he wants a tractable emu and a tractable roo who'll come up on either side, just like on the coins, right on the hour. He says he doesn't worry if they'll clear off afterwards. Just on the hour. All the families and school kids gathered. All the Japanese with their bloody cameras. They know it's going to happen, and their cameras are all focused. The coat of arms in the middle. Chifley on one side. Menzies the miserable bloody emu on the other. If they stand still for two seconds I suppose everyone will clap. Then Menzies'll clear off in his stiff-legged way. And Chifley will hop off, and I suppose that'll make everyone applaud all the bloody more.

—This entrepreneurial bloke (Gus continued) tells me sensitive handlers will entice them up to the coat of arms with titbits.

He shook his leathery, black-plumed head. He didn't like the arrangement anyhow.

—Different species with different attention spans. A mis-bloody-match. But no one gives a damn about that. Our founding fathers didn't give a bugger. And our founding fathers jammed the emu and kangaroo together on the emblem. *And* set up the system we live under, Jelly. Sadly the system's not adequate anymore to look after even one human being like myself living west of the Darling River. Poor bloody beasts.

His torch now switched off, he stared in the face at the darkness at the back of the van, that darkness in which you could feel the avian and marsupial long-suffering of the beasts.

—Well, said Jelly. You've got to make a living, Gus.

Jelly was shocked by his friend's anguish, and so in a way was Kate. She could tell that inveighing against the founding fathers of the Commonwealth of Australia wasn't Gus's normal style.

—Not me, Kate couldn't stop herself telling Gus, out of the blue, her head jerking. She wanted to be sure he knew she wasn't even by remotest impulse connected with the systems of judgment which ruled all the breathing world. She had been judged herself. Her license to be glib had been torn away from her.

Now she could see more closely into the interior of the truck—her eyes had got used to the dark, wide street beside the dark, wide railway. Past the avian skinniness of the hunched-down emu, she saw at a stroke the princeliness of the kangaroo. She was aware of the limpid eyes, though she could not actually see them reflect light. She had the evidence of muscular shoulders, of the brawny solidity of the lower limbs, the great hammer of a tail. A potent beast to be a cropper of grass, to be one with the sheep and the deer, to share no impulse with the lion. Through no animal chain had Chifley ever consumed his own kind. Yet he had a power which came from more than grass.

—We raised them like children, Gus said. And now we sell them. Or I bloody do.

Jelly wanted to salve the hour.

—That's the nature of business, old son, said Jelly, who knew nothing about the nature of business.

—*Tableau vivant,* said Gus. I told the Dubbo people no boxing for Chifley and nothing but the best treatment. I got the owner to sign a letter . . . And no bloody digger hats on the emu either.

The angular bird stirred and turned its head. It was vigilant, even in the limited darkness of a furniture truck. But the kangaroo called Chifley stayed immobile, fixed on Kate.

Kate said, Chifley.

—My wife's joke. Rest her.

—Bloody good woman, Jelly said hurriedly.

—Sadly missed I tell you, said Gus.

The emu gave a guttural moan, and the great muscular grass-eater, plague of graziers but friend of Gus's, seemed to join with him in reflection and fond memory.

Jelly spent more time on the question of the late Mrs. Schulberger, now that it had been raised by Gus.

—I was really surprised, Gus. I heard she had that problem . . .

—Yeah. Coccyx, Jelly. The cancer ate her up. It was a mercy when.

Jelly's voice took on a sort of liquid condolence.

—Guthega comes one day and tells me she's passed on. I mean, I had a get-well card all ready to post.

—Went quickly, said Gus, smoothing down the back of his wiry black hair.

In the truck Chifley seemed still to wait for further, more cogent news of where the hand which had raised him had gone. The bird Menzies bent down from his sitting position and picked up a feed pellet from the floor. He raised his narrow head on its enormous neck and stared and swallowed. If he had not been going off to dubious employment, Jelly and Kate would have laughed at the way he dispatched the pellet down the long tube of his neck.

Jelly nodded toward the kangaroo.

—Look at the balls on that big bugger.

But Gus was still reconciling himself.

—*Tableau* bloody *vivant*. It's supposed to be a flash park. There'll be a resident vet.

—Better than he'd get here, Jelly murmured. The cockies'd blow the shit out of him.

—Chifley, said Kate.

Something had been evoked in the stone behind her ribs. Some minor creak of wonderment.

Gus slid the door down as Kate waited oblivious of the bar inside. She kept a staunch sense of the presence of Chifley even while the door was still a hand span open, jammed for the second, demanding from Gus the deepest sigh of all and a more emphatic pressure of the hand.

She told Jelly she needed a quiet night and would not go home with him that night. He was easy about that.

—Need a bloody rest myself, love, he said, rolling his eyes in a way which did both of them the compliment of pretending they were insatiable.

In her sleep, a sleek marsupial pride uncoiled from her. She understood asleep that this was a joy she was not capable of awake. She made forward, bounding progress over a saltbush plain. There was an ecstasy in her pace, in the astounding assembly of limbs she had some sweet connection with. She found herself waking in the night with the first yelps of idiot laughter on her lips. They died at once, of course. Sucked up by the firmaments which hung above Myambagh.

A town in a plain, by a treacherous river, Myambagh was too massively lost in space to permit people to sit up in beds in wooden houses. Laughing aloud at nameless hours of the night.

But she knew her pleasure was significant.

Fifteen

SHE DID NOT AT FIRST recognize Burnside as the Kozinski retainer that he was. He had grown a sandy mustache which he hadn't had in the old days, when Paul used to bring him aboard the *Vistula* for reasons which were part of Kozinski Constructions' secret history. His belly had got looser too, but he still had his enormous shoulders—a weight lifter from before the time of the Nautilus machine.

In the bar he had taken off his suitcoat and his tie. The tie was folded into the top pocket of his striped shirt—all to falsely signify to the small crowd in the bar that he was just a drinker, that he had no other intentions.

Kate accepted him as a visiting salesman, but then identified him in a rush. Her flick of the head had diminished under the influence of the bounding dream, but it came back wildly now. She considered leaving quietly and finding Jack. But she went on stacking schooner glasses and answered the raised hand of a drinker at the far end of the bar, the man in Jelly's corner, which was available for casual drinkers to flex their souls in by day.

She cherished, in a fashion, the way men raised their hands like that, never certain that anyone would take notice. Each hand raising a tentative claim on the universe. And once they knew you'd seen them, they pointed downward into the residual froth of their friend's empty glass and then of their own. Who taught them to do that? Would Bernard have done that, in the end? And all without knowing where it came from?

Cleaning out two fresh schooner glasses—that too was set down in the liturgy of pubs: never the same glass twice—she set them on the drip tray and commenced the pour. She wanted the sweet, familiar act to be available to her for good, but there was every chance this was her last pour for Murchison's Railway Hotel.

Jack appeared from the direction of the saloon, and Burnside stretched his big hand out across the bar, a brawny lad asking a question in class. She heard him ask Jack in his plausible voice whether Kate Kozinski was here. No, said Jack, in a style meant to finish the conversation. But Burnside amended his inquiry.

—What about someone called Kate Gaffney. Kozinski's the married name.

Jack did not say: he had a sheet in his hand and was checking the bottles behind the bar for reordering. His manner was denial. Clear out. Who do you think you are interrupting people in the full routine of their business?

But Burnside pushed a card at Jack, which Jack took and placed on top of the reorder form and read fully, his eyebrows arranged crookedly.

Having finished her two perfect schooners, Kate delivered them down the bar and held her hand out to be paid. She wanted to stretch out each act to a great span of time. It was enough to strike time still, the idea that this man with a blond mustache who had once sunbathed on the *Vistula* with the children and Mrs. Kate Kozinski, might soon be dealing the Kozinskis' names to her across the bar. The wonder was that he or someone like him hadn't come and done it much earlier.

She had of course the bottleful of sleeping tablets to resort to but that wasn't the possible journey anymore.

On the night, outside the desolation of her home, Paul Kozinski had justifiably screamed, Why weren't you here? And she had agreed with that then and still did: she was a criminal through her absence. Just the same, even while voting for the idea with all her soul, she had come to sniff an air of ignorance about the proposition that her absence had destroyed the afternoon world. She had developed the idea that the Arson Squad chief inspector or the chief of Emergency Services might seek her out one day and give her something, an item, a plain sentence, to mute the blame. By one means or another, she must wait for that.

So would she slip away out the back where the nineteenth-century stables were, and flee to another town? Jelly might be confused by the suddenness of that. He expected a close of play, but a gentler one. To that extent she was a new woman. In the old state, she had been willing to leave Jim and Kate Gaffney without explanation. Yet the heart which had been torn out of her now had a bias to be kind to Jelly.

—What did you call her? Jack Murchison asked, still inspecting the man's card, looking for some little detail in the corner that would invalidate it.

He would in fact have made a first-class site boss. Cement wouldn't have gone missing. Likewise, people serving writs to the dogmen would have been sent to buggery.

Even head-thumping Burnside was careful of him.

—Kozinski. Married name. Gaffney, maiden. It's no problem. I just have some information that'd benefit her.

Jack appointed the saloon bar as the place Burnside could wait. It was empty in the daytime, since no one came to the Railway for confidential lunches, and the ordinary clientele considered drinking there a waste of money. Jack himself opened the door of the saloon for Burnside to go through. It was somehow meant to let Burnside know that there were stringent limits to what would be permitted to happen.

Burnside having passed through, Jack came back behind the bar and approached Kate like a parent who has just heard dubious news about the child's behavior somewhere else, beyond the normal reach of fatherly purview.

—Okay, Kate.

He passed Kate the card.

—Do you know this feller?

Kate hung her head. It was partly shame of course, given that Burnside was from the Kozinskis' hemisphere where her shame was well established. It was weary loathing of Burnside.

—He works for my husband, Jack.

—Wish I had a big dumb bugger like that working for me.

He went on looking at her. Had she given any sign, he would have taken her away and hidden her.

But of course she knew she had to face him. He was someone from the Kozinski world she *could* meet without peril to the new woman Shirley's steak and white bread was making of her. She was grateful to Paul for not coming in person. That would have been impossible.

—Sure? Jack insisted on knowing.

—Oh yes.

She took the card with her as she went through into the saloon.

□ □ □ □

He sat with his back to her. She walked round past his great shoulders and saw that he had one eye raised, as if she were a stranger, as if they had not floated together in the green water off the *Vistula*'s stern. His eyes were precisely as she remembered: those of someone who was used to terrifying people in a whimsical way. His arrogance came from the fact he thought himself a character, and because he had done good, frightening work for the Kozinskis, they told him that, the thing he wanted to hear. *You're really a character, Burnside.* A legend in the building business. People either shat themselves with fear or with hilarity.

—Your boss gave me a big welcome.

Jack had given him a glass of beer, and he sipped it once while assessing her.

—I love a bit of hostility. Mother's milk.

He showed his teeth. He thought all this stuff was subtle, but he looked melodramatically feral.

—Let yourself go a bit, love, haven't you? That Murray bloke who fancies you mightn't fancy you like this.

—Good, she said.

—No, I was just commenting, Mrs. Kozinski. *I* can get you back to where you were.

This stupid promise left her less frightened.

—We met a few times, I think. On that boat of Mr. Kozinski's.

—Pleasant days.

She would have made it sound sarcastic, less neutral and more edged. But she did not want to cause him to take one attitude or another.

He said, I've been honored for a long time by association with your husband's company, Mrs. Kozinski.

—Paul's mother is Mrs. Kozinski. She was endowed in that high office by the Blessed Virgin Mary of Czestochowa and by the Holy Father. Ask her and she'll tell you.

—But you're Mr. Paul Kozinski's wife.

—I reverted to my maiden name.

—Understood.

He'd begun nodding and was playing at being conciliatory. He had produced a thick envelope from the pocket of the vast suit coat slung on the back of the chair.

—Mr. Paul Kozinski asked me to give you these documents.

—Mr. Paul *and* Mr. Andrew.

—Well, yes. These are for signature. Maybe you'd like to look at them.

She did not take the envelope. She let him put it down on the table. There it lay. She would have been happy for it to get beer-glass rings on it.

—Mr. Kozinski's very appreciative of the fact that you're not seeking anything as marriage settlement, or at least he presumes that, since he hasn't heard anything from you. But he realizes he has a responsibility to you. Some of the papers to be signed are to do with relinquishing directorships in a number of Kozinski subsidiaries. It doesn't seem likely you'll want anything to do with them anyhow. And you'll see he hasn't been ungenerous. There's a letter of agreement in there which will entitle you to a two-million-dollar settlement payable in six monthly installments, the first within fifteen days of your signature.

—Yes, she said. Very nearly anxious, she distracted herself with the aftertaste of the delight in bounding over plains with Chifley. She relished the echo of that happiness.

High above the town, somewhere between the apex of the Railway Hotel and the roots of time, there was a prodigious, proud, languid bark of thunder. It seemed to her that Burnside blinked.

—God, listen to that. They get floods here, don't they?

—It's all they talk about.

—So . . . you'll see the documents of resignation. And you'll see also an annulment petition to the Archdiocesan court. Sign that, and you don't have to mess around with the buggers any further. Then the settlement document for when you've signed all the rest. There's a cross and a penciled K.K. where you sign each document. Katherine Kozinski. You mightn't want to sign them Kozinski, but you'd better, because that's the legal requirement.

She didn't care enough for all this to tell him the Kozinskis could take their settlement to hell. Why should she say something for the entertainment of the muscular servant of the Kozinskis? Who would add it to all his other smartarse stories of divorce in the private investigator business? For he was, it seemed, a licensed private investigator. At least his card said so. And she didn't want him to be able to classify the story. She would like him to be left with so little he didn't have a story at all.

Anyhow she knew her part-change, her mid-transmogrification, would be his story.

—Jesus, should see how she's let herself go.

Damn him.

—You'll be able to afford to leave here, he said. Of course, Paul wouldn't have wanted you here in the first place.

—Very kind of him. But this is where I am.

Burnside frowned since it all seemed to be going so easily. Something professional in him mistrusted the ease.

—Probably just as well if you sign now, he nonetheless urged her. You'll probably go on thinking about Paul Kozinski and the whole sad business while ever these papers are around.

—Don't mention the sad business!

—I was just saying . . .

—Don't say! Don't fucking say! *Don't say!*

—All right. Whatever you want, Mrs. Kozinski, but it doesn't look as if you and Paul will get together again. So why not sign? And the annulment . . . I believe your family's very Catholic too, and you'd want a Church annulment. So the document in there initiates the process.

—I know. You explained that.

—None of this divorce and annulment stuff is a big deal. Not for people like the Kozinskis.

—Old Andrew Kozinski is a Papal Knight.

—That's what I mean. So that document needs signing with the others. It'll go through like grease. Would you like me to open the envelope now?

—I wouldn't.

—Just that if you signed them, I could drive back to Wagga and catch the eight o'clock plane. We all have families . . .

But then a pallor, she saw, an awareness of having made a gaffe crossed his face.

—Oh Jesus, I know what happened . . . that business out at the beach . . . Please forgive me, Mrs. Kozinski. I didn't mean . . .

You could give forgiveness cheaply to someone like Burnside.

—We all have our families, she affirmed.

He thought she had let him off the hook and he was pleased to be able to resume his main argument.

—Listen, as I say, why not open these now?

He decided to be forceful, and picked up the envelope and was working at its flap.

—Leave them alone. They're my papers.

—That's right.

—Then leave them alone.

—Sorry. Look, I wish you'd—

Again a great elemental cough of thunder. The Railway Hotel itself seemed to move. The heavens ground their way across Myambagh like a river over gravel.

—You leave them with me, she said.

She didn't know why she'd want to delay things. What he said was good sense. Get rid of them and of him. He had interrupted her sea change, her change of form in Australia's most oblivious town. None of it could start up again until he left. If then.

Yet even at a cost to herself, she wanted to delay the Kozinskis' purposes. She remembered old Kozinski's story of the Pole and the lamp and the Chinese army. She had got to the level where relative balances of torment were what mattered, or where the lost took joy in minute gestures. She would *utterly* know her own shame, take it into herself, reinforce by decibels Paul's scream on the night, if Burnside were to walk into Paul's office and when asked if she'd resisted would be likely to say, No, there weren't any problems.

—You'd better stay here, Kate advised him. You'll get these in the morning.

—You know you'll sign them in the end, love.

—It costs twenty dollars a night, and—for that—steak until it's coming out of your ears.

—Since you know you're going to sign them, I *was* hoping you'd save me the trouble.

—The Kozinskis will pay your hotel bill, I'd think.

—Well, of course they will . . .

—Stay here then.

—I don't know what crowd you're mixing with at the moment, Mrs. Kozinski. But maybe you ought to tell them I'm licensed to carry a firearm. If I'm visited during the night . . .

—Don't be stupid.

—It's just there's some big bastards out in that bar. The publican himself is a big bastard.

—Yes. But he doesn't have your malice. Just stay here and shut up and I'll see you in the morning.

She remembered one last thing.

—You're not to eat with me. You're not to eat what Jack calls *tea*. Not with me. There are plenty of other men here you can eat it with.

—I understand, he said in an ironic way. In his general delivery, he had mixed objectives: sometimes he desired to sound like a cop, sometimes like a company law barrister. He was trying for the barrister tone now.

It came to her again that of course he would tell everyone where she was now. They would all come after her. Worst of all, her solicitous parents. So that perhaps all she wanted through her stratagems was one more night numbly embayed in Jelly's plentiful, radiant flesh, another evening to practice the two-pour schooner, another chance of the perfect marsupial dream.

Burnside. Capable of driving a few hours down the highway and catching a plane, of getting back to the place where people would ask, How was your visit to the bush? She had prevented that. He would stay, with his envelope full of consent forms which Kate would likely sign in the morning, and he would be thickened a little, coarsened by Shirl's spuds molten with butter and by plentiful custard. Given that, Kate thought, something might happen.

Since it was a night so blinded by rain that the police might have stayed home, Jelly took the risk of driving them home to his place.

It was vastly cold, the way a town in the plains can be. Jelly was sure the police would not be out tonight with their little breath kits.

He wanted to know, Who was that big bugger?

—Burnside. My husband sent him.

—What with?

—Divorce papers.

Closing one eye, he measured the significance of this.

As he drove, he kept saying, This could develop. Jesus, this could develop.

The rain he meant. Myambagh's streets looked negligible beneath it.

—They're all under their little iron roofs, murmured Jelly, and he stared out as if considering counting the thick beads.

Without asking more about Burnside when they got home, he slept for an hour in the dark. But she didn't. She enjoyed his bulk beside her. It still glowered from the night's intake of rum. When she woke him, he stirred in an uncomplaining way.

He said, Jesus, what in the bloody hell?

But these were purely token sentiments. In Jelly, genuine anger seemed to have been choked out by temperament, weight and history.

—What in the bloody hell?

—I want to put on the light, Jelly.

—Light?

Unlike city people, those in Myambagh were very particular about turning on lights at inappropriate hours. She noticed that they kept their houses black all night. No light burned in the Railway Hotel either, not even to deter a thief. The grandparents of the Myambagh people had seen the coming of electricity to the town's hearths. And a tribal memory told them, in the meat of the night, not to be flippant with light.

—The way it's raining, she explained, there might be a power failure later. I want to show you something, Jelly. While there's still power.

There was one bulb in the room, the overhead one. The bedside lamp she'd seen on her first visit was empty. No prodigality in Jelly's world. One source. One light.

She found the shoulder bag she brought to Jelly's every night and took her wallet from it. She knew the photograph was in there, though she had not looked at it since the catastrophe. She knew the picture would put the question and evince a guilty plea from her.

—There you are.

When she became the different woman, of course she would be able to look at the thing and meet their soft hopeful demand. She might even find tears, and be average maudlin at their faces.

She extracted the picture from the back pocket of the wallet and offered it to Jelly as the rain scarified his metal roof.

—Those are my children.

Taking the picture, Jelly shook his head to jolt his vision into the right mode—inquisitive, respectful, ready with the apt word of praise.

—I've lost them.

—Lost them? Their father take them away?

—Yes.

—Jesus. Why'd he do that?

—He argued he was a fitter person. His mother argued that too.

—Jesus.

After thought and still looking at the picture, he said, Lovely kids. I know there couldn't've been any cruelty, not with you.

—He said there was.

She told him that just to end the story.

—But I bet there wasn't. Was there?

—Nothing deliberate.

She saw him frown. He wanted the simpler answer, the motherly reassurance. She took the picture back out of his hands whether he was ready or not, replaced it, put the wallet back in her bag, and then went and switched off Jelly's melancholy light.

In the darkness, Jelly said, I don't know what to say, Kate.

But by his voice, he intended to go into the subject. She got in beside him. He felt deeply warm, but the surface of his flesh was cold.

—Don't start talking.

Her lips brushed something facial.

—But, listen . . .

—What were you going to say, anyhow? Something that would fix everything up?

—Jesus. I have a hard time fixing a fuse.

—There you are. Shut up then.

And indeed he seemed grateful to be acquitted of the task.

—Send her down, Hughy! he murmured on the edge of sleep.

An imprecation to the Australian god of weather, the god both of drought and of swollen streams. A prayer to the god of downpour from the god of the bar.

When she woke again, the light was gray-blue in the room. The rain was still in the same high voice. She was cold. Jelly had left her, and she had never been in his bed alone. She saw that he stood across the room, sighing his way into an enormous pair of waders.

—Jesus, I'll look like Donald Duck in these. You didn't hear the knocking at the door, eh? The sodding river's over its banks, and there's a tide of water on its way cross-country from Narromine. I'm signed up as an evacuation official. They need me on the books over at the old Palais Theatre. The Palais's built up a bit high, you know. Sorry, love.

She smiled at the curiosity of it: that he did her the courtesy of speaking like an ordinary lover, one who had a normal duty to rest at the beloved's side till dawn at least.

—You ought to get back to Jack, he said. I bet in no time they'll have you out at the racecourse filling sandbags.

He had negotiated himself into the waders at last. He looked slick and authoritative now, liberated from his daily duty as pensioner and servant of the bar. A temporary rescuer, and looking like it! She could visualize him saying to an old lady, Don't worry about the house or the dog, love. Water mightn't even get over the door-step. Take this cup of tea, and the helicopter will be here any second.

—There's something I want you to do, Kate. If I bring the stuff in here, I want you to take it over to Jack's.

She looked at him a time, not knowing what stuff he meant. He thought her solemnity meant agreement and was gone before she could ask.

She began to dress, and was into her shoes, which were still wet from the night before, when he came in slicked with rain and carrying a small Esky, the standard accouterment of picnics as enjoyed by *homo australiensis*.

Jelly was gasping somewhat in his glittering rain gear.

—It's not volatile, he assured her.

—You've got dynamite? You've really got it?

—Jesus, of course I bloody have, Kate. I *told* you.

He picked the Esky up again and did a demonstration of carry-ing it for her, creeping across the room and placing the thing softly on the bed.

—Carry it by the handle, see. You could drop it without any problem, but better not. The detonators are in there too, safe as you like. Wrapped up in foil. The blasting box I'll bring later. In this downpour, I don't want to overburden you, love.

—And where do I take it?

—Oh. Sorry. When you get to the Railway, you know upstairs? A whole walled-off section they open up in what they call civil emergencies. Just put it in there. Tell Jack. He won't mind. I'll be along later in the day.

Kate touched the handle experimentally. He thought she was terrified of the potential detonation still, so he explained further.

—See, if I leave it out the back it'll get drowned. Once it gets wet, you have to ask the police and the bloody army in to dispose of it.

He shook his head at the prospect. It was intolerable that his mission should close with such low comedy.

—I'm not worried, she told him.

Though she did want to live long enough to sign the Kozinskis away, and to see Burnside move out into an air blinded with rain.

Kate settled into her wet shoes now, ready to go. Not washed or rinsed, she presumed the day itself would look after that.

She lifted the Esky and found that it felt quite natural. Carrying it, she followed Jelly into the corridor. The front door was juddering in the wind. Jelly turned to her, a yellow frog king.

—That big bugger, said Jelly, a big bugger himself in some ways. The inquiry agent?

—Yes.

—All this flooding . . . he might get stuck here now.

—Damn him.

—Yes, said Jelly precisely and delicately. In fact he broke the word neatly off the body of language in a way he rarely did. It might be a sign that he was not finished with serious advice.

—Look, I've been meaning to say. You can't just expect to disappear, you know. It's not just enough to come to some dead place like Myambagh. I saw posters for you. Your family has put up posters all over the place. They decided not to call you a missing person, but they sent a poster to every police station. A photograph. Asking them to be so kind as to put them up at the Town Hall and the Post Office . . . A friend of mine who's in the police here brought them to me and says, *Isn't this your friend?* And I say, Yes it is. And he asked me if I think you want these posters put up. And I say I reckon you don't. He knows you've got no record, because he checked. So he just gave the posters to me and I disposed of them. There are pictures of you hanging all over New South Wales, except in Myambagh. Myambagh always wanted a distinction of its own, apart from floods. Well, this is it. The only bloody place with a council chambers that doesn't have your picture. Imagine!

She felt flushed with gratitude, though, and it was partly to herself. She had chosen her protector so infallibly.

The timidity she'd harbored about carrying dynamite across Myambagh vanished now. She imagined the detonators neatly packaged away from the explosive. The two lovingly insulated from one another. Instruments of high office.

Jelly left ahead of her, lumbering away into the murk. She had dropped the Esky to cling to him for a while before he left, and he'd said, Thank my friend the copper. He's took a bit of a risk. Though I suppose he could always say they were mislaid.

She closed the door but did not lock it, since Myambagh people feared not looters, only the flood. In the quiet, drenched streets she was delighted by the weight of the plastic-handled load, by the way Jelly's scheme had claimed her. Her gnarled shoulders ached and itched, as often when she carried weight. This message of pain from the old world could be examined for a while and connected by a thin filament to the new.

Burnside was waiting for her in the dining room at the Railway. He looked well settled in, as if he'd had a pleasant breakfast with the other guests and had diverted them with tales of the construction industry. Shirley had just finished cleaning up and wiping down the filigreed plastic tablecloths. The place was still. Even today all the Monks and Escapees were scattered around households and public buildings in Myambagh, repairing for time-and-a-half the water damage of the past flood even while this one brewed and threatened.

Burnside rose, leaving behind his coffee, and stepped toward her.

—Been on a picnic? he asked, but did not wait for an answer. I could get stuck here now if you don't . . .

—I'll get your papers. Wait there.

First she carried Jelly's Esky up the stairs and onto the upstairs verandah. Jack boasted that in the late nineteenth and early twentieth century graziers, cowcockies, drovers, sawyers and bullockies used to play cricket up here. The fieldsmen in slips and covers had to catch the ball clean to prevent it soaring over the balcony, into the street or onto the railway lines. A young Aboriginal was always employed therefore to stand in the street below and retrieve hoiked balls. Thus on the Railway Hotel verandah, and on other hotel verandahs in the antipodes, a three-dimensional game of cricket had been devised, height coming into the equation as well as length. A sub-fieldsman scouted the road and the steel lines, looking for the ball in thickets of paspalum grass by the goods yard, while upstairs the batsmen ran run after run and the fieldsmen leaned over the balcony screaming, Get it, you black bastard!

On this broad roof, the rain sounded like riveting guns. Kate found that someone had been into the annex—perhaps Shirley, who in between her high-cholesterol mode of cooking cleaned and set up rooms as well. Mattresses had been laid on the boards. Blankets and sheets were folded onto each mattress. On the orders of Jack and dark-eyed Connie, an emergency dormitory had been made. Kate wondered if Jelly knew matters at the Railway had reached such a degree of preparation?

A cupboard stood at the far end, suitable for the explosives. But Jelly had contemplated a vacant verandah. Nonetheless, for the moment, she decided to be obedient. He had said it was not volatile and it was his place to know. He must know of all these blankets and sheets, of the coming population of Murchison's Railway Hotel's normally unpeopled verandah.

Now she went to her room and closed the door. The air was cold and a dim blue, but she lay uncovered on the bed for a time and revived the flavor of her habitual Chifley dreams. No fur in the dream, though. No feather. Just motion above Australia's absolute surfaces.

Guthega had argued one night that the way a kangaroo's lungs hung down behind its ribs and the flab of the belly meant that the very motion of bounding sucked air in. Making light of the earth, or as Guthega had it, traveling like shit, itself caused the lungs to fill. There was never a gasp. All kangaroos, said Guthega, were marathoners.

Her throat closing up with desire, Kate imagined that state: the more you flew, the more you breathed. Flight made of you one continuous body of air.

After daydreaming about breath and flight then, she got up and took Burnside's envelope from the dresser. Blindly she signed every document, canonical and civil, wherever there was a penciled cross. She did not read them. She knew what they said. She was relinquishing all control, equity in and claim against Kozinski

Constructions, Kozinski Development, Kozinski Building Services, Kozinski Industrial Waste Corp, Vistula Trust and Cleaning, and so on. On the letterhead of the annulment document, St. Patrick trampled on a snake. She signed that document very quickly, loyally remembering Uncle Frank, his well-canvassed hatred of canon lawyers.

She put all the documents back into the envelope, stuffing some of them so that their neat creases were erratically rearranged. She carried it all downstairs. The malign exactitudes, she imagined, stung the flesh of the fingers.

Burnside was standing waiting for her. He smoked but he was not utterly at ease. She offered the envelope to him with a speed he didn't expect, so that he half fumbled it, clamping the cigarette in one corner of his mouth by contorting his lower lip. Opening the thing, he looked at every page, quickly. Seeing the repeated signature—she had even consented to sign the papers with her married name—he was pleased. But it was against policy to tell her.

—Wish you'd seen your way to sign them yesterday. Even if the highway isn't bloody blocked, I'll get stuck in Dubbo. Radio says the airport there's closed.

—It's a small inconvenience, she told him in a tone which implied he shouldn't think of making further complaints. Because signatures could be revoked at this stage. Envelopes could still be whisked out from under his elbow and documents ripped up.

She said, Don't forget to ask Jack for your bill before you go.

He stared at her, nodding his head as if reaching a new assessment.

—Whatever in the fuck did Paul Kozinski see in a slut like you?

But he held the envelope tightly in both hands. He would get a commission of some hundreds of thousands of dollars, and could afford to be offensive now he'd assured himself of that. She had an idea he was even wondering whether he should punch her.

—You should live with better people than this. Paul would be surprised to see you living here. I realize it's the shock of what happened, but . . .

She turned away, leaving him. It was time for her to begin her last short season at the beer taps.

She felt usurped to find dark-eyed Connie behind the bar.

Connie said, You settled things with that big bugger out there?

—Yes. He's leaving.

Jack emerged from the keg room. He said with a crooked smile, Connie's taken over the beer taps.

—Too early to start handing out free beer to flood victims. Jack'd start now if I let him.

—Darls! Jack appealed, offended to have his business sense so discounted.

—Australians don't understand business, Connie stated. That's why the country's in such a bloody mess. Jack's a sentimentalist. With my father's money.

Anger overcame Jack. His neck turned red and a stammer broke from his lips.

—Darls, I've never wasted a dollar of your old man's . . .

—Because I watch you, that's why.

Her bruised eyes were permanently wakeful.

—Man's got his pride, Jack reminded her.

—There won't be any business anyhow today, Connie said almost leniently. Better get going on the sandbag filling, if that's what you want.

Jack kissed her, whispered something to her and then went to dress for the outside world. The bulk of Connie's argument as he left the public bar was to tell those kids to stop that or she'd bloody well stop it for them.

In the dining room, pulling on the gumboots from Dunnegan's Country Stores while Connie's children stared at the big television set, Kate looked out under the long verandah across the pavement she or Connie hosed every morning but which was now hosed free of charge. Burnside was backing his car and turning its head eastward, very confident in that solid downpour. It seemed unlikely to Kate, though, that behind the veil the highway had sustained itself all the way to Dubbo. On the other hand, she could imagine him swimming the flooded sections, the envelope held in his teeth.

Sixteen

THE ROAD ahead of Jack's truck was at first empty, since the river had subverted the highway. But as they drove across town, they did encounter other vehicles traveling slowly, hubcap-deep and all within the diamond of space Jelly had once drawn for Kate on a sheet of paper by the bar. One end the Cobar railway line, its adjacent side the highway, and then the two lines of levee. The Myambagh parallelogram in the inland sea, by a deadly river which now had ambitions to swallow the earth. Against that possibility, people rushed by in their four-wheel drives and station wagons, spraying water, anxious about the coming night, unwilling yet to sedate themselves with drink.

The showground entrance boasted of the Myambagh Annual Agricultural Show, nominating dates from the previous April, the April which had been occupied by the other Kate.

The wooden produce halls amidst which Jack steered his truck showed the same patchy yellow as the railway station. He parked by the central ring where in brave days the prize bulls and stud rams paraded and the show horses reared and competed. Now the ring was covered with a hill of sand dumped there without much design by tiptrucks. More men and women and children than you would have thought Myambagh contained filled hessian bags by shovel from these mounds, or else tied the bags with twine.

This appeared to Kate like wonderfully hard work. She advanced with Jack onto the showground and reached for one of the wet shovels which lay unclaimed on one of the lower mounds, not waiting at all—as Jack had to—to pay respects to those who required it of him amongst the organizers of the melee.

Joyful at this last Myambagh labor, Kate worked all dim afternoon, as the flesh of her hands turned soft on the downpour, as the shovel and the bag and the twine with which she tied the mouths of her sandbags began painlessly to bear away her skin. Jack came around with medical tape again and again.

—Giz a look at your hands, Kate love.

He would tie up the damaged fingers, making small regretful noises with his lips. He tried to fortify the knuckles and joints, where the flesh was most at risk, with dressings of plaster. But the work and the rain defeated all that. Adhesive, clogged with sand and water, hung like strips of flesh from everyone's hands. The gloom grew astounding. It quenched all reflections. Kate began to shiver. An officious middle-aged man came around shouting that a new idea had been devised.

The French Revolution must have been like this, Kate thought, remembering something heard in a cool classroom in Sydney on a day of humidity. How Robespierre, shouting like this, possessed of a new plan, brought Danton to the blade.

At the transport depot, to which the man was pointing, there was a gigantic shed, a hangar. Sand was being dumped there, indoors, where volunteers could work out of the rain.

In near-darkness, under a sky choked by cloud, Kate loaded herself into a truck and sat amongst young women and high school students and beefy family men. The journey seemed to revive everyone, cause chatter and the comparing of damaged hands. Everyone was tired out, but in a feverish insomniac way. The communal efforts against water had put them in ecstasy. When they arrived under the great iron roof, they were eager to work again. They congratulated each other that the sand wasn't as water-laden and not as heavy to shovel. The sand was in the bag, the dynamite on the verandah. Her life, ignoring the nullity of it, was under startling control. For a woman on the edge of renouncing Myambagh, she felt narcotically static, an utter citizen.

An ambulance officer, Maltese crosses on his cap and the shoulders of his shirt! He came round dressing damaged hands more competently than kind Jack. He came to Kate and asked her to stop the shoveling, and he looked down at her unloosed grip and began to weep.

—You are all trying so hard, he stuttered.

He felt she had sacrificed her hands for Myambagh. For the integrity of the polis.

Jack had by now gone somewhere, out in the dark. Building a

levee of sandbags behind or on top of the earth levee. As Jelly had predicted, sandbags were essential to Myambagh.

A muscular sixteen-year-old came up with a mug of tea for her.

—You're a tiger, he said.

He made her stop and sit down on a cable spool. She drank the sweet tea. It made her imaginative. Somewhere the bags she'd filled were holding out the water. Down by the wheat silos, along Bardia Street, beyond Lusitania Drive, and by the fences of the cemetery behind which the dead all kept their soggy graves, strict in their denominations. Resting on her cable spool and exalted with exhaustion, Kate saw Gus Schulberger make a tentative entry into the shed.

His head was bare and his black hair spiky with rain. Judging from his hunted look, the peculiar stealthy gleam of his green eyes, he had not come to fill sandbags. A young constable from My-ambagh police, holding a quacking two-way radio, passed him, and Gus looked frankly furtive. The dead giveaway furtiveness of an honest man who lacks the front for deceit. He panned his face away and shaded his eyes till the boy had gone out with his bark-ing radio into the weeping dark.

Sideways then he saw Kate and rushed across to her.

—Tough weather, Kate.

She could tell that he was very pleased to have found her. He wanted to know where Jelly was. Wearing no raincoat, he steamed like a dog, and even smelled a little like one. He had a pleasant canine musk.

Jelly was at the Palais, she told him. Taking down the names of evacuees.

She could imagine Jelly at the desk, full of all the gravity of rescue, an electoral roll open in front of him, and telephones to connect him to the Emergency Services and the police. This was not his chief task in life. It was a holiday from his chief task. If you thought about it like this, pausing, you could taste in this dense, weeping night the rumor of Jelly's reduction to ordinariness.

Gus asked, Jesus, Kate, where's the Palais?

She told him Wrangle Street. An old cinema and dance hall. The Pentagon of Myambagh floods.

Gus shook his wet head. Fascinated, she watched the roostery feather of wet black hair which extended from the back of his skull.

—Listen, could you show me the way?

Amongst the sandbag fillers, she had earned such credit that she had only to mention to one of the middle-aged supremos that she was going.

—I'd think you bloody well would, love. Have a few hours' sleep, eh.

The rain had diminished in force, but could afford to now that it had gingered up the river and set waves of water moving across the plain. Kate was pleased in a light-headed way to find that Gus led her to the small furniture truck in which Chifley and Menzies had traveled to their employment with the Australian coat of arms in Wagga. In her dream catalogue of everything associated with Chifley, this truck had had its place.

Courtly in his way, Gus opened the passenger door for Kate. When he entered the cabin from his side and put his hands to the wheel, they trembled. He sat for a while, absorbing the good fortune of finding her, adjusting himself to the strain of not yet having found Jelly.

—I nearly got washed away crossing Tabramore. There's fifty yards of bloody torrent there, Kate. And I tried it and stalled in the middle. Desperate bloody times. High center of gravity, these things. It was beginning to shift and tilt. A bloke with a tractor drove in and hauled me out. I don't know his name. He's my brother for life, that bugger.

She heard a clicking, pawy stirring in the back of the truck.

—Do you have the animals? she asked in hope.

—It's all drenched in the back there.

—Is it the kangaroo?

—That's right.

Kate turned her head to the little window which gave into the enclosed back of the truck. It was jammed however about two inches open, and could not be pushed further.

—Bloody magneto's wet! Gus yelled as he tried again and again to start the engine.

When at last it caught he set the wipers going, though they made no difference, and drove away amongst the runny Impressionist images of showground and racecourse, past the Henry Lawson Primary School, up Dandibong Street and into Gunningbar, heading west past the Captain John Eglington High School. Kate tenderly rubbed her abraded hands. More than she expected: her dream coming back like this, smelling damp and sounding tentative, fixed in her presence by floodwater.

—So you have the kangaroo, you mean?

Gus said, Jesus!

He meant the rain and the condition of the world.

—Yes, it's bloody Chifley.

Kate did not ask anything more. She noticed gardens awash behind their picket fences. Drowned rhododendrons. The crowns of the streets, which had been clear of water this morning, were now covered. Yet the basic geometry remained. Myambagh's diamond of levees and embankments clearly held.

—I sold them to that bugger in Wagga, said Gus. He wasn't the right sort of person. I kept hearing stories about treatment from people. It started with a vet I know. He called me and said the bastard was starving them, you know, to make them tractable. Get them up to the coat of arms, either side, and they'd be listless, wouldn't hop away too quick. Bigger camera opportunity.

—Then I heard he was using the old electric prod, and he was keeping them in a garage too, separate from the animals in the open.

—Electric prod?

While she'd been having the dreams of night-bounding, Chifley had been pent up in a garage and bullied round with voltage.

—In the twentieth century, said Gus. But hang on, it gets worse. One weekend I drove down and had a snoop. It was all true. The stuff about starving them. You could tell they were in bad condition.

—Then I heard something in a pub that really made my blood boil. There's an old Australian welterweight champion lives in Wagga, short of cash. The owner was planning a big match with Chifley and this boy. Absolutely illegal. RSPCA would spit chips. But he was doing it. A hungry bastard. He was going to have big gamblers in—some of the Chinese, some of the Greeks, fellers from Sydney. Give them a swish dinner, and then the main event . . . Would have put a ginger-up drug in Chifley's tucker, to make him stand and trade blows . . .

Gus wagged his head and spiky hair continually while driving. The unimaginable, Dickensian motives of the park owner!

—Just verifies what I always bloody knew. No animal ought to be in captivity. It corrupts everything. The vets get corrupted. You know, like doctors in some bloody concentration camp . . .

Kate herself felt at once an affront to rival Gus's. Boxing matches were a blasphemy against Chifley's compact, bounding brain, and the electric prod a violation of his limpid eyes.

So Gus had borrowed his friend's truck again, and gone down there and got them out last night. From the perimeter fence he watched the security guard. A lazy bugger, the guard disappeared into his shack in the end to watch some football match telecast from Europe late at night, and that was the last seen of him.

To make his entry, Gus had cut an opening large as a door in the park fence, and on leaving it with the beasts had repaired it with wire. Gus, the earnest citizen, the man of good civil manners. I take your beasts, but you're entitled to your fence.

Gus coughed resonantly. The water had penetrated the points of his chest as well.

—This is a bloody ridiculous situation for a grown man to be in.

They passed the statue of the World War I soldier who kept his face set against the downpour, and his boots would be the last of any civic monument to go under. His companion piece, the humbler and lower statue of a merino sheep, looked hunched and ready for submersion.

—The road's closed now, east and west, said Gus. And Menzies and Chifley . . . They're a bloody inconvenient size to travel with.

Kate pointed through the windscreen: the art deco façade of the Palais. She found it hard to imagine an age in which Myambagh would have had time for such pretension. In front of it sat well-equipped four-wheel drives and police vehicles. Winches were attached and special lights, and you got a sudden hope that there was no emergency from which they could not haul people, no tragedy on which they could not shed a beam.

Gus parked some way from these opulently rigged trucks. As Kate closed the door behind her, she felt a strange phantom electricity, the negative impression of the pleasure of that efficient, bounding, marsupial breath beside which her own breath and Gus's were cramped, permitting nothing better than doggedness.

The first refugee from flooded low ground she found inside the door, right in the lobby of what once had been Myambagh's ritzy cinema, was Burnside the investigator, retainer and enforcer. He was altered in some way: he was wearing emergency clothing, donated stuff. Burnside in the weeds of charity.

Burnside grabbed her wrist. He seemed full of a heaving hysteric strength, and was trying for one or other of his practiced, gim-crack dignities, something to knock her flat with.

—Listen, I had a hell of a time, Mrs. Kozinski. Had to give up my rent-a-car in the middle of a crossing. Nearly got washed away as I waded out. My clothes are wrecked with stinking floodwater. What do you think of that?

—It isn't my fault, she said.

—Lost the papers of course. They're floating somewhere across the bloody plains. The bloody ink is running on them. So what do you think, eh?

She had his vanities at her disposal.

—I think you've got something really interesting to tell people about. When you get back home.

—I could have missed a child's birthday party, he accused her.

But she knew from Paul Kozinski that he acknowledged no children, had only ex-wives.

Past Burnside, she could see the highly lit section of the hall, down there by way of the aisle, past the remaining cinema seats, in the open space below the stage. Tables and telephones as she'd imagined, and Jelly, white-and-blue in the face with tiredness and plain duty, listening to townsmen and officials discuss something urgent. Jelly looked watchful amongst them in a special way, ex-actly like a man with a secret strategy which wasn't in their book of remedies.

—There he is, she told Gus, directing him onward into the lit floor-space of the Palais. But Gus was wary of the official look of some of the men. He dropped himself, in his wet clothes, in a seat three rows back. Burnside, who was helplessly stalking Kate and Gus, plumped down in his wet clothes three seats further back again. He called to Kate.

—You can't tell me you couldn't have signed those bloody things last night, Mrs. Kozinski! You can't tell me that!

Gus was confused by this side argument.

—What's this feller talking about? he wanted to know. But his attention fixed itself again on Jelly.

Kate said, Mr. Burnside, I'm sorry for your troubles. But I am entitled to take as long as I like with important documents. You're getting hysterical.

She loved saying that. To the Burnside of the construction industry, the one who made others hysterical by dangling them from the fourteenth floor by one ankle.

What a delight to see the way his professional air had been eroded. Without that betraying flick of the head, she simply walked away from him, this man without his own clothes, his own car, without the signatures for which he would be paid commission by the Kozinskis who rightly judged her but who themselves needed weighing and sifting, who needed the sharp end of their screams turned back on themselves.

At this stage Jelly saw her and broke away from the group and advanced up the aisle amongst the aged plush of the cinema seats. Arriving, he saw Gus's wet black hair, and the leathery Schulberger face cautiously raised to him. She believed it frightened him for a moment: all the mad people, himself counted in, in the one space.

He pretended they were all there for a routine report.

—They say there'll be some flooding in the low parts of town. But we won't have to move people out by helicopter unless the levees break.

Then he lowered his voice.

—See that fat fart Parkinson from Emergency Services? And old McHugh? They've got all the bloody first-class equipment to do it. But they aren't bloody up to it!

It was as if he was stating these ideas for the first time, as if an amnesia related to all his earlier dry-weather canvassings of the matter in the bar of Murchison's Railway.

—You ought to hear them. They say if the levees went, by the time you got permission from the Police Department and from the Minister of bloody Transport for the explosives experts to come in, the water would've subsided anyhow.

He shook his head. McHugh and Parkinson had between them, by taking this expected line against dynamite, confirmed their impotence in front of Jelly and left him stuck finally with the task. Even Gus, for all his curious problems, was shaking his head, unable to believe *this,* the old men's flatulence and lack of grit.

In his yellow overalls, Jelly began to shiver. He wanted others to take the cup from him. He wanted pillars of the community to be pillars of the community.

—You can't put your faith in levees. Nature abhors the bloody things.

—Jelly, Jelly, said Gus, trying to temper Jelly's enthusiasm for the one big question. He led Jelly aside by the elbow. In his cinema seat, the irrelevant Burnside had begun to sleep, his knees thrust out, his legs crooked, his head abandoned on his shoulder.

When Gus finished, Jelly began whispering very calmly. Judging by Jelly's magisterial air, all this was easily solved.

He had solemnity, and he turned to Kate, wearing an air of familiar command as if they had been companions from before the flood, not this one, but the one which instigated the messy, clamorous, arrogant business of history.

—Take Gus across to Jack's, he said. There's room for his stock there.

Stock. As if Gus had a truckload of cattle.

So now Kate traversed Myambagh the other way, accompanying bewildered Gus and the beasts, the stolen faunal elements of the Coat of Arms of Australia's Commonwealth.

—The owner'll be ropable of course, said Gus. He'll be after me for theft and loss of earnings . . .

They drove straight into the backyard of the Railway by way of the half-flooded side street, swinging into the pub yard as nineteenth-century pastoralists did on their bays or black mares, or else as now the carbon dioxide cylinder truck from Wagga regularly did.

—Look there, Kate directed.

All so familiar and eternal this yard was, like the landscape of a childhood. So she behaved like a proprietor. She jumped from the truck and opened an uneven door into what had once been stables. Gus summoned all his grace and backed the truck in so exactly. The lack of any need for communication between them marked him as a desperately applied being, the way she too was desperately applied.

In one movement she closed the stable door, and the dismounted Gus opened the back door of the truck. A unison, directed by the one brain.

Gus breathed with greater ease now. The stealth had gone from his green eyes. He had a kind of hope. He hauled out planks and set them to provide walkways to the ground for Chifley and Menzies. After an interval for reflection, both animals seemed about to avail themselves.

The first to appear was the great flightless bird, Menzies. He looked austere. He exhibited a primeval stiff-kneed suspicion, intensified by the experience of entertainment-park discipline. He moved to his left, fixed Kate with an eye, and moved to the right. Then he doubled a leg into his body backward, so that it all but disappeared. Only one leg supported him, yet he implied that now at last he was content and resting.

Chifley could have dismounted with one bound. He knew he had enough flight there, packed down in his lungs. But as if his life in Wagga entitled him to it, he was lazy. He tried to creep down the board on his tail and the heels of his great hind paws, and when it looked as if he might overbalance—purely out of the easy option he'd taken, not because of any problem to do with center of gravity—he made it to the floor of the old stables in one unhandy flop.

His descent of course enchanted Kate and utterly took up her attention. Again she verified the heft of his tail and hindquarters, and by contrast the supplicant, thin forepaws folded in some mimicry of prayer above his resounding gut and his brawny chest.

Behind him, from the back of the truck, came a stench of mud and of that dirty water which, Burnside had earlier complained, ruined clothes.

—Dry, Gus addressed the beasts. You're dry now. No more bloody complaints.

Though dealing with soundless animals, he apparently saw them as full-throated, complaining ones.

She was aware of her tiredness, and her night brain descended on her, with its nuances of easy movement and gracious air.

—I'll sleep in the truck.

—But it's water-fouled.

He insisted he would be warm. There was a ledge with blankets.

—Really, said Gus.

She had seen enough. She even wanted to get away from the shaggy-coated concrete Chifley, who seemed to have brought no fear or twitches with him out of his captive state, and go off to her sleep to contemplate the beast's abstract locomotion. She got Gus some bread and black tea—it was all he wanted, he said, and so she left at last and crossed the yard, where it was raining again, and moved in under the iron roof of the back verandah which raged with rain. She felt leaden yet had a sense of anticipation. One of the Escapees emerged from the Men's. He was drunk—he had been celebrating the goodwill he had shown in building My-ambagh's levees.

—Jesus love. We're going to be plastering and painting this fucking town forever.

—Good, said Kate.

Seventeen

IT WAS FROM THE DREAMS before dawn, crisper than
manna, that Jack Murchison woke her. Even on inundation
days, gentle apology was his way with women.

He said, They need us at the levee, love.

She washed her ruined hands and drank some water. Downstairs she found a raincoated, gumbooted and aggrieved Connie
waiting in the front seat of Jack's truck. They exchanged hellos.
Connie's seemed specially crafted for this dim, undeclared sunrise.

Kate wondered if Gus and the beasts still slept from their adventures, or if Gus was already up, feeding them their protein pellets,
giving them extra to make up for the barbarity of the owner of the
tableau vivant.

They crowded into the front seat of Jack's truck, their wet-
weather clothing creaking and crinkling. As they drove off, Connie
began to talk as if Kate's arrival in the front seat had been a mere
pause in a quarrel which had broken out hours before in utter
dark.

—I know we're going to be a target yet again. Just because we're
on the highest ground. Jack has to make a big man of himself. And
they impose on that. They impose on your good nature.

Jack's lips squeaked by way of appeal and reconciliation. Again,
his duty to prevent Connie from taking to her carotid with sharp
objects governed the noises he made with his mouth.

—No, love, look. You know we can put in a claim for anything
we give people in a state of emergency. Food, drink, shelter, everything.

—Yes. But you go crazy, and you build up a bill you know the
state won't pay for. So you halve your claim, and they whittle that
down by a third, and we end up with seventeen cents in the dollar.

Connie did not want Jack to put undue emphasis on this flood amidst all the other floods, fires, famines and human slaughters.

They parked behind the cemetery, and as the three of them walked to the levee at the eastern end of Myambagh, Jack seemed to make an earnest effort to adjust his demeanor to Connie's view of this one flood amongst many.

Trucks brought new sandbags from the depot where they had been filled, and people stacked them into the wall. Everyone was tired and talking berserkly, and a man who was clearly an army veteran of some kind came down the line saying, If you want them to hold, you've got to stack them army-wise, one lengthways, the next crossways. But people could not hold that much artifice in their head. They piled the sandbags up any way they could. Beyond the levee walls topped with bags lay the universal grayness of sky and flood, a sheet of breast-high undimpled foul water, on which little waves moved now and then across the drowned pasture! Myambagh was utterly beset.

As a team, one at each end, Kate and Connie carried sandbags to the levee. Kate noticed far away, along the ramparts of the highway, a string of aged and young and pregnant tottering with bowed heads toward helicopters from which men and women with cameras dismounted. Dropping a bag in unison with Connie, Kate pulled the hood of her jacket low over her brow. It was obvious though why cameras should be sent to behold this phenomenon, from the air first of all and then from the ground. To show Myambagh's pocket of color in the midst of the gray-water nullity. To show the wonderful unity of spirit of country people.

Soon the cameras were at the levee, perhaps three hundred yards along from Kate, at what they must have considered the water's chief point of attack. Kate, head down, lifted the sandbags with Connie as a light rain fell.

Someone cried out and everyone stood still and looked up. Connie and Kate looked up, holding a sandbag between them by its four corners. Amongst the tops of eucalypts a mile away, a new wave could be seen. It was slow and lazy. To a Palm Beach surfer like the former Kate Kozinski it would have been beneath contempt, a wave for a slack, still day. It traveled fast however. It came sucking up to the lip of the parapet and broke for a moment over it, splashing everyone's already glistening gumboots.

Some people began to reinforce the levee with driven-in angle iron spikes and rolls of fencing wire from the stock and station agents. They were all for a second the Australian Corps, those five brilliant divisions, rebuffing Ludendorff's assault in the Easter of 1918. They were connected in heroism to the putteed Digger whose memorial stood above the flood in Lachlan Street.

Kate had time to see that Jack worked with as much brotherly energy as any other man, though he uttered no particular opinions on the army method of laying sandbags, and at one stage he held his hand up bloodied and he laughed. He had taken a routine wound from the wire and the steel, and if nothing worse happened to him then he was no less fortunate than the others. And even if the town were not saved, they were working lovingly together in a dizziness of exhaustion, in a communal frenzy of love.

An ambulance had pulled up and Connie led Jack to it to have his wound dressed. A nurse who was a farmer's wife washed the damage and poured a stinging brown disinfectant on it and surrounded it with bandages. Her hood still pulled down to her nose Kate heard Connie and Jack asking the nurse how she had got into Myambagh, since she lived on a farm out to the west of the town, in the universe of water. She heard the woman say, I came in over the railway bridge.

Jack and Connie both expressed wonder.

—Jesus, that must have been hard.

—The gaps between the railway sleepers . . .

The gaps between the railway sleepers would have shown the furious water moving beneath.

The girl said, Yes. But she made little of it in her country way.

—I had to take it slowly, you know.

The news that there was this way in and out exhilarated Kate. The idea itself was all the escape Kate wanted for the moment.

Meanwhile she had gone on dragging the bags, two-handed, to the embankment. While she was engaged this way, her back to the levee, it gave way. She turned around and saw the little triangle through which the water flowed, filtered by its fall, almost clean. Calf deep, she and other women and men splashed around replugging it. She could hear behind her the enthusiasm of the news cameramen over this. The handsome men and women speaking to camera could be heard making up fables for people in other towns and cities about Myambagh's stubborn courage. Australians, she knew, would love the fact that despite all this tirelessness there had been a failure. That would stoke them up to demand the best for Myambagh. A new wave of Monks and Escapees.

She knew that the camera would very much like to focus on Jack Murchison's brave bandaged hand. Better that than her hooded shape.

The water topped the levee again, and then broke it in another place. Kate and Connie carried sandbags, Jack heaved them one-handed, using his thigh to direct them against the stream which gushed in amongst the unmilitarily placed bags. But nothing concealed the damage. Soon they were waist deep in cold, bad water, water full of the gray discontent of three thousand swamped farms, water fouled by dead sheep and by the fuel from Burnside's sweptaway car. Mundanely, it entered in a gush amongst the sand-bags, and now people stood back watching its flow and acknowledging to each other there was no stopping it.

Some began to wade home, knowing there would be an evacuation, that they should raise a few last things above the expected water line and grab a few last items to take away. A small de-mented man who tried to block the torrent with his knees was swept away and up against a fence a football field away. Strong men like Jack wallowed up to him and picked him up and advised him against any more recklessness.

Jack then and Connie and Kate waded to the truck before the rising water stifled its engine, and drove away. Squinting into the rearview mirror at the image of the wake his vehicle, boatlike, was making, Jack reflected on the nature of what had swept into the town.

—There's meningitis and all sorts of filth in this floodwater. People die of viruses no bugger can name. I tell you what. It'll be time pretty soon that Jelly was heard from.

—Long as you don't get that hand infected, said Connie.

Jack's truck emerged from water beyond the railway line and rolled up the slight but saving hill on which the Railway stood dry. There were already a number of camera crew outside the public bar, dressed in their paramilitary manner, sure they were at the front. None of them had cameras running but stood instead amongst silver boxes of gear, amongst tripods folded into black cylindrical containers. Just the same, Kate took no risks with them when Jack pulled up, and passed quickly amongst them, still hooded, pausing only when she had got inside. She did not take to the stairs however. For she was sure that Jack would have something pungent to say to them, and she needed to hear it. They were the limit to which Jack's manic charity would not reach.

While a television producer negotiated with Jack, she listened from behind the cover of the door, in the corner between the saloon and the dining room.

—My people need dry accommodation, like everyone else.

Jack didn't agree. He spoke in a terribly neutral voice. She found this listening delicious, the certainty of Jack's prejudice against the media, his heroic neutrality.

—I've only got room for orphans and bloody rescue workers. I'll have hundreds to feed within an hour or two. You jokers better get out by helicopter. That's what I reckon.

—Australia has always been very generous to Myambagh. Only because they see it on their television screens. That last flood . . .

—Look. I wouldn't be so keen to take credit if I were you. You blokes are a double-edged sword. Now I'm going to have police and rescuers and all the town's dogs and half the town's fucking cattle, all within yelling distance of here. I'll have to feed them and bed them down. They deserve to have their nights free.

—Free? What do you mean by *free?*

—Free of cameras, said Jack. You bloody know that's what I mean.

—Well, I'll have to tell people on camera you refused us accommodation. What do you say about that?

—I say go to buggery!

It was clear. Jack wanted his high, dry hotel to be available only for dynamiters, wanted it safe for kidnappers of the animal ingredients of *tableaux vivants*.

Jack and Connie appeared together in the lobby where Kate had been eavesdropping. She was too tired to flee. The licensees. They stood together a second at the bottom of the stairs of their high hotel, united for once in the disgust for the merchants of half-truth. On the threshold of his ark, Jack winked at Kate.

She knew she wouldn't be resting yet.

Later, godlike aerial shots would show Murchison's Railway Hotel thus, beached amongst Myambagh's drowned civic buildings and households, the houses swamped at least to their windowsills but often to their eaves. This aerial footage would likewise show the rows of dogs in the Railway's stableyard, all rearing on their hind legs in expectation of meat.

Despite his threats to treat Jack badly, the producer let his crew film the cattle and sheep teeming up to Jack's yard howling and bleating for fodder and receiving it from the hands of volunteers.

By the time these camera images would reach the rest of the country, the crucial question first uttered by Connie, of whether Jack would go *mad,* had been answered. As soon as he started the generator and turned the lights on in the bar, he had resumed his argument with Connie. Soon the men who had been defeated on the levees would be here. They would deserve beer. It defied decency to keep on hitting the cash register buttons on such a night.

—Jesus, love, Jack kept protesting, as if Connie were winning the argument.

In a low voice he told Kate to forget to punch the middy buttons and the schooner buttons and the buttons for nips of spirit.

—And if we're not going to do that, he argued with himself, it'll seem pretty bloody small-minded to punch the button for peanuts.

So instructed, Kate could feel the hotel fill up with the near-panic of Connie. Knowing you needed resources against a continuing history of loss, she couldn't get it through to Jack. He really thought everything could be expended on this one crisis.

—I am not feeding them all the steak out of my freezer, she cried.

—Love, love, the stableyard's bloody crawling with livestock.

—Then I want it hung. I don't want meat that hasn't been properly hung bleeding all over my kitchen!

—It'll get hung. Maybe not as good tonight as on following nights. But be a bit patient, Connie love.

European society in Myambagh was barely a hundred and fifty years old and looked for its myths, and Kate could tell that on top of the kindness, Jack had mythic ambitions. Generosity was his art form, and he *wanted* men to speak of the renowned openhandedness of Jack Murchison. During the Wrangle flood. Married to the Greek girl, you know. Connie. He wanted to be invoked in these terms.

This was how he disposed things in the Railway:

In the bar Kate poured her two-pull beers as the police and the evacuators came in, giving up Myambagh for the night, permitting the floodwater to enter all the town's cupboards, to inspect every drawer. Sometimes Kate punched the cash register buttons by mistake, but she received and put away no money, and the *ping!* and slide of the cash register drawer was only an occasional pleasant, sharp noise in the waterlogged air.

The stories the men told were of taking people along the flooded streets by life raft, persuading them to leave this and that behind: a wedding picture, a bucket, a packet of laundry detergent, a suitcase with a fifty-year-old wedding dress in it. Up past the Civic Centre and the Ambulance Station, right at the high school. Keeping the laws of the road in a rubber boat. Left at the railway crossing, bypassing the Railway on its hill and delivering townspeople to the helicopters on the highway.

Others told of emptying dead refrigerators before food putrefied, and of pacifying family dogs, the naïve protectors of the home, who could smell the coming water, the carrion adrift in it. Calling *There boy* and *Good boy* and getting a muzzle on the buggers and bringing them by boat to the high ground in Jack's stableyard for tethering.

None of the drinkers were aware, any more than the camera crews had been, that Menzies and Chifley occupied their dry shed and were now surrounded by the barking of dogs, and that they frowned at and tested the noise, at least in Chifley's case, by continuing shifts of the angles of the ears. Even the drinkers on whose sleeves were sewn the badges of the State of New South Wales, a lion and kangaroo in this case holding up an escutcheon, and *Orta Recens Quam Pura Nites—Recently Arisen How Brightly You Shine;* even those would not have been interested in who Gus Schulberger was and whether he harbored beasts. For their terms of reference were all to do with the flood. Stolen marsupials were *ultra vires.*

Kate noticed as she poured the beer, conscious of how many firkins and kilderkins of the fluid she was pouring out, that most of the Monks and Escapees were gone. She liked the rescuers better than those who merely painted and plastered the town and lacked a mandate to save it.

A sergeant of the Water Police—*Orta Recens Quam Pura Nites* —asked, So I put it to you, gentlemen? Can anything be permanently done for this bloody town?

There was a flurry of opinion. People couldn't wait to speak. In the midst of it, largely unnoticed though enormous in his yellow Emergency Service gear, Jelly entered from the saloon. To her he had so obviously now the aura of the-man-to-answer-the-question that she was astounded the police, the Water Police, the men from the Emergency Service, the camera people drinking off to one side, and the reflective crew of the air force transport plane which had landed at the Myambagh airport just before the levee broke, and which was now awash out there—that all these people failed to notice him! None of these men put the matter to him or even much adverted to him as anything more than a large presence, a Myambagh grotesque.

He asked her quietly for a middy of beer. He smiled palely at her. His beard was growing up bluely on his large, soft face.

His paleness was different from that of the others. They saw themselves back here again and again, every time it rained. Ferrying widows, pacifying dogs, cleaning out refrigerators. Whereas his duty was to demonstrate by dynamite that Myambagh did not need to be terrorized by the river, could be relieved not only of the fear of its own downpour but of the runoff from other people's. He carried such knowledge in his soft body, and of course it separated him from others. He would have considered it an enviable life purely to have to persuade old biddies and forthright country widowers into the rafts and across to the helicopters, to oopsadaisy them into the cabins and reach up and clinch their seatbelts.

His beer quickly drunk, Jelly disappeared looking for Jack.

Guthega and Noel, his shearing champion son, arrived. Guthega ordered beers by holding up two fingers which looked as though they had not been washed since before the flood. But he had gravity. He wasn't snide tonight.

—Noel and I put all the furniture up in the rafters and got the missus off in a helicopter. I don't know, I don't know . . .

He shook his head.

It was a legend that in some country game—Myambagh versus Narromine, perhaps—when Guthega had been playing hooker, and the referee had taken a long time to set the scrum, Guthega had got out his smokes from his back pocket and lit a cigarette. A cigarette in the scrum! They'd suspended him for life for that, and laid on him the duty to be forever a smartarse, whatever the ruin to his marriage and his liver. They had by their knee-jerk decision committed Guthega's forlorn son to tend him every night as well, even at the loss of championship sleep. Jesus, a man who had had a life suspension for smoking in the scrum owed a debt to society which could not be paid without sacrifice and the adoption of a given role!

Tonight though, the emergency had released him from his normal duties.

—Where's Jelly? asked Guthega, his eyes near-closed. Kate said she thought he was upstairs. Talking to Jack. She could in fact see it all with an interior but precise eye. She beheld Jelly's movements. The annex where the rescuers and the rescued would sleep. Where the swamped aviators would doss down too. Jack and Jelly were there, and Jelly inspected the explosive and, finding it in repose, moved it to another place, the far, unpeopled end of the verandah for a start. Every movement of this nature being an advance toward the actual use of the stuff.

With her internal vision, she saw him lumber downstairs then with it and put it in her room. She saw him then press his way down the stairs against the ascending homeless, going out then to locate Gus Schulberger the fugitive at his truck.

Guthega and his son drank quickly and also disappeared. The waterlogged night didn't offer them a truce either. They wanted to attend Jelly.

At one stage she excused herself from the bar, and walked along under the iron-roofed back verandah. She heard a shot; the dense air muffled it. She looked into the stableyard where the chained dogs—disconsolate on leashes—were beginning to compose themselves for the night, and she saw Jack and Gus and a friend of Jelly's, a Senior Constable Burns, without doubt the one who had consulted Jelly over her picture. Senior Constable Burns was armed with a rifle. A dead sheep lay near his feet. The men were pointing to steers who had come to the yard for its high ground but were now backing toward the gate, frightened by the shot Burns had just fired. She heard the men talking, pointing to this steer and that in the near-dark. Jelly could be heard clearly.

—Up that for the rent. Let's find a steer that belongs to that bastard McHugh.

McHugh, the Shire President, the anti-dynamiter. The Myambagh fable again: that the system of levees had been devised in large part to protect McHugh's pastures and divert tides of water onto the town. Not so much likely to be true, but widely taken as fact.

She saw Jelly and Gus approach the steers in the familiar, leisurely way which country people have with cattle. She herself could not have approached them in this way. For the brute force was on the side of the brutes, and it might occur to them for the first time in their history as you got close.

Nearing the cattle, both Jelly and Gus held their hands palm outward and wide. They moved amongst the beasts looking for McHugh's brand, and when Jelly found it he yelled and slapped the animal's hindquarters, and he and Gus drove it to Constable Burns. In one movement Constable Burns raised the rifle and shot the steer. Its legs flew from beneath it.

Kate wondered what Gus's beasts made of this stableyard commotion?

Guthega and his son had appeared now. They helped run a chain from Jack's truck, through a hook in the stable wall which had been used in pre-abattoir days to hang slaughtered livestock, and—very fast—they had the steer hanging, and Jack with one flick of his bandaged hand opened the artery in its throat.

The constant spouse Jack said, Leave it there as long as we can. Connie hates bloody steaks.

It was raining hard again now. One more inch for the drowned town. Gus was the one Jack passed the butchering knives to. Guthega said not a word; offered no advice.

Returned to the bar, Kate imagined Gus butchering with long, clean cuts.

An hour later she was drinking tea quickly in the kitchen when the meat was brought in, and Jack made the normal excuses to Connie.

—Look, we've got to feed these people some time before two o'clock in the morning, love.

Soon the smell of frying meat filled the bar, and men were pricked back to intensity by it and started boasting about their appetites. A number of men who by habit or temperament liked the work came to the kitchen and boiled potatoes and cooked onions while Shirley and Connie dealt with the great slabs of awfully fresh meat. It was utterly clear that the orgy of Jack Murchi-

son's kindness had well advanced despite Connie's warnings and
would be somehow compounded in the eating of all this meat.

Kate ate at the bar, and Jelly—plate in hand and giving off an
odor of dampness from his clothes—lumbered up to her.

—Listen, Kate love. I'm taking Guthega and his boy and Gus.
You must be tired. But if you want . . .

She found the invitation a little hard to believe in. It brought
fear and a brand of stupid pleasure. The Cornerman and the
Plaqueman, even if not helicoptered out on the grounds of age,
would never in a millennium have been asked to join Jelly in his
night's task.

Weighed with the burden and the grandeur of the idea and
barely breathing, she went to find her drying gumboots and her
torch.

Amongst the party traveling by Jelly's truck: Five people somehow
damply slotted into the front seat, Kate half sitting on Gus's lap
and Noel half sitting on hers and Guthega's; a short truck journey
to where they met the flood lapping across Commonwealth Street
and against the front windows of the abandoned Federal Hotel.

To one of the Federal's verandah uprights, Kate could see, an
aluminum boat with an outboard motor was moored.

In the truck Guthega had grown vocal and knowledgeable
again. There had been a lot of talk about fuses and pigstickers. She
didn't know what a pigsticker was. She had to pick up from the
way the name was used that it was some form of wooden splint
you ran into a stick of gelignite.

Gus said, Nonmetallic, see.

It seemed you could then run the wires either side of the pigsticker to the detonator. The pigsticker stopped them from touching and ending the world by accident. Jelly, Gus and Guthega
must have always known these things. Noel may have missed out
on learning them by becoming wide-comb champ.

Guthega kept saying he wished Jelly had something called a
shrike instead of the old-fashioned plunger box.

—It's got these two buttons on it and two lights, said Guthega,
and the charge can't go down the line until you punch both buttons and both lights come on.

Jelly advised him not to be fussy. The plunger box had been
good enough last bloody time.

They untethered the aluminum boat and pushed it thigh deep. Jelly loaded in the Esky and a heavily packed tarpaulin box which must have contained the rumored plunger box. It was required by all the men that Kate get in next. She found that the dinghy felt fragile in the tide. The others stepped on board gingerly, one at a time. Not even Jelly's weight gave the thing a feeling of substance.

Gus, who had a reputation even with these men as a mechanic, got the outboard motor going and they set off up the Eglington Highway and then left at the submerged rail crossing. After a while Gus asked Guthega's son Noel to take the tiller, and he came forward delicately in the ill-balanced little boat and sat beside Kate. The current was at least with them now, all the earth's water pushing west against the high abutment of the Cobar railway line. Its drift seemed of course to reinforce Jelly's argument, the old one, the one he had made high and dry in Murchison's Railway Hotel on Kate's first night of two-pour schooners.

Even afloat Guthega went on deploring the lack of a shrike, the latest in detonating technology. He seemed to believe that it had somehow been Jelly's duty to produce one.

—How much jelly have you got for a start? he asked in an aggrieved voice.

—Seven kilos.

—Shit, seven kilos, eh? That's what . . . fifty-six sticks of the stuff.

And he couldn't disapprove of that, though he took it as the minimum quantity owed to the chief supporters of a dynamiting fable.

Now and then Gus shone a torch onto near-submerged street names to verify where he was. The extra darkness of the railway embankment was bearing down on them. So they kissed the abutment. Guthega leapt ashore holding the painter, and Jelly came next. From the dinghy Gus handed the Esky to him and the tarpaulin bag which contained the blast box.

—Stay here holding the painter, Guthega told his son when everyone was out. D'you reckon you can do that?

—Yeah.

Guthega insisted.

—*Reckon* you can do it?

—*Yes*.

Noel felt he was fit to take a fuller part than this.

—So you won't get the willies and let the fucking thing drift off?

—Fair go, murmured Noel.

He believed he was being punished for his championship status which this menial task of hanging on to a rope and with the low accusation of fear of darkness.

—Guthega, murmured Jelly, unloading the Esky. Give the boy a go.

—Got to be watched. He's a bloody neurotic.

—For Christ's sake, Guthega. It's just bloody *you!* You make *me* bloody neurotic too.

In the end they left Guthega's unhappy son behind to hold the boat in place against the currents. He served too in the dark as a first-class landmark.

It was a comfort to be treading along the uneven railbed. The air was dark and still and the rain had stopped. You could hear the sucking weight of water dwelling somberly in all Myambagh's rooms.

—Where can I drop the plunger box? asked Gus, and Jelly said, *There!* and Gus dropped it. Then he and Kate and Guthega continued on with Jelly, who would not let anyone else carry the Esky.

Jelly took his mark at the meeting hall of the Myambagh Rifle Club. It had wisely painted its title on its iron roof, since it was now flooded over the eaves. Gus took rope from the same tarpaulin bag as the blast box and tied it around Jelly's waist. Pliers and electrical tape and coils of fuse had been lifted from the bag as well, and lay between the rails.

—Hold the torch, Gus commanded Kate, and she played light onto the preparations of Jelly and the others. Guthega at last now had a chance to handle the Esky. He opened it skeptically and took out the detonators, wrapped in their silver foil. The rope dangling from his middle, Jelly himself reached in and took up one of the explosive sticks from the Esky and one of those splints called pigstickers. He drove the pigsticker into the explosive. This initiating act caused Gus and Guthega to begin taping together eight or nine sticks at a time in bundles, and arraying them beside the Esky in the open. For Kate, all this was a compelling education. She didn't miss a movement.

Gus and Guthega and Jelly went on making their packages of gelignite, wrapping them together with many loops of black tape, asking where in the bloody hell the pliers were. When this was finished, Gus opened the foil package which held the detonators. He took out one detonator and gave it to Jelly, who strapped it to the wooden shaft of the pigsticker already embedded in the initiating stick of gelignite. This was an act of great weight and authority too.

—Don't be anxious, boys and girls, he breathed. The detonator's not even wired up yet.

But we are getting toward it, Kate wanted to say. We're getting there at an awful pace.

—Wire, he commanded.

Gus picked up a coil of fuse wire from beside the tarpaulin bag. Kate shone torchlight onto Jelly's grimy yet slug-white hands as he played one of the strands of the wire around the end of the pig-sticker—it was just as it had been explained to Kate before—and crimped it onto the detonator with pliers, and then the other strand likewise. Doing it, Jelly seemed so admirably light-fingered.

He completed everything then by binding the premier stick, the one with the pigsticker and detonator, onto one of the bundles.

So this was what there was now on the ground—half a dozen or so fasces of gelignite sticks bound together, and in the top stick of one bundle the pigsticker, and on top of that the detonator and the attached wires.

In the spirit of the expert status these grave acts endowed all four people with, Jelly gave Kate the fuse wire to hold and asked her to play it out a little. Gus and Guthega held the rope to which Jelly was tied, and Jelly backed down the embankment, carrying in his arms all the bundles of gelignite. When he got to water level by the submerged chainwire fence of the Myambagh Rifle Club he entered the water without flinching. She played the torch on him.

Guthega said, There's a blocked-off culvert down there. That's where . . .

Everyone associated with the fable except Kate seemed to know about this culvert. It had Jelly's name on it.

Jelly was up to his chest now in the water. He stored his bundles on a shelf of earth in the embankment, and he bent down into the water with one of them and strained to deposit it somewhere out of sight below the water. He did the same with each bundle, lifting it off the shelf of mud into the raised high crook of his left elbow, and from there into his right hand, and depositing it.

Kate shook her head, but it was not the involuntary flinch. It

was for the wonderful seriousness of these people, and the rite of
dynamite.

Before she would have expected him, Jelly was hauled out of the
water again, back up on the embankment, turning slowly from
side to side, trying to shake the water off his wet-weather gear.
Gus and Guthega somehow knew to drive a system of pigstickers
into the railbed here, and around it they separated out and hooked
the two strands of fuse wire which rose up the embankment from
the explosive below the water and which then hung from the apparently single coil in Kate's hands.

Without saying anything, Jelly took the coil of electric fuse from
Kate's hands.

Everyone walked backward up the railway line, Kate shining the
light as Jelly laid down the two wire strands, parallel and never
touching, across the sleepers of the Cobar line. Jelly's culminating
bang depended on this separation. That was the science of the
thing.

Trolling out his parallel fuse wires and accompanied by
Guthega, Gus, and Kate, he reached the point where he had left
the plunger box. He connected the two wires of fuse to their terminals very adroitly. These seemed to Kate to be lonely connections
he was making, even though he had company. As if alone, he
picked up the box and backed some way further again down the
line, very slowly, careful not to trip up his heels in irregularities in
the railbed. Once or twice he made little indicating gestures of the
hand that the others should keep behind him yet out of his way.
Yet for a man who would have such renown in Myambagh tomorrow, a man who would have rounded the circle of his own appointed fable, he did not seem excited.

This is how it goes:

They all duck down the side of the wet embankment, the western side of the railway, the side away from town, their faces, if
they should raise them, aimed over the rail line toward the sunken
municipality.

Guthega yells down the line to his son to lie down, to go down
the embankment a bit, to hold tight to the painter.

Wriggling in the dark, in the pre-shock of what is instantly expected, Guthega asks, Jesus, what's that? Kate herself feels a flurry

against her thighs. There is something feral and full of appetite about this flurry, and she can't stop herself kneeling upright.

—Rats, she says. And she and the others beat about themselves, Jelly himself hits out. But his tone is reassuring.

—Just some rats. Swam ashore. That's all.

Fat with terror, the rats have passed on down the line. They don't want a mere embankment. They are looking for Mount Ararat.

—Don't want any more of those little bastards, says Guthega. There is a shudder in his voice. He turns and calls to his son in the dark.

—You okay, Noel?

—Is it going to go off? cries Noel.

—We hope bloody so.

Jelly is all ready again and has the plunger box level with his face on the top of the embankment. His conscientious hands are so wet, he shakes the fat, hoary fingers with the terminal wires to see that they are securely screwed in and crimped onto the terminals.

But he doesn't depress the plunger; he struggles upright and cocks an ear. The wind has died. The flood comes sucking up against the Cobar line. But there is another sound too. It could only be picked up by that portion of the ear which is connected to the fright hairs on the back of the neck. It is the mob of rats straining against the god of waters and departing sourly down the line toward Cobar, their scouts sniffing for high ground to either flank and not getting any answer.

—Hope they didn't bugger up the wires, says Jelly.

Then, through a little contemplation, he becomes sure they haven't.

Prepare yourselves! yelled Jelly, sliding back into place and raising his hand to the plunger handle.

—You can switch the light out for now, Kate. On three.

He counted to three.

Kate couldn't believe that she was here at such a gravid moment. If only she were certifiably alive to taste the hour. He put the plunger down, and the wait for the great eruption went on to a point that even Kate raised her head to ask a question.

—Jesus, said Jelly. The bloody rats.

Guthega said, You needed a fucking shrike, old son.

Jelly pulled the handle of the plunger up again.

—I'll have to go and separate the wires. Some bugger trod on them.

—Fucking things're temperamental, Guthega told him, raging. Guthega was worried, though Kate and Jelly weren't. He had picked up the musk of imperfection.

—I'll go and attend to it.

—Wasn't one of us, Jelly, said Gus quietly. Must have been the rats.

Jelly rose.

—R'you going to disconnect the wires on the box? Gus asked him.

That sort of talk made Jelly strangely impatient. He shook his head heavily. The weight of it all had at last reached him.

—Yes, disconnect, Kate urged him.

—Look, if the thing won't go off with the plunger bloody down, it won't go off with the bloody plunger up!

So Jelly wouldn't do it. He took the torch from Kate and set off up the line, kneeling heavily in spots to finger the strands of wire. Moving back toward the center of his great task.

And so it continues:

As Jelly approaches the place where the wires debouch around pigstickers and under the steel rail and down to the underwater bomb, Guthega's son Noel comes running and whimpering up the railway line toward Kate and Gus and his father, dragging the dinghy with him.

The tide of rats which passed down the railway line earlier were simply the vanguard of all Myambagh's flooded-out rats. The genuine host of rats now pursues Guthega's son, not nipping at his ankles, having their own phantoms to deal with, but raising in him the fear for which his father has earlier persecuted him.

So many rats. A road of fur. A seething animal river. A railway embankment coated in moving rodent intent. It starts in Kate not only a fear for herself, but a concern for how Jelly will be confused when the phenomenon reaches him.

Noel the wide-comb champion is tripped up in his terror by rats or a sleeper and falls forward. What strikes the plunger handle? Forehead, inside of the elbow? Optional. As he comes down, Kate is sure that his fall is really serious business. The plunger is depressed. There is an astounding detonation as the known earth tears itself apart. Air is taken from her. Her skull and her chest and her invalid womb, a kind of echo chamber, take the terrible buffet from the noise.

Feeling the shock intimately and not as the mere shadow of experience she has had up to now from Chifley and from Jelly, she knows straight away that Jelly is saved now, easily and quickly, from the burden of his name and from the gravity of his parts.

The men are however too awed by the detonation, by the jangling of their heads, to begin mourning Jelly yet. But Kate has begun and she finds herself rocking on her haunches and uttering a sound she remembers from an earlier holocaust: Oooooooooo! All around her rats are falling from the sky. Some of them, she can tell, run off as they land. They want to come to terms with themselves far away from here.

The men gather themselves and go looking for Jelly with Gus's torch, exclaiming, Jesus! and Fuck me! They do not reproach Noel, who is going forward with them in utter silence.

They lack the authority to make Kate stay where she is, and so she goes too. Her grief is of a curious order now, as she cries out striding behind them. It is a quantity of grief. It has no quality. It oppresses her in a different, massive, blunt way.

They find with their boots a multitude of felled rats and pray they are not Jelly. It is brave Gus who encounters an arm and hand, and to prevent Kate seeing it clearly, puts it at once in the tarpaulin bag he carries, the one from which the plunger box came.

Guthega is getting efficient, though he does not have the talent to look after Jelly as briskly as Gus does, and he waves his arms and tries to make Kate stay with Noel, the big boy who is still dragging the dinghy with him and has been slowed and frustrated with it to the point that he now yells.

—What are we going to tell people?

Oh, how Guthega shudders and looks at the bag Gus is holding. To have Jelly so reduced! There is still in Guthega, she can tell infallibly, a hope that Gus is storing the arm to present to an otherwise integral Jelly.

Gus finds Jelly's large head, utterly white and contemplative on the edge of a gap in the railway line. The gap Jelly has made, and through it the flood is now gushing away loudly westward, precisely as promised.

—Bless him, yells Kate madly. Because they will tomorrow as their town drains and the Monks and Escapees return.

Gus lifts Jelly's pale, square head and puts it too in his tarpaulin bag.

—Hang on, Guthega protests. He might . . .

—What? asks Gus. What might he?

Gus goes on searching without result. Guthega yells punitively to his son Noel, You still got that bloody dinghy?

Uttering Oooooooooooo for Jelly, Kate knows she will leave Jack. The sweet triangle: Jelly, Jack, the unsated Connie, which kept Myambagh in place. Now it has been washed away. Now it is flowing noisily out through the gap in the Cobar line. Even uttering the long Os, she knows she has to get going. With the water flowing like this, Murray and her parents, Uncle Frank, the vengeful Kozinskis will not permit her to be static. Murray too hungry and devoted, the others bamboozled with grief. Her parents believing still she lived in a world where people sent each other polite cards.

—Please forgive me for disappearing . . .

After further search, Gus led Guthega and wailing Kate back to Noel. He took the painter of the dinghy from him and told him to go down the embankment and get into the boat and steady it. Then he told Guthega to embark. Stumbling down the embankment, Guthega sat down. He looked nothing, and he was. Rootless, no longer Jelly's smartalec. A smartalec instead deprived of his context. Noel put his hand out as if to straighten his father's posture. Guthega brushed the boy's hand aside.

—Fucking neurotic, Guthega said.

—Godsake, yelled Gus. Leave the boy alone.

It didn't seem to Kate, as she found her own way down the embankment, that the water had much receded. She reflected, finding a seat and looking up sobbing at Gus who still held the bloody remains in their tarpaulin bag, that she would have liked to be alive in a time when Jelly could live on in his fragments. Gus and herself lugging them from town to town and producing miracles. Saint Jelly the Detonator.

In a plain world however, it was hard to know what Gus would do with his bagful of Jelly's magisterium.

In spite of her ambitions to become unfeeling, she was not in fact an unfeeling woman. It was simply that she had accommodated herself to the principle that the order of the world is loss followed by loss.

They push off under Gus's direction. He is the only one of the three men who has any ideas about what is to be done, for Guthega and his son are stupefied. Kate sees a boat traveling off to her right. Its floodlight skims toward the embankment. Jelly's party does not call out or try to get the boat's attention and it goes singleminded on its way.

Without any other propulsion for the moment, they can all feel the current in the water; Myambagh voiding its flood through Jelly's hole in the wall. Gus lays down his bag in the bottom of the boat and smoothly starts the engine. This seems to be a talent of his. Getting motors to chatter away in the wet. Steering, he reaches his free hand out and pats Kate's knee. This causes her to cease her Os.

—What are we going to tell people? Guthega asks, taking up his son's earlier theme.

—What are we going to tell people? cries Noel.

Gus murmurs yet can be heard over the noises of water on the move and of the engine.

—You and the boy weren't even there, that's the first thing.

—Everyone knows we were.

Gus said, No, people like Jack know you and your son were. But the whole world doesn't have the sort of information Jack Murchison had.

—But they'll grill you and Kate, for Christ's sake.

—No, listen, said Gus. No one knew Kate was with Jelly. And me . . . well, why don't you say I was with him?

—Jesus Christ, said Guthega with a kind of reverence. But he was shivering.

—Say I was, will you? asks Gus. Go on. Say it.

—I'll say it, offered Kate.

—Good. You'll say it? Guthega? Noel?

He exacted quick promises as he steered the boat.

—Now stick to it, he said. Just have a bit of gumption and stick to it. And you'll all be clear.

—Oh Jesus, said the bereft, weeping Guthega.

But in their void of shock and in their shame, he and his son fearfully agreed with everything Gus said.

Shy of the Federal Hotel, the prow of the aluminum boat touched earth. Kate could see that Jelly had managed to empty out the water from the Federal, and from God knew what other institutions and hearths!

Noel the shearing champion got out and began to drag the boat with them all in it over the mud to the Federal's railings. He had not spoken much and he was madly eager. Gus rose while this was happening, picked up the bag, stepped out into the mud, and strolled beside the towed boat with Guthega and Kate in it.

—You and the boy weren't there, he repeated with even greater dogmatism, and Kate wasn't. I might've been but I'm missing. That's it, isn't it, Guthega? Covers everything. Fixes all the headache wafers.

Noel intended to continue hauling the boat along Commonwealth Street. He didn't want people saying he hadn't done everything possible. Whatever his faults with small animals, he had energy for objects of substance.

—Okay, Noel, called Gus. Enough's enough, son.

Guthega started weeping.

—You're going to have to clear out, aren't you? Pee-Oh-Queue. Aren't you?

—Well, I will, yes.

Guthega didn't want to be left to fend.

—Going to bugger off . . .

—Over the railway bridge, said Kate. She remembered the nurse.

—Yes, said Gus. The railway bridge's the go.

Guthega was still seated in the stationary boat in the mud, and he shuddered and asked, What about Jelly? What about poor bloody Jelly?

—I'll take him, said Gus.

—Jesus! And what about your livestock?

—I'll take them. You just keep things clear in that head there, Guthega. It doesn't matter what those who know us know.

Gus was already smoothing down his black hair; making ready.

Eighteen

SOMETIME LATE in this heavy night Gus, wiry and sober, carrying his tarpaulin bag, leads Chifley and stiff-kneed Menzies up the road, enticing the animals forward with pellets of stockfeed amidst houses draining of water.

No one has thought clearly about Jelly's awful accident except Gus. And he has made proper arrangements.

He has helped the crazed woman to her room and soothed her to sleep.

He has paid Noel forty dollars to deliver the furniture truck back to his accommodating friend in Wilcannia in the near future, once the receding ferment of mind leaves Noel clearheaded enough to make the journey.

He has woken Jack and tragic-eyed Connie and told them, and Jack too has ordered Guthega and Noel what to say, and they are all compacted together in the secret.

—But why did he take Kate? Jack keeps thinking. In his perturbation, he has to resist waking her now to ask.

Jack placates Connie.

—It doesn't have any bearing on your pub license, he has to keep telling her with something close to contempt.

Gus talks and talks and they become calm.

Then, very late, he and the beasts drive out of the old stables at the back of Murchison's Railway Hotel without anyone noticing, though there have been people, Burnside included amongst them, walking up and down the pub's verandahs, in the hard yellow of the light from Jack's emergency generator, asking if anyone had heard that bloody great bang about an hour ago, and speculating on the flood.

He parks the truck by the Federal. He persuades the beasts into the boat which Noel had dragged high in the mud there. Menzies has stepped in stiff-kneed. He has lifted Chifley's mighty tail in a way which has caused Chifley to yield up suspicion and jump into the aluminum tub.

Gus then reverses Noel's work, pushing and dragging the boat into the water. In the shallows the bird folds the stalks of its legs and settles to the floor. Chifley stays upright, broadly balanced on his tail. A kangaroo afloat, a sight which, if there were drunks to witness it, would cause them to swear off liquor.

Far away to the left, the water police and the rescuers have lit the gap in the line and run their engines in reverse to prevent themselves being sucked through with the water into the uncontained western plains.

He was in the water to his knees, ready to board himself, when he saw a shadow of Kate in the shallows four or five paces away. She seemed to be watching him, sharp-eyed from the little he could make out of her. She seemed to be carrying an airline bag. What of the exhausted woman he'd recently put to sleep? Where was she?

—How could I stay asleep? she asked him. What do you think the first thing I dreamed of was?

She shone a torch at him as a means of emphasis. She saw him close one eye. So clearly he wanted to be alone on the road with his charges. She switched the torch off.

—No. Listen, Jack'll think I took you off.

But she had the answer.

After packing her bag, she'd entered the Murchisons' bedroom to leave a little note, and heard their night breath. Connie slept with skeptical little intakes of breath, but Jack's was deep, slow, imperial. He had transcended the need for bar staff.

—He'll do well without me. He's got volunteers . . . They all want to be around him. He won't need anyone in particular for a long time now.

—Jesus, it'll confuse everyone. They'll think something's happened to you.

—Well . . . Did you see a man called Burnside? At the Palais last night?

—I'm not going to be responsible . . .

She began to weep on the edge of the flood, but there was something not supine but imperative in her tears.

—Please, she told him. Now Jelly's gone.

He was in a sense the inheritor.

In the end Gus lacks the power to rebuff her, and so asks her to get into the dinghy with the beasts.

The leaving of Myambagh is so unexpectedly easy.

Gus could reasonably expect that the fall in the water level has left a gravelly beach exposed below the embankment, just where it meets the line going west to Bourke. A beach of gravel and shingle. Gus grounded the aluminum boat here, and Kate trod ashore with her airline bag, accompanied straight away without hesitation by Chifley the incarnate marsupial joy of her dreams, the shadow of her shadow. How she welcomed this far shore. If she had tried to utter her gratitude for not being left, she would have been defeated. There was no idiom available to her for a task like that.

In a different world, Gus might have looked comic carrying Menzies ashore, hefting the abdomen high so that the long legs would clear the gunwales of the boat and the shaly patch of beach. Such trust the bird showed: deposited on the little beach, he stood waiting.

Gus reached back into the dinghy to fetch the tarpaulin bag.

—Come on then, Kate.

Scrabbling up the embankment, she was watching the kangaroo, already briskly away and up there on the railway line above her, the line which traveled away from Jelly's hole. The main line to Bourke. *Out to Bourke,* people said, to signify great distance, great dry distance, great dry interior distance. Not dry tonight though. *To Bourke and back,* people said to the same effect.

Gus's rescued beasts moved as companionably as dogs in the company of Gus and Kate, sometimes going ahead along the embankment, sometimes lagging. Essential company for the night of Jelly's obliteration. She was their dependent. She prayed nothing more would be taken before morning.

A little comradely walk, and Kate could hear but not see the surge of water below her, and feel the steel presence of the bridge's superstructure. The vacancy between the sleepers was opaque in this light. Chifley's paws overhung the gaps. Sometimes there was a slippage of one of his hind legs. But the great tail spanned four or five spaces, and Chifley would adjust himself like a man pulling his foot out of a bog. The lack of vertigo displayed by Chifley, high-stepping Menzies and Gus as a group imbued her with the means to make progress too.

Halfway across, Gus stepped out to the edge of the bridge-works, carrying the tarpaulin bags in his hands. He showed a steeplejack's lack of fear.

He calls, Kate!

Kate sees and approves the aptness of his intention. Yes. Okay.

For from this woman who once was a girl in Loreto Convent there comes no glib formula, no *Requiescat in pace.* Jelly won't rest in peace. Jelly will be an unquiet spirit in the river. He will hold it in a kind of equipoise, tugging it down with the weight of his spirit.

Gus lets the remnants of Jelly fall. An instant after Gus's hand lets go, there is only a uniform abyss. Country selector, railway clerk, invalid pensioner, bar priest and dynamiter, he is plainly gone. Since the engorged river is putting out its own rhetoric, there is no noise of an entry into the water. To assert his presence, Jelly might need to wait for the level to fall and the current to slacken.

Across the bridge and a little way from the river's racket, the line declines into a flooded cutting, and to Kate's surprise the beasts are happy to wade or lollop their way through this. She wonders can they see or smell the hill on the far side? Jelly has barely been dropped from Gus's hand, but this speculation is throwing a shadow of exaltation on her in the liquid black of the cutting.

Where the silver rails emerged from the water and took some of the minute light available to surfaces tonight, the Schulberger party located themselves between the parallels and climbed the slow rise.

Gus was reflecting on Jelly's history.

—A tremendous prop forward, you know. Got a trial with a city club. But his wife wanted to stay with her mother. So Jelly was persuaded out of it. Typical of Jelly's poor bloody life. He stayed in town for his wife's sake, and his wife left him anyhow. And now look.

Gus's hard life on a Soldier Settler farm near Bourke had given him perfect wind. He did not seem to pause for breath as he reached the crest and concluded Jelly's encomium.

—When he was a country selector, he said, politicians used to queue up to shake his hand. Now his hand's in the river.

—Yes, said Kate. A few strange shuddering tears broke out of her. They felt as if they were a long distance from her, glaciers on the moon's face.

Making his way along the lines, Gus confessed he didn't know what they should do. Keep on this path or cut across the paddocks to the road? Partly flooded, it was off to their right hand, but if they took it, how could they explain themselves to the police or to anyone likely to give them a lift?

Not reaching any answer for the moment, Gus began complaining about the beasts.

—These poor animals will follow me like dogs. They've lost their nationality. They think they're related to me or something. Better for poor bloody Menzies if someone had blown his egg and etched a palm tree design on it. He might have been a bloody sight happier as an ornamental emu egg.

She was uneasy to find him hoping the bird back into the egg.

—Yet you rescued them from Wagga, Kate argued.

—Of course, with Chifley, it's hard to wish him the slow death he'd've had in his mother's pouch. We ran her down by accident one dusk. And we find Chifley's still alive in the pouch. So we felt a responsibility. But this is bloody hard now, too. Look at him.

Chifley had waited behind a moment sitting on the rails and taking thought. Soon he would bound ahead, sit and contemplate again, earnestly domestic, eager as a cattle dog.

—Bugger's so pleased to be out of Wagga. And he thinks he's a member of the bloody union.

Kate has had a sharp though short education in floods, and she is considering their position in this light. Again, the question is slow travel by a railway track, possibly faster by road. If they could negotiate the flooded paddocks between the line and the road, she thinks, the road would be the go. On the western side of any flooded low point, there may be discovered a half-drowned car which Gus in his cleverness would know how to revive.

So the stratagem she offers to Gus is that they should watch the pastures either side of the track. If they find a flooded region, they should cross through it on the relative height of the railway track and then, when they get to the shallows on the far side, take a right-hand course directly across the fields at that very point, along the inland edge of the dip of earth where, it could be hoped, someone's car had choked.

Not of course that a car is much use for conveying Chifley and Menzies, with their odd antediluvian design.

Gus and Kate in their gumboots and with the beasts and the still palpable presence of Jelly, traversed the shallows of someone's lucerne field. Floodwater had spoiled it.

—Who'd be a farmer? Gus asked of the universe, though himself a farmer and cowcocky.

Kate grew weary. To her it seemed an unconscionably, a maliciously more-than-average distance from the rail to the road. She had thought the two were meant to echo each other. But this was no echo. It was a long picking of the way. Coming to one after another barbed wire fence, always part awash, parallel to the railway line but presenting no parallel highway!

At the fences Gus seemed to become overtaken by anxiety about Menzies' thin legs. Again, as at the boat earlier in the evening, he would lift the large eccentric bird by the bowl of the abdomen and pass him across the wire to Kate. Menzies seemed extraordinarily at ease with this arrangement.

Chifley was an eccentric case. He could have cleared the fences at a bound, even on this ground. Instead he broached them lazily, humanwise, lifting up a strand of wire with a shoulder, pulling down lower ones with his great hind feet. Inserting his head through. Delightful to see, it was the negative of bounding. It was the whimsy of a great bounding beast.

—See the way he gets through fences? Gus asked Kate. See?

Gus pretended to be annoyed at Chifley's laziness.

At last their hard progress brought them to an embankment, and on top of it a road.

The top of the road was very dry. Gus took her apologetically by the elbow. They must return a little way now, back toward the flooded town Jelly had relieved.

Soon they could see the vehicle waiting for them, a white van, almost luminous, its rear high, its snout stuck into a broad arm of flood. The van had red and blue lettering on its flanks which said that it belonged to a particular signwriter, O'Riordan of Bourke.

Someone to the east of Myambagh, in Dubbo or Wagga perhaps, had lured the signwriter down here under swollen skies, promising him a contract, and when his engine choked in the water across the road, he'd sworn blue Jesus on the side of the road, and someone had given him a lift back to Girilambone or even perhaps Cobar, where he had to stay in a pub or motel, and knew that in the morning—even if things got no worse—he would need a tow truck and a mechanic.

And he would sit on his bed with his head in his hands, or buy himself a middy in the bar and complain to everyone.

—This fucking job is really going to cost me the earth now!

The water the signwriter's truck was stuck in had a strong current, and it was hard to believe that it was not affected one way or another by Jelly's great releasing of the Myambagh waters. Gus had to wade in tentatively, hauling Kate behind him by the hand. He wanted her to sit in the cabin and release the bonnet lever. She did it. The truck opened its maw. She could see in the side mirrors that Menzies pecked in the gravel on the edge of the water and along the broken tar of the road. But Chifley was leaping westward. That easy lope which delighted Kate in spite of everything; and then he sat back on his tail for a while and thought, and then loped east and sat again back on the thick, stupendous tail to regard Kate through the open window.

—Well, she found herself telling him. Well, where are the bloody tears?

Chifley went on staring at her indirectly, largely through reflection off the side mirror. She had found herself entertaining this fantastical idea that he had her tears held somewhere and would release them to her some time or other. Where did such a notion come from? She was engrossed by it anyhow. But Chifley did not stay long enough for it to become fixed. He loped away again to the west. All this thought seemed dependent on movement.

She got out of the cabin to discover if she could see a little of what Gus was doing. The water came up over the top of her boots and she felt the shock of its cold. She bent down and scooped up a handful and drank it. It not only smelt of, but tasted too of mud and the rankness of dead cattle and sheep and foxes. It was water of substance.

□   □   □   □

Gus talked to her about magnetos. He held spark plugs up toward an utterly shrouded moon, and blew at their apertures, cleaning them with the flame of a Bic lighter. He promised to open and clean the carburetor.

—No sense in your standing there in the water, love.

But she kept standing there, turning numb, hearing the beasts pace and shift behind her. Their habits would have brought imperfection into the Wagga man's *tableau vivant*. The six medallions of the founding states of the Commonwealth of Australia could be made to stand still indefinitely, secure in their bush heraldry. But Chifley would have needed to lope aside for contemplation, and Menzies must work the earth, forwarding and backing over its surface.

And in the significant waters, flowing so coldly around her, in a scene where the only decent light was Gus's torch, she saw without warning and with a casual but exact sharpness, down to the last nuance of their hair, their scent, the faint and particular musk of their womanhoods, the women with whom she had shared the last Sunday she ever spent aboard Kozinski Constructions' yacht, the *Vistula*. She saw as well the young Mrs. Kozinski, not transmogrified yet by the raw protein of Jack Murchison's kitchen, not even seriously threatened with change.

In thin torchlight reflected by the inside of the signwriter's hood, she felt her shoulders itch, a different sting from the normal rankling of her scar tissue. It was a shadow not of the sun's assault on her, but of the way it had more jovially nipped those children, bit Siobhan and Bernard lightly through the fabric of their shirts.

Before they'd left the house for the *Vistula* Paul had been cautious in describing the coming day. He said the guests would be a consultant and three building union officials. They were going to bring along what he wrote off as *their party girlfriends*. It seemed to Kate a ridiculous phrase, and she threatened to stay home. But he pleaded. He wanted to see the children.

A competent sailor, Paul took the helm, and the young deckhand the Kozinskis used for weekends worked the shrouds, and they tacked their way up lovely Pittwater, the Palm Beach houses flashing light from their picture windows across plum-blue water. On their left, the great cliffs of West Head, thickly dressed with Australia's eccentric botany, a hanging garden from before the flood. No more beautiful place: that was established between Kate and Paul Kozinski, and was a proposition subscribed to without prejudice by all O'Briens and all Kozinskis at once.

The unionists were apparently some powerful triumvirate from what Paul called with reverence *the peak council* of all builders' federations council. One small and very muscular. The other two large and strong yet flaccid. Their skins were pale with what the young Mrs. Kozinski took to be the pallor of conspiracy. They might have argued with some justice it arose from a working-class raising in Newtown or Alexandria.

In the flood by the signwriter's truck, with water in her boots, Kate could still imagine their pallor, and the traceries of minute purple veins they showed either side of their noses.

They were jovial enough. They had a nice little patter going with Paul. He was a capitalist bastard they got on well enough with.

All of them drank steadily as if they knew that was what they were here for. Their three girls sat in bikinis on the coaming of the forward cabin, the one in which old Mr. Kozinski and Paul sometimes said they'd be happy to live while sailing the Pacific. None of the women were shy, but the young Mrs. Kate Kozinski noticed that they didn't know each other at all. They were trying out each other's unfamiliar names, whereas the men standing around Paul at the helm closely knew each other's names and were onto other matters: reflections and anecdotes.

These women who had never before spent any time with each other all smoked hard, just as the men around the helm drank hard. When the young Mrs. Kozinski went forward to socialize with them, she could smell the cigarette chemicals which their hair had filtered out of the air.

Even with her boots full of the serious waters of the Myambagh flood, she remembered the names of two of these women. She handled both names as if they were flat stones. She saw both sides of the stones. Denise and Chantelle. The name of the third would not come to Kate on this spirit-laden water.

For some parts of their conversations, they dropped their voices. For others they were boisterous. Their main talk with Kate Kozinski was about how they liked the boat. She saw that they all seemed to shave their pubic hair, for some of the shaven spikiness of it was in each case visible above the line of their bikini bottoms.

Extraordinary that she should now have such a sharp memory of three women with shaven pubes, two of them called Denise and Chantelle. Extraordinary that the day of the women on the *Vistula,* along with the memory of Mrs. Kozinski screaming at gravesides, was all she had brought with her on the road.

All three women made a casual loud fuss of the children. The children had tested the fuming, near-naked, loud and discreet girls with a couple of their best tricks. Siobhan stood on her hands on the roof of the forward cabin, extending her legs in the air, so that the V of her body could have served as a navigational directive to her father at the wheel. Bernard Kozinski showed how fast he could do half a lap of the deck, pounding forward on his flat feet to the bows, then aft to level with his father, who applauded him from the helm.

The girls twisted on their thighs and yelled at the children, Clever boy! and, I wish I could do that!

The children could tell all this was just politeness, a break in the women's absorption in each other. And so both went down into the cockpit instead, to get an occasional flurry of notice there, to listen to the men's stern, barking chatter.

And again this choice made by the children showed that the women on the forward coaming wanted to give most of their attention to getting to know each other, whereas the men already did and had therefore space to devote to handstanders like Siobhan.

Paul and the deckhand hauled the *Vistula* around West Head and anchored in a limpid bay called Jerusalem. They let down the platform aft. From it it was possible to go swimming. The prospect prompted the three women to put their shirts back on.

—Aren't there sharks? they asked at various stages. Paul assured them as he assured all visitors. No one had ever been taken by a shark in Pittwater or in this part of the Hawkesbury. Look, his own children were already in swimming. What long clean strokes Siobhan made. She knew the water was sharkless. Bernard swam more hectically, bobbing upright every twenty frantic strokes to take breath, but getting a smile on his face, tickled pink to find the kindly air was there, and utterly unafraid of predators.

The woman called Chantelle hugged her shirt to her.

—They're so lucky. Living near the water. Makes all the difference to kids.

Paul came down to the galley, where Mrs. Kate Kozinski had now begun shelling prawns and sundering chicken for lunch.

—You know, you don't have to be anything more than polite to them, he told her as if he was worried Kate and the women might become friends. They aren't lost cousins.

She got a little peevish and argued that anyone who came on the boat, anyone it was worth spending Sunday with, deserved a basic courtesy. She asked if the women knew each other, it didn't seem they did?

—I don't know, he said. I only asked them along to keep the boys happy.

She was going to ask what that meant but he smiled excessively, the disarming Slav, and thundered up the companionway again.

When lunch was ready and she went on deck to tell them, Paul had already gone. She could see that he was rowing the three union men and their girlfriends ashore to a little beach beneath the nearly vertical façade of bush and sandstone. Everyone had then vanished into the bush except Paul and the deckhand, who sat on the beach like servants, chatting. Of the unionists and the others there was no sign now. Both the children sat listlessly in the cockpit.

—He didn't let us go with him, Siobhan complained to Kate.

Kate said it didn't matter. You come swimming with me. So she stepped with them onto the grating which had been lowered from the stern, and all three of them took to the water. Habitués, both children. The union officials and the shaven-groin women did not have that competence.

Soon they all descended from the bush: the three unionists, their girlfriends. Dropping down through the ancient flora, amongst the banksias, olive green and black and gray, knobbly and bristling with black cones. From her buoyant place amongst the swimming children, Kate saw them on the beach, saw Paul and the deckhand rise to greet them. While her husband and the deckhand were rowing the guests back to her, she took her mouthful of the deep, brown, brackish, clay-laden estuary water, retained it in her mouth for long enough to give a sense of its full character, and then released it.

The night of the *Vistula* day, once the children were asleep, she told Paul that she would not go on any more cruises like that. Not with Siobhan and Bernard, and not without them either. They were procured tarts, she said. Chantelle and Denise and the one whose name, by the time she drank from Myambagh's flood, she could not have recalled.

She remembered this argument not in the painstaking way in which she had remembered the women and her mouthful of brackish water. She remembered it only in general terms. It was the standard argument between them.

Paul· Kozinski Constructions was the basis of their lives, above all of her leisure to be the supreme mother. Yes, you could call the women whores if you wanted. That *was* why she'd heard one of them say, as they made themselves up and combed their hair in the bedroom behind the galley, that she had always worked for Kozinski Constructions. But did Kate think the world was an idyll? Did she think her children could be protected for good from the commerce of the flesh and the allied commerce of bricks and cement? She kept her children hostage in an unreal world, and for one day, without knowing anything about it, without suffering any harm, they had inhabited the true world. So if the union officials had had small erotic adventures up on the sandstone ledges, that sort of goodwill went into Kozinski projects and paid for Mrs. Kate Kozinski's great motherhood project, which was strangling her children to death!

This was the question, then in Palm Beach and tonight on the Eglington Highway: Had she been the one who took her children's air from them? In Myambagh she had been growing out of that idea, not fast enough but fueled at least by all Jack Murchison's old-fashioned food.

Waiting for Gus to vivify the signwriter's engine, she lowered her hand and stirred the cold waters of Jelly's dissolution.

Kate, arguing on the *Vistula* evening: She believed the Kozinskis liked doing business the way they did it. Would not have wanted to operate under any other system. The snaky corruption of the old world dancing along nicely with the hairy-arsed corruption of the new! She wasn't afraid of the realities of life in the construction business. She believed Siobhan and Bernard should be exempt though from being patronized by women bought by the hour to perform favors for building trade unionists in Jerusalem Bay.

(Becoming heated)

The next time he wanted to award union officials a boatload of women, he ought to provide one for himself!

But again, calf deep in floodwater, stirring it with her hand, she remembered the women and the estuarine water far more intimately than she remembered the fight with Paul. Maybe he was right: he always counted for less.

She did remember one point she had made: that old Mr. Kozinski wouldn't have put his own wife aboard a boat where the frank exchange of bodies was the order of the day. Old Mr. Kozinski might be corrupt, but he knew the protocols, the decorousness necessary for doing business that way. Paul was too Australian and did not have any grasp of the etiquette of tainted business.

Gus seemed to be enjoying himself within the limits of this astounding night. He said he was now ready to start the engine by any means necessary, but would she look under the rear bumper bar to see if the signwriter had taped a spare key there. And yes, wading out of the water to the high and dry rump of the vehicle, she ran her hand along the underside of the blade of bumper bar and the key *was* there.

Carrying it thickly in cold fingers, Kate got into the cabin and turned on the ignition as instructed by Gus. There was a throaty shudder from the engine. Hearing it, Gus laughed. He knew that after a few more convulsions, the engine would start outright. And so it happened. Gus shut the hood, the triumphant slam of a man used to having his way with machinery. With him urging her with hand motions and taking care of where the beasts were at this stage of their inquiries into the earth, she backed out of the flood.

She got down then from the driver's seat to see to the loading of the beasts. Gus fed Menzies into the back of the truck in that peculiar way, lengthwise, since there was barely room for him to stand. Menzies reclined on his backward-bending, tucked-under, sticklike legs. He had been trained to do this by the dimensions of so many of the vehicles which had come Gus's way. Chifley, similarly well trained, stood sagely amongst the paint pots. He had entered a new phase of meditation. He sunk himself for the journey by truck in a style of thought for which no movement was necessary.

Gus rolled down the back door on them, and then as of right, went around to the cabin and took the wheel. Kate in the passenger seat, they drove west. They had a sense of the wide swamps and seas of the western sheep pastures. Semi arid farming they called it. But not tonight. Rice paddies tonight. Fens.

Gus turned on the radio, and the newsreader began to read statistics about the flood. The unfortunate town of Myambagh. Twice stricken in the one year. Two hundred-year floods in twelve months.

Gus said, The centuries pass bloody quick in Myambagh.

—On a lighter note, said the newsreader. On a lighter note, a kangaroo and an emu up to now employed by the owner of a Dubbo entertainment park to provide the living elements in the tableau of the Australian coat of arms have been stolen. Chifley is a mature, male big gray kangaroo, eight years of age. Menzies is a male emu, nine years old . . . A police inspector from Dubbo was recorded as saying that this was not being treated as a light matter.

But that did not take the levity out of the news item. For Gus had heard the announcer say, *On a lighter note* . . .

—People bloody amaze me. Out of the back of the Railway Hotel, Jack has every dog in Myambagh that hasn't drowned, and that's big news, part of the bloody headlines. An act of humanity. That's not on a lighter note. But a kangaroo and an emu? That's comedy in some people's book.

With the aftertaste of the floodwater still in her mouth, Kate considered the issue of what was to be done with this truck in the end? As far as Girilambone, it was licit: a truck Gus had rescued from the flood. After Girilambone, it could be considered stolen. It had the owner's name—O'Riordan—on the side. The name was a personal plea: don't take away my instruments of trade just when I'm hardest hit; just when flood, and the decline of towns along all Australia's aged waterways are narrowing down all business. She could still guess at the desperate feelings of Mr. O'Riordan, prickling with insomniac fear, watching the bush's one late-night television channel.

It was apparent that Gus too thought of O'Riordan, both nobly and practically. About O'Riordan's convenience but also about his red and blue name on the sides of the thing. A dead giveaway.

She watched Gus slide his jaw sideways away from his upper mouth, making a crooked gate of teeth.

□ □ □ □

A tall hayshed presented itself, open to the road, piled high with what even in half-light could be seen as strata of old, brown fermenting hay with blond bales, recently cut, on top. Around such a shed Chifley and Menzies, even if seen from the road, would look *au naturel*. Even if one was spotted by a passer-by, they would not present themselves to the eye as kidnapped performers.

Kate and Gus abandoned O'Riordan's van and crossed the wet paddocks to climb in amongst the bales in the hayshed and mount from level to level of stacked hay. As they rose, Menzies stood by the glossy trunk of a she-oak and seemed utterly detached. He might be able to fend for himself in what was sentimentally called *the wild*. Chifley kept a distance, off amongst the tea trees, but Kate felt the shock again, the phantom of pleasure who always stood there by Chifley's shoulder.

Gus said, Just watch out for tiger snakes.

Everyone knew tiger snakes spent slothful winters in places like this.

Gus erects a little cold- and windbreak of hay bales. It is a blind, a vantage point. Behind it he and Kate can sleep amidst the blue, pungent miasma rising from the bales. Moisture, heat, the furious bacteriology of cut hay.

Gus has brought the signpainter's dropcloth with him too, and now spreads it across the surface of the bales.

—Best I can do. Sorry to say, it's pretty spiky. Not the Hilton bloody Hotel. Sorry to say.

About to sleep, Gus remembers Jelly every few seconds.

—What about poor Jelly, eh?

There seems to Kate to be a large black-blue space in the corner of the shed which is Jelly's absence. She feels the substance of his loss, the changed world, rather than any active frenzy. It is the weight that is awful. Again she looks to the idea that Chifley might lift it.

Kate and Gus, utterly dusted, have crept into each other's arms, Kate in the chaste widowhood of the detonation she can still feel like a block of wood in her stomach and in either eardrum. Gus is reliably a gentleman, following the virtues which he picked up together with his farm mechanics from his battler father. Out in the seeping coldness, Menzies is asleep on his locked knee joints. Amongst the tea trees, Chifley sprawls for a moment, his enormous legs spread. Kate is always aesthetically offended by an image of Chifley in repose. Never did he look so much like a beast of hindleg-heavy imbalance as he does now. She wants him to give her the consolation and easy air of bounding, the air which over-brims with every bound instead of, as in the human model, being emptied out. There is no air for her in the image of his repose.

North of the Darling, on the Schulberger farm, now owned and tended by Gus and his sister-in-law, stands a 1920s derelict building. It dates from a time of hearty intentions. Australia contributed to a fantastically remote war in Europe a larger number of its youth than did most of the *real* combatants, two out of three of these boys from the bush being casualties. Trying to say: here we are, here we are! Europe in the South Seas! Redeemed convicts! True Britons all, even the Irish!

The nation rewarded its returning heroes by giving them slabs of desert and the proud name Soldier Settler. Most of them farmed bravely on, sticking in the agrarian trenchline until the crash of 1929, or in some cases until the great drought at the start of another World War in the 1940s.

Gus's and his late brother's place has one remaining Soldier Settler homestead standing on it, and is in fact made up of two abandoned Soldier Settler farms of about two and a half thousand acres each. The abandoned house, far from the homesteads of Gus and his brother, has timber floors with ancient linoleum still stuck on them, and beneath the linoleum the newspapers of a hopeful year. The family who gave up the homestead in the end has left behind very few exhibits or artifacts, but the most notable is a white and black banded snake preserved in kerosene in a large jam jar.

Occasional iron bedsteads still stand as well—they belonged to children who perished of diphtheria or pneumonia or polio, and whom the parents were too weary to replace. Such are the beds to which Gus and Kate travel.

In Australia movement is not westward to the center but eastward to the coast. Australia is periphery. It dreams of and yet abandons the core. So that the furniture removal trucks, when met, and even discounting the flood, are moving all the time in the wrong direction for Gus and Kate and the beasts.

The sleeping Kate has with better success than she imagines

become the woman she wanted to become. Her hands are be-grimed still and cut about from shoveling and bagging sand. Her hair is lank and damp, and the roots would not tolerate too exact an inquiry. She smells of sweat and unchanged underwear and mold. If the Prime Minister saw her, he would not know her now. He would not be able to say, Gidday Kate, still voting for me?

While cutting up vegetables in Connie Murchison's kitchen, Kate, coming across references to Kozinski Constructions and small pictures of Paul or his father, would quickly enough start to fold the paper on itself over the scraped skins of carrots or the tops of onions or turnips.

But one brisk morning, she did see something she wanted to read and it was not to do with the not-so-Reverend Frank. She moved an eggshell to see the item better. It had to do with a man already mentioned in this account: Frank Pellegrino, film-maker and early lover of Kate.

Pellegrino was an anomaly, an Adelaide Sicilian. In some senses there was no more un-Sicilian a city than Adelaide. It started not as a convict settlement but as a yeoman-based experiment in progress. It had always lifted its skirts clear of the mad Irish-cum-Cockney convictry of Sydney. It prided itself on its British probity rather than on its Sicilians, except that Pellegrino couldn't be ignored. He was one of the young directors who had emerged in Kate's early adolescence and who sometimes expressed gratitude to Jim Gaffney for giving them a run in his cinemas against the advice of his board, and whose talent made a claim on everyone.

There was a pre-existent bond—to do with Jim Gaffney's reputation—between Kate and Pellegrino.

Pellegrino's youth had been spent making television commercials but dreaming, of course, of the feature film. He unleashed his cameraman, a Croatian from Melbourne named Rapotec, on the sublime desolations of Central Australia, and he confessed always to wishing that what they saw through the viewfinder of the Croatian's camera could be employed to narrate tales rather than to sell petroleum products. He had made his first feature film for less than half a million dollars in one of the old Cornish copper mining towns in the South Australian wilderness. His film was chosen by the international jury for showing at the Cannes Film Festival. No sooner was it seen and misunderstood by Hollywood than he was desperately yearned for, and within a few years he was living in Beverly Hills and making studio films, two of which won Academy Awards for various of his technicians and actors, and one of which earned him an Oscar for himself.

Kate met him when the winning film reached Australia. She took him over in fact at the airport, as was her job, led him through a press conference, got him into his hotel, supervised his itinerary and accompanied him to every large city in the Commonwealth for premieres of his film. A number of women in Bernard Astor's office and in the film distribution business in general warned her at cocktail parties to be careful of him. He had a pleasant, larrikin style. In it he liked to conduct the whole palaver of seduction.

She found him however to be a defenseless, short man, negligently dressed. He was exhausted by the flight from California. He confided in her in an urgent whisper how he had been kept awake by the terror of coming home.

—This is a bloody tough country to come back to, he would say again and again.

She told him that all the nation was proud of him and felt included in his success.

He said, That's the ordinary people, love. What about the culture police? They're going to ask me why I went to America, why I made American movies, when I'm going to come home. As if Australian bloody films had been available for me to make, once *they'd* worked the industry over. I know I'm going to get the big question, and there's no answering it.

All the critics who met him at press conferences were genial however, and didn't ask the questions he feared.

—Jesus, love, he confided in her. I think this bloody country might be changing for the better.

His tentative exhilaration began to color all the meals they had together, all the jokes they shared in the lifts and corridors of all the good hotels. She began to indulge that perilous feeling that she'd known him since childhood.

But he was still tremulous about the premiere in his own home city.

—Not a big Dago city, love. Not even a big Irish one either. The only bloody state of Australia where the Anglos still hold the redoubts.

But the Adelaide acclaim was so full-throated that she could see the final ropes of tension dissolve in his face. His parents attended a great post-screening melee in a vast marquee by the banks of the Torrens. She'd been expecting to see workworn Sicilian market gardeners, but they were in fact two stylish retired restaurant managers. Their quiet, well-ordered elation reduced him safely in her eyes to the status of son rather than director. She forgave him the slight vanity by which he'd represented the parents to her as hapless and bewildered peasants.

Back in the hotel, in the corridor, he took her easily into his arms. She could smell on his breath the sourness, the enormous amount he had drunk to protect himself from failure.

—Marry me, he said with vinous ardor.

He meant it of course, and she knew he would continue to for the rest of the tour. He was the sort of man who said these extreme things easily, and then went to a lot of trouble to believe them for a day or two. He remained a devoted lover from Adelaide to Perth and then back to Sydney. Sitting in planes he would touch her helplessly and gaze at her and praise her. It was all of such a high octane that there was a kind of relief when at last, with a keen but feigned wistfulness, he got on the plane to go back to Beverly Hills. He had to face up there to the berserk expectations he had raised by winning an Academy Award.

An altered Kate moved an eggshell to read in the kitchen of Murchison's Railway Hotel a feature on her old three-city lover, Pellegrino. His picture on the page on which she was about to roll things brought back a reminiscent dry flutter behind her ribs, a serpent turning over in husks of corn. The feature said his last film, *The Reaper,* story of a *crime passionnel* on a Texas farm, had done poorly. It had received no nominations at all, and had lost money and been badly reviewed.

The feature quoted Pellegrino as saying, I think my impetus as a director was based on the fact that I came from so far away. Now I've probably been too long absent from my Australian wellsprings. I want to go back, gather myself, and make one beautiful Australian film.

The beautiful Australian film he wanted to make was a novel by one Bruno Casey. In summary it didn't seem so surefire a story. An Australian woman runs a farm in western New South Wales during World War II while her husband is away in the Southwest

Pacific. Her husband's elderly parents are also partners to this arrangement: her husband's older version therefore helps her run the place. Assigned an Italian prisoner of war as a farm laborer, the woman falls in love with him. Her husband is crippled in a jeep smash on Bougainville. It had all to be in the telling.

The film was to be shot in western New South Wales on a property called Craigholme northwest of Cobar.

Kate wakes, feeling at first tireder than the aged western plains. But her remembered information restores her all at once.

Gus wakes too and groans and says, It's cold.

But he lets go of her and is embarrassed for what she will think of him.

She asks, Do you know the properties around here?

Gus confessed to having worked on some of them. He was a remarkable man, willing to answer any question in good faith on first awakening.

—Do you know one called Craigholme?

—Oldest bloody property in the district, said Gus as if it were one of the fundamental data of geography.

Nineteen

CRAIGHOLME, the set of *The Italian Visitor,* sat framed by bare imported poplars beneath a moist dawn. It has not been too easy for Kate and Gus and the beasts to reach it. They have walked more than two hours through the predawn, negotiating seventeen wire fences and crossing five sloppy red clay roads gouged with the marks of bogged tires.

Craigholme itself was a white wool-palace with broad verandahs. Its poor-relative litter of outbuildings in aged brick and slab timber hunch wetly around it. A string of caravans, where cast and camera crew were clearly living and—at the moment—sleeping, connected the big house to the shearing shed and the shearers' quarters, which sit on a bare knoll parallel to the wooded one the big house takes up.

From beneath dripping stringybarks, Gus, Kate and the beasts observed this present capital of Pellegrino's imagination.

A man in a yellow wet-weather jacket emerged from the end room of the shearers' quarters and made his way with fuming breath to a long white catering truck. His hunched back and the vapor his breath made reminded Kate of her own coldness.

—Let me talk, Kate told Gus. The power to issue commands had shifted to her now. She expected though that the beasts would do most of the talking.

They all walked like habitués down from the last fence amongst weeping eucalypts into the film location. Stars and cameo roles, cameramen, soundmen, boom operators, grips and best boys, electricians, drivers, carpenters, continuity women, makeup artists and costumers slept all around them as they progressed.

The hunched, steaming man had by then entered the catering truck and Kate knocked on the door. The man reappeared, rubbing seamed hands. From within an early morning radio quacked resonantly on a stainless steel bench. The noise bespoke a warm studio, a newsreader with coffee close to hand.

—Police are interviewing a Myambagh father and son about the death of one man and the disappearance of a further man and woman.

Would they have Guthega and Noel under hard inquiry in separate rooms? If Jack had anything to do with it, they'd be treated gently, as shocked survivors.

—It is now believed that Myambagh man Barry McNeal (Kate was astounded to hear Jelly called by his civil name) perished in an abortive attempt to blow up the Myambagh–Cobar railway line. Two associates of Mr. McNeal's vanished later in the night, when they set off across the flood-swollen township of Myambagh in an aluminum boat. The names of the missing couple are a Mr. Gus Schulberger of Bourke and Miss Kate Gaffney of Myambagh. Grave fears are held for their safety . . .

—Yes? asked the canteen man again. He had not heard the content of what the newsreader had said. He had heard only the general contours: Myambagh, flood, the normal cast of missing persons. Every flood gathered its quorum of the missing. No foul play was ever suspected; foul water took all the blame.

—We brought the animals Mr. Pellegrino wanted, Kate told the canteen man.

—Oh yes. I don't know much about that.

—He needs animals for today's shoot, said Kate. Or it might be tomorrow's. Anyhow, we've brought them.

The man caught sight of Menzies and Chifley.

—They aren't caged.

—Yes. We don't confine them. They aren't lions and tigers.

The man laughed without any ill intent.

—Free range, eh?

—Mr. Pellegrino told us to contact him soon as we got here.

—They had a night shoot last night. Give him another quarter of an hour's sleep, love. Have a cup of tea with me. Christ, they just stand there.

—They think they're members of the family, said Gus, still honestly deploring the fact. My wife and I raised them from the egg and the pouch.

The man was not to know the wife was gone, and he thought the wife must be Kate, and the reference calmed him a little.

They drank tea, giving Frank Pellegrino and his American wife a last quarter-hour of sleep.

—What agency sent you? the canteen man asked. He was casual. He was not prosecuting them.

—Bernard Astor, said Kate, flying automatically so to speak, with thousands of feet of thinness under her wings.

—I thought he was in promotions. I didn't know he was an agent.

—See, said Kate. We did this job for him at a film premiere in Sydney.

Young men and women carrying metal boxes or battery belts or holsters for spanners and screwdrivers round their waists came and went, making themselves tea and coffee. A man with a light meter round his neck on a black cord arrived rubbing his hands and yelling, Oh Jesus, it's a cocoa morning, boys and girls!

This fellow Kate recognized: Pellegrino's boyhood friend, Pete Rapotec, who had shot all Pellegrino's films, the good and the bad, just as Marty Fenton, graduate of the Adelaide University School of Music, had written all Frank Pellegrino's scores. Rapotec was a walking index of Pellegrino's loyalty to the talents of old friends.

The canteen man grabbed a woolly-headed boy with a belt full of tools around his waist and said, Rabbit, take these people over to Frank's caravan.

Frank. The egalitarian film set in the egalitarian bush in egalitarian Australia.

The boy led them across open ground on grass which crackled—its moisture had frozen overnight. The beasts at this or that stage either followed, led, or outflanked. They got to the caravan with PELLEGRINO stenciled on its door and the boy knocked. Opening up, Frank Pellegrino was wearing a towel around his waist. His upper body had an olive smoothness which Kate remembered, but which had aged a little and acquired with success and failure baplike slabs of fat around the chest.

—Jesus, Rabbit, he said. This is worse than fucking Alaska.

He *had* once made a film in Alaska. With his childhood cameraman Rapotec. Music by his childhood composer Fenton. He stared

toward Gus and Kate and the loosely associated beasts, and moisture steamed from his undried shoulders.

—Do those two want a job? he asked, nodding toward Chifley
and Menzies.

—We brought them for that, Kate told him.

—For what scene? I didn't order them.

—My name's Kate, Kate told him. I knew you. I worked with
Bernard Astor.

—Kate?

—Kate Gaffney. You might remember. Adelaide.

First he looked over his shoulder, widening his eyes, shaking his
head slightly within the boundaries of the wider, more sweeping
movement.

—Listen, wait there. I'll just get dressed. Wait there.

Naturally enough, he didn't want his wife to hear the utterance
of old lovers' names.

While Pellegrino got dressed, Kate led Rabbit and Gus down the
hill a little. In this process Chifley and Menzies were still outriders,
keeping watch on the limits of the known, tolerable, breathable
world.

—I might, suggested Rabbit. If you don't mind . . .

He nodded to the steaming knot of men and women around the
catering truck.

—You go by all means, said Kate.

She watched him dance off to breakfast, and the cold burned
within her like a flame and caused the old itching of the shoulders.
Soon Frank Pellegrino emerged from the caravan, wearing untied
sneakers and pants and a leather trenchcoat of the kind which
must have cost him some thousands of dollars in New York but
which he wore like a Myambagh Escapee wearing overalls.

—Kate? he asked afresh.

—Kate Gaffney.

—I heard the radio. I wondered, you know. But you weren't
washed away? Some other Kate Gaffney . . .

—Yes, some other.

—I think it'd be a bloody mercy if this fucking location flooded.
But listen, there was talk about an explosion . . .

—Not us, Mr. Pellegrino, said Gus firmly.

—What about those animals we brought, Kate asked him.

—Christ, you've changed, love.

And then, being the decent or at least sentimental man he was, he put his hand out and touched her clogged hair by her cheek.

—I mean that without prejudice. Naturally you don't work for Bernard anymore?

—No. This is Gus, Frank. Gus, Frank Pellegrino.

—Augustus Schubert, or some name like that? asked Frank, ever attentive, ever a student of news broadcasts.

—Schulberger, Mr. Pellegrino, said Gus, hoping Pellegrino liked battlers.

Pellegrino, who looked more of a crafty Sicilian than his parents did and who probably found it wise to cultivate his ancestrally wise peasant air, assessed Gus. Gus did not meet his gaze but fixed his eyes frankly on the misty hill behind the caravan. Pending judgment.

Before long, Frank gave up being an employer and spoke quietly to Kate.

—As I told you I would, I always remembered how you were kind to me in Adelaide. You were my guide in the bloody nether-world, Kate. I'm pleased you didn't drown. I mean, I can't help wondering what happened to you since . . . You know what's happened to me, anyhow. Every bastard's been dancing on my grave, but I won't bloody die for them. And I've got a bloody good wife, Kate.

—Can we stay here? asked Gus suddenly, since the reunion dance was taking so long.

—I don't know about incognito, Gus. Kate's a well-placed woman. There'd be a lot of people sad if they couldn't celebrate her survival. I think we ought to let people know.

By common consent Gus and Kate kept silent for a while. Kate said, Make room for us in the budget, Frank.

Frank Pellegrino scratched a worry sore on his lower lip.

—Come on, Frank, Kate insisted. Be a sport.

—Oh Jesus. A sport. Is that what you want?

He shook his head, but in a way which added up the old loyal-ties and debts.

—Okay. Report down to the production office—it's the one closest to the catering van. I'll ring ahead. Use any names you like. Tell them I sent you. You're the animal wranglers. I reckon you'll need accommodation. You've got to see the executive producer about that. Klaus. Next to the production office.

Menzies walked right past Frank Pellegrino.

—Reassure me though. What are these two like with actors?

Gus said quickly, The roo doesn't box people.

—I don't want him to box anyone, mate, said Frank. What I want is for him to wander up to our Italian leading man and give him one hell of a great bloody epiphany. The spirit of Australia eyeing the bugger off. I mean, he's big, your roo, and he's got that archetypal look. Would he stand still for a shampoo, do you reckon? Rapotec'll want to give him one.

—Shampoo's okay, said Gus.

—Our Italian leading man can have a bloody epiphany with the emu too. You know, the best things in the script are often things that befall you at the time, on location. So, Kate, you can hang round here while we film the grace notes with these two. You ought to dry off and get some breakfast. I'd better get back to the missus.

And with a small wave which gave them the liberty of the location, he turned and went back to his caravan, the sodden laces dragging, the leather coat crackling in this dry winter dawn.

It was in this way that Chifley and Menzies were not so much written as injected into the shooting schedule of the new Pellegrino movie.

The Italian prisoner of war is left by his charges at the gate of the sheep station. He asks in broken English where he is to go.

—Up that way, mate, say his departing Australian guards. Up at the house.

Walking up the long red road, he encounters Chifley blocking his path, a tutelary deity. Chifley weighs him in that direct contemplative way. It is not exactly the epiphany Frank Pellegrino wants, but it inhibits the Italian—at the threshold of the farmhouse where he'll meet and become the lover of an alien woman—with a sense of the level, terrible strangeness of the country. At various stages the Italian encounters Chifley again, and Chifley's gaze is to return to him frequently in flashback throughout the film.

Likewise Menzies' enormous striding speed cuts across his vision, especially in a crucial early scene. The vehicle in which the Italian star and the female lead are traversing the great, vaporous plain encounters Menzies, who scoots along on an indifferent, uncompetitive parallel, in the end outspeeding the truck. Excellently shot. Not overdone. The lead actors are required to occupy the truck during this long-range shoot: Pellegrino rarely permits stand-ins. Kate and Gus attend the screening of the rushes every evening in the freezing shearing shed, where rugg-ed actors and crews pass bottles of cabernet sauvignon around from mouth to mouth and exclaim about Rapotec's camerawork.

In the rushes, they see too the separately shot truck interior scene. The Italian prisoner turns to the woman in the truck—at this stage they don't know each other well—with a wide-open and inappropriate smile on his face, because he thinks she has seen and been amused by this startling progress of great, flightless Menzies. But she has not even noticed Menzies. The bird is simply an un-remarked item in her landscape. She wonders what this Italian is grinning at. She is hostile to the size of his grin. Gawp-eyed Men-zies is a catalyst of hostility and so, in the end, of passion.

—Get the bloody marsupials while they're hot! Frank Pellegrino would regularly yell during the shooting of these scenes, and his New York wife would smile and shake her head at the same time for his combined loutish speech and filmic gift.

He would stride out onto the set after a shooting had stopped and sling his arm around the Italian star's waist and yell, Listen you old Eye-ty poofter. We've got to have a conference!

Pellegrino always seemed tickled with Gus. He was delighted with the way Gus could get Menzies to run by pressing a point on the bird's nearly nonexistent hip. As for straight-gazing Chifley, he needed no coaching and no cues.

In the caravan she shared with Gus, Kate washed and combed her hair but did not dress it. She showered, but always put her clothes back on inside the bathroom. She would have been ashamed for Gus to see her scarred shoulders. She wouldn't share the news of them with him as she had with Jelly.

On Gus's urging, Chifley and Menzies were permitted the free-dom of the location, except during those scenes where they were not needed and during which they were corralled for a time in the small stockyard behind the big house. Often, drowsing in her bunk, Kate could hear them ambling and weighing the earth out-side the caravan, the dry flutter of flightless Menzies, the heavy, casual shifting and loping of Chifley.

Still hoping for mutation by carbohydrate, she ate vastly from the covered catering truck's hearty breakfasts, lunchtime soups and pastas, evening roasts.

One lunchtime the star, an Australian woman whose reputation rivaled that of any of America's cinematic women, came stamping up to the catering truck in her 1940s jodhpurs and riding boots. She was attended by a young production assistant, and raged at her.

—Though I don't know why he wants *me* in for all these fucking long shots. That's what he's got Sharon for. He's filming from four hundred meters away and he says he needs me! Why's he so bloody funny about that? I know what he says. The soul is the fucking soul, and the talent's the fucking talent, even at four hundred meters. But I'm freezing my arse off in the summer long shots. I just won't do it today. I've got a bloody cold coming on. He can go to hell.

The Sharon the star spoke of was a young Sydney girl who rode well and who resembled the actress. But as the female lead implied, Frank Pellegrino believed temperamentally in soulprints and in the capacity of a presence to be discerned from another one at a great distance. It was said that movie stars, who did not believe in the unswappability of the spirit, always got the flu in Pellegrino films.

But for Kate, the meaning of the movie star's passing the dressing tables where technicians and lesser actors were eating was that her eyes settled for a cold moment on Kate and did not see her as a sharer of the same air. Kate had sat beside her in press sessions when they were both young. A witty, self-absorbed woman, but with enough sharpness of mind to scan faces in passing and become aware of cues from the past. She picked up no cues from what she saw of Kate.

In muttered sentences during the shooting of the animal scenes, and as if he was instructing her in some technical matter, Frank had told Kate that he would provide a truck and driver when the Chifley–Menzies combination had finished its work. The day of Chifley's last scene Pellegrino pulled her out of the luncheon queue and asked for a word.

—Do you know young Kevin? Frank asked. The red-haired kid, the gopher? He'll drive you wherever you like.

He looked away at the line of his people, the tribe required for the making of any picture anywhere. They would be fueled by the catering to cohere together in the making of sublime images, or so Pellegrino hoped. He returned his gaze to her.

—Do you know a bloke called Burnside? Would have worked for the Kozinskis and people of that ilk. When I used to make documentaries as a kid, he was always turning up. A frightening feller. Adelaide people aren't used to men like him.

—He wants me to sign papers.

—I heard you married that prick Kozinski. Why did you do that, Kate?

—Well, she said. She could have given the supreme reason: I wanted children. But he wouldn't have understood the force of her old desire for motherhood. She found it hard to remember herself.

—He was here just after dark last night. Shower time, before dinner.

For Frank was a great showerer and she seemed to remember that they had spent a lot of time together under cascades of water —the bed resorted to only for exhausted sleep.

—He doesn't believe what was on the radio. He thinks you're on the road. He came right up to the door of my caravan, and I thought, *Shit!* because, as I say, I remember him when I made a little documentary, and I interviewed him as a colorful figure and he said, *Yes, it can be a rough business. It's full of rough bastards.* And then he put a grip on my arm that made the tears come to my eyes. I kept hoping you wouldn't appear from your caravan, but you were acute as always, Kate, and you stayed low. You must have known somehow.

—I didn't know.

—On a commission. He told me that he was offering a quarter of a million dollars for information leading to your location, Kate. I looked at him and I said, Whose money? and he said, My money, Mr. Pellegrino. Part of my fee.

She had had a dream about lushly, *heartily* uttering gratitude to Frank, but by the day's light she still spoke in her flat way and the heart was mere steak. Just the same, he deserved to be told something.

So she explained that she owned a lot of her husband's business. Burnside wanted her to sign papers handing things back to Paul so that he could put them in his new woman's name or more likely keep them to himself. Once bitten, after all. She'd signed papers for Burnside, but Burnside lost them when his car was washed away.

—So do you want to meet him? Sign the things? Get a settlement out of the bastards? I'm not asking because of the money he mentioned, love. I'm wasting so much money here, his little payoff counts for buggerall. But do you want to be free and clear?

She felt a pleasant flutter of anger behind her ribs.

—I never want to meet him. I don't want anything, but I don't want to help Burnside or anyone from the Kozinskis.

—What did they all do to you, Kate? You were a lovely woman. What did they do, love? I could have married you, not that I'm complaining—I'm *not* complaining. But I could have married you. Saved myself some anguish too.

She laughed at the stupidity of his vain world scheme. *I could have married you.*

—So I've let you down?

—No, I didn't mean it that way.

But in part he did. She had reneged on the duty of old lovers to maintain a sort of continuum of charm against future chance meetings.

But all that was contrary to the truth: Uncle Frank's dogma about the *necessary* roles of people, a dogma she had seen fulfilled with Jelly and all the attendant deities of Murchison's Railway Hotel. That not everyone was on the earth to save themselves anguish.

So Kate said, You couldn't have married me.

Pellegrino had the good sense not to insist.

He said, I did read what happened. You've got to forgive me for not writing to you. Something like that intimidates people, you know. Makes them think there really is nothing they can say. But Kate, are you going to spend all your life like this? That man Gus. Lovely fellow. But a fucking ghost, Kate. A bygone figure.

—No. He's alive. He's okay. The world's the ghost. It's gone sour around him. But he's not sour.

He shrugged. Furtively he took a card from his pocket. Sicilian from South Australia, an Academy Award winner, commander of camera technicians, actors, horse wranglers, caterers, electricians and costumers. *Furtively.*

—You can always reach me through *him,* he told her, nodding to the card. He's my agent. Ask for anything. Money. Are you okay for money?

Kate would not take the card.

—I won't need to call on you. The animals have made Gus and me a living. Thank you. *Thank you.*

She found she childishly stamped the earth with the ball of her foot in her gumboot. Emphasis. Now she was going to leave. But he held her back, furtive again, by the elbow.

—I know you don't feel you're in the land of the living. Jesus, you've got to change that.

She shrugged.

—I'm going along all right.

He shook his head.

—I hope you get through all this okay, he said finally, hitting an abrasive basso in which a suggestion of tears lay over the surface of the hormones. He was a sentimental man too. The bad reviews must have near killed him. The terror of the mockery not just of Adelaide but of the world might even now make him drift away in the midst of his wife's caresses.

Driving off the next morning in raw, bright air, amongst paddocks dun with frost, Kate—seated beside Kevin the gopher in the cabin of the truck—smelt the vegetable musk of his red hair and hoped a vegetable innocence was there as well. For Burnside might offer him so much for news of her.

Sitting by the passenger window, Gus was occupied by such things too. For they both knew only Jelly had the sublime innocence, an innocence of the order which shone in the air the truck parted, which slithered down the flanks of their journey and then applied itself to the rear of the truck. The shoulders of departed innocents, Kate was certain, impelled the truck forward.

She knew that it could be a mistake for her to read the whole universe as abetting her escape in this way. But her faith that the universe, having gutted her, would now help her at every small turn was reinforced by breakfast time on the edge of the town of Byrock, when a broad constable stopped red-haired Kevin and accused him of being ten kilometers over the in-town speed limit.

The beasts were in the back, but there was not a tradition in Australia of cops searching trucks. Kate did not feel too great an anxiety about it.

—But constable, said Kevin, we're not even *in* town.

—The speed is posted.

Byrock, to fortify its existence, had spread its town speed limit for miles either side of its modest main street.

The cop asked who owned the vehicle. It was leased, Kevin told him. Who by? Kevin pulled out the papers from the glovebox. Paramount Pictures, they said. That made the cop pause. He had never thought of Paramount Pictures and Byrock as existing in the one universe.

—You with that picture down near Cobar?

—That's right. I'm taking these people home to Wilcannia. They've finished. Transport home's in their contract.

—What did you do on the picture?

—Animal wranglers, said Gus.

The cop was appeased. It sounded good.

—Okay. Next time you're through here, I want you to obey the signs.

He patted the truck familiarly, as if as a vehicle of cinematic glory it was bound to traverse the limits of Byrock again and again.

Pulling away, Kevin wasn't grateful at all.

—I told him Wilcannia, he explained, because you never tell them the truth. Not in a one-horse town that's got bigger boundaries than New fucking York.

They shopped at a country store south of Bourke in the early afternoon. Gus put the food he bought in a gunnysack not unlike the one in which Jelly's remains had been dropped into the flood, and deftly gave some confusing information about his supposed destination to the talkative grocer, who claimed to know him and his sister-in-law.

Then Gus had Kevin drop them all, himself, Kate, the beasts, at a gate in flat saltbush country. The gate said T. P. MCGLAGLAN. From this point they waved Kevin away. Kate saw the redhead leaning out of his cabin waving, radiant between his freckles. A coconspirator, at least till Burnside approached him and offered him the Kozinski incentives.

Standing on the red dirt road which led off through the McGlaglan gate, Gus put his hand on Kate's forearm. A gentle hand to her thickened, inhuman self. She was astounded by it and hoped it did not mean he was trying to bring off a habitual tenderness.

—Not our gate of course, Kate. We're cross-country, twenty miles from here. Easy stages, Kate.

She was happy in a way. As always she enjoyed the prospect of covering cold ground with these worthy and philosophic animals.

The earth here had once been a seabed, and had the absolute flatness of a great seabed still. Over this sea, with its screens of stringybark and its pointillisms of saltbush, within this landscape of sparse tribes and defeated farmers, Kate and Gus and the beasts hiked to the Soldier Settler farmhouse.

Twenty

MISSA DE ANGELIS. The Polish clergy who were friends of the Kozinskis said the Mass of the Angels for the occasion. The pale, not-so-Reverend Frank attended in a surplice at the side of the altar. He was already under his archdiocesan cloud, and demented in any case with grief. He would at the end of the Mass cling to Kate so closely that she could smell both the starch of the surplice and last night's whiskey part denatured by Uncle Frank's boilermaker's body.

—It's an utter visitation, said Uncle Frank.

She knew that a more orthodox priest might have said, It's the will of God.

The vestments for the *Missa de Angelis* are white. The first cold night at the Soldier Settler's farmhouse, lying for warmth in Gus's arms, swathed in saddle blankets which may have been thirty years old, Kate was all at once and without reason overcome by a craving to see these vestments again. She saw the Polish monsignors standing amongst the eucalypts in their bland, waxwhite faces and snowy-breasted chasubles and felt that she wanted at any risk to put her hand to the fabric, the white hot dignity of her children's departure.

Gus hiked off to visit his sister-in-law, leaving Kate time to loiter over the idea of the white vestments. The two of them took some time to arrive back in a red utility truck loaded with food and crockery and more blankets from Gus's own homestead. The sister-in-law helped him carry it in, but she did not seem utterly happy. A large, muscular woman with a hook nose, she wore a red cardigan and gray skirt, and flying boots for warmth over her stockings. When she'd first dismounted from the red utility she'd cried, Jesus, Gus, it's high time you got those beasts put down!

Gus and his late brother had equally inherited their father's place. Their two houses were over to the east somewhere, Gus's normal residence and his brother's, within hailing reach of each other. Gus's brother had been killed in a stock truck smash, Kate would discover, perishing with a load of sheep when he lost control and steered into an irrigation canal. Cancer had got Gus's own wife. Now brother and sister-in-law rounded the communal stray cattle and fixed the bore pumps. The sister-in-law, though visibly not an enthusiast, seemed fairly content about his recent absences. She must have taken or felt entitled to absences of her own. She seemed either not to have heard or not to have got into a state at reports of his drowning.

—Well, when are you coming out into the open again? she asked over a mug of tea.

—Let the dust settle first, said Gus.

—I like the look of this Kate here, said the sister-in-law with a little edge. Why don't you marry her and make an honest man of yourself?

The implication was, *She's using you, Gus.* Kate couldn't have denied it.

Throughout this sparring and veiled complaints, Kate went on thinking of the white vestments, seeing herself make contact with them. Touching the mollified children in the fleshwhite brilliance of that fabric.

—Are the coppers watching my place? asked Gus.

—Come on, Gus, said his sister-in-law. Don't fancy yourself. It's not the Great bloody Train Robbery.

She took a deep draught of tea. Kate looked at her and judged that she was discontented in a jovial, back-of-Bourke way. Hard work and cash hunger had made her face craggy.

Kate washed the cups while Gus drove the sister-in-law away in the truck they had turned up in. Hoary with dust, its engine had a clean growl as if Gus kept it honest. Gus would be back with the thing soon. It would be their truck.

—Come for a walk, Kate? he asked.

A clear evening under an immense sky. A few streaks of white vapor on the horizon. He walked toward the only hill you could see from the farmhouse. This was a knob of stone, a rare bump left over in the flatness by some old play of forces.

—This is very hard rock, Gus told her, pushing against the surface, out of whose crevices trees grew in postures of great determination.

Gus pointed to a long dent at the base of this stone plug. It reminded her of something from her adolescent travels: the sort of indentation the carriage wheels of the Romans had made in the cobbled streets of Pompeii. It looked equally historic. She was tired and her head, still full of holy white fabric, did not at first take in what she was looking at. But the rut ran all along the stone plinth of Gus's only mountain.

Gus said, See there's a water hole amongst the rocks here on the far side.

There was a sort of academic reproof in his voice.

—Only in good seasons, of course. That's when kangaroos come here to drink. Imagine, Kate, how long it took to make this dent in the rock? How many kangaroos it took, traveling in file, to make this rut? I reckon it took thousands of years to make this little road. That's millions of generations . . .

He loved the idea of it.

She looked around and Chifley was considering her. He had followed in a random sort of way. He didn't seem as impressed with the indentation in the stone as Gus was.

—See, said Gus, it means buggerall to him. I bring him to places like this and it doesn't trigger anything. I'm the one who gets excited. You know, thinking how many kangaroos it took. The does following the bucks. The young men kangaroos with their eyes on the does, sly-like. Not ready to make a move yet.

A laugh broke out of him. He was a little abashed at its lack of control.

—He *did* go chasing after does once, but he was too young and an old gray beat him up. He did it a second time. And he was still a little too young. He could do it now and be a success. But he doesn't. He's sticking round as if he wants to look after me in my bloody old age.

The not-so-Reverend Frank had, on first coming from Ireland, served out here in this sparse diocese around the Darling River. I remark on that because of its bearing on white vestments.

On the Soldier Settler verandah, where Gus sat reconstructing an old rifle the Soldier Settler had left behind as useless, Kate remembered sitting up to dinner tables in her childhood, staying there long enough to make the adults forget she was there, or slipping down off the chair and camping amongst the legs of guests and parents, in their adult musk, part animality, part dry-cleaning fluid. And then Uncle Frank would begin tales of his youth in the diocese of Wilcannia–Forbes.

Those were his celibate days. The seminary and the Ten Commandments still cast a shadow over him, and he was pure and fresh-faced. Yet quick to punt at country race meetings, on the dirt racecourses (rainfall wasn't adequate for turf) where the Abo jockeys and their crooked trainers had the races all arranged but where God too had a hand, as Uncle Frank believed, in the placings, and an influence amidst the clouds of dust.

Under the table, Kate became recipient to Uncle Frank's mysterious tales of his first bush diocese.

So Father Tim Brady, parish priest of Wilcannia some time after the birth of Christ and before the birth of rock'n'roll! While the bush was still innocent and full of Gus-like battlers. Brady dies, twelve thousand miles from his brother's farm in Offaly, Republic of Eire. Priests come from all over the enormous diocese to watch Tim lowered into the Australian earth. The bishop, Kieran McDonagh, drives all the way from Forbes with his curate-secretary. By the time the priests all get there, the nuns have had to close the casket, but they tell Tim Brady's arriving brethren that Father Brady had looked tranquil and had died well.

So there's the coffin in the big church of Wilcannia. In the nineteenth century when wool was worth so much in Liverpool and Huddersfield, when paddlesteamers took Wilcannia's fleece away down the Lachlan and the Darling to the sea, it had seemed that there would be nothing but growth and growth on this distant river. But by the time Tim Brady's corpse sat surrounded by his brother priests, the Sisters of Mercy, and his parishioners, Wilcannia's church was already too big for a shrinking town.

Frank O'Brien and his friend Michael Cassidy file with all the others past Tim Brady's closed coffin, and Mike Cassidy whispers, You know, Frank, I wouldn't be so sure Tim's in there. I think he might have run away to New Zealand with a woman. He was never one for the washing, Tim, and I've never known him to smell so good.

Tim is taken out to the graveyard and put beneath the alkaline-streaked alien sod—if he'd died earlier they could have fitted him

into the churchyard, but it was full up by now with nineteenth-
and early twentieth-century Irish clerics. After the interment, the
bishop and all the priests come back for the mother of wakes at
Tim's enormous and empty presbytery. They do not get together
frequently, so that even death must provide a social pretext. And
would you believe it, it starts raining? The drought ends. The flood
comes. The Sisters of Mercy maintain that this is due to Tim
Brady's intercession before the throne of God, though if he had
such power with the Deity he had kept it something of a secret
from his bishop and his fellow priests.

In country where the yearly rainfall is eight inches, they get *that*
by breakfast the next morning. The town is utterly cut off. The
sanitary truck cannot get through to take the full can (which Uncle
Frank describes in his telling at table as *heavy with the wastes of
mourners)* away.

By the second morning His Lordship Kieran, Bishop of Wilcannia–Forbes and of Neapolis Trojanos *in partibus infidelium* (the
bishop's phantom diocese in infidel Turkey) appears at the table
and thunders at his clergy.

—You boys are going to have to do something about that shit
can. A man's balls are dragging in it.

It gave an electric excitement to the young Kate Gaffney to be
told that a bishop spake thus. That was the special scatological
merit of Uncle Frank's tale for her. She would sit rocking beneath
the table, while hilarity jerked the knees of all those around her.

The memory of the white vestments of the *Missa de Angelis* was
sustained in Uncle Frank's old diocese by the grown and bereaved
Kate, hidden in a forgotten farmhouse on marginal land. *In partibus infidelium.*

The beds were made now in the room off the kitchen, the old stove
creaked and ticked with heat, a family of possums having been
driven from the chimney where they must have nested for thirty or
forty years.

Outside, Chifley and Menzies prowl without intent a cold, elec-
trically radiant blue night. While in that small room off the
kitchen, the two iron-frame beds are jammed close together, which
suits the fellow travelers' need for warmth. Fully clothed in the
darkness, they find they have huddled close, each to the inner rim
of his bed.

The air outside seems to chime with cold, and in these cold-to-the-core conditions Kate is to receive the final revelation concerning Chifley and the dreams of flight and air. In the dark, holding on to her frankly in a way which they have both agreed to consider good manners, Gus begins to talk about an old blackfeller who'd worked for his father. At first it seems a casual story. Folklore. An effort to charm.

But from the earliest words, at the speaking of one word in particular—*language*—Kate understands straight away that it will be a grievous tale, more than Gus knows.

As gently and breathily told by Gus:

—The old feller said how the gift to talk had been out there, on the plain, a separate animal, looking for an owner or a friend or something. All the others were scared of it, because they thought it was a dangerous beast, a troublemaker, a real meat eater.

—So there was a sort of committee made to decide who was going to get stuck with language. And someone said, some animal, some totem creature, Give it to the humans. They're vain and they're stupid, and they'll like it.

—The animal chosen by all the others, said Gus, to persuade the humans to take on the talking business was the kangaroo.

This story on the edge of drowsiness and the possibility of drowsy caresses wakes Kate up fully. It is that she knows now in an instant what Chifley's placid intensity meant. It was a kind of persuasion. It was the urging of language upon her. It meant she cannot merely bellow in distress. Through Chifley's bestial cunning, she is faced now with the duty of defining her misfortune in words. She is stuck with language and with the awful business, the fussiness of definition. The cruelty of this stings and distracts her. At once she begins weeping.

—What's the problem, Kate?

He is panicked and presses her shoulder to find out.

What she most bitterly hates is to find herself stuck with language now, in the rump of her life, when it is a futile implement. She understands now the transaction behind the Chifley dreams, and so the viciousness of dumping talk upon her. Though she knows she will still exult in him, she has an awful, rankling, bitter sense that he owes her more still, and better.

—What is it, what is it?

The way he pushes against her shoulders, which he has never seen bared, about whose scarring he is ignorant, will lead by degrees and ultimately to gentler touches still.

She is pacified. It's no use arguing the matter. The panic at owning tongues subsides. Gus's arm goes all the way across her for warmth's sake. He desires her too, but that is no excuse in his book for intruding upon her. He is an antiquity of vanished values, poor Gus, and artless in a way unknown elsewhere.

Not properly asleep, she beholds the remote ghost of her own desire in the room, substantial enough, together with Gus's more robust animal presence. She wishes she could be absorbed in that wordless urgency. But it stands off a little way from her yet. It is just as well. The thing has to happen by degrees, by random caresses. Gus would not be able otherwise to accept the shame.

They needed to heat their bathwater on the fuel stove. Ruminating on Chifley's language trick, Kate did it, taking a long time over it, and then ultimately bathing herself. She saw how her hips had expanded—they were now what people called ample. But she wanted more dimpling of fat around the inside of her thighs. She hadn't yet achieved the amplitude of Connie Murchison's cook Shirley. She washed her genitals and felt the unfamiliar blood in them. Like a postcard from a distant place, she thought. Because of that she came out dressed only in her worse-for-wear bra and a blouse on her shoulders, and a slip which had once been cream and had turned yellow from washing with rough soap. Gus said with fear, Aren't you going to put something warmer on?

When they put out the storm lantern, he held her as usual but tentatively, from behind. To let him know that all was permitted, she reached behind her, one-handed, and stroked as best she could —not flesh but the hard fabric of old army pants. Soon she felt and was pleased by his solidity. She helped him raise the yellowed slip and he entered her with that gratefulness which is the better part of the male spirit.

She now had more time for recollection than she'd been permitted in Myambagh, or had permitted herself.

The memory arose of how at one time Bernie Astor's office had been employed a little oddly to conduct American astronauts on a tour of Australia. The Australian tracking station at Tidbinbilla had been their only link as they crossed the earth's southwestern corner; the city of Perth had kept all its lights on till the small hours to provide a navigational fix! The astronauts had been sent by NASA to thank a friendly nation.

One was a Christian of fundamentalist tendencies, and the other was a wild technocrat reasonably assured that Australia's pleasant women would be anxious to reach out to the flesh he had carried to the moon and back. At first Kate was repelled by him, but when he discovered that Kate was not one of those who wanted the astral experience which was his to offer, he took it with an unexpected style and settled down to become a mere companion.

So that one night, drinking late, she had been able to raise with him the friendly, hackneyed question. Had he learned anything of God in space?

She asked him because by now she expected from him a novel answer. He had already disproved the accusation that spacemen were humanoid. He had told her, for instance, that he hated the jungle training and suffered a childhood phobia of insects. When dumped with the others north of the Panama Canal in rotting rain forest where they were expected to live off the land, he had become ill when served iguana, and had huddled on a muddy slope watching the mulch of leaves beyond the door of his pup tent for fear that they might disclose a spider or a scorpion.

His frankness about his refusal as a certified superman to countenance lizard meat had gone together with his brotherly acceptance of Kate's rebuff, to generate a kind of friendship. So, both their brains tinted with whiskey, she could raise with him the question of space and the ultimate principle.

The astronaut grew somber and said he—like the fundamentalist who had already gone soberly to bed—believed in the Incarnation of Jesus Christ.

She looked for a twitching of his joker's lips but there was none. So he believed in the Incarnation. How strange he'd say it just like that! Raging at his own reflection in a mirror behind the bar. Real Hound of Heaven stuff; wrestling with divinities. And playing out his startling argument.

—God was made flesh in Judaea, said the astronaut. God made Jewish in fact. Imagine. I believe it. I wish I didn't. It has what you could call important implications for my lifestyle and my future . . . I realized in my spaceship—really had it come home to me—

that we, the earth, the race . . . we're a suburb. A little corner. A cul-de-sac.

—It is therefore in my opinion obscene to be stuck with the idea that the only intelligent life in the universe is here, here in this dead-end street. What I believe is . . . Christ has been throughout the universe, to many, many constellations. Otherwise there's no sense. Okay, that's number one.

—Number two. Number two: our idea of aesthetics and of what is noble in the body of a man or a woman is based on gravity. Gravity makes us. Gravity made Marilyn Monroe. Gravity made Jesus Christ. If we lived on a planet where the gravity was 1.5, Christ would be four and a half feet tall and have an enormous flat brow to stand the extra pressure. Marilyn Monroe would be four foot two and her ankles would be seven inches through, and we would still think that was damn marvelous. Because gravity would've given us our idea of beauty as well.

—But imagine (continued the astronaut to the now enthralled Kate Gaffney). Imagine a planet where the gravity was three, Christ and Venus would be hunched over, they would drag their forepaws along the earth. And again we, made by that same gravity, would think they were beautiful, worth dying for, worth our souls. And then a planet with gravity eight! Christ and Venus would be serpents or multipedes, and *he* still would have died to wash us in his blood and we would still have wanted *her*.

She remembered the nature of the awe she and the astronaut had shared then. Reverence for the serpentine Messiah. The vision of the serpentine Venus. It took much headshaking to rid the imagination of these images.

The Kate who made love to Gus knew she was Kate from a planet of gravity two. Her skull had been pressed flat by the weight of events. She had turned herself by will into a Venus from an alternate planet. She had let the gravity of Murchison's Railway Hotel thicken her. Yet Gus clearly came from a similar planet, because entering her and caressing her from behind, his mouth near her ear, he writhed and jerked with cries of praise.

As Chifley had had one or two great and foredoomed glandular adventures, Kate imagined but she may have been wrong—that this was a rare excursion for Gus's body. In tune with this belief Kate herself felt certain waters breaking and flowing inside her.

She approved of it all distantly, a Maharani approving of the coming of the monsoons.

Flung with abandon across the frost outside, Chifley waited, owing her something for the pain of being shackled to language, even for the milliliters of painful breath, the ounces of broken words Gus uttered against her ear.

But though Chifley had the lungs and sinews, he couldn't provide everything. Toward the edge of sleep, she said, Would you let me go to Mass?

—What do you mean, *let?*

—I want to take the truck if you'll let me. I want to go to Mass in Bourke or Wilcannia.

—Bloody long way to go to Mass, Kate, he said.

He was very wary with his affection now the frenzy had ended. Again, being proud, loath to offend or presume.

—But it's okay by me, he added then.

—And if I meet Burnside, I might sign. Just for peace. But I wouldn't let him follow me back here. This place wouldn't be found or anything . . .

—Your business, Kate.

Twenty-one

AMONGST THE DWINDLED NUMBERS of devout in Bourke, she attended the Mass. The church in Wilcannia where Mick Cassidy had cast aspersions on the then and forever late Tim Brady was, as Gus had persuaded her, too far to go, so Bourke must serve.

The cast of the rite:

The Catholic doctor and his placid wife and handsome and mannerly country children.

The Catholic lawyer who looked Lebanese, and his young freckled-Irish spouse.

The elderly women, and the runty little men called Kelly or Mahony who had worked on cattle or sheep stations and retired in town, wearing everywhere, perhaps even to the bathroom, the sweat-glutted Akubras they had worn in their days of labor.

And although the congregation was smaller than the Irish monsignors who had built this church would have ever foreseen, it was in some ways as if nothing had changed since Uncle Frank had been a cleric of this diocese. The young priest could have been a bygone not-so-Reverend Frank. Though Frank and the others had come to Australia because there were too many devout for even the native Australians to supply the sacerdodal need, this lad was here because no one cared anymore, because Madonna had acted and Jack Nicholson had slickly taken the souls of the young. The crass but complex world would in the end distract even the country doctor's wholesome children.

The priest was wearing green vestments, for that was the season of the year.

She sat through the Mass and numbly through the sermon. The young priest had been to some elocution teacher who had taught him to hone the final consonants of words. She listened to the shape of his words and imagined where he came from. The standard green lane in mid-Eire? A pub in Meath? Or judging by the burr, a pub in Derry.

Numbly she took communion from one of the town's remaining nuns. Not a galleon of a nun, full habited in the manner of the year when Tim Brady had perished in this diocese. A nun in a calf-length dress. A modern woman.

At the end the priest with the sharp-honed words blessed them in English. Divesting himself of his green chasuble at the altar, he made for the front of the church to intercept his departing parishioners and peck some of the women on the cheek. Such Protestant folksiness wouldn't have characterized the wrath-of-God, I-might-shake-your-hand-but-God-will-still-damn-you Irishmen of Uncle Frank's youth.

Only a few aged faithful, dissenting from the folksy handshaking and kissing in progress outside, stayed behind to make their private devotions. Kate stayed with them. She could hear the young priest being genial around the doors of family vehicles, sticking a head in to rib one of the children on intelligence from the parents. He seemed so remote that the world—at least the world as it existed in Bourke—was tearing him further and further out into the secular streets. His green vestment lay barely remembered on a chair.

Kate left by a side door. She passed the graves of monsignors called Cullen and Fitzgerald and entered the sacristy from the outer door. The smell of Uncle Frank and all the others was there. The highly scrubbed and beeswax scent of the catechism. The smell of Uncle Frank's soft hands on race day. Long before he thought of applying them to Mrs. Kearney's whippet body.

There were long, brown varnished drawers with brass brackets to hold a label. *Albs. Tunicles. Surplices and Stoles. Chasubles.* Two drawers of chasubles.

She pulled out the lower of the two. Red and black assailed her eyes. Blood and desolation and burnt offerings; martyrdom and loss. She kicked this drawer shut with her shoe. She was affronted by even the chance idea that the black of the Mass of the adult dead applied to her case.

A new drawer. With the green and yellow, there were two sets of white—a modern silken chasuble, made for the weather, and a heavy brocaded and braided one built without reference to Bourke's mean summer temperatures. She pulled this one out. She inspected it, felt its texture, and then folded it to herself, against her breasts. The young priest appeared in the sacristy doorway coming from the church, carrying his green chasuble of today's Mass, but not as intimately as she carried the white.

He was surprised, but he said pleasantly, Is there anything I can do for you, madam?

Kate walked toward him. Yes, she said. These white vestments . . .

—The heavy set, he said, still pleasant and willing to humor. Probably eighty years old, that one.

She hit him in the stomach with all her force twice and then ran away, clasping the thing to her. The churchyard rang with the Jansenist disapproval of dead monsignors. The street was empty though except for peppermint trees. All the faithful had vanished.

She did not wish to have to explain to Gus what the vestment for the *Missa de Angelis* was doing in his truck. It sat beside her on the front seat and she felt it one-handed and was satisfied. Ultimately, she was pleased to encounter an irrigation canal, well before the turnoff to Gus's place. She laid the white chasuble down into the water, and it floated away like an august living thing.

—That's it, she said reassuringly, standing on the edge of the canal, on the limitless bottom of a once inland sea. It was well known from the classroom: two hundred million years too late the English gentleman Charles Sturt came with certainty to find a sea that had so long stopped lapping, and had found instead the harshest light off white objects and been blinded instead of bathed.

She inspected her hands with which she had taken the wind out of the Lord's anointed. She did not know why she'd done it to that poor, jovial man.

Back in the truck, she drove home on spidery trails amongst the stringybarks to the Soldier Settler ruin, and went inside to sit by the stove and listen to Gus's quiet inquiries.

Gus turned on the radio news in the still afternoon as they sat content, she with her morning's work done, he with his veneration of her and the old rifle to work on.

The radio said:

—Well-known racing identity, the Reverend Francis O'Brien, was arrested in the early hours of this morning at a hotel in Ermington, Sydney.

Letting an unwise yelp loose, Kate saw that Gus had noticed nothing. She composed herself. She knew the name of the hotel after all. The Partridge and Grapes. A massive barn of an Aussie hotel to carry such a cozy name. Mrs. Kearney's hotel.

—Also arrested was an associate of Father O'Brien's, Mrs. Fiona Kearney. Father O'Brien and Mrs. Kearney are charged with taxation fraud, illegal gaming, and with violations of the Federal Telecommunications Act. Mrs. Kearney and Father O'Brien between them have interests in at least ten Sydney hotels, of which Mrs. Kearney is nominee. Mrs. Kearney is the widow of well-known East Sydney alderman, Mick Kearney, who at the time of his death was a witness before the inquiry into illegal gaming. The Reverend Francis O'Brien was suspended from duty by His Eminence, Cardinal Fogarty, Archbishop of Sydney, in November 1988, at a time when the Reverend O'Brien's connections with starting-price bookmaking were revealed before the Independent Commission into Corruption.

Morosely gratified Fogarty, who had managed to move in on Uncle Frank before the police did. Though there was no sense to it, she felt something like a fury at the righteousness of His Eminence Fogarty.

Gus heard all this newsreading static too but knew nothing of what it meant. Chifley, beneath the stringybark, heard it and gazed at the verandah.

—There, she believed he placidly said. The gift of sodding language. Keep the bastard.

—Thanks a lot, said Kate.

At least the radio was too prim to say what Kate knew in her blood: that Uncle Frank was dragged half-naked from the same bed as half-naked Mrs. Kearney. Neither of them beauties, Frank in his tousled plumpness, she angular and her face blurred. As she had heard someone, probably a friend of the Kozinskis, say, If he was going to break his vows, you'd think he'd get better value than Fiona Kearney.

What is required of me now? she wondered. Whatever it was, there wasn't any chance she would provide it. The not-so-Reverend Frank was not dependent on her favors.

The bottle the shocked young fireman had pressed into her hands.

—Reached inside the door, but this was all I could get before everything went. Sorry. Sorry.

Even in prison, Uncle Frank would be Uncle Frank, a god who would know where the bottle was. In a cupboard at Mrs. Kearney's at Ermington at the worst. In a cupboard at *his* house in Abbotsford. It wouldn't be right to ask him now, burdened as he was.

Just the same, she wondered should she write to him? He would have the best of counsel. His ten hotels would pay for it. His tax-evaded earnings. If not that, his loyal brother-in-law James Gaffney, or his tame mortician O'Toole.

Siesta: an unlikely event in Gus's life. It is midafternoon on the day after Kate stole the vestments of the *Missa de Angelis,* and still she cannot think of anything Uncle Frank needs from her. Somewhere Jim Gaffney is discussing bail and lawyers with him, while Gus has yielded to drowsiness and is languorously entwined with Kate.

—Man's getting bloody lazy, leading this life.

Half-asleep, they could hear the engine of a truck and both got up on their elbows to get a view through the window. Soon two distinct motors could be heard.

The first vehicle to appear by the farmyard gate of the vanished Soldier Settler was Gus's sister-in-law's red ute, tinged a sallower red by its permanent dust.

Gus's sister-in-law dismounted and opened the farmgate. By then Gus and Kate had reached the window. They were mystified: having opened the gate she backed away from it, did a complete U-turn and parked with the tail of the truck toward the farmhouse, leaving the track clear to the black sedan which had followed her to enter the yard.

Kate dwelt on the ecclesiastical black duco beyond the window.

—Uncle Frank? she asked. Uncle Frank?

She was still caught in the tail of something like a dream. Gus took no notice. He put his boots on without socks, in the manner of people of the old bush, the battling bush of the vanished Soldier Settler who wore socks only in the trenches of Flanders and for his wedding.

—It's someone, Gus told her.

Barefooted still, she reached for her gumboots. She would have liked to have washed. This had nothing to do with the normal etiquette of visits however. Of what a visitor could expect in a farm wife, if that's what Kate was. It had more to do with her delight in the image of a thread of cold water from the water tank by the front door. The white fabric had sharpened her delight in the seeing of such things.

She could hear the visitor's car pull up by the steps. One look of alliance, and she and Gus went out to greet it. When they got to the verandah, Burnside was already out of the car, inspecting some knee-high native plant which had encroached on the shade of the verandah steps. He was no longer in the charity weeds they'd given him at the Palais in Myambagh after his rescue, but in his accustomed clothing—razorsharp slacks and a windcheater. He looked up as Kate emerged.

—Well, don't you think you two ought to call the police and tell them you're safe? They'd like to talk about what happened to the big fellow . . .

The big fellow. The biggest. Jelly.

Standing by her truck beyond the gate, Gus's sister-in-law was waving something. It was an envelope. Burnside was the master of the envelopes.

—Fifteen thousand in cash, Gus. And a check for fifty thousand. All so that Mr. Burnside could have a talk to your friend. Legal documents. Fair enough in my book.

Gus's face reddened. Perhaps even from that distance she could get that whiff of his shame, for she got uncertain and threw the envelope into her truck.

—Leave you to it for the time being.

She entered the truck herself, then she drove away homeward, dragging with her a light red squall of dust.

There was a makeshift table and two chairs on the verandah. Gus had set them there so that he and Kate had somewhere to sit and drink tea in the afternoons. Slowly in this landscape aching of slowness, Burnside set his eyes on this rough furniture.

—Can I come up? he asked as if he was very tired.

—No you bloody can't, said Gus.

Burnside went back to his car, opened a door, then his briefcase which sat on a seat, and took a brown envelope from it. It was of course the twin to the one full of the papers Kate had signed in the

Railway Hotel. She felt an intimate anger. With a shudder, she felt it slither from her. She believed she could perceive it glittering handsome as Satan on the verandah boards.

She said, Now I'm not signing. I'm not signing now.

He did not realize that he was up against a living thing, where in Myambagh he had had to fight only inertia.

—If you'd signed them last time when I said, I wouldn't be still after you.

—Get out of here. I'm not signing.

—So you only signed in Myambagh, said Burnside almost plaintively, with a thug's genuinely hypnotic sense of grievance, because you knew the floods would get me. What a bitch of a thing. I can't stand people who think like you do!

—Listen, you used to make me sick when you were on the *Vistula*, Mr. Burnside. Fuck off. I'm going inside.

—Well, you weren't in such good taste yourself. You were all sewn up like a fucking Lebanese virgin. But we're not here for insults. Mr. Kozinski senior is willing to pay you an extra $300,000 over the two million for your signature.

She heard Gus whistle or at least express breath despite himself.

—No. No way.

If the fury hadn't broken from her body and made things simple, she could have said more rhetorical stuff than that. Something like: They haven't printed the check large enough to carry the digits to pay for getting rid of me! As it was, she was so ruggedly angry she didn't need to.

Burnside appealed to Gus. I don't think she's reasonable. Do you think she's reasonable?

—Not for me to judge. But a sum like that . . . there's got to be some dirty work.

—There's dirty work, said Kate with her new passion. He's the dirty work.

Gus put his head on the side. Light could be seen through his feathers of black hair. He said, I don't know who invited you onto the property. I'll have to speak to my sister-in-law.

Moved by his herbivorous curiosity, by habits well tolerated in his de-pouched babyhood by his friend Gus, Chifley had come in close.

Burnside mounted the stairs opening the envelope. He took papers out as he went, and offered them to Gus.

—You read them then. There's a fee in them for you too. She already signed their identicals in Myambagh. What a town that is!

Stepping forward to receive the papers, Gus was at his most defenseless. She meant to tell him about Burnside's renown, but Burnside was quicker than utterance. He dropped the papers on the verandah. They would not blow far in this still, dry air. With both hands he took Gus behind the neck and dragged his face down onto a raised knee. She heard Gus's already skewed nose crack like a twig.

Omnipotent Gus who had led her out of the floods and rescued the beasts! Rescueless himself, he tumbled to the boards. Burnside's knee then landed in her stomach, taking her breath, making her brain reach hugely for air.

Even without air Kate was abashed by the way Burnside spoke in cliché, not because he could not do better but because tough guys loved clichés, and Burnside wanted the tough-guy niche in the building industry of New South Wales.

—Don't leave bruises on a lady, she heard him inform her. Work on the soft tissues. I've been bloody wanting to for some little time.

Her legs gone, she sat beside Gus. She could hear herself whooping for air. There came from between her legs a hateful brown stain; a stench of helpless resentment.

Burnside was collecting the Kozinskis' papers again. *Now I will die rather than,* Kate was still airlessly saying.

What took up her mind while she barked for breath was a sort of admiration of the sister-in-law's innocence. Here was a woman who certainly believed that money fell from heaven or—the same thing—came unsullied from the hands of scoundrels. If she hadn't believed that, she would surely still be here, keeping an eye out for the way things went on the verandah. The eye, one of many, Burnside deserved to have focused on him.

He lifted her by the scruff, without effort, and somehow the movement gave her back her breath.

—What a great girl you are, Mrs. Kozinski! The *real* Kozinskis, particularly old Mr. and Mrs., despise you. You want to have kids by this fucking bushwhacker? I can neuter him, love! Listen: Sign Paul Kozinski's papers so he can live the full enriched life he wants to, and you can live the shitty one you want.

Gus was trying to lever himself upright. Holding Kate still, Burnside kicked him casually in the side of the head. Had Burnside been wearing those heavy, metallic soles in Murchison's Railway Hotel? How had she missed them?

At the thud of the impact, Gus's arms flew from beneath him. Kate saw Chifley, a placid witness, ten paces from the base of the stairs. Menzies paced the fringes of the bush with an avian indifference, but Chifley *saw* and misread it all. He had the same brand of grass-eating innocence which Gus's sister-in-law possessed. You push the gift of tongues upon us, thought Kate beyond reason, and now Burnside beats us to death with it.

Burnside said, I will fucking cripple your friend, and the lawyers Mr. Kozinski hires for me will tell the courts it was self-defense. They'll even argue he was beating you. Your behavior will disqualify you as a witness. I've had cases like this before.

He sat in Gus's chair. Shuffling the papers, he grew ruminative.

—This is an old road to me. It's only new to you.

He watched her raise herself from the boards and flop into a chair. She wanted her breath back to tell him that the womb didn't matter. For the fury was gone—it had its own will. Oh the weariness of his catching her up, and all the people who would be in his wake! But she had the resources to help Gus. Nothing to help Uncle Frank with. But she had the papers and, no doubt, Burnside's pen, to hand.

—I won't sign for money. I'll sign for nothing.

He produced his pen, set the reshuffled papers before her.

—The cover document says you have accepted an upfront and additional fee of $300,000, which I am authorized to write a check for. It's up to you whether you cash the check or not. But I don't want the legal problem of altering the documents.

She signed even that letter of agreement, and then started on the swath. There seemed to be even more companies than last time, not that she had ever taken definite notice. Some rang bells from the time in Myambagh, some she had not adverted to since Paul Kozinski's courtship. Vistula Hotels Group Pty. Limited. Clean Cut Linen Service. Cracow Holdings Pty. Limited. Kozinski Residential of Western Australia. Kozinski Mineral Exploration Company Ltd. Kozinski Shopping Centres of California Pty. Limited.

These papers of resignation which might soon be matched by parallel letters of appointment. Papers waited in Sydney perhaps to enable *La Belle* Krinkovich to take up the wealth and unconscious power Kate was relinquishing on a verandah at the bottom of the sea outside Bourke. They may already even have been signed. But their force depended on Kate signing these.

As she signed, Burnside grew philosophic.

—Look at that, he said. He laughed an unfeigned laugh. That bloody roo. Symbol of Australia. Small brain, enormous balls and all its muscles in its arse. Kept in the dark all its childhood and fed dairy products. Advance Australia Fair.

He rose and walked down the stairs with a swagger, his old Rugby jauntiness. The jauntiness too of course of a man feared without question on building sites.

He shaped up like a boxer to Chifley. As Gus had said, it is because of their pugilist posture that kangaroos had suffered this indignity for two hundred years or more, from the days of Georgian bare-fist fighting, imported on the same transports as the fly boys and girls of the East End. The first European ashore had wondered if the European soul could live here and if the flow of Christ's blood had touched the place. The second European ashore, slackmouthed and a joker, had shaped up to the continent's antique marsupial. Gidday, mate, want to fight?

The tradition of oafdom which had found its high-water mark in Burnside was about to take that old and hackneyed direction. Was about to box Chifley's ear to punish him for his delicate forepaws and the appalling delicacy of the way he held them. Didn't the bloody thing know what Burnside knew: that this was a tough bloody country.

Kate saw now with sweet foresight how Chifley would repay her for the tricky business of imposing tongues. Gus himself would have given out warnings on the subject, even to a man who'd broken his nose. But Gus was still gray-white and without bearings. Burnside had silenced his one possible warner.

In the opening passage of the contest, Chifley looked confused, flinching, leaning right back on the sturdy tail. Soon he would either flee or bring it all to a serious close. Burnside believed that what was needed was an increasingly stern approach. This supposition had made him a career. Old Mr. Kozinski and young Paul would pay him a quarter- or perhaps a half-million for smashing Gus's face and exacting signatures and sparring with kangaroos.

Chifley leaned further back on the broad base of his tail. The great hind paws, partly raised, looked useless in this mode. You could see by the tension in the tail that it might be used at any moment to swing Chifley into sideways flight. All Chifley's poundage and dynamics at the moment suggested bounding away. And in all her dreams he had never presented himself as a show boxer. Flight was his mode, and he was about to take it. Then even Burnside would need a gun to catch him.

—You great fucking zoological joke, said Burnside, jabbing now, a sting to every jab. Chifley's ears. Chifley's shoulders and chest.

Burnside struck Chifley a straight, fearful blow, over the nose and between the eyes. And as the encyclopaedia she had read on her first night at Murchison's Railway Hotel had foreshadowed, the beast's hind paws, driven by the energy in the base of the tail, sped forward, fast as something thrown. Struck by these enormous paws in the abdomen and pelvis, Burnside folded up forward and sideways and struck the ground.

Now Chifley fled. He could tell that something had happened, though he wouldn't have been able to define it from experience. He scudded past stiff-necked Menzies. For the first few halting bounds—the ones in which the forepaws were also involved—his hind paws left dark traces of blood on the ocher ground.

She went down the stairs and bent to Burnside. Chifley had torn the front of Burnside's trousers and made a wound in the lower stomach.

Burnside said in a thin reverent voice, Mrs. Kozinski, my pelvis is gone.

In the shock of the damage done him, she had been restored in his mind to membership of the family.

—Oh Jesus, he admitted then, bloody silly thing to have done. Get a doctor, eh?

But he'd put himself beyond any usual, suburban mercies. In any case he gasped and seemed to go comatose. No more reflections or requests. She went back up onto the verandah and knelt by Gus. Gus, not certain where he was, but better in color. Regularly and with his eyes opened he would begin to snore without first going to sleep. She would get him a cool cloth soon.

She picked up Burnside's signed papers from the table. She began tearing them to pieces. She worked them into small wads and fragments. They fluttered down to her feet in a straight line in this still country. At some times of year, of course, tides of wind moved across this ocean bed. Today nothing moved, and the seafloor was stagnant.

Old Mr. Kozinski's check vanished amongst the other bits of paper.

She got Gus his cool cloth.

After Gus had been awakened and been held during his confusion by Kate, and been sick on the boards and slept again and again been grayly awoken, the first he said was that he would be having a word with his sister-in-law. He was still not aware for some time of the exact form of Burnside's apparent absence. When he first got up and saw him, flattened and perhaps gutted in the still, fading afternoon, he grew desperate, a state alien to Kate's experience of him.

—Christ, Chifley hit him!

—Yes, Kate admitted, wanting to sound cool. He says his pelvis is broken. He had everything he wanted. He'd broken your nose and I'd signed the papers. But on top of it he wanted to box Chifley. That bit didn't work.

Gus began to weep, anguish bubbling bloodily at his nostrils. To Kate, these tears were an even more alien phenomenon.

—Chifley? he asked.

—He's run off.

—He'll come back. He doesn't know better.

They went together down the stairs and inspected Burnside. His color was poor. Kate felt contemptuous toward him.

—He wanted a doctor. Where did he think he was? Boxing a marsupial and wanting a doctor. *Kangaroo strike. Item 123C on the Medical Benefits form.*

Giddy again, Gus told her his vision was full of splotches. Her voice echoed and seemed black to his demented optic nerve.

—My bloody sister-in-law, he kept saying.

—Her check will be cancelled now. The Kozinskis don't pay for unfinished work.

—Well, said Gus. Staying here is all bloody finished.

This was suddenly so clearly the truth that she began to weep.

—You'll drive to town, Kate.

—What? Get a doctor?

—Get everyone.

So Burnside's power to bring others in his wake was unimpaired by a smashed pelvis.

—Drive to town, Kate. Keep the truck for a borrow if you want to then. I'm a big enough truck-borrower myself, aren't I? Keep away till all this is settled . . .

—No, she told him. No, I want to keep going with you.

This was the ménage she wanted to be associated with. Jelly's shadow. Gus and the beasts. That was the ménage.

—Okay, Gus told her, flushing with pleasure. But you can see it's temporary, the way things have been here.

And they kept arguing and Kate dreaded the descent from bounding which lay before her. But Burnside had to be treated. Tetanus injections would be needed too. If he perished he would create even greater havoc.

Barely clear-eyed, Kate was in the car, and was turning it toward the gate, when she saw Gus emerge on the verandah with the farmhouse rifle he had spent hours of idleness reconditioning. For a second she had the shocking thought that he intended to add a bullet to the mess which had been made of Burnside. But she saw Gus sit down at the verandah table and take up a dolorous waiting posture, rifle on lap. She stopped the truck at once and as a sign that she would not easily go on again, she shut its engine off, got out and went up the steps to the verandah again.

—The police will need him, said Gus. You know, for forensic purposes. Blood matching. You know. He'll be in the sideshow again. All along I've tried to save him from the sideshow. It was a disgrace I sold him to that oaf in Wagga. That was a lapse. Can you imagine what it'll be now. *Mankiller Roo!* On all the television news. *And* . . . he'd become police property. And they'd do it to him in the end. Without an ounce of affection. *Police shoot killeroo!*

Again tears came effervescing out of Kate. She said, not very clearly, Please. Please, he's my only joy.

—Well thanks a million, said Gus, and then more leniently, I know, I know.

She knelt in front of him and grabbed both his wrists.

—If you shoot him, I'll be finished.

—No. That's not right.

—It is. I'll be finished. With my children.

—Children, Kate? he asked, a huntsman's gentleness. I didn't know about children . . .

Twenty-two

I N AN EFFORT to distract Gus, to show that she could not
bear further bereavement, and so to save Chifley by indirect
means, she found herself offering up with some speed the story of
Bernard and Siobhan. She was confused by the dangers and yet the
ease of this. As we know, she had spent so long futilely trying to
become another, slovenly woman whose cells were gorged with
steak fat and whose hair was unwashed. A woman who had never
had *that* kind of child, never even known golden children whose
bodies, when washed at dusk, shed orange grains of sand from
between the toes and brine from out of the hair. Children studiously reared. Who on special sweet-toothed occasions were directed not to fried protein of the kind which came from the Murchison Railway Hotel kitchens, but to honey and nectarines.
Children who would carry the habits of childhood into a place
where at full height they would slimly catch and turn.

Was she the mother of such children? Apart from her one confession to Jelly, she had been on the edge of disbelieving it. Now,
for Chifley's sake, she began reclaiming them.

When her father Jim Gaffney told her that night they had still half
an hour to drive. She could argue herself out of the news two or
three times in that distance, so thoroughly that Jim said in the sort
of gentle despair with which he treated Mrs. Kate Gaffney's tan-
trums, Do you think I'd lie to you? Do you think I'd try a joke like
this? For pity's sake, Kate, prepare yourself!

The narrow cliffside street was crammed with shiny civic vehicles whose lights flashed red and white and blue: blood, mercy,
sorrow. Only the roadside end of the bridge which ran to the front
door was still standing. The sandstone walls of the garden fell
away briskly. An oily fallout seemed to coat them. The house itself

lay in a moat of ruin. She could see in the charred collapse of the garage the black framework of her car, the one which had refused to start, devoured to a skeleton. Paul stood amongst the singed rubber plants and oleanders on the edge of the road. He roared.

—Why weren't they at dance class?

Ambulance men held Paul back from Kate, as if privy to the Kozinski marriage problem. Jim Gaffney's arm stood round Kate, preventing any answer. But at the time Paul's question sounded to her a cogent one. Why not go to the dance and catch a treatable pneumonia? Better than to be consumed.

A little off to her left, Denise the baby-sitter's mother was on her knees crying *No,* while Denise's father and a policeman tried to raise her. There was still that frightful feeling that Denise and the children were there, hidden or hiding behind the angle of sight. Even that, though, was shocking, and the weight of blame shocking too. Every mother, as Paul Kozinski had remarked, sent her children to the dance rather than to the furnace.

Ambulancemen carried three stretchers up the hard way, up the slope in the corner of the garden. There was a risk that they would stumble, but they did not want to bring them the easy way, in front of people. Kate heard her own wailing and was held forcibly. Jim Gaffney, many policemen and other ministers of heaven pinioned her.

—Why weren't you with them? Paul Kozinski roared again and again. Again it seemed utterly reasonable. What sort of mother will not step off the edge with her children when the dance ends?

The other parties to this frightful night began to appear. The other Kozinskis, mother and father, white-faced. Their tears could not be gainsaid, and when Paul saw them it spurred him toward uttering those questions again, just at a point when grief had threatened to strike him mute.

—Why weren't they at dance class? Your car was here? Where were you? Why weren't you here?

Her father Jim Gaffney, holding her close, sometimes put his hands over her ears, a hopeless and—she thought—hysteric act to guard her from the justice of other people's questions.

—God, she said, accepting but demented by Paul's screaming.

Uncle Frank and her mother arrived in the one car, staggering forward from it to join Jim and Kate. Seeing the black hole where the children had vanished, Uncle Frank also at first fell to his knees. By habit, he uttered the words of absolution in the direction of the ruins from which the angels had already in any case been carried away. Then he got to his feet and put a hand on Kate's shoulder. He was anxious next to shut Paul Kozinski up.

—Why doesn't someone give that gobshite an injection? Kate heard him asking Jim Gaffney.

—Where were you? Paul kept challenging.

In the light from the emergency vehicles, his face was redly glossed from tears. It was too much for Uncle Frank, who walked over to the Kozinskis. Seeing him coming Mrs. Kozinski, weeping quietly, turned half away, sustaining the mean little daily feud no matter how horrible the night.

Paul yelled to Uncle Frank, She should have been here with them!

Uncle Frank took his hands and strove to look him in the eye.

—Now listen. Now listen my good man. Would you prefer you'd lost your wife as well as your small ones? Think of her. Think of her for Christ's sake!

But Paul evaded Uncle Frank's repute as a soother.

—Her car was there! Why was she out when her car was there?

A young doctor from Avalon, who had treated the children and referred Bernard to the coordination clinic which had made him a catcher, appeared. He began muttering to Jim and Kate Gaffney senior about sedatives. He himself looked so stricken that Kate thought madly something grievous must have happened to his family too, that this was like the curses of Egypt, and all the first-born gone. She was so focused upon this site that she did not know what was happening in others.

She noticed that ambulancemen were pushing a cup of hot tea in the direction of Paul's mouth, but he shook his head, avoiding contact with the rim of the mug. He did not want to be paused in his yelling.

—Why weren't you with your children?

Uncle Frank made a last attempt with him.

—Oh think of how your wife feels, for Christ's sweet sake.

But there wasn't any getting through to him. With Paul still fretting in the arms of ambulancemen, and the senior Kozinskis averting their eyes, Uncle Frank gave it up and returned to her. She was so pleased to see him coming back. She hoped he had the spells for this moment and could interpret things to her.

A young fireman with an ash-smeared face held something out to her. A bottle of vodka.

—I got my hand inside the door, he said.

He was shaking. He needed ambulancemen himself.

—This was all I could get before everything went. Sorry. Sorry.

He put it in her hands. It was no more than warm. The residue of her household, her academy, her gentle forcing school for excellent children. Jim Gaffney offered to take it from her but she clung.

Uncle Frank murmured, We should take her home. The bloody Kozinskis are utterly beyond reason. Of course, they've an excuse, as we all have.

Tears broke from him. Helpless ones. Did it mean Uncle Frank himself was helpless?

She was confused when they started marshaling her back toward Jim's car.

She thought, But who will look after the children?

A plainclothes policeman flanked by two uniformed ones intervened tentatively between them and Jim's Jaguar. He simply said that he didn't know what to say. She had his sympathy for what it was worth. And that he might talk to her when she was feeling better.

Unless this awful night was reversed, there would be no *feeling better* left.

Her mother Kate Gaffney got into the back seat, going ahead as one will with a child, to make sure it knows it's safe to follow. But Kate balked. For Murray was standing there, under the escarpment which made a suntrap of her vanished house. He stood amongst the banksias and the tea tree and the palms, and he stepped out fully into sight now. He had nothing to say, but extended his arms, an extraordinary public act for a plain man like Murray. She hurled herself into them and gagged with the horror. It was the first sound she had made. She had been keeping quiet in case the whole drift could be turned around. The sight of Murray —like Uncle Frank's tears—somehow indicated to her that there would be no alteration to the nature of the night.

She was aware of her parents and Uncle Frank milling around, even of their sense that she was playing into the hands of the enemy by flinging herself at a man other than screaming Paul. This was such a picayune item beside the mass of her loss, however, that she wanted to tell them all, while she choked and hawked in Murray's grasp, to go to hell and lose themselves.

You could not deny though that the Kozinskis would make much of the fact that she had not wailed early and had then thrown herself into the arms of some neighbor. So Uncle Frank moved in at Murray's shoulder.

—Come on, young feller. Better she gets away now.

He had got back the old capacity to make shocked people obey him.

Even when they had her in the Jaguar, and she saw Jim seeking *Drive* as fast as he could, the lack of street lighting for once supplied by all the flashing red and blue and yellow, she could still hear Paul Kozinski asking, Why weren't you here?

She was distracted though by someone groaning and wailing inside the car. Her, but it was too profound to be merely derived from lung capacity. Nothing at all, she found to her dread, lay beneath the base of that wail. She had become a pillar of loss, bereavement incarnate. And at some stage, at some point in the column of grief, culpability set in. Paul Kozinski her husband, lover of Mrs. Krinkovich, was absolutely right of course. Who could doubt he deserved a more observant woman?

He was quite right saying she should have been there.

At last the gentle chief of the Arson Squad, who had stopped her with his condolences on the way to Jim's car, took a statement from her. This was in her parents' wide-balconied apartment in Double Bay. It looked out on a Harbour which had never been without interest to her or to the race in general. The Harbour into which Captain Phillip had stumbled in a whaling boat on a morning in January 1788 and exclaimed that a thousand ship of the line could ride here in perfect serenity. The Harbour of Slessor's *Five Bells*. The Harbour Bridge, of which she had learned in the February classrooms of childhood that it was the biggest single span on the planet.

Ferries rounded Middle Harbour and headed up past Fort Dennison toward the Opera House and the Quay, the whole scope of this action visible at a glance from the Gaffneys' wide glass. The Opera House with its great ceramic sails shining, semaphoring a generous intelligence of light toward the parallel glimmer of the

Gaffney glass. Wonderful. All managed through bounty Jim Gaffney had earned his family by unassertive cleverness.

None of it meant anything to drugged Kate Gaffney-Kozinski,
whose mother kept trying to distract her daughter's attention from
the cognac behind the cocktail bar.

Drain it all away and fill with ashes the great pit, the pit of
harbor dug by glaciers. And it wouldn't hold the ashes she had. A
fact of physics. It would not hold them.

The chief of the Arson Squad told the Gaffneys things they already suspected. It had started in the electrical box. An arc. It had
devoured the sun-dried, beach-salty red cedar facings of the house
too readily, leaping quickly from them to the sun deck, which was
massive and combustible. It had also entered the roof and consumed the insulation. The insulation above all gave off noxious
gases. The children and Denise had not died in pain. They had
been asphyxiated. He wanted them to know he wasn't just saying
that. It would be proved by the coroner's report.

In her crazy state, she thought quite kindly of the forensic men
and women who had uncovered in her children the evidence that
no sooner had they opened their mouths to ask where she was
than the fumes had numbed them.

The chief of Arson further explained it was likely Bernard had
actually been asleep at the time, since Bernard had been found in
the remains of the bedroom. Denise and Siobhan had been together. The way he spoke implied companionship and merciful
sleep, and she watched her parents be consoled by such fragments
of promise.

On the Soldier Settler verandah at the bottom of the sea, pale
Kate, trading all this history for Chifley, found that she had finished the first account she had ever uttered to how her children
had been lost through her absence. At points throughout it they
had heard Burnside raving and demanding, but they knew he
could wait. She had had to concentrate on the narrative, expecting
at each step the solidity of things to give way beneath her. It was
not so much a minefield—people often said that: Emotional
minefield. It was more a series of steps in space. Every image a
precipice. Gus too seemed to be aware of these perils. His lips were
thin beneath his smashed nose.

But at the end he used the word they had all used. The word

beyond belief: *accident*. She heard him fumbling for something to say, conscientious even though Burnside's knee had done his face so much damage. And he said the plain things. Oh love! and Jesus love! Even more trite for emerging nasally from his sick, leathery face. And he said *accident*.

Burnside's body seemed to attract darkness to it and lay in a pool of early night. The complaints from that source were dim. The rifle in Gus's hands was held so loosely that soon she was sure she would be able to remove it. He wanted to grasp the sentences of condolence more firmly, and in his condition couldn't manage two things at once. His intention to finish Chifley had dropped from him.

The price for this result was that she felt too bitterly how much of her biology was still that of the superb mother of Palm Beach. How much irreducible Kate Kozinski was still there! How the hated, culpable woman still clung on, lingering like damned Ophelia in her bloodstream. Rigor, she thought, rigor would be needed! Reformation, which she'd thought was pretty well advanced, had only just begun.

Gus stood. He had released the intention to murder Chifley now. He said he wanted to be ill. For some reason he staggered into the house instead of out amongst the dark dots of tea tree and saltbush. It was all right. She could face cleaning up a little mess. While he was away, she opened the breech of the rifle he'd left and emptied the bullets out, dropping them into the pocket of her cardigan.

He soon returned. His ruddy look remained but his mouth gaped. He said he had no balance, that he had to lie down. She helped him into the bed, covering him. For it was getting late and the level of cold was rising up from the heart of the Pleistocene sea.

He said, For God's sake, you've really got to get the police and the ambulance now. You can't leave Burnside there overnight.

Holding the bullets in her pocket and watching his lolling head, she considered him a neutralized force. She would need to bring back the doctor not only for Burnside but to him too.

Murray telephoned every day in the demented week she spent with her parents after the funeral. There was no word from the Kozinskis in those days lit and alleviated by the garish yellow comfort of booze and sedative drafts. Brandy and sedatives kept the wailing down, and her dreams sleeping and waking were unnaturally full of children after all restored, and of the reproofs of the Kozinskis by the ruin, at the church, by the graveside. The old man had needed to be helped to his seat in the church by two Kozinski executives. She had seen that. Somehow it had confirmed her responsibility. And the son yelled by the wreckage, and the mother yelled in the cemetery, sustaining the blame. And justly so, of course. No argument. She kept on putting her hands up. No argument. And her mother pressed on her wrists and said, No, there's no need, darling.

Because Kate Gaffney senior knew that this lifting of the hands was always the start of some paroxysm.

In that week when Murray called politely each day then, she still waited to be convinced that the thing had happened. Maybe everyone was conniving with the Kozinskis for her own good to ensure that from now on she *would* attend Australian-Polish presentation dinners and subscribe to Mrs. Maria Kozinski's proposition that this Polish pope was greater by factors of three or four than Uncle Frank. Once she was utterly sure there wasn't a chance they would say to her, There you are. Now you've had your scare. Go and be a good wife!—then she would certainly go and kill herself. She had the means to hand.

But Murray kept calling. One who was certainly not in any conspiracy. And he talked in his normal, un-Gothic Sheffield Shield cricketer way, and she was astounded and confused by that.

Murray who would usually have needed stretches of time to make informal telephone calls, telephone calls out of season. Who had taken so long to call the number of his wife's lover, politely maintaining to the point of lunacy the idea that of course his friend was a decent fellow, and his wife would certainly return. He who had had to rehearse anger at his young wife the scuba diver. *He* wanted to know would she like to go out for some coffee?

Her mother said she should. Given that nothing had been heard from the Kozinskis, and that they had returned no calls from the Gaffneys, not even a crazed call Kate herself had tried to make. Whatever damage had been done to Kate's repute there, was beyond repair.

Sitting at the Cosmopolitan at Double Bay, drinking Vienna coffee, Kate was barely conscious, looking without understanding at the refugees from South Africa and Eastern Europe, eloquent and busy wives coming and going, well dressed. Unlike the cloistered Australian born, talkative about the condition of the world.

And Murray pushed his lawyer's lips forward and he had a small, kindly smile on his face and said, Kate, you just have a little mustache of cream.

To get off more hurtful subjects, she planned a sentence and then had her mouth—which had been borrowed from some other person—utter it.

—Has your wife come back home?

There was a frank blush across the tops of his cheekbones.

—No. She's with her new friend. Had to be expected. They were very taken with each other.

She watched his extraordinary lips—made as they were for confidential information about money, share and property prices, about unit trusts and currency notes—push further forward still.

—Kate, we had a holiday booked, my wife and I. Since last year. One of the islands off Fiji. A private one, quite luxurious. South of Viti Levu. I wondered, if I could get you a room of your own, would you like to come as my companion?

She looked at him, trying to fix on his face. She could focus on his discomfort. That was apparent even to the dazed and drugged.

—All you need do is sit in the sun, and perhaps read if you want to.

She wondered how he could be so innocent as not to know she was contagious.

He said, My shout of course.

—The coffee?

—No. I meant the airfare and accommodation. Least I could do. Already paid for.

She didn't think that that was quite a logical claim.

—Unless of course you're worried about the divorce settlement. But I don't think there's any problem there. Not in the sort of faultless divorces we have now. In any case, he started it first . . . forgive me talking like this. I'm not trying to suggest anything you do is the equivalent of his involvement with Mrs. Krinsky or whatever her name is . . .

He began coughing.

—Listen, forgive me talking like this. In the circumstances.

She laughed at that too, more heartily.

—In the circumstances. In the fucking circumstances.

She thought she had said it softly, but other coffee drinkers were looking.

Murray said, I don't care if your behavior's embarrassing or if you talk like that most of the time. I mean, a bit loud. To hell with it. You're entitled to.

—Yes, I'm drunk and I am drugged.

—I know that. You might even get less drugged and less drunk on holiday. Or less drugged anyhow. Liquor's permitted on holidays.

She started to laugh and she was sure now the laugh was under control. He sounded like a schoolteacher: *Liquor's permitted on holidays.*

She asked, What if there's a Q.C. there? On the island? Or a federal judge? Or the Solicitor General?

—A good reputation gave me no leverage at all when my wife left. To hell with the Solicitor General.

She stood up in her place laughing.

—Why would you do it, Murray? Why would you fucking well do it, mate? Do you love me or something?

The idea tickled her so much that she couldn't stop an automatic laughter rising in her, gushing out.

—Yes, I believe I do.

Everyone was certainly speaking loudly on the terrace of the Cosmopolitan, though she was aware now that they were not loud in the way she was.

—And will we have children? Eh, Murray? Will we have children, mate?

She had turned cruel and she wanted to rout him. She wanted to make his eyes slew sideways. She wanted him to gallop away, back to the legal secretaries in their runless pantyhose. But his eyes took hers on. He wasn't going to be thrown off by her loud voice and the attention of the other coffee drinkers, who were saying, Isn't that the woman . . . ?

—I don't go as far as children, Kate. One thing at a time. It's hard enough getting used to things the way they are.

Since he couldn't be stampeded, she sat down again.

Now she realized she had an opiate of her own; something to fight her parents over. They were edgy about Murray's proposal, as if it was up to them. Kate Gaffney senior had this idea, from his behavior on the night, that he was some wild man. She kept asking how it would all affect the divorce settlement? She knew Mr. Andrew Kozinski was already talking to tame canon lawyers with a view to divorce and an annulment on the grounds of deficient consent.

Joke stuff, as Uncle Frank had always said. She wondered whose consent it was that the canon lawyers would find deficient?

She told her mother she didn't want a settlement, and her mother argued that the time would come when she would, so that in the end Kate had the chance to bay at the ceiling over her mother's stupidity. Mrs. Kate Gaffney née O'Brien: consistent excellence at passionately misjudging the issue.

Through conversations the others had, Kate heard that Uncle Frank had actually been to see Murray.

—A decent man, said the not-so-Reverend Frank. A decent man. And there's the question as to whether you really want your daughter to take the charity of the Kozinskis for the residue of her life?

—But she bore him children! cried Mrs. Kate Gaffney, and realizing what had been said, drowned in tears.

Kate paid for her own ticket, and one morning she and Murray took off strapped side by side, wheeling over that Botany Bay renowned in convict songs, nosing forth over that most dazzling misnomer: the Pacific. They traveled at the front of the plane, and both of them drank crazily, Murray doing her the favor of matching her frenzy. They hurled two Armagnacs in on top of everything else. A chauffeured car took them from Nandi to Sigatoka. There a launch with a cocktail bar met them, and they were ferried out across a withering blue glare of ocean, the sea's uppercut complementing the sky's overarm haymaker. Kate insisted on sitting in the stern, her blouse pulled low on her shoulders as if this were a kissing sun rather than a brutish one.

As he had promised Murray had reserved her a separate room. Not simply a room however. It was what they called a cabana, a thatched roof, air-conditioned hut with a living room and a bedroom, all looking out at an ultramarine sea. In the living room she and Murray drank together before and then after dinner. For by that hour of the night they did not trust themselves to the public scrutiny of the bar, or of the band of sweating Melanesian musicians. Here in the living room and in the bedroom is where they coupled, hectic and sweating, punishing each other, gouging out pleasure. Not certain whether it was transport or punishment they were seeking, punishment certainly coming into play once their sunburns began to bloom.

With a lawyer's certainty that things came to litigation in the end, especially if the Kozinskis were involved, Murray commuted from his cabana to hers. He showered for example in his own. He went back there early in the morning to try to impose on his sheets what looked like the indentation of a single, virtuous man.

He was very muscular, she had noticed even in her stupor. More so than Paul Kozinski.

Murray blamed himself, but all the experts said that in the tropics it took only half an unwary day to induce third degree burns. She had strung together many unwary days. Pretending to block the sun out with a raised hand and reading nothing at all, she sat by the lagoon with a book. Once she went out with him in the stern of an aluminum boat and waited near naked while he dived briefly. When he surfaced she had become ill from heat stroke and was shivering. The liquor had probably dried up the nutrients in her skin in any case. One Sydney doctor would ultimately and sagely tell her so.

Fijian boatmen carried her to her cabana on a stretcher. She lay shivering in a blaze of heat. At first she felt too ill to appreciate anything except the grateful pain, as the flesh of her shoulders howled and blistered and then shrank, becoming black, sloughing. Later it would seem so trite, such an unworthy gesture to her children. But for the moment she was pitiably satisfied.

She could read the silliness of what she had done however in the bemused faces of Indian doctors as she wafted in and out of a conscious state in hospital in Suva.

Murray stayed on with her, though the time of his holiday was over. When she was well enough to travel, they dressed her shoulders, and Murray took her home. He knew what pills to give her if she had trouble. He knew that she was not to drink liquor on the plane.

In Australian terms it was a short flight and she was full of tranquilizer and opiates for it. The Gaffneys had an ambulance waiting for her at Sydney Airport.

They never thought as much of Murray after that. For Uncle Frank had become too busy with Mrs. Kearney and her affairs to stand up for Murray's cause again.

Twenty-three

RUSHING TO TOWN with news of Burnside's injury, wanting to be fast to save Chifley from Gus's mercy, she careered all over the red dirt road, dragging the russet bottom of Gus's ocean behind her in a cloud. Rattling over bullbars, opening and closing gates, restless and competent. So many saltbush miles to the frontage road, to the final gate. She felt that she had been so long cloistered from the normal offices of civil life that she wondered in what language she would speak to the police or the ambulance people. She would open her mouth and Aramaic might come out.

A band of cloud in the west had flattened the declining sun to a molten ingot. The world was full of still light. Light which waited upon an event. Something abominable was growling across the slant of the light. The sky descended to suck her up. She drove fast to evade it. Top gear. Seventy-five miles an hour and in something like terror. Rattling over culverts. The shadow of the sky passed over the windscreen and darkened her hands on the steering wheel.

A genuine but minor surprise, a blue helicopter, glittering, its navigation lights already switched on. Tentative, taking pains to be sure she would brake, it edged groundward in front of her. When she did slow it came to rest on the common pasturage along the side of the road, the strip where battling farmers grazed their sheep free of cost in drought time. It looked as sweet as a cerulean egg, this helicopter. O'TOOLE on its side, in serious white picked out with black.

The door of the thing swung open and Uncle Frank, tearing himself from its wind, wearing a black aviation jacket, delivered himself out of it. Hobbling to the middle of the road, he blocked her way to town.

It was O'Toole the undertaker, Uncle Frank's friend, with hands white as the sacraments of Christ from committing to rest the souls of the faithful departed. He and Uncle Frank had known each other even before their arrival in Australia, that well-known missionary country. For they came from the same place in County Limerick.

She was somehow unsurprised to see Uncle Frank there in the road, in his paramilitary jacket. If Burnside's intelligence could reach the back-of-Bourke, all the more so the not-so-Reverend Frank's.

As she remembered him doing in her childhood he gestured vastly with his large soft hand.

—Come here now, the hand said.

An instructional gesture too. He needed to impart something to her, a little way away from the full blast noise of the rotors. Some mystery of faith.

She went up to him. Perhaps thinking it was still tender, he gently touched her shoulder and surveyed her. She saw his mouth make the sound of her name. Kate. Kate.

No question he wanted her to join him in O'Toole's sky-blue contraption. In mime she tried to tell him the story of the business she was on. God knows if he understood. He shook his head, and then kissed her impetuously and wetly on the ear and roared into it.

—Bourke, Kate. No kidnaps, my darling! All aboveboard.

She had never in her waking life needed so much a means of flying over the earth. But she wasn't sure this one was it. Just the same, it oddly pleased her to obey Uncle Frank. She eased her truck into a ditch and took the keys, leaving the windows open to the dusk. She climbed up into the cabin of the helicopter by means of the little stirrup step. There in the pilot seat was triple-chinned O'Toole in a flying jacket covered in far more militant patches than Uncle Frank sported. Skyhawk O'Toole. She wondered but blessed whatever vanity it was which led him to own a helicopter.

In fact O'Toole used it for rare ash scatterings over the sea, now that Catholics were permitted to cremate themselves. This had enabled him to get the whole thing off tax. It was another example of the way, because eight hundred years of rule had misused them, the O'Tooles and O'Briens practiced their anarchism.

In the days when Uncle Frank was in something less than climactic trouble with His Eminence Cardinal Fogarty, Archbishop of Sydney, he had done grief counseling for O'Toole and might even be doing it now, even under release on bail.

O'Toole's sky-blue hearse came down on a football field by the Darling River, right on the white-limed halfway mark; like a referee from on high. Already Uncle Frank knew by yells and urgent gestures that there were matters to be attended to before they went into the question of Uncle Frank himself, or of how she had remade herself in the bush, changing herself to an extent in Jack Murchison's frying kitchen and at Frank Pellegrino's hearty location canteen.

At last O'Toole cut the engines. His rotors went on churning still, though he had switched off the power to them. All the racketing of the machine dropped to a mere whir.

Surprised by silence, Kate herself fell quiet.

O'Toole turned and said, Hello Kate.

He looked at her under his brows, in a way which he had developed from thirty years of facing the bereaved in the first full-blown frenzy of their grief.

—Mother of God, she heard Uncle Frank cry. Did you say to me —back there—Burnside?

Despite all the explosive force of their arrival, they failed to find a telephone and had to walk into town looking for police and ambulance. O'Toole dawdled behind, leaving Kate and Uncle Frank to their reunion. Needing of course to get back before Gus was well enough to murder Chifley, Kate walked too fast. Since Uncle Frank had never been a man for exercise and had recently spent some sedentary time in cells, he did well to stay on the pace. Long-legged though fat-hipped, he kept by her side, uttering sentences one and a half words at a time.

—Kate, he reassured her, I know you didn't . . . understand . . . how thoroughly you . . . were persecuting us. Your parents got the word . . . from that nice publican in Myambagh, but before they did there . . . was eight hours or so of . . . anguish you couldn't imagine. I tell you so you'll . . . know that if you yourself . . . don't believe in . . . your own existence . . . there're people who do. No, no, Burnside isn't the issue you think he is. If you killed that gobshite, we'll all stand up for you. Mother of God, half Sydney will give you a testimonial dinner!

He told her too how he'd found her: through her theft of the white vestments. *Missa de Angelis.*

Earlier in the monstrous year, he had written to every parish in his old diocese, enclosing a picture.

—The boys still like me, Kate . . .

That young feller in Bourke had got the letter two months back and put it on his refrigerator with a magnet. It stayed there as things will, and he had gone from his kitchen to his altar that Sunday morning, and then to his sacristy, and there was the face from his refrigerator door, willing to do him harm and steal his vestments.

Still they found no phone box they could call from and the first sign of agencies of state was the chain fence of the police station. Within it a nineteenth-century sandstone building, the majesty of Britannia on a deep-set Aboriginal river, on a rainbow serpent named Darling. Victoria's stone lion and unicorn still stood on the cornice of the police station.

Uncle Frank paused.

—I should tell you. I've had my experiences lately with these lads.

—I know.

She felt impatient and wanted to be inside now.

—I heard it on the radio.

—Kate, I want to tell you seriously to your face that I never bribed a single soul.

For Uncle Frank's chief pride was in getting favors done out of love.

—Of course, she said urgently, shaking her head. Both because she did believe him and because she wanted to speed matters up, though to exactly what end for her she was not sure.

With a sort of divinely annoying expansiveness, Uncle Frank presented his bail documents to the police, straight up and as if he cherished the things.

—I'm playing straight with you boys . . .

He had been looking for his niece for some time, he told the senior constable on duty. A big man, up to Burnside's weight, but more flaccid.

238 · THOMAS KENEALLY

Kate recounted her truth to him flatly, without any desire to engage her narrative skills, to extenuate or embroider. Burnside had been injured. It was on the Schulberger property. No, not at the main house. No. Not at his late brother's. She would lead them in then, since they didn't know it. Who hurt him? He hurt himself. He fell.

Arriving at the police station behind them, O'Toole explained that he would offer his helicopter, except that darkness was coming and he was not good at map coordinates.

After a lot of police drawling into radios and loud instructions, they were all at once on the road to Schulberger's, traveling in a police car followed by an ambulance. Uncle Frank had his arm lightly around her shoulder, and she both welcomed that and didn't. For again it showed how much was unaltered. It was a vanity, all this dream of transmutation. She was still the small Kate Gaffney, who had inherent in her the risk of becoming Mrs. Kozinski junior. Corpuscles of blame in the bloodstream hadn't been altered into dull mute bush corpuscles.

If she took the blame for Burnside's condition, she could get bail and then skip further west with Gus and Chifley. But she must be rigorous and travel a great deal if she really wanted to change. There was a furnace at the Centre that would alter her. She wasn't the only one to harbor that suspicion. Though not a suspicion, a conviction. She believed it. She had sensed it just beyond the horizon of the bounding dreams.

So she had to try to do that. Make her way, breathing lightly, to the great renewing fire.

Meanwhile Uncle Frank's arm, laid there carefully just in case the scar tissue still smarted, was pleasant enough in itself. It did not make a claim, as other arms in her family would have.

They saw a truck coming the other way. It was flashing its lights and even pulling into their path. By the last light you could see that its main color was red dust. Gus's sister-in-law's truck. Gus's dismal eyes became visible by the police headlights. The police car and ambulance both halted and people got out, the ambulance driver, and Uncle Frank, Kate, senior constable and sergeant. Gus himself was waiting for them now on the red and black dirt road. The spike of his hair at the back jabbed the air dejectedly, like the plume of a defeated brave. He led them with movements of the hand to the back of his sister-in-law's truck. On its tray lay a groaning human form wrapped in a tarpaulin, and naked to the air the still, shaggy-furred body of Chifley.

Uncle Frank later reported that he heard a mechanical noise from Kate, something like the shifting of a gear.

Her breath departed. With nothing to elevate her, she gave up to the magnetic drag of the things which had befallen her. Her vision closed off like the closing of a shutter. Coolly dying on a godless star, she knew that her uninformed legs were writhing in the red dust, giving a show of resistance. The limbs of one who does not want to ascend from the bottom of the sea.

First Gus shot the returning Chifley to deliver him from notoriety on the evening news. Next, convinced of the futility of rescuing Menzies, he tried to shoot the bird too. But Menzies, named for a survivor and narrower in the head and throat than Chifley, evaded the bullet through one minor repositioning of his neck. He fled of course, at the same pace which had competed with the heroine's truck in Frank Pellegrino's film. And so at last Gus gave up.

He wrapped Burnside in the tarpaulin and gave him water, which caused him to go into a fit. Then he set ablaze the Soldier Settler farm with its coral snake in a jar, its ancient furniture, its 1920s copies of the *Sydney Morning Herald*.

It is hard to say why he did this. It consumed the remnants of the Kozinski papers of course, or sent them flying charred out over the flat earth. It served as a beacon to draw his sister-in-law in, and as a sign of surrender. It served sentimentally as a pyre for Chifley.

So the naïvely treacherous sister-in-law saw the blaze, the black column of smoke so different in hue from the smoke of bushfires. She drove over in a panic. What she feared was that Burnside had set the fire.

When she got there she forced Gus to give her explanations through his smashed nose. That was how daunting her innocence was. She thought she was still entitled to every piece of information her brother-in-law could give her!

On the road between Bourke and Schulberger's Gus knelt by Kate —so her uncle would later tell her—and he kissed her on the cheekbone, and in front of the hardened police of what could be called his home town, wept and said he'd never do anything to harm her. Uncle Frank had an eye for this sort of thing, but did not consider him a soul imperiled however. Kate was the soul imperiled, so convinced of it that she had begun swallowing her tongue. Uncle Frank did not understand the signs. The senior constable was trained that way though, and dragged her clenched jaws apart. He brought forward that same tongue which Chifley had cursed with language.

The police remarked that Burnside's blood was visible on Chifley's hind paws, the long opposed toe with the savage claw.

Though Gus was required further by them, Kate was not. Around sad Gus however there hung very little atmosphere of condemnation. He was simply asked about Jelly, and then about the beasts, and finally, the morning after he shot Chifley, released on his own recognizance.

Kate was not in Bourke to see this however, since Uncle Frank took her *home*—as Uncle Frank himself chose to call it—quickly in O'Toole's helicopter. The killing media would pass her coming the other way in their light aircraft and in helicopters of their own. For what a story! Heiress divorcée of Kozinski, mother of dead children, thought once to have drowned in a flood of Myambagh, succored by Frank Pellegrino, involved in kangaroo injury to the notorious Burnside. Time for the kangaroo court of their own bludgeon headlines and frightful cameras! Imagine her destiny if they had found her in Bourke, with nothing to protect her except her conviction that she could no longer breathe!

—I wanted to warn Burnside, she would have pleaded with them. But he kicked me in the stomach, and I didn't have the . . .

—Sorry, Mrs. Kozinski. We're out of film . . . the batteries are flat . . . the light's wrong . . . a plane's going over . . . Could we just do that bit again?

For the flight home, she was stupefied with legal drugs, full of medicaments normally prescribed for epileptics, though probably she wasn't one. Something heavy had to be used to distract her from her belief there was no air.

Gus was left to do all that press stuff, and he did it in grief, having lost his beast and his companion. But he was a dutiful interviewee. His directness won him support during the next week, while Kate lay drugged in a leafy, plain private sanatorium near wooded Kuringai Chase, beyond the normal range of scrutiny of Sydney's frenetic press.

During her stupor, Murray visited her. So did her parents and, filling in his bail period and curing her soul, Uncle Frank. He was the one she noticed. In a brief wakeful period in which she did not speak, she was aware that he carried an airline bag, as if he had a gift for her. But he put it by the wall. He wanted her to be clear-headed to receive it.

Gus, since he did not even try, had the basics to become what the media call a folk hero. When he refused to sell his story to any newspaper, it made them double the price.

He served as a catalyst too. Feature articles appeared about Burnside and his repute for terror, and his long retainership to those prize Australo-Poles the Kozinskis.

In sympathy with Gus, the Royal Society for the Prevention of Cruelty to Animals raided the Wagga entertainment park which had featured the *tableau vivant* and served writs on the man from whom Gus had retaken Chifley and Menzies. People queued in newspapers and on television and radio to say they didn't think Gus's was the sort of prosecution on which taxpayers' money should be expended.

His life has made him a practical, play-the-cards-you're-dealt sort of man. His *known* Kate was the Kate of Murchison's steak kitchen and front bar. His Kate was Jelly's Kate. Not a woman of whom so many bewildering things were said: heiress (an old-fashioned term Gus had only ever encountered in books of a certain kind), Kozinski Constructions, shopping malls in California, tragedies on the Northern Beaches. Events on a yacht called *Vistula*.

He causes so much distress to the half-conscious Kate Gaffney that Mrs. Kate takes him aside and tells him it would be better if.

He is aware too of course that he has had his choice. He has chosen saving Chifley rather than take any notice of Kate's idea of where her breath and phantom joy come from. A true lover, he accepted, waited out, served, handled gently all the beloved's mad ideas, especially those about air and the uselessness of the human lung at certain points of history. But then, despite all that, he shot Chifley.

Kate, cleaned by experts and stunned medically in a sanatorium bed! She knows she is dead, but is never awake long enough to actually set her compass in that direction. It is clear to any ob-

server that her ideas about air are utterly crazed and that she will
go on living.

Kate now tends to see the same person in the room whenever she
wakes. It is never her mother and father. It is never Murray, who
is rarely allowed to be alone with her anyhow because of his part
in her injuries. It is always Uncle Frank. It is clear that Uncle Frank
waits on after others leave. He is looking for the moment that his
airline bag can have its part.

But he always speaks to her too. He speaks at greater length
than she has consciousness for. He understands that that is effective. She will sometimes answer him without knowing it, her
mouth will clot with the few words she has to play with. She
doesn't know at any stage what she has said. Somehow she knows
what Uncle Frank says though.

What most of his talk is about is still that he has never bribed
anyone. Since it is his chief claim, the claim which in his mind
qualifies him as comforter and guru, he is as desperate to tell her
this in her sanatorium as he was amongst the pepper trees outside
Queen Victoria's remotest police station in Bourke.

SP (Starting Price) bookmaking. It was as old as the anarchic
island continent and as ancient as convictism. It was harmless too,
in some lights, part of the unofficial democratic rights of the Australian working men and women. Except that there were some
rough boys and even some gobshites involved. The intention upon
coming to Australia to serve the diocese of Wilcannia–Forbes and
then the archdiocese of Sydney had been pure and he had involved
himself in it. But he loved the races. If he hadn't had a vocation—
he still thought of himself as having a vocation, a better one than
His Eminence Fogarty—then he would have certainly been a
trainer or at least an owner.

And then love. He hadn't come to Australia from loveless Limerick for love. Yet love was something he was not ashamed of
claiming. The late Alderman Kearney had been in SP bookmaking
since boyhood. When he died too young and left his widow, she
appealed to her friend the not-so-Reverend Frank to help her to
run things.

Kate probably knew—and if not he certainly told her during her
convalescence—that you needed to be able to get phones on quick
if you were a controller, the central figure of an SP network. You

needed a bank of a dozen phones at least in a series of given locations. Just in case the authorities, with nothing better to do with citizens' taxes, became concerned about the number of calls being made from an individual number or string of numbers. It was something they checked on. Hard to believe. But they did. So you needed a dozen or so in each place to bear the volume of traffic, and then alternate locations in case of raids.

If one of the controller's offices came under threat—and say there was a friendly local inspector and he said, Frank, Fiona, I'm under pressure from above . . . ! Or if Telecom investigators got close, using their spying methods . . . you moved your office to a new place lying ready, phones already installed. That was Frank's idea. The eight hotels (or as some press reports said *ten*) were eight locations under Fiona Kearney's (and Uncle Frank's) control. They even had subcontrollers who rented the locations from them. And the central controlling office itself could be moved from hotel to hotel at will. So it depended on getting new telephones put in quickly and on having plenty in place.

And Uncle Frank could attend to that. He had friends who would do it for nothing, and thus—in his mind—it was clean business.

He had friends in the banking business too who would, if he asked them, as he sometimes did, let him use their own addresses as a home address on various accounts. To Uncle Frank these accommodations were the normal accommodations of friendship. She came to appreciate in her stupor that though he was a saint he had a profoundly criminal soul.

Again she would have liked to have argued with him over his peculiar idea of what corruption was. In his world it did not exist if it were amongst the friendly and the loyal and was a token of love. He was not ashamed, in fact shamefully unashamed, to ask for favors based on crucial words of consolation he had offered in some presbytery front parlor or at O'Toole's. She was reminded of the minor graft of O'Toole's hearse-helicopter. What it said was that government was a joke and deserved to be laughed at through the exhausts of cerulean helicopters, as through batteries of book-making telephones.

So prison would be futile for Uncle Frank, in a different way from the futility which applied to habitual criminals. It would not cure Uncle Frank of his tribal premises. She wondered where he had got his confidence in her: his belief that she would see the reason of his argument. As if in her childhood too she had seen the Black and Tans go by in their armored vehicles. As if she had not in fact spent her childhood in the Harbour's utterly equitable sunlight and come to believe in law and order.

These questions lay idly and flat between Uncle Frank and herself though. They were not living issues for him. She did not have a living issue.

Whenever she woke, she was always amazed after an early flutter of breathlessness that the air went in, turned itself sour, was emitted again just as with any living beast.

Her skin felt altered, and she washed it with a tissue dipped in a water glass and found traces of cosmetic there, applied by her misguided mother.

She stayed awake long enough to greet Mrs. Gaffney as she came visiting:

—No cosmetics, she told her mother.

—Just to freshen you up.

—No. No cosmetics.

But then she lost her hold on the argument.

Once she woke and found that Mrs. Fiona Kearney was there, smiling. Kate thought, Yes, in some lights, a handsome and generous woman. A hostage Frank had taken back from the Black and Tans. A soul saved from the straitlace and the narrow way.

Kate found with regret of course that she was waking hungry. Instead of asking for food she might ask where Gus was.

—He's been on television, said Uncle Frank as if that exempted her from further regard for him.

—You'll be on television too, Uncle Frank.

—Yes, darling. But dead against my will.

She told him she wanted to see Murray, and she wanted to see Gus.

—Both at the same time? he asked her, trying to confuse her for the best of motives.

So Gus's flower-bearing visit first:

He was anxious that there might be a scene, and he wanted to show her as fast as he could that he knew himself disqualified, that he understood it all without rancor.

—I might be going home soon, Kate.

—Nothing to stay down here for, she agreed.

—Well, I started going out with a widow. She's one of those
. . . animal liberationists. Not one of the mad ones though.

He smiled madly and touched Kate's wrist.

—One of the ones that believe roos shouldn't box, anyhow.

Gently he talked her into drinking a cup of tea with him. She
looked around for something to give him. There were only two
novels, which Jim Gaffney had brought and left there, believing
that she would achieve focus imminently. It wasn't going to happen.

—Will you take these, Gus?

He made all the polite refusals, but it was established he *would*
take them, and would handle them reverently on the bottom of the
sea beyond the Darling.

—We were just stumbling along, eh? Lost bloody souls.

Before kissing her goodbye. It was the last multisyllabic thing
she would hear him say in the flesh.

Murray's visit then. He came on the first day that she realized
what day it was. She realized it was a Saturday. It was race day,
but Uncle Frank was banned from all race tracks and so was there
as well. He tried to linger in the room. Kate surprised herself by
managing a warning look, something of more vigor than the mere
warning looks that occur in most novels, one which threatened
riot and exasperation.

After Uncle Frank left, Murray kissed her slowly and gently in
the middle of the forehead.

—Has my mother put makeup on me?

—Oh Kate. How are your shoulders? How are your burns now?

—I don't know. I haven't referred to them.

He chose to take this as a little joke.

—For an hour or two, when the flood was on . . .

—I know, she said. I know.

He held her hand and seemed to get much from the experience.
She herself felt little of it all. Her hand might have been a curio
somewhere in the room. He had decided wantonly to cherish it.

—Kate, he said, I'm so pleased to have the chance to speak to
you. I'm talking to you as a friend now. Your mother and father
are all in favor of suing the Kozinskis to the limit. They've spoken
to me of settlements in excess of twenty million. It isn't greed.

They want to see Paul pay for his bad behavior. In my opinion, you shouldn't be persuaded by that. There's a kind of intimacy about court hearings which you will find painful. And you know what they say: if you lie down with dogs, you get up with fleas. In my opinion, you should settle with the Kozinskis for an immediate amount now, payments spread over a strictly limited period. There might be nothing left of Kozinski assets by the time you've been through the courts. They're in considerable trouble with this inquiry into the building industry. Both father and son could face charges over improper practices of various kinds, from false prospectuses to extortion. As a matter of good sense and of self-respect, settle with them as soon as you can.

She was somehow tickled by his mixture of hard monetary advice and moral hauteur. She let him stroke her frazzled hair.

—I will marry you at any stage. Nothing that has happened to you frightens me away.

—That's a boast, she said, and fell asleep.

She woke in the afternoon and Murray was gone. But Uncle Frank was sitting on a chair on the left side of her bed. From a small radio in his lap came the static of a race meeting turned down low. An Australian voice with that peculiar adenoidal twang of racing announcers was recounting the finishing order of horses Uncle Frank had now been forbidden to place bets on.

He saw her and seemed slightly embarrassed to be caught at his passion like this. He switched the radio totally down but not off.

He said, There's a three-year-old, Diamontina. I tell you, it's going to be one of those wonder horses. They've got it set to emerge in the spring carnival. Next Melbourne Cup, Kate, they'll have to put a truck on its back to stop it. It's a beautiful beast. Put some money on for me, Kate, if I happen to be unavailable for the purpose myself.

He laughed but his eyes were narrowing in a way which had nothing to do with hilarity. He was measuring her, as he'd measured her every day since their reunion.

He came to his conclusions and rose and went to the door where his airline bag waited. He unzipped it and produced a bottle. It was a vodka bottle, full, and it produced fear in her. Ah, she thought, he has drunk or lost or broken my bottle and now intends to pass off a substitute.

But the one he held up was the one from the house. She recognized the unforgettable tear in the label.

—I kept this at home. Faithfully, Kate. As requested.

The memory of the request gagged him for a moment. But swallowing he resumed.

—I took it out one night from the cabinet, for reasons to do with a kind of nostalgia, and I stared it hard in the eye and I noticed a yellowish tinge which didn't seem right at all for vodka. I am after all a publican, they tell me. So I have this friend, a chemist with the police . . .

Another client of Uncle Frank's talents of condolence. Or else a customer of the O'Brien–Kearney Starting Prices ménage.

—He says there's a solution in this vodka of some great thumping amount of something called Vallergan. If you took two mild slugs of this vodka, Kate, you would be asleep within ten minutes, and you would sleep for ten hours or so. Mark what I'm saying. It'd be fanciful to say that this bottle was poisoned, Kate. But it was certainly heavily doctored.

At this news she felt the near-dead glands of her curiosity come to a peculiar chemical life. This was a strangely painful and delicious revival.

—Who? she asked. It was so hard but intriguing to believe in.

Uncle Frank shook his head, as if he were the one most afraid of knowing.

—It was hard enough telling you any of this, Kate, without saying who. But it does tell you something, doesn't it? That you are free of blame. There are all sorts of stories, Kate, about your husband being overextended. He's been on with that woman perhaps as long as three years, and something about her must have given him delusions. He financed all those malls in Southern California, and put up properties here at inflated valuation as security. You know the phrase *heavily geared?* Your husband has liquidity problems. That's the background landscape, Kate, to what I'm going to say now. Two incomplete Kozinski Constructions development sites have had fires. While you were out on the road. Out of our midst . . .

Uncle Frank put the vodka on the bedside table, and the radio. Abandoning horseflesh for the day. Somewhere perhaps faithful servants were taking bets on behalf of himself and Mrs. Kearney. No, she had a sense of the hollowness of the man. He'd been closed down. But listen, she told herself. Listen. Come back to the question. It's not his level of operations that's the question at the moment.

—Remember, said Uncle Frank, how on the night he yelled, *Why weren't you here?* He said, *Your car's here. Why weren't you?* And everyone forgave him because of the terrible time, Kate. But there is a device now, Kate, utterly combustible, which you can put in electric boxes if you have a mind to. Expensive, it overrides the circuit breakers. It causes arcing. It produces a merry bloody combustion.

Drugs did not confuse her now. She understood the reasoning. Since it had a familiar feel to her, it was clear that in some ways she had always understood it.

—The only thing in his favor is that he wanted you to go off without any pain.

—Aaaaaah, she said, before taking in more air than she needed. But there was a new and awful confidence in all her functions. As Chifley had given the certainty of breath, Uncle Frank had given her the certainty and high natural chemistry of hate.

Yet he had his hands up now, counseling against too strenuous a use of it.

—He's in utter hell. Your successor in his arms, Kate, is said to be unhappy on two fronts: his drinking and the threat of his fall. And she's not an evil woman, though it would be better if she were. And she wonders why he can't be happy, apart of course from his loss. She's told friends that she admires him for the intensity of his grief. But she knows it's more than intensity, more than average, even for such a non-average loss. She knows there's something grandly wrong with it. And so do you now. We can leave him to it, Kate. We can watch him die and go to hell.

She found herself half out of bed. One leg, limp as string, was searching for the floor.

—I want to see a chemical report, she said. She suspected the one done by Uncle Frank's friend. Not in itself, but in its informality. She wanted a printout.

—I want a proper analysis done.

—Sure. We'll send it to a commercial lab.

She groaned and shook her head. The weight of something new. It *did* need to be painfully accommodated now. She had not thrown her children away, as the old version told her. The point of the question, *Why weren't you here?* had been reversed. She had not thrown her children away. They had been snatched. This unfamiliar equation made her sit up, chatter, cover her eyes. She could feel the strain in her skull. It was not the blessed gravity of air she stood to lose, but the gravity of blame.

Since loss and the drugs had so dried her out from the teeth down to the pit of the stomach that he could not understand what she was saying, Uncle Frank went and got her tea. She was asking, as it turned out, Who did it for Paul Kozinski?

Not the doping of the vodka: he had the stomach for that. Who put the arcing device in place?

Asking, but she knew the answer. Burnside. She was already used to vengefulness, it was as if she'd always lived with it. She wished she'd known all this on the day Burnside suffered. She wished Chifley had really struck, clawed Burnside's guts out and strewn them across the bed of the sea.

When the tea came and she unlocked her tongue from her palate with a quick scalding mouthful, she asked, Are they open on the weekend?

—Who is that?

Uncle Frank seemed to be secretly listening again now to the fluttering and twittering voices of the tuned-down radio; for the signal that they were at the barrier for the next. It couldn't be so. Though it would be in his nature to attend godlike with equal ear upon the flippant and the barbaric.

—The chemical labs, said Kate. The chemical labs.

She had made the words so precisely. The *l* and the *b*.

—Well, that's an idea, Uncle Frank conceded. He took his attention right away from the radio and turned fully to her. He said he'd see to it.

—Don't humor me, she told him.

—No. No. But I'll check.

Kate, not being able to calculate what Burnside is owed, is soothed somewhat by Uncle Frank's news: not only does Burnside walk with a stick, this taking the sting out of all his threat and all his manner, but he is as good as neutered too. She does not know if this last news is reliable, or if Uncle Frank has made it up to cosset her. But to have lost her signed release forms twice, she thinks, must be a torment to Burnside, and she takes satisfaction from it.

And then above all the walking with a stick. Murray has verified that for her. An enforcer with an inability to enforce. She savors this as she waits for the vodka to be analyzed, and for the chemical report to be made.

By contrast she knows that Paul Kozinski must be exactly punished, and she will apply herself to that question when the results arrive at her bedside.

So while she waits for the chemical analysis, Murray takes a day from work, collects her from the sanatorium and brings her to McCarr's Creek, an arm of Pittwater. Waters familiar to the *Vistula*. But Murray has taken her on board a more modest boat today, one belonging to a friend. Thirty-two-footer. Very manageable. He uses the donkey engine to get them away from their mooring, and then he cuts it and hoists a foresail. It is wonderful, she thinks, how a little boat pitches so honestly in a slight swell with the breeze astern. How cleanly. She notices how delighted Murray is that she raises her chin to the sun. As if he thinks that, even though she knows now not to give herself up too utterly to that vicious, blazing star, once given a full reprieve she will sometimes risk her face briefly and without fear. Her hair is shampooed, since her view of entitlement to shampoo has been changed by Uncle Frank's news. On her cheeks sits a mixture of makeup and sun lotion.

So Murray sits at the tiller and feels triumphant. He is aware too how itchy the world is for a photograph of Kate. News editors are utterly sick of the old stills. He relishes the idea that she is safe from cameras here. He has delivered her from the electronic snouts. He glows with frankness and with love.

Provisionally—subject to the chemical analysis—she recognizes this in him and is provisionally pleased. And on the same grounds she accepts the dazzle of these waters where she picnicked with her children and with Burnside and with girls hired by the Kozinskis to please those who would do them favors.

Murray has at home his collection of Paul Kozinski press clippings. He likes to think of each clipping as yet another leaf of the Polish onion boiling free and sloughing away.

The most effulgent recent addition has to do with Queensland, where a former state cabinet minister has told a government inquiry that he received a political gift of $250,000 as reward for building a bridge specifically to service a Kozinski Development Corporation's shopping mall. At the time of the exchange of money, the mall had not yet been built, but the Kozinskis were careful planners.

In New South Wales, shamefaced union officials of the kind who sailed aboard the *Vistula* and lunged at the Kozinskis' proffered girls, had already confessed to extorting gifts of money and kind from Paul Kozinski; and a political donation from Paul Kozinski had been put into the hands of a party official in the expressed hope of favorable decisions in the matter of a marina-hotel development at Tweed Heads.

These admissions have been made before various state and federal inquiries, including the Commission into the Building Industry, whose address Murray keeps close at hand, since there is some talk that Kate might be called as a witness. If so, he would like to mediate.

On top of this, the financial news. Kozinskis, *père et fils*, have had to go into meetings with bankers with a view of restructuring the Kozinski debt. The indignity of these meetings, Murray explains to Kate, is acute, particularly the fact that the press waits gloating at the door for reports.

But both father and son keep a composed demeanor. It is reported around Sydney that Mrs. Kozinski has frequently said that the only people not in trouble now are the Jews. It is Christian recklessness and spaciousness of soul which have brought her husband and her son to troubled times.

They tacked into Jerusalem Bay, where other boats were moored. People were lunching aboard, seated deeply in the stern, passing wine bottles. A woman's birdlike laughter rose up the cliffs.

—No liquor for us. Though we gave it a shake in Fiji, eh? The hospital staff warned me. It won't go with your medication.

These were *Vistula* waters also, though Murray could not be expected to know that. Siobhan, drifting in the water, had looked up at this stratified bush and said, Where are they going?

Murray went down into the galley to cut chicken up, as Kate used to do on the Kozinski craft. He kept an eye on her up through the hatch.

—Something I ought to tell you. Nothing to be concerned about. Burnside has taken an action against Gus Schulberger.

Some form of criminal assault to do with negligent care of animals. A nineteenth-century Act of Parliament with twentieth-century amendments.

When she looked stricken he ran up the companionway.

—No court will give him a judgment. Honestly.

But the writ itself was an abomination.

—You told me to make a straight settlement with the Kozinskis?

—Well, that was personal advice. Though it's not bad professional advice either. Take what they offer, while they have it. Sign their papers and forget them.

But of course Murray did not understand the size of their ill will, and how unforgettable Paul was.

—I want to make my own document. Could you draw up a document for me?

Of her own will and her own drafting, she wanted to hand over to the Kozinskis the assent Burnside had been neutered trying to gouge out of her.

She said, Very important. Very important.

—I can't draw up a document for you. I'm too close to you, Kate. It could be challenged at a later date. Undue influence. After all, you're in a sanatorium. And I'm showing kindnesses to you. That's interpreted one way by us, but in court it looks like a plot. Besides, if I drew up a document like that, it would finish me with your parents.

She looked at him in a studied way, hoping there was a tremendous weight of demand in her eyes, like the weight of grievance in Connie Murchison's.

—Well, I could send someone independent to talk to you and draw up a document like the one you suggest . . .

—The one I suggest . . . What you must do is send me someone who will shut up and write what I want. It's all rubbish and it burdens my soul and my children's souls. I want to return the whole shitty mess to the owners.

—Of course. But you have to think of your future welfare too.

—Go to hell, Murray. I'm very hungry actually. You should have seen me eat in the country. They know how to eat there. It's different . . .

He brought chicken and unshelled prawns and orange juice up from the galley.

—Perhaps you should rest awhile after lunch. While I sail back. There are bunks below.

She repeated it.

—There are bunks below.

It was a sentence of sweet contours.

In the midst of shelling king prawns and dropping the carapaces over the side, he reached to her and kissed her, holding his arms open-handed and away from her, not wanting to mar her clothes with the rank sea smell of the prawns, clasping her shoulders with his wrists.

—I want nothing from them, she told him.

Murray tested that idea. You could tell he was thinking, What a concept for a lawyer to hear. I should say something. But he couldn't manage it.

She said, Yes. I mean it, for Christ's sake.

She smiled at her luck in finding such men. For the steak-eating woman, there could not have been better men than the sainted Jelly and then Gus. And Murray for the sanatorium patient. It was all beneficial for her purpose. She must be utterly quit of Paul Kozinski before she could begin to think of which way to punish him.

Uncle Frank did not turn up as often now. He had become busy— *conferencing* with his lawyers, as he liked to say. His telephone calls stood in place of his presence. He always sounded in good heart: she could tell he congratulated himself on having safely changed her idea of what had happened to her, all without damaging any of her tissue. His pride in this was at least as spacious as his pride in not having bribed anyone.

Kate was visited by a youngish lawyer, her age, but young in the way in which men to whom nothing has happened except the expected are young. She told him to be quiet and to take down to dictation her demands. Without consideration (she said) other than that no employee, casual or permanent, of Kozinski Constructions should take any action for damages against Mr. Gus Schulberger of Bourke, New South Wales, she released all her interests in and claims on all the Kozinski businesses. Specifically the writs issued by Mr. Burnside against Mr. Gus Schulberger should be withdrawn as a condition of the release.

She said she wanted him kindly to draft the letter in the terms she had given him. She wanted no argument. She would sign any exemption he wanted. If he would shut up and do it, she would pay him any price.

Old Kozinski would of course be cheered to receive such a document. He would not see anything but her sense of shame behind the lack of demands. Mrs. Kozinski would attribute the good outcome to the intercession of the Black Virgin of Czestochowa. But Paul would be arrested by it. Paul would correctly disbelieve it. What is she trying to say? he would ask himself.

A good thing.

Twenty-four

WHEN IT ARRIVED, the chemical analysis was twelve pages in length. Inside a cover blue as O'Toole's helicopter. According to its summary, some 450 milligrams of Vallergan, trimeprazine, had in fact been dissolved in Kate's vodka. Trimeprazine was an antihistamine of extreme potency; the maximum recommended dose of thirty milligrams produced in a male of average height, weight and age an extreme drowsiness followed by profound sleep. The effects of the drug would be—to quote the analytic summary—*potentiated* by its mixture with alcohol.

A mixture of vodka and trimeprazine would have produced in the first instance a clear solution, and only over a time could the substance react with the clarifying agent to produce a faint yellow coloration.

And so Kate remembered the ballet class. Denise's job to take the small dancers. Vodka time for excellent mothers.

Kate's first impulse on reading the report's summation is a motherly one, a strange onset of futile tenderness toward Paul. She can see him locking the door on the boardroom and beginning to experiment with sedatives and glasses of vodka from the corporate cabinet. Mrs. Kozinski's junior chemist. One drug turns the vodka immediately blue. Another alters it green or yellow. He may even have had to make notes: he couldn't have had such a success without bringing methodologies in.

Burnside would have without question got a whole battery of sedatives for him. Since there were kingdoms and fortunes involved, Burnside would have been paid exorbitantly for the service.

The problem of the chemical analysis for Kate is that having painlessly yielded up to the Kozinskis all that Paul had tried to achieve through mixtures and then through sending Burnside to the bush, how could she punish him without entering the whole mean question once again; debasing herself and sacrificing her breath?

She wishes of course that Uncle Frank was there. She would like him to sit down and relieve her with talk about three-year-olds and the spring carnival. When she wakes at the end of an afternoon's sleep, her body prickles and is covered with hives. Only the scarred shoulders are exempted from this panic of the flesh. They coat her in lotion, but then the heat of it all enters her mouth and she begins to gag, and they have to put her on a drip of adrenaline.

When she woke the next morning, Uncle Frank was found to be standing at the end of her bed reading the chemical report—his own copy. He had written neatly on it: *The Reverend F. O'Brien*.

—Heard about your episode, Kate. A rash . . .

As if accusing her of sending obscure messages, he shook his head.

—I want you to get well, Kate. Because in two days the madness will start. Cameras will follow me and Fiona Kearney everywhere. Going to court, coming.

He sighed. A put-upon Irishman.

—I don't think I can do much for you or anyone just now.

She inspected her arms and saw that they were white and clear of blemish.

—Your man Murray tells me you *have* given everything back to the Kozinskis. It could turn out to be wise, Kate. By one view you've doubled his wealth. By another, you've doubled his indebtedness. You can't give a damn about how the man feels. He's put himself beyond.

—Then how can I touch him? If he's beyond?

—Kate, he's pretty thoroughly touched himself. Except . . . to be honest . . . Michael Collins would never have let a man like that live.

One of Uncle Frank's ambiguous saints: Michael Collins. Director of operations in the old days, when the IRA had all been good people and Ireland was facing its indisputable destiny. The best of men with the blessing of most of the clergy upon their heads, except for a few pre-Fogartys in the west who tried to excommunicate them. In those days they went to the church after ambushes and prayed for the repose of the souls of the Black and Tans they had just felled, the British agents they had just shot in the head.

So she wondered was Uncle Frank arguing Paul Kozinski had moved out of the zone of civil justice into the militant zone? Summary punishment appropriate? Uncle Frank a possible participator in the militant?

—I want to forget it all, she rushed to lie. You have your own case to settle, Uncle Frank.

—Mother of God, do I!

He walked the room, hitting his arm with the rolled-up chemical report. On it, that perfect copperplate: *The Reverend F. O'Brien.*

—I wonder if His Eminence Fogarty will abrogate my damn suspension to permit me to say Mass in Long Bay.

She smiled.

—I think he might let you.

—The apostle to the crims of New South Wales. It won't be the first fooking time a priest has worn chains in this place, let me tell you!

That was his saving delusion again: that he was some sort of political prisoner, a saint of anarchy, a successor to the rebels of 1798. Someone kind should deliver him of that notion so that he could have a tranquil old age. Or someone cruel should. She didn't have the space or strength to do it herself.

—Are you going to wear your canonicals in court?

The glory of his black alpaca and his virgin white collar.

—Of course. I don't yield to the gobshites, Kate. I'm as much a priest as the next feller.

She had been thinking of trying to argue him out of this perhaps inflammatory mode of dress. But she imagined him in a plain man's lounge suit, and the idea lacked such credit that she said nothing.

She was aware of thinking of her mother too, in an unlikely, intimate way she thought she had sworn off for life; in a way her shame for the lost children had until recently invalidated for her. Her mother was not well; suffering from lack of sleep and complicated family shame. The shame of the tragedy; the shame of Kate's vanishing and return; the shame not of Uncle Frank's crime but of a society, sober when it suited it, that judged her brother to have behaved illicitly.

They had arguments though about whether Kate would go to

court. For Uncle Frank had told Mrs. Kate Gaffney that her daughter shouldn't go. Uncle Frank said Kate wasn't ready to leave the place yet, and his authority with his sister hadn't been lessened just because he was facing charges under the Gaming Act.

—Murray will take me, Kate argued. Murray will protect me from the press.

—And then the press will say, *Missing heiress Kate Kozinski with her friend Murray Stannard* and the whole world will be left to guess what *friend* means. Including the Kozinskis.

Mrs. Kate Gaffney didn't understand that they were all now free of the Kozinskis.

Mrs. Gaffney left and Murray arrived, Kate asking him to stay on in her room after dark to watch the footage of the not-so-Reverend Frank and Mrs. Kearney walking into the New South Wales District Court. The woman commentator said, Still wearing his clerical costume . . .

Nothing much seemed to have happened after that, the day apparently spent on legal palaver. The big news: Uncle Frank's clerical collar.

No sooner did the news item end than she and Murray began devising a time for her to go to court. Early afternoon on Thursday say, when after lunch the press would be less vigilant. By 2 p.m. too her morning dosage of sedatives should have partially worn off and left her less thick-tongued in case the unspeakable took place. She would in any case sleep all morning to prepare herself.

Early in the week a member of the Legislative Assembly of New South Wales, a one-time parishioner of Uncle Frank's, founded a Father O'Brien Support Group, all the more startling a body given that no one doubted the not-so-Reverend Frank could well afford his own legal fees.

This development helped to generate in the bright winter's day through which pale Kate and Murray walked bravely hand in hand an atmosphere of favor toward Uncle Frank.

They waited for the lift amongst the melee of solicitors and barristers, many of whom nodded to Murray and murmured his name. Their eyes flicked too across the face of Kate's sunglasses. The barristers wore their wigs and gowns with the same amour-propre she'd seen in academics. Yet you'd think they must be used to it by now. Perhaps the presence of Murray, a woman's hand uncustomarily in his, had set them off, reminded them somehow of who they were and how they were different from him. Look at me, some of them might have been suggesting to Murray. Acned and uncertain in law school, now at least a wigged barrister if not a silk.

It was a modern court. Imperial red fabric and Australian hardwood paneling. Late-twentieth-century architects had reversed the trouble their nineteenth-century counterparts had gone to and tried now to make the courts look no different from a fashionable accountancy firm. In this milieu, as they mounted the stairs to Uncle Frank's courtroom, Kate and Murray were ambushed by a single young journalist, perhaps a sentry.

—Mrs. Kozinski, the young man addressed her.

Murray dealt with him briskly. He pushed her through into the court. Protected ground. Sanctuary. With a red and blue carpet.

Three open galleries surrounded the pit of the court.

—Theater in the round, Murray whispered.

The hearing was already in progress. The prosecutor muttered about something procedural. Murray bowed to the judge, a token of reverence in which Kate didn't feel bound to join.

Two of the galleries were occupied by a scatter of spectators and interested parties and press. Mr. and Mrs. Gaffney were not amongst the interested spectators. In the third, the police who guarded the court and who were there to protect Uncle Frank and Mrs. Kearney from the impulse to escape, lounged. Everymen. *Orta Recens Quam Pura Nites* on their shoulders.

Tight in under a gallery facing Uncle Frank, the jury. Seven men, five women. One of the men had a Polynesian face. Two of the women looked Greek. No necessity that they would share Uncle Frank's comprehensive view of what morality was.

The not-so-Reverend Frank wore the milk-white jacket which Roman clergymen reserved for social occasions. It set off the pure black breast of his clerical stock. Its appearance here was a kind of bravado. Elegant clergy from the North Shore wore that sort of coat on visits to Rome in the European summertime.

Above the judge sat the lion and unicorn. The kangaroo and emu who sat above normal Australian institutions were excluded from the court. It was under the lion and unicorn that all Irish heroes had been sentenced. Uncle Frank therefore was at least given a pretext to consider himself one in the line of Robert Emmet, Wolfe Tone, Michael Meagher of the Sword, Padraic Pearse, James Connolly, all of whom had been savaged by the lion and gored by the unicorn.

A youngish man in a gray suit was ready to give evidence to the prosecutor and had been sworn in. Uncle Frank, his face animated but in a thoughtful kind of way, was in the process of passing a note out of the dock to his lawyer Eric Tandy, Q.C. Uncle Frank looked up, saw Kate, winked once sagely—to an outsider it could have been a tic—and returned his attention to the witness in the gray suit.

The prosecutor began asking questions of the gray-suited witness.

—Mr. Teece, you were till recently the assistant manager of the Mortdale branch of the Eastern Australia Bank?

Mr. Teece said yes.

—You are acquainted with the accused?

—I only know Father O'Brien.

Mr. Teece was very nervous. He had an old-fashioned working-class face and his freckles blazed, and the white between them was quite slick with anxiety. What did the anxiety mean? That was the question on which she could see that Uncle Frank's attention was fixed.

—So how did you meet the accused O'Brien?

—I first met him when my youngest aunt died. She was only thirty-seven. A husband. Two children . . .

—So the Reverend O'Brien first approached you in the role of a comforter?

What a stupid question Kate thought that was. As if it were a role which made blame all the more certain.

—He was very kind to our family, said Teece staunchly.

—And he kept contact with you after he met you?

—Yes. We had a bit of a wake. Father O'Brien and I got on well. He was exactly the right sort of priest for that sort of thing.

Yet Kate feared, a bubble of panic rising in her throat, pricking the roof of her mouth, that Teece spoke as if he would soon switch gear and render a different picture of Uncle Frank.

The prosecutor asked, Did the Reverend Frank O'Brien seek any special favors from you?

Teece took pale thought.

—One day Father O'Brien called and wanted to see me. I said I was available. He came in and asked if he could open a bank account in the name of Edith Timms. He said it was an unregistered trust, and there were problems in using his regular accounts. I didn't ask him too many questions about this. I had no reason to. I thought he might be just wanting to open an account for a widow or for someone injured . . .

There was indulgent laughter from the press and, Kate was comforted to see, the women in the jury in particular.

—And you know, he didn't want to go through the legal fuss with founding a trust. And then I asked him what address this Edith Timms account should be in. He hadn't thought of that. He didn't want it to be *his* address. He was looking perplexed. So I said that if he wanted he could use my address for a time.

The prosecution acknowledged that this was very generous of Mr. Teece and asked how much ultimately came through the account.

Teece said, About thirty-seven thousand dollars.

The prosecutor remarked tritely that this was something more than a widow's mite. Mr. Teece said it was not beyond the bounds of possibility for a trust based on donations to raise as much money as this, if raffles and dinners were held.

—But you never knew who this Edith Timms was?

Teece said, No.

—Even though the address of the account was yours?

—I thought that was a technicality.

—Did your superiors ultimately point out to you that it was more than a technicality?

Teece admitted that they had. He did not seem utterly shamefaced about it. But he admitted he had been suspended.

Would Mr. Teece have been surprised to know that a number of accounts under the name Edith Timms had been established at other branches of various banks, that they had been established by Mrs. Kearney and that all of them used his address?

Teece shook his head. This is where he thought the Reverend Frank had let him down a little. He'd been ignorant of all this.

So—in a way—was Kate. Ignorant of the style and cunning and scope of Uncle Frank's operations. Astonished by it and overtaken by a kind of wonder.

The chief question then:

—And you say that the defendant O'Brien offered you no direct inducements for this service you had done him?

A month after the account had been opened, Teece remarked, the Reverend Frank—who knew he was a keen punter—called him and gave him three telephone numbers. Father O'Brien said that if Teece called any of these numbers, he would discover that he had a credit of three thousand dollars.

Did Mr. Teece think this was a bribe?

No, said Teece. He knew the Reverend O'Brien was a wealthy man. It wasn't such an astounding thing for him to give another punter a little credit.

—So it wasn't an inducement, Teece said. It was a gift.

Through this, Fiona Kearney kept thin and composed, but she wrote no notes to Tandy Q.C. She was an old-fashioned woman and had taken her direction from Alderman Kearney and now from her spiritual director and lover, the not-so-Reverend Frank. It was Uncle Frank who held his head on the side, seeing at every step the trick behind the prosecution's drift and firing off the notes to Tandy.

—Are bank officers encouraged to accept gifts from wealthy clients? asked the prosecution.

—Not in theory. But it happens.

When it came to Mr. Tandy Q.C.'s turn, he seemed to understand Uncle Frank's disposition as thoroughly as Kate herself did. He asked Teece the right questions, or at least the questions which Uncle Frank wanted asked.

—When the Reverend Frank O'Brien told you of the three thousand dollars credit, did you consider it a reimbursement for your having let your address be used in this way?

—No.

For Teece as for Uncle Frank, it was all in the spirit of the premature burial and wake.

—Did you consider the extension of credit as connected with your duties as a bank officer in any way at all?

—No.

—What did you consider it?

—A gesture of friendship. From a generous sportsman.

Happily Teece's ignorance remained as invincible as Uncle Frank's. The next witness called was however so likely to be damaging that Murray suggested they leave now.

—Soon, said Kate. Soon, Murray.

This witness was older, a former manager of a bank in Milperra. He had a jovial, beefy look, but was wearing an old-fashioned brown suit. For he was serving a sentence for embezzlement, a matter quite separate from the matter before this court. He had however received visits during his banking career from Mrs. Kearney and the Reverend Father O'Brien. He had opened accounts in the name of Edith Timms and Edmund Kelly.

—Did you have any reason, the prosecutor asked, to believe the names were fictitious?

—Well I wondered about Edmund Kelly. In view of the fact it's the name of the bushranger.

Ned Kelly, hanged in the Melbourne jail, in Uncle Frank's worldview another victim of the lion and unicorn.

—What address was used for these accounts?

—There wasn't any actual account. I kept the amounts informally for Father O'Brien and Mrs. Kearney.

—What do you mean by *informally?*

—Well sometimes—temporarily—I'd keep them in my bottom drawer, or else in my office safe.

—Was bank interest paid on these amounts?

—No, said the fallen manager. I was doing it as a favor.

Kate noticed with a pulse of fear that when the witness said this, Uncle Frank had nodded. Good answer! Good lad! Judgment might come as a vast surprise to Uncle Frank, a terminal confirmation of the lack of civil good humor everywhere on the planet.

Tandy Q.C. spoke to the witness.

—How did you first meet the Reverend Frank O'Brien?

—My wife approached him. She was worried about my gambling.

—Did she have cause to be?

—I wouldn't be serving a sentence if not.

—Why would your wife go to the Reverend Frank O'Brien, who was known to be something of a gambler himself?

—My wife believed that Father O'Brien was the *beau idéal* of gamblers. He had his gambling under control.

This caused the jury and the press to guffaw, and Kate was grateful that her mother was not there.

For Tandy and the judge did not laugh.

—Did Father O'Brien ever give you any advice?

—Yes, said the fallen bank manager. The Reverend O'Brien sent me to Gamblers Anonymous. Just as an observer at first. To get the idea. Even though it was all meant to be anonymous, I didn't want to declare myself in case word got back to Head Office. So Father O'Brien gave me three telephone numbers. He said I'd better ring those if I *had* to bet. He said that I would find that I had ten thousand dollars credit if I called those numbers.

—At the time of your arrest, how much did the people who answered those telephone numbers tell you you owed them?

—They told me I owed them $17,737. I spoke to Father Frank about it and that was the last I heard.

Seeing the prosecution rise in a way she thought predatory, she asked Murray if she could go. After all it was an odd minute, when again the press might not be so watchful. But it was painful for Frank's sake to be a witness to this—the drift of judgment. Even his friends were—with the greatest respect—condemning him, and he construed it as praise.

Murray helped her as she struggled upright urgently.

Waiting for the lift outside, he said, This is a remarkable family you belong to, Kate. You are yourself a remarkable woman.

She said nothing. She was palpitating for Uncle Frank.

—I never thought I'd be mixed up with a family like this.

He began to laugh.

Two barristers appeared, talking secretly to each other and nodding at Murray. Murray too spoke as in a conspiracy when he turned to her.

—Come and live with me, Kate. Now. I've been a negligent friend. But I'm very patient. If that's what you like. My first wife couldn't stand it.

—I have to get out of the so-called sanatorium first.

—Come and live with me when you do.

As they were leaving the building, a press photographer in wait took their picture. As it appeared in the next morning's Packer tabloid, they seemed designed for each other by their parallel thinness.

Twenty-five

WHEN THE SANATORIUM SEASON ended, it had to be either her parents' place or Murray's. Her mother had a surprisingly poor sense of how little a woman deprived of her children wanted to go back now to her childhood hearth. Jim Gaffney understood it though. He understood the obvious things: such as that her burns had had nothing to do with Murray.

So she moved to Murray's city apartment. She laid her few clothes out in a chest of drawers. She had begun to use simple cosmetics again, but only the most simple. She wanted to mask the harsh effect all the sedative had had upon her skin. She established a modest beachhead on a vanity table the former Mrs. Stannard had no doubt used more spaciously.

She went to day therapy for a week, sat and listened to men tell how loneliness or ambition had unhinged them, to women speak of how a lust for possession had entrapped them. She listened to them talk each morning of such ordinary treacheries. As a means of convincing everyone that she was whole, she made up eminently sensible advice for all parties. She enjoyed creating these salutary little near-fictions about other patients, salting them with items from socio- and psychojargon, frowning and hesitating before uttering each Californian cliché. The burden of her advice was: You mustn't blame yourself. It seemed to satisfy everyone eminently, and she believed it was benign advice anyhow.

And so the sanatorium let her go with a set of prescriptions and a list of emergency phone numbers.

She had ambitions to work, and one Sunday afternoon she and Murray went to drinks at Bernard Astor's.

How her son's godfather had aged!

She went back to Bernard's to do itineraries—the plain business of flights and hotel bookings—and to write press releases. She did not set up or attend press conferences, as she had when she was young, and she did not travel with actors and directors. Yet Bernard paid her as if she did. She chose not to argue about it. She would earn it all soon. She could foresee a time when she *would* appear at press previews and move amongst the reviewers with a casual skill.

Soon she was able to call Murchison's Railway Hotel. Jack seemed to be a man harried in a new way, a less comfortable one. He said that Connie had had a little time in hospital, but she was improving now. She was learning not to blame herself, he said.

—What for?

—You know. Her sister. Beats me to be honest.

He changed direction then, and she heard his laugh.

—Jesus, we had to keep a straight face telling lies about you the night you and Gus took off. We didn't know what to say, so we said the least we could . . .

Guthega was a town hero, said Jack. But men really spoke volumes of Jelly, and Jack was putting up a plaque for him in the bar. It was sad, Noel and his father had fallen out and Noel was off doing shearing exhibitions at country shows. It could be the making of the boy.

Though of course he would always remember that through no fault of his own he had fallen on the plunger.

—And have you seen Gus? she asked.

—Gus's engaged, said Jack, and this struck him as utterly hilarious. He's traveling round New South Wales in his fiancée's caravan, and they lecture and show slides on Australian wildlife to schoolkids.

At night Kate reclined back against Murray's body. He placed his cheek against her scarred shoulders. He said that she was beautiful. It was a preciously ordinary word. She was aware of hollowness, but her daily work was done and Murray enfolded her. She fulfilled responsibilities and observed herself doing it. She believed there would never be a connection between the observer and the task. She was sundered in two for good.

The black onus of punishing Paul Kozinski never left her, and she was not delayed by anything as minor as reluctance to act. Even as she wrapped herself into Murray's embrace, she was utterly willing to arrange a conference with Paul and to reach out in the midst of cool exchanges and plunge a knife into his abdomen. Everything she could devise failed to come up to weight however. As with all committers of unspeakable wrongs, the punishment should bring the culprit himself deliverance, but not too easily.

Paul had bought himself a new house for the new marriage, not that the new marriage was achieved yet. But there would be a wedding as soon as the annulment was delivered, and Monsignor Pietecki—Kate knew—would officiate. She knew that this new place had been bought in part with the insurance money from the hecatomb at Palm Beach, her share of which waited for her somewhere, in some lawyer's office. A charred reward she intended not to touch.

The new Kozinski house stood in Woollahra. No more commuting from great distances for Paul. Woollahra was ten minutes from the city. The house was hidden behind a high ocher-painted wall, in the midst of it a heavy gate faced with burnished brass. A small bell to the side was marked with a brass plate which said KOZINSKI.

Murray used to broach, tenderly, the idea that the case might not go well for Uncle Frank. Having never been near a jail, he tried just the same to convince her that things would be pleasant for Uncle Frank there.

—Nobody wants to go to prison, of course, he conceded. But he'll be respected both by the screws and the cons. No one will touch him or assault him. He'll have a better time of it than Paul will. Besides, a lot of the prisoners will have had Catholic childhoods.

Beside the Kozinskis' crimes, she cherished Murray's unheeding and homely bias. She was charmed by the certainty that he could be depended on to utter the mild, unfashionable prejudice.

But she was disturbed by the thought of Uncle Frank constrained. *Immured* was the word which filled her head. Uncle Frank socketed amidst walls.

A relentless dreamer still, she woke from images of immurement, and she yelled and grabbed for air in the way Murray was familiar with, and he would wake and switch the light on and stroke her scarred shoulders. She would gently test her recovered breath. At that hour the idea of Uncle Frank's locking away and of her mother's shame seemed hard to tolerate.

She went to court the final day, and Tandy was eloquent. He had little to go on though except Uncle Frank's services to the community, a claim the prosecutor could undo by referring to His Eminence Fogarty's suspension. A cardinal does not suspend eminent priests!

Uncle Frank wore his white jacket, however, just like an eminent priest. Mrs. Kearney wore a floral dress. They were a handsome enough middle-aged couple. She could not understand why they were so composed. Did they know something the judge and counsel didn't? Were they safer than anyone thought? Or did they have the calm of martyrs?

The jury went out and did not return that day. Leaving the court holding Murray's hand, Kate waded in a surf of journalists. Murray made the comments for her, an arrangement she was not fully happy with—since Murray could not be expected to understand a phenomenon like Frank—but which on balance she chose.

Then she and Murray took Kate Gaffney and Jim for dinner, they felt so sorry for them.

The jury comes in just before lunch the next day. At the utterance of guilt, Kate's face contorts in the same pulse as her mother's. They have become the one woman for a second. They rise hand in hand, and Uncle Frank who is standing looks across the court at them, raises his eyes, makes a whimsical bunch of his mouth and lifts both arms. Robert Emmet did not go to the scaffold in Dublin with greater grace or more certainty of a kind of immortality. And Kate realizes that what has brought its own reward to Uncle Frank is not virtue but style: his idea of style, which is not removed by more than a whisper from a kind of lawlessness and subversion. The style of all this will keep him alive under judgment.

For example, and as if to demonstrate, he kisses Fiona's hand before he is led away.

Again it is Mrs. Kate Gaffney *née* O'Brien who lacks something like that to fall back on.

Sentencing will be within nine days. We all know that it will not be a suspended sentence. The judge however will say that in no construction of justice can Uncle Frank's sentence be greater than that of an ordinary violator. The one thing the prosecution had not successfully argued, the judge will say, is that Uncle Frank had violated the expectations of society in some way that was extra to his violation of the New South Wales Gaming Act. In any case the Reverend O'Brien still had many admirers amongst the wide community and amongst members of his denomination. It was society at large which he had offended.

In another place and under another jurisdiction, said the judge, his illegal earnings would be estimated, action would be taken for confiscation, for payment of fines.

Five years in prison.

Uncle Frank's sentence drove her to take up a kind of surveillance. From a given parking space in a laneway facing onto Ocean Street, she could see the house. For as long as an hour and a half after work each day, she could watch it from her car. One early evening she saw Paul's Jaguar, KOZCON, pull up before the garage which was at one end of the long ocher wall. The sight of this wall somehow returned her to the red dust road outside Bourke, where Chifley slept in the back of the sister-in-law's truck beside the tarpaulin-wrapped Burnside.

As Paul drove into his garage, she lost and refound herself again in the accustomed way, gasping for a while in the front seat of her new car, a modest little Japanese thing to match the modesty of her survival. In it, on the bridge where people crazily changed lanes, she achieved an almost pleasing sense of fragility.

Bring the Sydney spring to us, with its bright, effervescent air. Safe in their knowledge of who Uncle Frank really was, sharing the secret, Kate Gaffney and her daughter began to meet more frequently. They became familiar with cappuccino bars around Bernard Astor's office in Woolloomooloo. The ceremonies of being a good daughter pleased Kate.

Send Kate to David Jones's department store on the corner of Elizabeth and King Streets to buy a present, at an end of a frightful year, for Mrs. Kate Gaffney's fifty-seventh birthday.

Follow her as she ascends the escalator, making for the gallery on the top floor. She steps off at the second, amongst the couturier clothing, and comes close to colliding with Perdita Krinkovich.

With all else to distract her, this was the first time that it struck Kate: Perdita coveted her name. Kozinski. Kate was surprised to find herself loath to give it up. There was flesh invested in that name. She had paid for the stretch of desert it stood for.

A terrible meeting, both in the same instant coming eye to eye, both parties bereft of a moment to prepare themselves.

Kate saw Perdita's mouth open and the lower lip draw back ferally. She saw too that Perdita was well pregnant, in the phase they called *showing*.

That is my child, she thought. She has captured my child.

She staggered sideways, in the direction of the handbag counter. If she got her balance back she might flee. But there was a chance she would attack Perdita.

—Oh Jesus! she heard Perdita murmur.

Paul Kozinski's lover turned and began to hobble away amongst the counters. Slotting herself in athletically between the shoppers, women older and younger, she wanted to lose herself behind their average flesh and the padded shoulders of their coats.

Kate was startled enough not to pursue. Besides, humanity and a sense of sisterhood asserted itself. Behind her stood the down escalator. Briskly she excused her way past the plump companionable women who wanted to descend two by two, talking as they went. Women with the spaciousness of their achieved motherhoods.

Downstairs was a doorman the store still used, even in hard times, in imitation of Harrod's. She told the man she needed a taxi at once.

—They've just taken my mother to hospital.

He took her through the melee of other women awaiting taxis.

—Excuse us, ladies. I'm sure you don't mind . . . this woman has an emergency.

She was fortunate that the cab driver was a Korean. He understood enough to know there was an urgency, but not enough to hear the doorman's lackey blather about hospitals. He forced his way through the traffic of Elizabeth Street, driving in the swashbuckling mode of his race. He jousted his way up Parramatta Road, making for the address in Abbotsford which she had given him. Uncle Frank's place.

Mrs. Prendergast opened the door to Kate. She had been the not-so-Reverend Frank's housekeeper for seventeen years, this thin woman who shared none of her employer's vices.

She knew Kate at once, and went on calling her Miss Gaffney.

As she led her down the hallway, she turned to Kate and her eyes filled with tears.

—It's dreadful what has happened to Father Frank.

—He's taken it well. He says he's very comfortable.

—I know. He *says* it.

Kate could see that she would have to talk to the woman for a time, to console her.

Mrs. Prendergast said, If they seize his property to pay tax, this house will go and I'll be on the street.

She had a memory of being destitute, after her husband's death in 1959. A repeat episode was the dread of her life, and Uncle Frank her only guarantee against it.

—It won't happen. My father says that if they sell, he'll buy.

Though she had not heard her father say this, she must remind him that it should be so.

—He'll buy it for Uncle Frank.

Mrs. Prendergast was rendered ecstatic so easily.

—Oh, everyone knows Mr. Gaffney is a saint.

—That's right. A very loyal man. Could I see Uncle Frank's study? My father is handling Uncle Frank's affairs. He's given me a list of documents he'll need . . .

Mrs Prendergast would open any door as long as it was for Jim Gaffney, the saint, the deus ex machina of her life's history.

Kate entered Uncle Frank's study alone.

There was a long ovoid mirror inset above Uncle Frank's mantelpiece. It was familiar to her from her childhood, from the days Uncle Frank had the Gaffney family here to his off-duty house, where he could operate free of the scrutiny of his parishioners. To the side of its beading sat a little block of varnished wood which seemed like a small blemish in the general carpentry. She knew from having pressed it in childhood that something as magical as a small compartment lay behind the mirror. She had been so delighted to find it at the age of eleven. A secret compartment. Even in Abbotsford, New South Wales. It had meant that the real world and the world of secret places encountered only in film and television were continuous at Uncle Frank's house and that drama, which at that age she thought was confined to another hemisphere, was therefore everywhere.

This slight nodule of wood was still easy to find, and locating it she pressed it, and the mirror swung as if on gimbals just as it had twenty years past. There was revealed—as there had been that day in her childhood—a clutter of dusty papers. Perhaps they were precisely the same papers which had been there when she was eleven. And at one end, at the corner of the cavity, a large revolver lying upside down along its barrel, butt against the wall. Beside it was a dusty little box which said .32 *caliber* and she picked the box up and rattled it and found it was near full.

She knows by instinct that there is no documentation for this weapon. No means that it can be—as the cop shows have it—*traced* to Uncle Frank.

It was very likely that Uncle Frank had acquired this weapon from some sergeant of detectives whom he had consoled in bereavement.

Kate tried to pick the gray-blue weapon up by its brown-hatched handle. She lifted delicately at first, and failed to move it. She tried it again with a greater firmness of grip. It was terribly heavy in the hand. She walked up and down the study, training with it, so that it would come to feel a more accustomed weight. As she had been taught to do by the cinema, she opened the weapon and inspected the chambers. Four of them were full. Surely, she thought, this could not mean that Uncle Frank has used two?

Though very dusty, a fact which strangely consoled Kate, the weapon seemed well oiled. It had the efficient look of something that would work.

Uncle Frank's revolver fits precisely into her office handbag, though it makes the sides bulge and may stain the satin lining.

There is nowhere in a city that one can test-fire a revolver without drawing attention. But she has emptied the chambers and fired the mechanism. Six authoritative, businesslike cracks. The mechanics of it sound and feel very heavy, suitably potent. She has been satisfied and she is confident therefore at this hour.

An evening hour.

She sits in a cappuccino bar opposite Paul's ocher-walled villa. She intends to wait in the street if the coffee bar closes. It does not prove necessary. A little after seven Paul comes home to the mother of his potential third child. From within the Jaguar he opens the ocher garage door, and it slides up with a ceremonial obeisance.

He does not move the car on and under cover until the door has risen with robotic slowness out of sight and into its socket beneath the ceiling.

This is the point at which to greet him. Seeing her coming he would not wind down the window, or at least could not be depended on to. She would shoot him through the window. She would load all the chambers. It would be frightful for Perdita, but people lived beyond the frightful. Not as frightful as his way with children. And even if grief consumed you, it was still a lifetime's work to attend to all that must be attended to.

Her excuse to Murray, to cover this vigil as earlier ones she has maintained into the meat of the evening, is that she has been to a screening. Murray never displays narrative curiosity: What was it about? He only wants to know was it good or bad? A cricketer's question. In or out? Won or drawn?

She was sleeping very soundly now, with confused dreams but without medication.

The evening she intended to finish Paul, he was late home. They closed down the coffee shop around her and she was reduced to sauntering up and down the block. She studied the pictures in the window of the real estate agent and had it confirmed to herself that Sydney was an expensive city. She read news posters. Her devices were those one uses when waiting on the other party to an assignation. Sheltering in the shadow of spotted gums, she smelt the tang of dog's piss from around the base of the trunks. She waited like a lover for the unutterable second, the instant of encounter which would never but inevitably come.

From shadows she sees the Jaguar come home toward its ocher walls. It halts at the curb, its burgundy hindquarters still stuck out in the stream of traffic which would never dare strike anything so impeccable.

She walks out toward the Jaguar with her hand in her open bag and around the pistol. She wants to resemble a woman fumbling for makeup in her purse, her posture credible and nothing to cause alarm. From behind, from the darker shadows of the trees, she feels someone tug at her left elbow. The tugger is a large man about her own age. By the street lighting she can see that he wears an ordinary suit and a blue tie and has a preventive look in his eye. Looking from him to the Jaguar, she can see that Paul Kozinski's smooth electronic persuasion has made his garage door slide right up. But two other large men in suits have moved in on the car and are hammering with casual power on its window. Faced with them, even Paul would feel compelled to wind the thing down.

The man at her elbow introduced himself. He was a Commonwealth police inspector named Winter. Whereas the two speaking to Paul were from the New South Wales Fraud Squad. Or so he told her. So that Paul had sinned against at least two jurisdictions, state and federal. And domestic too, she could have reminded them.

They let Paul drive in under his door, and they entered the garage, attendant on either side of the car.

The inspector of Commonwealth police told her, We have a search warrant. It'll be messy, Mrs. Kozinski. Why don't you let me get you a taxi?

She brought forth Uncle Frank's revolver. The man closed one eye.

—I was going to shoot him with this thing.

He took it gently from her hands. After unhinging it, he looked in the chambers and then at the wall against which the revolving mechanism clicked into place. He pointed at this wall, though she could not see anything in particular.

—You would have scared him, Mrs. Kozinski, though I think we've done a better job. The firing pin's been taken out of commission. By a professional gunsmith too. Where did you get this?

—I borrowed it from a friend, said Kate.

He returned it directly into her handbag.

—Too much bureaucracy if I took it from you.

She liked the man. He had a gentle manner. By various movements of his eyebrows, he implied that they had a secret. He might be hell to know if he were forcing a confession from you.

As she closed her bag, she felt thwarted, and yet re-enamored of Uncle Frank. She felt no crippling disappointment though. Angels had descended from Canberra and Macquarie Street to take over the punishing of Paul Kozinski. Winter was mere chorus when he spoke.

—Listen, Mrs. Kozinski. He'll get enough shit from us. Okay?

He stepped into the street and raised his hand and a cab stopped. Behind her the door in the ocher wall opened, and half a dozen uniform policemen had appeared around the corner and were entering. Perdita Krinkovich was wailing somewhere inside.

Twenty-six

I T IS TIME to relinquish our grip on Paul Kozinski. Perhaps Kate is in part appeased by this degree of vengeance. Perhaps we are.

But if not we might want to forecast that she will write to Perdita. Perdita, soon maybe to be Kozinski. She still lives in the ocher house, even though it is now in the hands of a receiver and in fact belongs more to a merchant bank and to the Australian Taxation Office than to Paul. She writes the letter not from meanness of vision perhaps so much as from the necessity of separating Paul from all life's staples. In the text of the letter Kate commiserates with Perdita. For Paul Kozinski had complained to the press of police brutality at the time they searched his house. And the proof is that his wife-to-be miscarried with the shock and fear of it all. There are grounds for compassion there.

Kate has coffee with wan Perdita in the cappuccino place across the road from Paul's—or the Commonwealth of Australia's—villa. Paul, though still living at home, goes to court daily. At first Perdita has gone every day with him, but now he has asked her to stay away for her own sake and for his. The court—as Paul understands—is not a place for those who want to show love. It pains him, he tells her, to see her looking so stricken in the visitors' gallery.

So she drinks cappuccino with his truest enemy other than himself.

He stands trial for bribing a cabinet minister, for a series of violations of the Local Government Act, and for contravention of the Land and Environment Act. What was worst for him, Perdita tells Kate, was that he knew it was all just beginning. After the state of New South Wales had finished with him, he would need to appear in a succession of federal courts.

It is on record that Paul gets five years from the state, and old Mr. Kozinski four years.

Mrs. Kozinski comforts herself with a novena and tells friends that the Nazis are everywhere and that their spirit lives on. Kozinski Constructions remains in receivership but hopes to trade out.

The ocher villa is sold for thirty percent less than market value, and Perdita moves to an apartment supplied by Mrs. Kozinski.

Without telling Mrs. Kozinski, Perdita begins also to attend meals at Murray and Kate's. Murray praises Kate for her generosity toward her betrayer, though there is a trace of doubt in his eyes as he says it. Wisely he cannot quite believe this is routine kindness, average sisterhood. The doubt becomes more marked when Kate invites Murray's most outgoing friend, a banker named Ferris, to join them in suppers for four. Perdita, an honest woman, fights Peter Ferris bravely off for some months but succumbs at last. For Ferris is pleasant and untormented, he has earned his money in accredited ways, and no curse of lost children lies over him. Perdita plans to tell Paul only when he has left prison and is in business for himself again.

Kate visits her uncle at the Central Industrial Prison and talks with him and hears from him the news that she is Queen of Sorrows. Later, in the exercise yard, maybe the not-so-Reverend Frank mentions the matter of Mr. Ferris to Paul Kozinski. Kozinski assaults him with a cricket bat—which happens to be Murray's weapon of excellence as well. Paul receives another two years for assault. The judge tells him that if he had thought of himself up to now as a white collar criminal, his assault on an older and well-behaved prisoner should shatter his self-delusion.

That should just about bring this narrative to the rainy night from which the tale began. It is obvious from the poster in the newsagent's window that Uncle Frank has not passed up the chance for notoriety even from his prison hospital bed. He hopes to be out in a year with good behavior.

And at least Murray waits at home for Kate, beyond the rain. Kate has reached that illusorily static point appropriate to the closure of a tale.

We all wish her nothing but well.

ABOUT THE AUTHOR

One of Australia's leading literary figures, Thomas Keneally has won international acclaim with his novels *Schindler's List* (winner of the Booker Prize), *The Chant of Jimmie Blacksmith*, *Confederates*, and *Gossip from the Forest*, among others. His most recent works include the novels *The Playmaker* (which was adapted for the stage and ran on Broadway), *To Asmara*, and *Flying Hero Class*, and two travel books: *Now and in Time to Come*, about Ireland, and *The Place Where Souls Are Born*, about the American Southwest. He has served on numerous government councils and commissions in Australia and has taught at universities there and in the United States. Currently he is a Distinguished Professor in the English Department at the University of California, Irvine. Thomas Keneally is married and has two daughters. He divides his time between California and Sydney.